NEVER HUG A MUGGER

Never Hug a Mugger
ON QUADRA ISLAND

Sandy Frances Duncan & George Szanto

TouchWood
Editions

Copyright © 2011 Sandy Frances Duncan and George Szanto

All rights reserved. No part of this publication may be reproduced, stored in a retrieval system, or transmitted in any form or by any means—electronic, mechanical, recording, or otherwise—without the prior written consent of the publisher or a licence from The Canadian Copyright Licensing Agency (ACCESS Copyright). For a copyright licence, visit www.accesscopyright.ca.

TouchWood Editions
www.touchwoodeditions.com

LIBRARY AND ARCHIVES CANADA CATALOGUING IN PUBLICATION

Duncan, Sandy Frances, 1942–
Never hug a mugger on Quadra Island / Sandy Frances Duncan, George Szanto.

Issued also in electronic formats.
ISBN 978-1-926971-48-3 (bound).—ISBN 978-1-926971-49-0 (pbk.)

I. Szanto, George, 1940– II. Title.

PS8557.U5375N46 2011   C813'.54   C2011-904164-2

Editor: Frances Thorsen
Proofreader: Lenore Hietkamp
Cover image: Els van der Gun, istockphoto.com

We gratefully acknowledge the financial support for our publishing activities from the Government of Canada through the Canada Book Fund, Canada Council for the Arts, and the province of British Columbia through the British Columbia Arts Council and the Book Publishing Tax Credit.

The interior pages of this book have been printed on 100% post-consumer recycled paper, processed chlorine free, and printed with vegetable-based inks.

This book is a work of fiction. Names, characters, places, and incidents are either products of the author's imagination or are used fictitiously. Any resemblance to actual events or locales or persons, living or dead, is entirely coincidental.

1 2 3 4 5 15 14 13 12 11

PRINTED IN CANADA

In memory of Marilyn Wood.

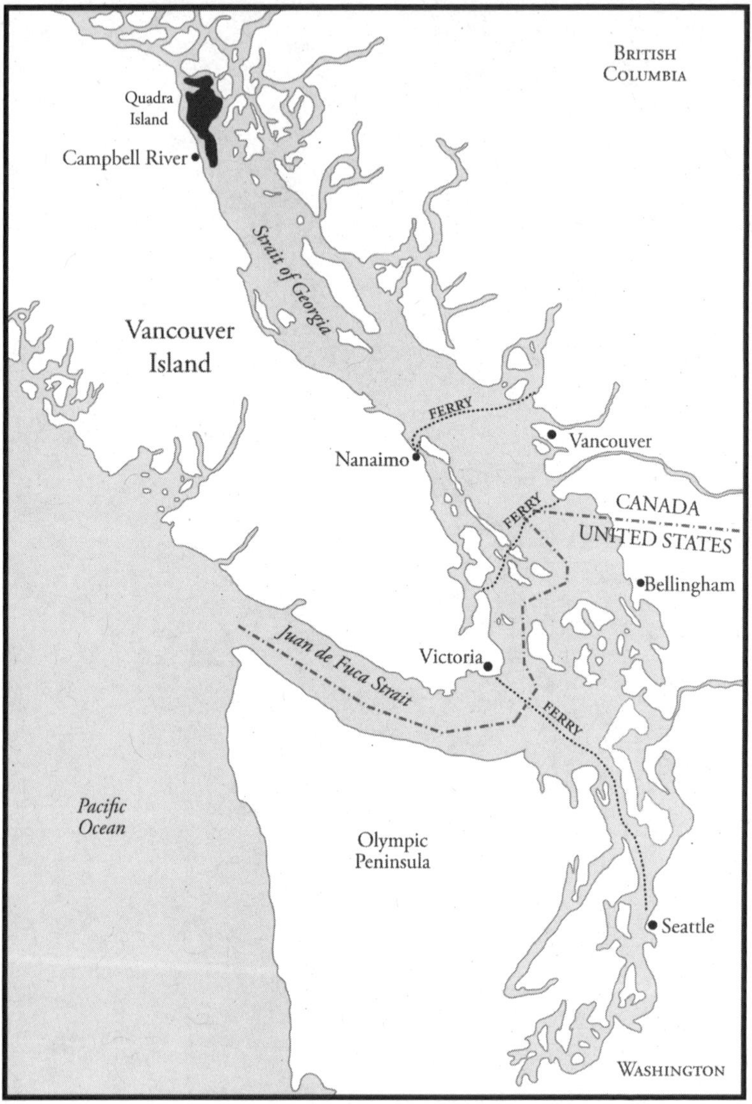
British Columbia
Quadra Island
Campbell River
Strait of Georgia
Vancouver Island
Ferry
Vancouver
Nanaimo
Ferry
Canada
United States
Bellingham
Juan de Fuca Strait
Victoria
Ferry
Pacific Ocean
Olympic Peninsula
Seattle
Washington

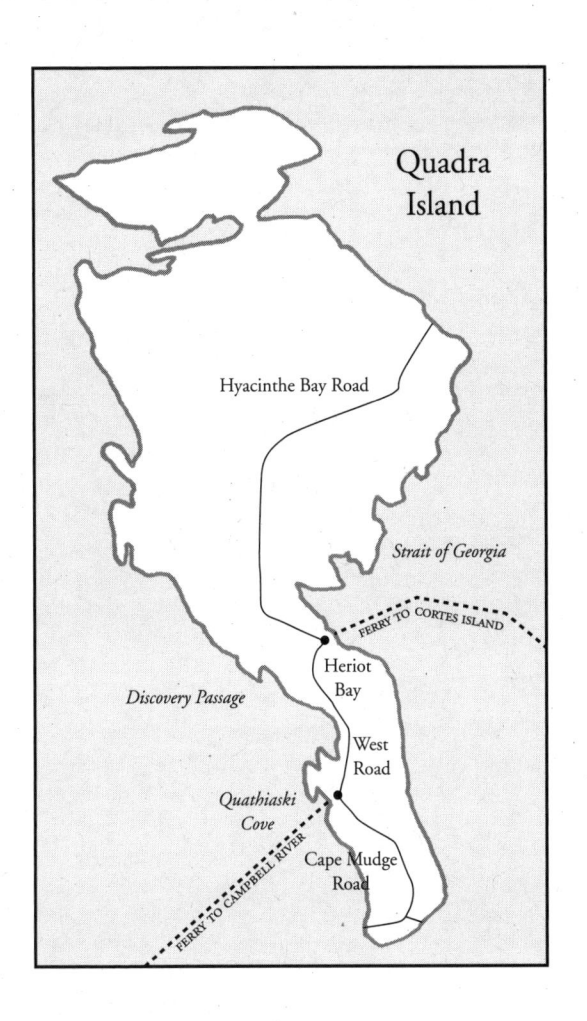

PROLOGUE

DEREK COOPER DROVE his eighteen-year-old Mazda pickup onto the 10:00 PM ferry. This late in the day, only four cars were leaving Quadra Island. The ten-minute crossing to Campbell River was a first-rate moment to think about nothing—an in-between time. Well, ten minutes if there weren't any storm, fog, log booms or cruise ships passing—however long, still in-between time. Twenty hours since he'd thought about anything other than Cynthia. She'd been gorgeous in her yellow grad gown, auburn hair sparkling in the ballroom's throbbing lights. Even more stunning with the gown on the floor beside the bed in her parents' guest cabin. Hadn't been their first time, just their best time. Soon as they got to the room, first thing she'd said, they had to—

No. Think about nothing. Clear the mind. Soon as the ferry docked he'd pull off the road and then he could think. Shape things to make sure there was no chance for anything to go wrong. This'd be his biggest deal ever and if it worked there'd be way more to come. His buddies had set up the connection— Damn! Thinking again.

Hard not to. He closed his eyes. Not thinking, just seeing pictures. Dancing slow, Cynthia's long hair along his neck, her cheek against his, holding her tight with both arms, around her shoulders and around her waist, could feel her ribs under the dress and skin, her leg between his... He floated on the image.

He'd be with her again tonight after the deal was done. She'd told him to park the truck at the end of Trask by the turnaround, usually a couple of cars left there by people going for a walk up the trail into the Beaver Lodge Lands, and his truck wouldn't stand out. Then head back to her place. If the cabin was dark, let himself in through the sliding door. If there's a problem, she'd said, she would leave the deck light on. But her parents weren't expected home for at least three days. At first she'd been pissed off at them for being gone for her grad, but with Gran so sick they'd had no choice. So it turned into the best kind of luck. They should use the cabin though, she'd decided—more like pretending it was their own house.

She liked it when he called her Cynthia. It was after all her name. But most people called her Cindy.

He felt the ferry slow. He opened his eyes. Nearly dark by the time he'd get there. Yeah.

The ferry slipped into its berth with a clang and a thud. Two workers tied the ferry fast. Ramp down, and Derek drove off. Low tide so the ramp met cars at a sharp angle, a problem for a low-slung sedan, but Derek's pickup rode high. He turned left at the traffic light, pulled over to the curb behind a parked car, and stopped the engine. He glanced at the box on the floor beside him: his passenger. Hide it? Too big.

Was he scared? Course not. You're not scared, Derek? Okay, a little. He said to himself, I'm doing it for Shane. Without support Shane couldn't compete. And Shane was damn good. Derek had admitted this for the first time, grudgingly, a couple of years ago. Years before, Derek had figured the three of them, him and Shane and Timmy, they'd become hockey stars, maybe all three brothers playing for the Canucks. But Shane went in a different direction, figure skating, who'd have thought? And, Derek realized, his own hockey skills weren't overly impressive. Timmy? Too early to tell. But Shane was world class. Or would be soon. As long as he kept getting the right coaching. So the deal was for Shane. The weed in the box was thick and rich. Worth $8,000. Half that to the supplier, $500 each to his buddies, the rest Derek's. Shane's. Eight weed deals a year, enough to supply Shane's skates, costumes, coaching expenses, travel. If Austin had to drop him, that'd cover it.

What if the buyers said it wasn't worth the eight? Then they don't get it. But Gast said these guys were in for the long haul, if the stuff was good they'd want more, and they'd pay right for it. His buddies had never had any complaints, and Derek had been supplying for nearly a year. Small-scale, sure, but they knew the value of what they got. It'd be okay.

Derek knew he was playing the iffy role here, the mule always did. The growers don't show themselves, specially not on an island that's nearly all forest like Quadra. But the guy who transports is out in the open, cops stop the truck for any reason it's all over. So his Mazda had everything working fine, lights, exhaust, even the windshield wipers, and he hadn't hotted it up like some of the dudes at the college. He was cool on all that.

He checked his watch. Twenty after ten. Couple more minutes, didn't want to get there with the stash before Gast and Joe arrived, his good buddies—let alone the buyers. In half an hour he'd be gone, cash in his pocket, on his way to Cynthia. His parents knew he'd be overnighting in Campbell River. He hadn't told them where. If they worried about him, they didn't say.

Derek started the pickup and pulled out into the traffic lane. At 5th Avenue he turned north. Then a left onto Dogwood, past the other high school, the one he hadn't gone to, and then just before the rink right on Evergreen Road. Straight on down, past the little kids' school, *Mer et Montagne*, French immersion place, Sea and Mountain.

Evergreen ended in a T. Ahead, a semi-open area. Immense cement blocks stopped any four-wheel vehicle entry—take an excavator to lift them. To the right a narrow dirt road—not even his Mazda could have got in there easily. A big white house on the corner. Part of the reason why Derek had suggested this place—friends of Cynthia's parents lived there, and they were away for three weeks. To the left an unused dirt road, overgrown. Across the road, blocking it, a locked yellow gate held a notice saying this used to give access to Twinned Holdings Pit. They'd do the deal around the curve a few meters beyond the gate.

No other cars yet. Damn, first here. He shut off the engine and looked over to the box, as if expecting it to have disappeared. He got out, locked, and walked around the gate up to the curve in the overgrown road. No one. Well, there shouldn't be. Not till Gast and Joe got there. Late twilight, nerves on high alert. A chill in the air. He slipped on his windbreaker.

Cynthia kept coming into his mind. He blocked her body's image as best he could. He checked his watch. He heard a car. 10:34. It drove toward him and pulled up beside his Mazda. Joe's Merc. Good. Gast got out the passenger side, Joe from behind the wheel, both wearing T-shirts and jeans. For a second Gast's shaven head looked unfamiliar, something threatening about it. And Joe's groomed shoulder-length hair seemed too thick, as if hiding something. But they grinned as they walked toward him and immediately everything was cool. "Hey, guys."

Sound of a motor. Headlights. A dark Saturn Ion stopped half behind the Merc, half behind the Mazda. Accident, or statement? A tall light-haired man got out of the driver's side, a woman nearly as tall from the other. She waited for him and they approached the gated road together. She had short curled hair, wore a sweatshirt and light pants over a slight frame, and carried a large purse. The man wore a black T-shirt, jeans and construction boots. Joe introduced them: "Derek Cooper. David Soy and Christine Gagnon." Nods, no hand shaking.

Soy said, "Nice night."

"For making a deal," said Derek.

"Right to it, eh?" This from Gagnon. "You got the stuff?"

"Yep. You got the money?"

She pointed to her purse. "Right here."

Derek said, "Let's see it."

"When we see the weed."

"Get it, Derek," Joe directed. "It's okay."

Derek walked back to his Mazda, unlocked the passenger door and pulled out the box, closed the door without locking. Still that sense of some kind of presence. Stupid—of course a presence, four other presences. He returned to the group. Gast took the box from him and opened it. A large clear plastic bag, held closed by a twist-tie.

Gagnon said, "Open it."

Gast untied it and pulled the plastic down. A flashlight shone from Gagnon's hand. She beamed it at the bag in the box. Two beautiful kilos of thick green marijuana, Quadra's finest. Gagnon nodded at Soy. He reached for a leaf, sniffed it, put it on his tongue, waited, closed his mouth, chewed. Nodded again.

Gagnon opened her purse and pulled out a thick manila envelope. She handed it to Joe. He opened it, took out four wads of bills. Gagnon said, "Fifties. Forty to a pack."

Gast said, "Count 'em."

Joe fanned each pack. "I trust Christine and David."

Gast shrugged.

Derek said, "Christine. Want to shine your light on the bills?" She did. He thumbed it through, one pack at a time. It took a couple of minutes. He nodded. "Okay."

Gast handed Soy the box. He took it and glanced at Gagnon. She said, "Nice doing business with you gentlemen. See you around." Back to their car and Gagnon opened the trunk. Soy placed the box inside, she closed the trunk. They got into the Saturn, backed up, turned, drove off.

Derek let out a long breath. Joe nodded. Gast grinned, "First of many, Derek."

Derek took one hank of bills and counted out ten fifties for Gast, ten for Joe.

Gast said, "Want to go for a coupla brewskies?"

Derek returned the money to the envelope. "Thanks, guys, but I got a date."

"Okay, man," said Joe. "Two or three weeks, they'll be wanting more."

"Got to give me time to get to my man."

"Much as you need." And to Gast, "Come on, I need a beer. See ya, Derek."

"See you, guys."

They got into the Merc and drove away. Derek realized he was shaking. Not fear now, but relief. He reached for his keys. His hand trembled. He was sweating. Shaking. Get rid of this tremor before driving. He shoved the keys into his pocket, the envelope in his armpit under the windbreaker, and walked back down the path. He spread his legs wide, and stretched. His mind burbled with the relief of a done deal. So he didn't hear anyone come up behind him, didn't sense anything till something hit him hard on the back of the head, saw only a man with a pink bear head swing at him again. Derek went to one knee, two, holding his head as the bat struck his hands, his back, his head, till he lost consciousness.

ONE

THE PHONE RANG. Noel Franklin looked around for it. Lost as usual. He followed the ring, found it on his bed. "Hello?"

"Hi, Noel. It's Jason."

"Jase. Hello." Noel's best friend in high school, but until their school reunion last spring, nearly twenty-five years since they'd seen each other. "Hey, how are you?"

"Actually, not great."

"What's up?"

"It's awful. I can barely handle it. And Linda—Noel, we need your help."

"What's going on?"

"Our son. Derek." Jason's voice was ragged. "He's in a coma. Beaten up. Badly."

What would it feel like to have a son beaten and in a coma? What did it feel like to have a son? He couldn't remember which son Derek was. "The figure skater?"

"His older brother."

"Jase—that's awful. When did it happen?"

"Three weeks ago. Hospital can't do anything, they say we have to wait." Jason sounded close to tears.

"How'd it happen?"

"Nobody knows. A lady and her dog found him, police say they're still investigating—"

Noel heard a sob catch in Jason's throat. "They getting anywhere?"

"If so, they're not telling us. And I don't know anybody who could look into what happened. Except—maybe you. And—your partner?"

Not a good time for a job. "You mean now?"

"Soon as you can. Linda and I'd sure appreciate it."

Noel's next few days involved nailing down some documents for a case in Nanoose before his brother and sister-in-law arrived to visit their parents in Qualicum just up the coast. "It's complicated, Jase. My brother's coming in on the weekend—remember Seth?"

"Yeah. But for a couple of days before then? Please?"

What could he and Kyra do in a couple of days? He and Jason had been close, but way back when. Still— "Look, I'll phone Kyra, maybe we could come up for a day or two. Don't know how much use we'll be." Noel rubbed his eyebrow. "I'll get back."

"Thanks. Thank you. Uhmm—you've got to tell me how much you charge."

"Let's wait till we see what the situation is." Noel's new standard response. "Anything more you can tell me about the beating?"

"That's everything I know. Derek's a good kid, going to the college, getting good grades. The way the doctors were talking, I'm scared maybe his brain's fried."

"Your other two boys are fine?"

"Taking it hard." Again a catch in Jason's voice. "We all are."

"Okay, I'll be up. Maybe both of us. Let you know when."

"Thanks. I appreciate it. Really."

"I can't promise anything."

"Just to know someone's trying— Thanks, Noel."

"Yeah. See you." He disconnected, dropped the phone back on the bed— No, put it where it belongs, base on the kitchen counter. He walked through the living room to the veranda overlooking the Gabriola ferry terminal and Nanaimo harbor. A soft summer afternoon. He watched a floatplane skid to its dock by the pub.

Jason. Best friend through grade twelve. Since then they hadn't talked until last spring's reunion. Noel had never been to a reunion but figured maybe a quarter century was a big deal. See what all those people had been up to.

At the reception he'd talked to ex-fellow students. Then, across the room, a man who had to be Jason. He'd been a scrawny kid, as had Noel, but the guy had muscled and matured. Hey, a bald spot. At his side, an attractive dark-haired woman.

Noel sipped his drink and crossed the room. "Hey, Jason."

"Noel?"

"The same."

"Hey!" Jason stood, reached out his hand. "Great to see you." It hadn't been great twenty-five years ago. Just before their grad, Noel had explained to Jason that he was gay. At first Jason wouldn't believe it. Quickly he did. Until Noel went off to university in the fall, Jason had mostly avoided him. They'd not seen each other since. What to say? He took Jason's hand. "Great to see you, too."

They stared at each other for a moment, their hands falling to their sides.

Jason said, "I wondered if you'd be here."

Noel realized he was glad he'd come. "Yeah. Me too. About you, I mean." Which was not a lie. He'd been badly hurt by Jason's rejection. Over the years he'd thought about Jason often, but with a lingering sadness. Seeing him now, it didn't hurt anymore.

"Introduce me," the woman said to Jason.

Jason put his arm around her. "My wife, Linda."

"Hello, Linda." Noel shook her hand. "Pleased to meet you." He looked at Jason. Might as well put it on the table. "My partner died last summer. A year ago now."

"Oh, I'm sorry," said Linda, and excused herself. "You two'll want to talk."

Noel and Jason greeted ex-classmates as they glanced at their name tags, but talked mainly with each other. After three stiff drinks Jason said, his tone heavy, "Noel, I'm sorry I wasn't a better friend."

"You were a good friend."

"But I didn't understand."

"It's okay now."

Twenty-five years of catching up. Impossible in one evening. Headlines: Jason ran a couple of woodlots on Quadra Island. Linda, a nurse, worked at the hospital in Campbell River. They had three sons. The middle son was a promising figure skater. Noel told Jason he'd been a reporter for the Vancouver *Sun*. Jason said he never read it. Noel explained that he and a woman friend had started a detective agency, Islands Investigations International, concentrating on the Canadian Gulf Islands and, in the US, the Puget Sound and San Juan Islands. He lived in Nanaimo, Kyra in Bellingham. They joined forces when a case needed both of them. "Keeps the mind occupied," Noel said. "And we like working together."

As they all left the reception, Linda said, "You'll have to visit us on Quadra."

Noel held the door open. "I'd like to. Meet your boys. Take in a cold ice rink."

"That's where we mainly live," Jason had retorted, with a wry grin.

They'd talked twice on the phone since, but hadn't seen each other.

Noel had been looking forward to spending time with his parents while his brother's family was there. They didn't get up from southern California often. His mother, in particular, was looking forward to having her two "boys" together, chatting about this, that, and other important things as they used to. Maybe, with Kyra, they could do this job quickly.

He phoned. She sounded strange, not her usual light teasing self. Sure she'd work with him on Quadra, she didn't know that island. She needed some distracting. From what? She didn't say. His parents would be pleased by her visit too. Okay, they could all have lunch together, including his niece Alana who had come up early. Then he and Kyra could drive north to Campbell River, couple of days to ask questions about the boy in the coma. Back on the weekend when Seth and Jan arrived.

He also called an old friend, Albert Matthew, one-time member of the Nanaimo contingent of the RCMP, a bit of a gay-basher when Noel first met him. Noel had had to, well, educate him; they'd become good friends. Last year Albert was promoted to General Investigative Services, the plainclothes division, headquartered in Victoria. Noel had seen less of him since, but they kept in touch. A couple of hours after calling, Albert got back with the names of the investigating officers in Campbell River, Dorothy Bryan and Harry Latiche. Albert offered to pre-introduce Noel and Kyra. Noel declined.

Then he sat down at the computer, called up the Islands Investigations International website that he'd built, made two small adjustments on one of the hyperlinks, and felt pleased with himself. The site, plus their ads in five different phone books, had brought in a number of well-paying but dull cases. Finally he did some preliminary computer research on Campbell River and Quadra Island and went to bed early.

Kyra Rachel threw black jeans, brown pants, a tan skirt, four tops, some underwear, and a pair of low heels into her bag, collected toiletries and her purse, checked it—yes, the Mace was there—locked the door of her condo and took the elevator to the garage. Driving to

Nanaimo was a major improvement over sitting home brooding. She could fret in the car. Or not. A plane would get her there too quickly. She had a decision to make.

Noel had heard it in her voice. "What's the matter?" he'd asked. Damn, was she so transparent? "Nothing," and she'd tried to laugh. "Just haven't exercised my voice this morning." Kyra did not want to tell him until she had to. And not on the phone.

Damn speed dating! If she hadn't gone to that get-together— If she'd continued seeing Jerome— If she hadn't gone on those dates— Yeah, right, if wishes were floatplanes, beggars would fly.

She pulled onto the I-5 and let the Tracker galumph over the concrete slabs that paved this part of the interstate.

All right. The speed dating reception had been fun. Twelve men, seven minutes with each. At the end of the evening she had two matches, men she wanted to see again who also wanted to see her. That part was okay.

And she couldn't blame Jerome; she'd broken it off over his goddamn dog. Nelson had bitten her ankle. Again. "It's either the dog or me!" "But Kyra," said Jerome, "my son gave the dog to my wife before she died. I can't just give him away." Then Jerome took up with Ann Blair who'd taught the art history course where Kyra had met Jerome. Well, she didn't really mind that either. Except he'd done it within days. And phoned her to tell her. And that damn Nelson liked Ann. And Ann liked damn Nelson.

The problem is: I am Pregnant. With a capital P. The problem is, what am I going to do? The problem is further complicated: who is this baby's father?

She reached Blaine and slowed for the border. She'd driven half an hour without once noticing the intense blue sky or the vibrant green grass, or felt the full heat of early July. Just after the national holidays in both of her countries. Kyra hadn't given any real consideration to summer border traffic; maybe she should have flown after all? But every booth was open and the traffic bumped along. Her turn.

"Nationality?"

"Canadian." Kyra handed him the correct passport.

"Your car has a Washington license plate."

Kyra smiled. "I'm working in Bellingham temporarily."

The young man—did he have children?—scowled at her, but didn't pursue the point. "Purpose of your trip?"

"Family."

"Anything to declare?"

"No—"

"Have a nice visit."

"Thanks."

—except that I'm Pregnant and don't know by who. Whom.

At a rest stop after the border Kyra pulled in to use the washroom. Did she need to pee more frequently already? At least with her Canadian passport there'd been no delay. As a dual citizen she carried two passports—American for getting into the US, Canadian going in the other direction.

She re-entered the traffic flow. Two choices: have an abortion or have a baby. How do you explain to a child you don't know who its father is? Kyra remembered a friend telling her about a friend of a friend who had a baby by a sperm donor and said she'd tell it, *Into every life some trauma falls and not knowing who your father is, that's yours.* Could Kyra do that? Would she want to?

Abortion. Of course every woman must have control over her body. Of course in this imperfect world, women have the right to terminate pregnancies. Of course in her perfect world no woman would conceive an unwanted child. Could Kyra have an abortion? Did she want to?

Turn it off, dearie. Think about something else. She'd purposely left her juggling balls at home. They often relaxed her when she had a knotty problem to deal with: juggle the issue into clarity. But two balls were too easy, and in this case the only possibilities were in the air at the same time: baby or abortion. Damn!

Kyra took the overpass and drove on to the Tsawwassen ferry terminal. The parking lot looked crowded. July. Of course. "Will I get on the next ferry?" Kyra asked.

The woman at the fare booth gazed around the lot, back to her computer. "Probably." She smiled. Kyra smiled back. Her first smile of the day.

She drew up behind the car in the appointed lane, turned off the engine. Silence, of a sort. Screams of seagulls, music from cars, laughter, demands of children, admonishments of parents. Nothing she had to deal with. Yet.

Damn. She'd forgotten her book. She turned the key. The radio came on. A discussion: reduced fertility in women since the turn of the century. Damn. Kyra wrenched out the key, got out, slammed the door and crossed the parking lot to the ostentatious new building that contained coffee and restrooms. She used the latter—again—and bought a skim latte. The interminable wait for the coffee turned her mind off. Temporarily.

Back in the car, sipping, she forced herself to bring up the two men's—now putative fathers'—names: Mark and Brian.

Mark: about six feet, styled collar-length brown hair shiny from shampoo, pleasant face with regular features. His dark blue eyes leapt out with singular immediacy; that's what had grabbed Kyra. He worked from home as an accountant for a Seattle firm. He hated dogs, yay. He made her laugh. Kyra had a drink with Mark. Two days later, Kyra had dinner with Mark. Three day later, Kyra had sex with Mark. The condom slipped off as he shriveled. Too bad. Kyra had had a nice time until then. Then in the morning he was gone. A note said, *Thanks*.

Brian: tall too. Thick curly hair, quirky grin, strong chin. A paralegal. He'd been to Reed College, Kyra's alma mater, graduated a couple of years before her. They had dinner at an upscale restaurant. They had dinner again. Back in his vintage Ford convertible, Brian put his arm around her, kissed her. She kissed back. But Mark's note still flamed in her brain. But Brian was awfully nice. The next day she invited him up for a glass of wine. He didn't have a condom and he wanted sex. He had it. Kyra couldn't call it rape, exactly. How much had she led him on? He was polite, and he told her he thought she was lovely. Although he refused her condom. In spite of that she did have an orgasm, which was very nice.

Which was the father? She'd gone off the pill seven months ago and her cycles had become irregular. She checked her calendar and her memory. As far as she could think, sex with Slipped Condom had happened two days before the peak of her cycle, Naked Sex two days after. As far as she could think.

So here she was, alone with Pregnant. The drugstore test had confirmed it. And her breasts were extremely tender and if the ferry didn't dock soon she'd head to the restroom again. What the fuck to do? She'd pick a delicate time to tell Noel.

She parked in a guest slot in Noel's parking garage, used her key to get to his condo.

"Hi," Noel said, leaping up from his sofa. "You made good time."

"I'm pregnant, I'm keeping the baby, I don't want to damn talk about it." Kyra's eyes filled with tears, from joy or desperation. Her head fell onto Noel's shoulder.

"Oh." He hugged her. Oh dear.

One of the advantages of traveling first class, you were off the plane quickly. Austin Osborne hated sitting in back rows, standing sardined in the aisle as the plane slowly emptied. First class, few passengers, he could stretch. The hatch opened and he moved.

He punched in his cell phone as he strode past boutiques and coffee outlets to the stairs to the luggage carousels. Ringing, click. "Hi Austin. You on the island already?"

Osborne disliked call display. He tched. "Hello Steve."

"Just like to know who's phoning. Eliminates the surprise."

"I don't like surprises. Thought you didn't either." In fact, Austin knew Steve hated being caught unawares. "I just landed in Vancouver."

"Going over tomorrow?"

"Floatplane, first thing. When are you arriving?"

"Oh, end of next week."

"Get serious, Steve. We have issues to resolve. The season is approaching."

"You think I am not fully aware? No worry, I'm booked on the Friday 1:10 to Campbell River."

"I'll get Randy to pick you up."

"Thanks, Austin. You are too gracious."

"Damn right I am," said Osborne.

"When does Shu-li get in?"

"Thursday afternoon."

"How nice for you. Direct from Calgary? Or is she gallivanting?"

Of course direct. There are direct flights between civilized places. Austin said, "Direct."

"See you Friday."

Austin broke the connection. He should call Shu-li. Even with her successful if abbreviated career, which had taken her to competitions around the world, her nerves got panic-attacked before any flight. Luckily her recuperative power was strong. Without it she'd never have taken all those silvers and golds.

No luggage yet—the carousels weren't even turning. He poked in her number. Answering machine. He broke the connection.

Shopping? She liked doing that. Visiting someone? A consultation? No, definitely not. Shu-li was far too careful. They all had to be careful.

Ten AM and Kyra and Noel, down in the underground garage, got into his Civic. Suitcases in the trunk, on her lap her big sack purse containing her needs: make-up, camera, iPhone, Mace, flashlight, tissues, Band-Aids, tampons. Which she really didn't need, now.

Earlier they'd futzed about with breakfast. Kyra didn't want much, piece of dry toast and milk. Thanks. Last night she'd drunk milk at dinner. No wine, Noel, really. She'd flopped onto the chesterfield and taken control of his TV remote.

The elephant in the living room, Pregnant, swished its tail but fortunately not its trunk. Noel respected Kyra's desire to not talk about it so the only conversations took place on the TV screen. What had she been thinking? She'd gone off the pill after nearly two decades when she read about terrible side effects on the body as it responded to synthetic estrogen. She'd detailed them to him in vivid and gruesome disgust: she wouldn't do that to her body any more. He hoped she'd be careful. He thought: Pregnant.

For a few minutes Kyra flicked channels and complained, Nothing on. Then she pleaded fatigue. She took herself and her fetus to Noel's study sofa-bed. Early.

Before turning in Noel manoeuvred around the elephant to phone Jason. He and Kyra would meet him at the Campbell River hospital around three. The elephant followed Noel to his room. He lay flat on his bed. How is she going to manage a baby? What will Triple I do with a baby? Where do I fit in? What happens to Triple I? The elephant moved into bed with Noel. A long time before he fell asleep.

What with Kyra's fatigue, Noel's insomnia, and the elephant, it was late by the time they got going. He drove onto the street. "We have to talk about this baby."

"Yes, we should." Kyra sounded academic and distant.

"What are you thinking about it?"

"Not."

"How do you feel?"

"Ehhh."

"What may I do?"

Kyra sighed, a deep blow-out of breath. "What can you do? All I know is I think I'm keeping the baby and that's as far as I've got."

Noel sighed too. The elephant in the back seat patted his shoulder with its trunk. "Want to talk about this case or about visiting my parents?"

"Your parents. We'll talk about the case between Qualicum and Campbell River."

"I didn't tell you, Alana's been there for a week," Noel said.

"What is she now? Thirteen?"

"Seventeen."

"No!"

"Yep. Graduating high school next spring. She came down to Victoria with Mum and Dad and me when I drove Dad to his treatment last week. Alana and Mum shopped while Dad and I went to the clinic."

Over the past month Noel had been driving his father to Victoria for prostate cancer treatment. Over that time she'd taken on a couple of small cases for Triple I, one on Lummi Island, one on Mercer—not much of an island, it had two bridges. Minor problems, low fees. Bad in two ways—reducing the balance in her bank account, giving her lots of time to worry. Now she thought, Noel can run the business while I have a baby. She breathed deeply against a wave of nausea. "And how is your dad?"

"Well, they say the treatment's working."

"And your mum?"

"It's been hard on her. And she can't do highway driving because of her eyes, and Dad can't drive with the chemo."

Driving. They both looked out the window at the road, the cars and trucks whizzing by, a July-blue sky, black sheep and white sheep in the browning green fields. Kyra pressed a switch and her window descended. Real difference in outside color, the tinted windows easier on the eyes but distorting too. Warm scented air blew in.

"My parents are delighted you'll be there for brunch." Noel said.

"I haven't seen them in ages. And I haven't seen Alana since she was about six."

"They don't come up much." Idle chat. The elephant, taking up a lot of room.

"How far is Qualicum?"

"Oh, thirty minutes."

"I have to pee. Pretty immediately."

They were passing Nanoose Bay. With the tide out, the mudflats were ripe. "Hang on," Noel said. "There's a gas station at the stoplight."

Kyra did not like Pregnant having such control of her bladder. She tightened muscles. Goddamnittohell.

Of course the stoplight was red. Kyra tightened more muscles. Noel whirred into the gas station. She got out, walked swiftly, collected the restroom key, peed with relief, returned the key. Satisfied. "Thank you."

Noel wondered if needing to pee abruptly grew from pregnancy or anxiety. The elephant in back was momentarily asleep.

Tim Cooper enjoyed working their woodlot, and being with his father was great. But did they have to decide today what to take out in the fall? And parts of the southern lot, over 386 hectares, hadn't been checked on in a year. They should walk the land, see what had happened, before making any firm decisions. But not this morning.

His mind kept wandering from their fir, maple and cedar, heading in only one direction: over Discovery Passage to Campbell River, up to the hospital, to the bed his brother lay in. Derek hadn't moved in three weeks. Would he ever move again? Those were the issues of the moment, not a bunch of trees. His dad was planning on the noon ferry, still a couple of hours away. His mother, in the same hospital as Derek, wouldn't be at his side, but wherever a nurse was needed. Though she couldn't do much for Derek right now. But Derek needed someone with him. Someone other than Cindy. Cindy was—oh, okay, and she did care for Derek but she wasn't family. Tim had read that people in comas can maybe hear what's being said or feel someone's hand, they just can't react or talk back. If he had his driver's license, he'd take Derek's truck and be there right now. But that had to wait eleven months. What's going to happen to Derek before next year? He glanced at his watch again—

"Hey, Timmy! Come look at this!"

He jogged ahead and spotted his father bending over, staring at the ground. "What's up?"

"Here." Jason Cooper pointed a little way into the woods at a heap of earth nearly five feet high. It seemed to be moving. "And here," he gestured down to their feet.

"Wow." A trail of ants three wide marching across the dirt road, many carrying tiny white eggs. They were transporting them from the heap which, as Tim looked closer, was actually a huge ant hill. "Neat. What are they doing with the eggs?"

"Probably starting a colony somewhere on the other side of the road."

"Should we let them?"

"Course. They break down leaf matter."

"And maybe trees?"

"Only when a tree's down. They'll speed up new soil production."

One of the things Tim most admired about his father was the precision of his explanations. His father hated waste, in language as in most aspects of daily life. "So ants are good for the woodlot."

"Part of the system. Take them away, the system's that much poorer." Jason looked his son square in the eye. Tim and Jason stood about the same height, each half an inch under six feet. They both had high foreheads and blue eyes. Jason's beard was going white, Tim had yet to grow more than fluff. They both wore jeans and thin long-sleeved shirts. Jason said, "How come you were hanging back?"

"Thinking."

"Derek?"

"Yep." Tim dropped his father's glance. "You think—he'll come out of it?"

Jason lay his hand on Tim's shoulder. "Yes," he said. "That's what I think."

"But you don't know, do you."

"I can't see the future, son. Much less control it. Except here on the lot." He dropped his hand to his side. "This I can plan. We can plan."

"Can we go over now? I'd like to."

"Let's take another half hour here. We're too late for the 11:00 anyway."

Tim looked at his watch. If they pushed, they might still make the 11:00. But he didn't argue. More than anything Tim wanted Derek to get better, and quickly. Right after that he wanted the mystery solved, why his brother was so god-awful beaten. If he could be the one to solve it, even better.

They walked for ten minutes to the northwest sector, the only sound the tromp of their boots on the forest floor among the big firs. The high sun was penetrating the thick foliage canopy, raising the tangy scent of newly growing branch tips and warming duff. A squirrel chittered and a pileated woodpecker rat-a-tapped. His father, staring at the near distance, said, "Oh dear."

"What?"

"Over there." He gestured forward, then crunched through brush and downed branches. The woodpecker and squirrel went silent.

Tim saw his father's concern. Half a dozen big fir, each maybe twenty inches in diameter, lay aslant, uprooted, crowns of downed trees interhooked with branches of upright trees. The root masses, spreading fifteen to eighteen feet, showed how shallow the roots had grown—very little topsoil here, old volcanic rock. "Must've been that windstorm in April," Jason said.

Tim nodded. Roots intrigued him. Tim had learned the details of photosynthesis in his biology class but had been prepared for his lessons by his father's explanations when he was small. "What're you going to do, Dad?"

"Don't think we can get lumber out of those. Have to buck and split it for firewood." He stared ruefully at the uprooted trees.

They'd be worth less than what they'd get for logs that went to the mill, Tim knew. Which these days was little enough. Sure hoped Derek would be okay by then, and willing to pitch in—Tim didn't want Randy around helping out again. Randy gave him the creeps. "Dad, you aren't going to hire Randy again, are you?"

"I've been thinking I might get Zeke to help out."

Relief. "Great. Randy's bizarre."

"He's not bad. A hard worker. Knows what to do without always being told."

"Anyway, I like Zeke." He glanced at his watch: 11:10. Plenty of time to get on the noon ferry if this wasn't July; with all the summer people there might be an overload.

Jason may have been thinking this as well. "Come on, let's get going."

They walked back the fifteen minutes to the house, a rambling early 20th-century farmhouse in a clearing, surrounded by small barn, workshop, a couple of storage sheds. Eighty acres of the land had been a working farm—hay, cattle, a few sheep, and a kitchen garden—when Jason's mother's father, Harry, was a young man; then Harry had turned the pastures into more woodlot, way less drudgery, soil hadn't been great in the first place. He'd planted cedar and fir, and found work on the big island. Tim wanted to grow up the way his grandparents had, the farmhouse the comfortable place where Grandpa had lived, where Tim and his family lived. A happy place. Till three weeks ago.

Tim changed into shorts and a T-shirt, Jason into khakis and a short-sleeved shirt. They each took a banana and an apple and climbed into Jason's Corolla, deep blue, five years old, and drove down the long dirt drive to the macadam of Gowlland Harbour Road. The woodlot on the farmhouse side of the road belonged to Jason; across the road was Crown land held by Jason on long-term license. Good trees on both sides.

It was ten minutes to the ferry dock at Quathiaski Cove, four miles. But Tim felt nervous. Sooner they got to Derek's bedside the better.

Jason said, "Going to stop for a paper."

Tim glanced again at his watch—11:38. He thought, Get the damn paper in Campbell River. He said only, "Is there time?"

"Sure."

Tim felt the car speed up. Good. He leaned back and closed his eyes. Usually if something seemed wrong, he'd scan it and most often be able to figure out where or how that bit of out-of-placeness leapt the tracks. Not this time. Whoever had beaten Derek couldn't have had a reason because Derek was simply a nice guy everybody liked. Nothing stolen from the truck, the change in the glove compartment all there in the old film canister, even the ferry ticket card was there, and the truck itself hadn't been stolen or bashed around. For the dozenth time Tim said, "I'm not getting it, Dad."

"Derek."

"Why?"

"Yep, that's the question."

"You'd think—if it was robbery—"

Jason shook his head. "Doesn't look like it."

"You think—somebody was mad at Derek?"

"Maybe."

"Derek couldn't make anybody mad."

"I don't know, Timmy. I just don't know."

At West Road they turned right onto Heriot Bay Road. A couple of hundred meters along, at the school Tim had gone to all his life until last year, they turned right again, passing the Village Square and Niko's Sushi Bar and Grill, great restaurant once, closed now—Tim hadn't cared for the sushi but the steaks were great—and on to Q-Cove Plaza. Jason parked in front of the Drugmart, jumped out, went inside, came back in less than a minute with the *Mirror*. Tim noticed his father check his watch before climbing in behind the wheel.

Jason started the engine and winked at Tim. "Plenty of time."

They drove downhill to the ferry line-up, the *Powell River Queen* there already. Two and a half rows of cars ahead of them—not that many, usually more on a summer morning. The 8:00 and the 9:00 would've likely been overloads, Tim figured, maybe the 11:00 too—Oh, but they were already loading. Maybe they wouldn't get on? Damn!

"We're fine," said Jason.

Was Tim that readable? He wished he could be more secretive. He wished he could see into the future. Heck, he'd settle for seeing the past—to see what happened out where Derek got beaten up. And why. Maybe if he could figure out why he'd learn who.

He'd done everything right and it felt good. Almost as good now as actually doing it. He sat in the big chair and realized he was smiling again. Even after three weeks he still felt, in his hands and arms, a bit of the satisfaction. Kid was a big shot, bruiser hockey player type, thought he could handle himself. But no, didn't happen, not against him and his bat. Did that ever feel weird, good kind of weird like he was born for it, bashing the kid with the bat, way the wood went slap into soft skin and flesh, hard where it hit bone. He could feel the rib-cage cracks happening, plunk of the bat and a little pop fly fell in safe right between the ribs, crack of the bat at the forearm and thigh and the breaks were sharp singles, then a coupla doubles, clean into the outfield, out to the warning track—that was good, warning track—and that big swing when he got the kid in the head it had to be a heavy-duty man-alive home run—over the fence, into the woods, outta there.

And hey, he'd watch the exchange, grass for cash, seven thou, who'd'a guessed the kid coulda got that out of them. Seven thou that didn't have to be reported. And specially not to the boss. Seven thou, no sharing. Who'd'a thought. Well, six now that Charlie had taken that pot.

He snapped open the can and drank down half the beer. Holy delicious on a hot day, best thing in the world. He'd kinda like to do it again, with a bat like that. Not the same bat, that bat was ashes now. Burned, just like the boss would want it. Had to burn his T-shirt and jeans too, good thing he'd brought others, but not the shoes, they were clean. Lotsa blood on the bat. And inside the plastic bag he'd stuck it in, after. Woulda looked funny, anybody saw him hiking through the woods, baseball bat in his hands. Hey, you got a bat? won't find no pitchers here! Smart, bagging the bat. And the mask. Musta looked weird to the kid, seeing a pink bear. Look out for the bear swinging the bat! Except nobody saw him. Only the kid with the seven thou. Friggin' pink bear in the woods. The bat and the mask, ashes to ashes. If he ever got to do all that again, he'd need a new bat. Mask too—different mask. He had lots of masks.

He finished the beer and went inside. Another beer and a pack of cards. Waiting to see what was dealt, figuring how to make it work for you. Any kind of gambling for that matter. And with that seven thou he'd been able to pay off half his gambling debts. Hah!

He sipped beer and belched. Nothing much to do till the boss started talking about all the problems, the boss'd sure do that. Soon, too. Figure how to solve the problems, yeah. He wondered what it'd be next. He mixed the cards three times, put the pack down on the table, and cut it once. Placed the lower half on top of the upper. Set up for solitaire—good draw: black king, red seven, ace of hearts, the two red deuces, red queen, six of spades. He sipped his beer. Time for the ferry, the evening at Saddleman's, always a few guys there ready for a game. He finished his beer, cleaned up the front of the cabin, washed his face and hands, water-combed his brown hair flat down to his ears, and set out for the afternoon chores.

TWO

TWO CARS PULLED onto the *Powell River Queen* behind Jason Cooper's Corolla. There was still room for one more. "See?" said Jason. "We got on."

One tall and one stocky ferry worker waited till exactly noon. Tall slid the guard across the rear of the ship while Stocky pressed the button on an electronic switch that raised the last three feet of the steel boarding ramp to create a protective barrier. Slowly the ferry pulled away from the dock. Out of Quathiaski Cove and into the burbling water of Discovery Passage.

Tim left the car and stood in the rear, in warm sun. He looked back at the island he left every day to get to his new school, Timberline High, attached to North Island College. His island was a good place to come back to, afternoons or early evenings, depending on whether there was hockey practice. Usually he rode his bike that his parents had bought after he'd grown seven inches last year. If Derek was driving to college he'd throw the bike on the truck for the trip home—sometimes Derek stayed in town with his girlfriend. Shane used to ride with Derek until he went to Vancouver to train for Juniors with the great Carl Certane, a silver and a gold at the 1988 Calgary Olympics, a bronze and a gold in Albertville in 1992. When Shane left home, the Coopers, each in their way, cheered him on while finding themselves saddened (Jason), devastated (Linda), jealous (Derek), or abandoned and relieved (Tim).

Now Tim watched Quadra Island recede, the powerful wake of the ferry cutting across the churning water of the passage at an acute angle. Tim loved living on Quadra. Walk in the woods with his family or by himself, plan with his father the future of the woodlot, read in their living room by the fire in the winter, on the deck in the summer. He'd made some good friends at Timberline, liked half the guys on the hockey team, still got along with most of the kids he'd grown up with. But a lot of the time he enjoyed hanging out at home by himself.

Except for the last three weeks. Without Derek it felt a lot less like home. Shane had come back four days after the attack on Derek. But not for his brother. It wasn't a holiday for Shane; the technicians had re-iced the smaller rink at the Campbell River arena and he had been using it every day. Having won gold last winter at Juniors meant he got *carte blanche* from the rink. Quadra and Campbell River each claimed him as its own.

In the past weeks he'd been a black presence, brooding or in a constant twitch—Jason, Linda and Tim at first hoping it was on account of Derek. Wrong. It had become clear that Shane was obsessed with Shane—his status, his need to get back to training and practice. Moving up to Seniors meant he had to work even harder, as he'd explained. Not that Shane didn't care about Derek's condition, but they knew Derek's coma was only a secondary cause of Shane's agitation.

Tim loved watching Shane skate. He remembered Shane's first double axel when he was eleven, and his first triple in the short program at the Juniors two years back—Tim felt as if the jump/spin had lasted a full minute because it seemed he'd held his breath that long. Shane in a simulated tuxedo had been a miracle of moving perfection. And he would be again. If he didn't fall when there was no reason to. But that'd never happen again. It couldn't.

The ferry slowed as it approached the Campbell River dock. Tim ambled back to the car and found Jason reading his paper. "Anything exciting?"

"Another land settlement up north," said Jason.

"Zeke's going to be pleased."

"Or really ticked off at how slow it's going here." Ezekiel Pete and Jason Cooper had played and fought together all the way through elementary school, had fallen out of contact with each other when Jason's parents divorced and his father had taken him to Vancouver, way better schooling there than he'd get in Campbell River, his father had insisted; and besides, Jason's mother, Sue, was taking up with Richard, like her a member of the Cape Mudge Band. Zeke and Jason re-met summers when he came back to Quadra from the University of Victoria; they formed a friendship stronger than the one they'd left behind. Jason rediscovered his love of the land his mother had left him when she died of cancer, Jason only fifteen.

Halfway through UVic he'd changed his major from engineering to environmental studies, and after his degree had gone to BCIT for a certificate in silviculture. With no immediate profession and little income from part-time forestry jobs, he decided to live on Quadra in the old farmhouse that he fixed up for himself. And soon after, for himself and Linda. Zeke Pete was his best man, even if, as Zeke liked to joke, half of Jason's blood was that thin pallid stuff—"Too many white blood cells there, Jason"—one of Zeke's beloved lines. Zeke was one of the Cape Mudge Band's chief negotiators trying to move toward settlement, hoping to transform the reserve into the tribal land it had once been. Now Jason added, "But it'll help Zeke put more pressure on."

The barrier lowered. The row of cars beside theirs rolled off the ferry. A minute later car brake lights in their lane went red, Jason started the Corolla, and in five seconds they too were driving off. They took 9th Avenue up to Dogwood, turned left, and headed up the hill to the rink. Jason pulled across the oncoming lane into a parking lot. A perfect summer day, the air clean as rainwater. Tim stared at the mountains across on the mainland, crests of snow above brown and green layers, a child's icing colors, as they rose hard-edged against any encroachment on BC's interior.

The façade of Strathcona Gardens, the sports complex, featured two green pipes about a meter in diameter: water slides for the indoor swimming pools. The larger of the two ice rinks had once been the venue for the Junior Women's Hockey World Finals, its ice of professional quality. When Shane had begun figure skating, he'd been one of only two boys who'd taken lessons. Of course they'd both been teased, Queers! Girly-boys! Faggots! The other boy had dropped out. One day, before that first triple axel, three guys attacked him after practice but by then Shane had grown so powerful he'd beaten their faces in. After the first triple axel the thunderous applause was a warning to anybody who'd ever think about challenging Shane again. Outside the rink, anyway.

They pushed open the big glass door, glanced through more glass at men and women swimming laps, and carried on past the information desk: "Hi Coopers!" This from Kay, the cheery large young woman. Tim reckoned she knew him and his father in their own right, but Shane's fame reflected off anyone in his family. They pushed open the door, felt the icy blast, walked past the big rink over to the smaller one. No Shane.

The Zamboni made its cleaning rounds, growling softly as it dragged the conditioner. Driving the Zamboni was the legendary T. Shorty Barlow—as Shorty called himself. He was a tall skinny man, maybe late thirties, maybe early fifties. Standing between tank and conditioner, he called out, "Heya Timeee!" and brought the Zamboni over to the rim of the rink by Tim and Jason.

"Heya, Shorteee!" yelled Tim. The only person outside the family he accepted calling him Timmy.

"Good to see ya." T. Shorty's blue eyes blinked, exaggerating the crow's feet that stretched to his ears. He might be grinning except under his walrus mustache it was hard to say. "Gonna look good on the team again, kiddo?"

Tim said, "Gonna try."

"Hey, can you believe this new machine I've got? Electric, like the Montreal Canadiens have. Plug it in overnight and you're home free."

"Nice, Shorty" Jason said. "Glad to see you. Shane around?"

"Yeah, he was out here. He's with Osborne. How's Derek?"

"The same. Just going over to see him."

"Damn effin' dreadful thing." Shorty pointed to the office. "Shane's in there."

The office door stood ajar. Tim heard heightened whispers. Jason knocked. Silence, then the door opened wide.

Shane said, "Hi Dad, hi Tim." As tall as his father and younger brother, short brown hair, red shirt, khakis and sandals, Shane carried himself like a young man who usually owned the space he walked in but today only rented it. His face, despite its smile, looked strained. "Come on in. Austin's here."

Half sitting on the desk, Austin Osborne, Shane's guide and sponsor. White-blond hair, handsome face, eyes green, tennis shirt, khakis, running shoes. Osborne stood. "Hey Jason." They shook hands. "Hello Timmy."

"Hello." Damn him. *Timmy* was reserved for family and Shorty.

"Hello Austin," said Jason. "Didn't know you were in town."

"Just arrived and headed here, see if Shane was skating. I lucked out." A grin to Shane. "He looked great. Smo—king, that's what he was, Jason, king of the smoke."

Tim felt his usual relief around Austin: Shane had to deal with him, not Tim. He'd known Austin for four years, since Austin had offered to act as Shane's sponsor, covering his training and competition expenses. Shane would never have come this far without Austin, not on what their mother made as a nurse, not on what the woodlot brought in. He'd overheard his parents: how would they repay Austin. But it was impossible because Austin had made it clear all he wanted was to support a great talent. He heard his father whisper, Twenty-five thousand a year, Linda. Costumes alone cost over four thousand.

Austin was saying, "... no leads, no suspects?"

Jason said, "Mounties are at it. Dorothy said she'd keep me informed."

"If there's anything I can do—"

"Yeah. Uh—did we interrupt you? Sounded like the middle of a conversation?"

Austin glanced at Shane. "Talking about the season."

Shane nodded and turned to Jason. "We going, Dad?"

"Yes. See you on the island, Austin?"

"I'll look forward to it."

Austin walked with the three Coopers to the parking lot where he'd left his rented blue Porsche.

Noel's parents, Paul and Astrid Franklin, lived on the ground floor of a condo building near the beach in Qualicum. They'd moved there five years ago. In spite of Kyra's promises to come up, this was her first visit. She'd known Noel's parents since she was ten and her own parents had rented a cabin for the summer next to theirs on Bowen Island. The Franklins had taken her into their family as the daughter they never had.

Astrid opened the door. "Kyra, my dear! It's been far too long!" Their hug was intense. Kyra blinked back tears. How come she'd gotten so damn emotional... His mother hugged and kissed Noel.

Alana was next. "Hi Unc." A jocular almost-adult, not quite

willing to call him Noel without uncle, not willing to call him Uncle Noel as she had since she was two. On her eight fingers and two thumbs, maybe fifteen rings.

Paul remained in his chair in the living room. He'd lost a lot of weight, Noel had told Kyra. She remembered he stood a couple of inches taller than Noel but with the same slim build. "Hello, dear! Long time no see." His voice was still strong.

"You're right." Kyra grasped his hand. She leaned over and kissed his forehead. "My fault."

"You're correct about that." Paul smiled and squeezed.

"I hope I will eventually be forgiven." How quickly she'd adopted the patter she usually brought out for Noel's father.

"You could get on your knees for a thousand obeisances."

"Oh creak, creak." Kyra half squatted.

"Now, dears," Astrid said, "brunch is ready and Alana's starved, aren't you?"

Alana rolled her eyes. Everyone filed to the table.

"You can tell us all the news," Astrid said.

Kyra followed Astrid to the kitchen. She had produced artichoke frittata, a small ham covered with chunks of pineapple, cinnamon buns, fruit salad. Kyra ferried them to the table.

They sat. Kyra studied Astrid's face. How has Paul's cancer played on her? Suddenly thinking, How had she managed motherhood? She pushed that thought aside.

Astrid's skin had gone grey too; normal for people in their seventies? Slim like Paul, a narrow attractive face, her thin lips enlivened by an occasional wry smile. A couple of times while serving she sent a worried glance down the table toward her husband. Kyra noted Noel tracking them. Now he stood, pulled out a cell phone and took pictures of them all. Kyra had made him upgrade. A picture was more powerful than any verbal description, she'd insisted.

"Smile," he said again.

They did, a variety of grimaces.

As he sat down again, Alana asked, "Are you two working on a case now, Unc?"

She was a pretty young thing, Kyra decided, bottle-blonde hair, even features. Though the plucked eyebrows, dramatic black eye shadow, and pierced nose didn't do it. And all those rings. I am getting old, Kyra thought.

"Yeah," said Noel. "We are."

"What's it about?"

Should he be telling a seventeen-year-old kid about this? Well, seventeen seemed older these days than back in Noel's own dark ages. "Kind of messy. A young guy, beaten badly, he's in a coma. Dad, Mum? You remember Jason Cooper when I was in high school?"

Paul said, "Sure we remember Jase."

Noel turned to Alana. "We were close from grade six on. Now he's got three sons. The eldest, Derek, he's the one who's unconscious. Has been for three weeks."

"How dreadful." Astrid's hand covered her mouth.

"Jase asked if Kyra and I could help. They live on Quadra but he was beaten in Campbell River." He cut a small piece of frittata. "The middle son's supposedly an impressive figure skater." To Alana he added, "You still skate, Alana?"

"Yep, but just for the fun of it. What's the skater brother's name?"

"Shane Cooper."

"No—" her eyes bugged at Noel "—way! You know Shane Cooper? He's Worlds! He's maybe Olympics! He's great!"

"No," Noel said testily, "I don't know Shane. It's their oldest son who concerns us. We don't know a thing."

"Oh Uncle Noel, Kyra, may I come with you, please, please, please? I really really want to meet Shane Cooper!"

"Alana. We're dealing with the brother in a coma." Uncle Noel gave her a severe frown. "Not the skater."

"Gran! Can I go with them. Please please?"

"Noel?"

"Please, Unc?"

Paul said, "Alana, I don't want you near a case where a man's been beaten up."

"I'll be with Uncle Noel, it'll be completely safe." And to Noel, then Kyra, "Right? Can I come with you? Please?"

Noel stood. "A word, Kyra." He led her to his parents' bedroom. "I'm not hot on having her along. We need to investigate, not babysit."

"She's hardly a baby anymore." Kyra mused. "Maybe with a family of teenagers she'd sense things we didn't."

"Hmm." Noel mulled. "We're too aged to understand the young?" He shrugged. "Maybe." Back at the table he said, "It's up to your grandparents, Alana."

Astrid folded her hands. "I'm not sure this is a good idea." To Noel she said, "Can you deal with her for a couple of days?"

Okay, just maybe this tough-looking young woman would note things he and Kyra didn't. "I guess so."

"Back by Friday, Alana." said Astrid. "I don't need your parents angry with me."

Now Kyra was thinking, what have we let ourselves in for. And Derek wasn't technically in his teens anymore. Alana Franklin, teenage detective.

"Jim! You in there?" The voice came muffled through the thick plastic wall.

"Yeah! Be right out!" Jim Bristol wiped smudges of soil from his hands and glanced across the four-hundred-plus heritage tomato plants in the shed. Still small but the second crop of the season; he rubbed his chin through his thin beard and headed down the narrow aisle, stepped over a pan of shoe disinfecting liquid, and opened the door. "Hey, Dad. What's happening?"

"The bank's what's happening." Brant Bristol, late fifties, once a tall athletic man, stood stooped forward with osteoporosis. He wore a dress shirt tucked into his jeans. "Got to go over to Campbell River and have another argument."

"Hey, I thought we were golden."

"I think they want us to refinance."

"They don't trust us?"

"That's what I'll find out. Sheds thirteen and fourteen may need less water. Plants seem to be growing too fast. Can you check it while I'm gone?"

"Sure, Dad. Shit. Damn bankers."

"I'll be back before dinner. Defrost a couple of steaks, would you?"

"Sure." Jim watched his father walk over to the car beside the house, a simple double-wide they'd trucked in three years ago and put together on a concrete slab. Funny and sad the way his father moved, like a man who was forever falling forward as he strode on to catch up with his shoulders. Firkin' bank.

He didn't know where Ben was, hadn't seen him come in this morning. Didn't matter, Ben put in his time. Which was important, because Bristol Greens needed at least three full-time people—good thing his father could still keep up his load. He walked away from shed seven, one of three tomato sheds along with eight and nine. They also grew bell peppers, five kinds of lettuce, spinach, kale and chard. And in thirteen and fourteen, the cannabis. Two years ago they'd received their federal license to grow medical marijuana, last spring shipped out their first crop.

Jim had convinced his father three years back that they should apply. With the greenhouse just barely breaking even, they needed a crop to jump them far enough into the black so that they could breathe more easily. The marijuana project was Jim's primary concern.

But the bankers didn't like holding a mortgage on what was in their petty minds little more than a grow-op. That twelve of the sheds produced plain honest organic market vegetables made only a small impression. Legally the bank couldn't call in the mortgage but they might try to shift the terms. Jim's greatest wish: Get rid of the mortgage quickly and pay no more damn interest.

He opened the plastic door to shed thirteen, stepped into the disinfecting pan, drew the soles of his running shoes back and forth twice, and walked over to the nearest row of plants. They looked tall and healthy. Maybe, as his father suggested, growing too fast for the water/nutrient mix they were getting? Speed was good, but height wasn't the only criterion. They needed strength as well—in both senses: sufficient fiber manufacture to maintain good leaf production, and a high level of potency. The Compassion Club, of which Bristol Greens was a member, had produced a study making it clear that AIDS, glaucoma, and cancer patients much preferred high quality cannabis. Who wouldn't, Sam had thought. On reading the details of the report he learned that patients preferred to take fewer puffs, smoking it for its pain-relieving effect rather than for pleasure. Bristol Greens would put only the best product possible on the market.

He checked out the gauges on the vats providing water and

nutrients to the plants through an irrigation system of bleeding pipes he, Ben and his father had put in the year before. He had researched the Federal Medical Cannabis Program handbook, a loose-leaf collection of studies and reports that were constantly being updated, for suggested ratios of nourishment and liquid. The Program recommended a small but allowable range of possibilities. He increased the nutrient side by point-four. In shed fourteen he found precisely the same conditions but here he left the balance as it was. He'd check again tomorrow, see what happened.

Goddamn firkin' bank. And goddamn Derek, too. Sam had gone to see him in the hospital, found him looking more like a mummy than a human. Poor guy. A close friend since grade one. Sam'd trust Derek with just about anything, including a few kilos of marijuana. And Sam would've trusted him a lot more times with weed skimmed off the crop. What the hell had happened, Sam thought for the thousandth time. He'd heard from Gast that the deal had been made, Gast had gotten his cut. So whoever worked Derek over did it for Sam Bristol's four thousand dollars. The government paid okay for marijuana, but from private buyers you got much more. Money to give to his father to reduce the firkin' mortgage. And now, shit. He closed up shed fourteen and headed to the house.

That was another thing, their house. Until five years ago, before his mother died, they'd lived in a big house down on Discovery Passage, a perfect Quadra house. He'd grown up in it. Then his father had sold it, paid off his mortgage there, started the nursery here. They trucked in, and moved into, the double-wide to be close to the sheds. But then bringing the nursery up to an ever-changing code first cut into the profits then threw them into debt. Which meant the new mortgage.

Yeah, it'd take a few years, but they'd make this place profitable. If he could find somebody to replace Derek, that'd happen faster. Going to be hard. He'd trusted Derek absolutely. Maybe Derek would pull through. And if he did? Sam figured Derek wouldn't ever deal dope again. Not for any money.

Noel and Kyra, with Alana, set off up-island after brunch. They drove up the Qualicum connecter to the new Island Highway. A well-engineered road, speed limit 110 kilometers per hour. Noel's Honda wanted to go 130, not much traffic so why not. Except he'd heard from friends that the Mounties were fierce with tickets on this stretch. Didn't make sense: build a beautiful road, put a fast car on it, then penalize the collusion in speed between road and car. But an accepted way to finance municipalities and regional districts.

Alana sat beside Noel, earplugs in residence. In the back, Kyra had a hard time looking out the front window between the two headrests. She leaned forward. "Alana, how do you know about Shane?" She spoke in a voice loud enough to carry over road noise and earplugs.

Alana turned her head, fiddled with something, probably the volume control. "A friend met him at Juniors, last year. Lucy. She told me about him and I've followed him ever since. He's cool, Kyra, just so cool. He's going to be champion. Worlds. Even Olympics!"

"What makes that apparent?"

"Oh, he's just awesome! Wait till you see him. He's a bundle of talent."

"I hear you're a good skater too." Kyra knew nothing about Alana's skating.

"I can stay on my feet, sure, but he's awesome." Alana pulled her earplug out and turned off the machine. "He's just miles better than anyone else. I can't describe it, you'll have to see him." She half turned toward both of them. "Remember Toller Cranston?"

"Not really," said Kyra, thinking: how old does this kid think I am?

"Yes." Noel flicked a glance to his right. "Your grandmother watched him every time she got a chance. Your gramps grumbled, but Mom and I found Toller gorgeous." Noel raised his eyebrows and smiled. "Fluid, artistic, a whole new style."

"You think Shane could be another Cranston?" Kyra asked.

Alana fiddled with her earplug. "I don't know. Shane's his own skater. But he could set a new style like Toller." She stuck her earplug back in, fiddled with the gadget, then leaned back. Kyra caught Noel's half smile in the rearview mirror. His niece, back in teenland.

This new inland highway was zippy but boring. Kyra watched trees, fields, fences, an occasional mountain whiz by. The peaks of Mount Arrowsmith on the way from Nanaimo to Qualicum; now it was more trees, hydro tresses and No Hitchhiking signs. New-growth Douglas fir clad the sides of the highway. Beyond them, clearcuts.

Jason, thought Noel. Jason's son in a coma. What had happened to him? And to Jason over all those years? The pain of Jason walking away when they were eighteen was long gone. But now Noel didn't know what Triple I, what *he* could do for a kid in a coma. For an ex best friend.

When they were fourteen, fifteen, pimples covered Jason's face. Noel, six months younger, still had a clear complexion but worried about acne lying in wait. There'd been a burly, tall guy with a little moustache and acne scars, he was sixteen, in their grade ten English class, who picked on Jason: "Hey, Pimple Face! Hey, Jerkoff!" One day toward the end of term he strong-armed Jason against the lockers. A teacher came by, frowned and the confrontation ended. Next day, outside the corner store that sold candy and newspapers, where Jason and Noel had agreed to meet, there he was again—Matt, that was his name—and he had another go at Jason: "Yo, Pimple Fuck! Zit Heaven!" He poked Jason in the chest with his fist.

Noel appeared, saw them, let loose at Matt: "Hey, leave him alone or—!"

"Yeah? Or what?"

"You get those scars from picking at *your* zits?"

Matt went for Noel's throat. But his hands didn't make it that far. Jason pulled at him from behind, Noel backed away. So did Jason. So did Matt, saying, "Two against one in't fair!" His shoulders slumped and he turned and kicked the shit out of a bench. Noel and Jason walked away fast. They glanced at each other, a silent thanks. That was the look Noel now remembered, driving up the Island Highway.

At the best of times, Kyra couldn't read in a moving car. She didn't have morning sickness, she refused to have morning sickness, besides, it was afternoon. She crossed her arms beneath her tender breasts and stared out the side window. The highway crossed a bridge, abutments on each side and a sign: Nile Creek. She couldn't see any creek. Immediately another bridge, another sign: Crocker Creek. Again, no visible water. Kyra had always thought of creeks as little trickles, yet these were long bridges. Enough to span the Mississippi—or at least an arm of the Fraser. Another sign: McLaughlin Creek. Soon Rosewall Creek, then Waterloo Creek. Noel zipped along. Furry Creek, Buckley Bay—not a creek, an exit—Hart Creek, Bloedel Creek, Trent River. Ah, a river! That deserved a bridge but it didn't look any different from the creek bridges. Damn engineers built this new highway to get from point A to point B fast and safely, so no quaint wooden bridges a meter above sparkling creeks. Nope, stay up on the ridge, cruise along, pretend you're in a plane.

"How you doing back there?" Noel called.

"Creeks! Hell of a lot of creeks. Makes me need to pee."

"Half an hour till we're there. Can you hang on?"

"I'll try." She was going to say, you've never been pregnant. But she knew Alana's earplug wouldn't block conversation. She wanted to say: When you have to pee, it seems you have to pee. "Oh now they're promising us elk!" She crossed her legs. "Look, they've built a fence"—she looked out the other window—"on both sides. No worry about elk on the highway." She leaned forward and said around Noel's seat back, "Tell me more about our client."

Noel thought. "Can't tell you much. Derek's got broken ribs, a smashed tibia, a shattered cheekbone, possible brain damage, internal injuries. Linda, she's a nurse, got him medevacked down to Victoria. After ten days they brought him back. Middle son's the figure skater. Youngest son I don't know anything about."

Kyra's bladder made her cross her legs the other way and tighten her pelvic muscles. "Would you speed up a bit, please."

Noel looked ahead, behind, and obediently did.

Kyra, to keep the demands of her body at bay, went back to reading creek and elk signs.

They turned off the brilliantly engineered boring highway—stunning mountains around them now—onto a narrower new road leading down into Campbell River.

"Gas station," said Kyra. "Quickly, please."

"First one," Noel replied, semi-sympathetic. Bloody hell, is pregnancy nine months of demands? What if we're doing surveillance?

A gas station at last. They all used the restrooms. Noel filled up with gas, couple of cents a liter cheaper than in Nanaimo. In the store Alana, still plugged in, picked up a small bottle of unsweetened fruit juice. Kyra, who'd been thinking about pop, thought, oh shit, and grabbed the same. Uncle Noel smiled at both of them and paid.

Jason had said the hospital was on 2nd Street. Back in the car Noel appointed Alana official navigator and gave her the map. She took it, releasing neither music or juice. Noel turned left, as he knew he had to.

Here you go, baby, Kyra thought. Drinking juice for nine months. Already you're changing my life.

A couple of blocks off Dogwood they located the hospital and a parking space. Lots of green space. Splendid setting for the sick. They entered the hospital, a three-storey building of far greater antiquity than the highway. At Emergency they asked for directions to Intensive Care. Elevator to the third floor. At a nurses' station Kyra said, "We're here to see Derek Cooper."

A plump middle-aged nurse asked, "Are you relatives?"

"Yes," lied Kyra without hesitation.

"He's in 311."

"Not ICU?" Noel asked. He hated hospitals. He knew them too well.

"Telemetry. Just outside ICU."

The three headed down the hall and into a room. In the bed a bundle of body lay under a sheet. Wires and tubes stuck out of it, connecting to bags and monitors. The scalp was bandaged. The skin of the face was deeply bruised, some of it still purple, much of it gone yellow. No one else there, but seconds later three men entered the room, one after the other. Jason and the two brothers, Kyra figured.

Noel confirmed it by grabbing the older one's upper arms and holding them tight. "Jason, I'm so sorry." He glanced toward the lump.

One son had gone around the foot of the bed to the other side. He picked up Derek's hand. "Hi Dee, it's Tim here. Your favorite pest." His voice choked, he cleared his throat, he blinked hard. "You're gonna come out okay."

The other boy must be Shane, confirmed for Kyra first from Alana's intense gaze, then immediately by Jason's introduction. Noel introduced her and Alana to the men.

"I've been following all your successes," Alana said to Shane.

"Right." He sounded deeply uninterested. He stared down at Derek.

The family resemblance was strong. The three were about the same height. The two sons had dark brown straight hair, one day likely morphing to Jason's brown-grey. The three faces were long, with firm chins and narrow noses; pleasant faces. Kyra glanced at Derek. His nose was blunter and his lips fuller. No way to tell anything about his hair with his head bandaged.

Many bodies in the room. Then another body arrived, in a nurse's uniform.

"Hi Hon," Jason said. Linda, the boys' mother, Kyra realized.

"Hi." Linda smiled at them all quickly, then looked to Derek.

"The doctor saying anything new?" asked Shane.

"Nothing different."

Jason asked, "They should do another brain scan."

Linda shrugged. "They're waiting for an indication of some change."

"People come out of comas even after years," said Tim. "We've got to keep him in touch with us. He's got to hear family voices."

Noel introduced Kyra and Alana to Linda, whose smile was tight.

Another person entered the room, a young pretty auburn-haired woman carrying a big purse. "Oh, hi, guys. I just went for coffee."

"Good to take some time away," said Linda evenly.

"Yeah, I've been here since ten. Talking to Derek. Playing his music." She put down her purse and pushed to the bed. "Hi Derek, I'm back."

"This is Cindy," Jason said. "Derek's girlfriend."

Kyra noted the irritation on Tim's face. Shane remained expressionless.

Linda said, "People in comas don't need to be stimulated all the time." Her tone was mildly admonitory.

"Derek likes his music," Cindy defended.

"You checking in with the nurses' station?" Linda's tone was still mild but Kyra caught a fleeting sense of glee from Tim.

"Sure," Cindy mumbled.

Linda pushed by Jason and stroked Derek's forehead. "Too many people in this room. It's just after staff change. There'll be rounds."

"We'll be in the waiting area until you're free," Kyra announced as she motioned Noel and Alana out. Shane came too. After a minute, so did Tim.

"I'm really sorry about your brother," Alana said to Shane.

"Thanks."

Tim slumped on the orange plastic sofa. He took off his cap, put it on backwards.

"How long's he been in a coma?" Alana asked Shane.

Shane sat too. "A few weeks."

"Twenty-three days." Tim pulled the bill of his cap around again, and down so his eyes were shaded. Alana's concern was only for Shane. Kyra, coming to stand beside Noel, said quietly, "What now?"

"We need to see where Derek was attacked."

"And talk to his doctor."

"And go to Quadra?"

"We'll find a motel or a B&B for the night." Kyra looked at Alana, still trying to talk to Shane. He'd crossed his legs and was flipping his foot up and down. Tim's cap sat halfway down his face.

Noel said. "Kyra, find out who Derek's doctor is and when we can see him. I'll go to the car and look up bed and breakfasts. I bet there's a wireless leak around here."

Kyra crinkled one side of her mouth. "I'm your social secretary?"

"Please." He'd learned to despise hospitals when Brendan was dying. "If you don't mind?" He had to get out of here. Her face appeared resigned. He left.

She sat down in a hard lumpy chair and picked up a magazine. Over it, she studied the three teens. Alana, limpid eyes still on Shane. Had she been wrong casting Alana their teen detective? Tim, under his ball cap, aware of anything in the room? Shane, all but immobile.

Linda came in, followed by Cindy with her large purse. Linda looked tired—and though a generation younger than Noel's parents, nearly as grey. Cindy looked what? defiant? sulky? chastised? What had Linda said to her?

Jason arrived last. Kyra said quietly, "Noel and I would like to talk to Derek's doctor."

Jason glanced at Linda. "Doctor Pierce."

"He'll have the reports from Victoria?"

"Yes, he does."

"Where could we find him?"

"Do you have a—?" Linda made scribbling motions.

Kyra pulled out her iPhone. Linda gave her the number. Kyra punched it in. "Thanks." In the hall she pressed Talk. The receptionist said, "The doctor could see you for a few minutes—" she stressed *few*—"in about an hour."

Back in the waiting area she said, "We'd like to see where Derek was attacked."

"A dead-end road." Jason pursed his lips. "I better come with you. Linda," he put his arm around his wife's shoulder, "why don't you take the kids and go home. I'll show them the attack site. We'll come over later."

"We're to talk with Dr. Pierce in about an hour," Kyra reminded him.

"Oh. Okay."

To Alana, Linda said, "You can come to Quadra with us if you'd rather." And to Kyra, "I've got a place for you on Quadra. A friend with a B&B had cancellations. Won't you have to be on the island too?"

Yes, they needed to interview whatever friends and maybe enemies Derek had on Quadra. In the morning. "That's very nice. Thank you."

On Alana's lips, a confused scowl. She glanced over at Shane; he stared beyond her. To Kyra she said, "If Noel doesn't mind, I'll go over with Linda." Linda nodded. "You'll tell me what you find out?"

"That's okay?" Kyra said to Linda, who nodded. Then to Alana, "Sure."

"Come on, everyone. Cindy, take some time for yourself, dear." Linda's tone just wanted to go home. "Derek's getting the best care he can have."

Cindy played with her purse strap. Fear, grief, anxiety, confusion flitted across her face.

"If you do something for yourself this evening, you'll have more to report to Derek tomorrow," Linda stated.

Cindy's eyes teared. "I just want him back again."

"We all do, Hon." Linda patted Cindy's shoulder. "Do you have your car?"

"No, I walked."

Linda smiled. "Jason and the others can give you a ride home."

In the elevator Linda told Kyra that her friend, Barb, had cancellations because she'd informed her bookings that the attic had been invaded by carpenter ants. She only needed the people away for a few hours but they spooked and cancelled. "City people don't know, in the bush you live with lots of critters. If you want I'll confirm the rooms from the ferry. The ants are gone."

"Great." Ants?

A couple of years ago Harold Arensen decided the weather in Victoria far outranked humid Ottawa summers and ice-laced winter streets, so decided to move his base. In Victoria, too, the skating community treated him with appropriate respect. Not that he'd lacked respect in the east, simply that the natural rivalry between the BC skating world and that in the Hamilton-Toronto-Ottawa-Montreal stretch had the west believing they'd brilliantly won Harold away from his haunts for the last thirty-plus years.

Though he preferred Victoria to Vancouver, sometimes it was necessary to spend time on the mainland, especially this year leading up to the Olympics. He'd been a proud supporter of the Canadian faction that had won the 2010 Olympics for Vancouver; if he'd been living on the west coast then he would've been a leading partner in the effort. Now, since many of Canada's superior young skaters trained in and around Vancouver, he'd been following a select few through their coaches, offering advice, sometimes even wisdom, as best he could. To the very best he would offer his unique expertise. They would profit from it, and their success would reflect with burnished grandeur Harold's own place in Skate Canada.

He held out a great deal of promise for several of them, Miranda Steele and Tak Lee in Calgary, Dan MacAdoo and Graham Pauley in Toronto, Danielle Dubois on Montreal's West Island, and especially Shane Cooper from Vancouver, an extraordinary performer. As well he might be, considering Carl Certane had selected the boy, as much for his natural abilities as for his imagination. That faun sequence he'd performed had been remarkable. And with each competition his routines became increasingly polished—in fact, they sparkled.

Today Arensen would watch Shane skate. His preferred manner of observing was from a distance, without announcing his presence. So this morning found Harold driving his vintage Lincoln Continental onto the ferry from the Swartz Bay terminal at the tip of the Saanich Peninsula, heading across Georgia Strait. Ferry time was, he had discovered, a good time to be out of time. An hour and a half of giving himself, like his couple of thousand fellow passengers, over to the good guidance of the ship's captain. He always tried to get a place at the very front of the boat. There he could look up from his book to follow the ship's passage. Now they were passing between Portland Island and Salt Spring, the so-called Satellite Channel. Massive dark-green Douglas firs rose on the Salt Spring side. A sunny summer day and the sea sparkling brilliant blue, wind-blown breakers snow-white as they smashed against the shore on both sides.

Excitement took him as he wondered how much Shane had progressed since his last competition—a fine performance until his dreadful fall. What could have distracted him? Shane had no answer. A bad placement? Possibly, but why? His mind wandering? Shane hadn't thought so. A bad night's sleep? Shane thought he'd slept okay. "Well, don't worry about it," Harold had told him. And added with a smile, "Just make sure it doesn't happen again."

Approaching Harold Arensen's favorite part of the trip across, a narrow boomerang-shaped passage between the southern tip of Galiano and northwest Mayne Islands, called Active Pass. Active it was as the sea roiled between the land masses, smashing against shale shoreline. Past Bellhouse Park, and the ferry was in the open Strait, the last leg before the flat drive from the terminal into the city.

He and four-hundred and fifty other cars and trucks drove off, along a reinforced spit of land, past the Tsawwassen Band reserve, under the Fraser River, through Richmond and into the city. Along to Kerrisdale, home of the Cyclone Taylor Arena. Arensen had pushed Certane hard—get Shane ice time at one of the Olympic venues. But Certane had rejected the suggestion: Stop breaking your head over it, Harold. Wasn't breaking his head, just making a logical suggestion. It took a couple of months arguing with Carl that Harold had learned Carl really was doing the best for Shane—ice time at an Olympic site, when it could be had, was strictly limited from 11:00 PM to

7:00 AM—the rest of day needed to prepare the rink for the Olympic events. Instead, Carl, who was a consultant to Cyclone Taylor Figure Skating Inc., purveyors of skates and costumes to champions, requested and was given prime time daily at the Kerrisdale Arena.

Well, why the hell didn't Carl say so in the first place? Dumb ass.

But that was in the past. Long forgiven. Today Arensen pulled into a space reserved for the arena's brass and parked. He strode through a side doorway. At the information desk he noted a woman in her forties with a strong chin and a mass of blonde hair. "Tell me when Shane Cooper is skating."

The woman checked her schedule. "Don't see his name on for today."

She glanced backward in her schedule. "Don't see his name for anywhere the last couple of days." And forward. "Or later this week."

"That's ridiculous. He has to be training."

"Maybe. But not here."

Arensen exploded a puff of irritated air, started to stride away, turned quickly. "Carl Certane in?"

"Should be. Down the hall to—"

"I know, I know."

To Carl's office, then. Even had Carl's name on it, black lettering. He grabbed the knob, turned it, pushed. A large cluttered desk, computer and papers. A tall man, broad in his hunched shoulders, sitting with his back to the desk, walls covered with photos and posters of skaters. One paper-filing cabinet. Couple of chairs. "Carl, where the hell is Shane?"

The man turned—a frowning face, narrow nose, thick shock of white hair. "That's a door there, Harold. They're made to knock on."

"Sorry, sorry. But why don't you have Shane in training?"

"He is training."

"Where? I want to see what he's doing."

"Well, head up to Campbell River."

"Campbell—? What the hell's all this about?"

"Sit down, Harold, before you explode."

Yeah, Harold could feel his face had gone red. Damn blood pressure. But not something to worry about now. He sat. He spoke slowly, deliberately. "Okay. Campbell River. Why Campbell River?"

"Because that's where he's from. Quadra Island."

"So what, is he on vacation or something? There's not much training time left and—"

"He does have a bit of a personal life, Harold."

"Hey, what's this? Some girl?"

"He doesn't know what a girl is, so just relax. He's got a brother who's in a coma. Shane's spending some time there."

"Yeah, but what about his work?"

"There's a pretty good rink there. I got him excellent ice time."

"Pretty good rink? Gimme a break, Carl."

Carl shrugged. "It was used a couple of decades ago for a world's finals—junior women's hockey. He gets whatever time he needs, whenever. And he's not far from his brother. Close by he worries less about what's going on."

"Women's hockey, for pissake! That's no figure skating rink." He got up, stared down at Carl. "You trying to ruin him?" He stormed out of the office.

"Where you going?" called Carl.

"Home. Where I should never have left." Back to the Lincoln. Back to the ferry. The return trip began to soothe him. Then, in Active Pass, he thought: Shit on it! Campbell River, that's right next to Quadra Island. Which, if he remembered right, was where Austin Osborne had a home. Osborne had been supporting Shane, Harold knew this. Goddamn Osborne! Always dangerous.

THREE

JASON AND KYRA, Cindy trailing, walked downstairs. Jason pushed open a side door. "Car's parked in the next lot," said Kyra.

"We can cut through the garden."

The garden, a quiet green space that featured mown grass, scattered trees and benches, also held a number of sculpted pieces—a figure of a despairing woman in chiseled wood; a ten-foot metallic serpent rising from its coiled tail, called River Spirit; a hand rising from the ground that stood taller than Kyra, holding an enormous egg. Noel snapped pictures with his cell. "What's with all these?"

"No idea," Jason said, and led the way.

Kyra felt unclear regarding Jason Cooper. She granted him his distress—son in a coma with no end in sight would be upsetting. But if she and Noel were to learn anything about the comatose kid, Jason would have to be more forthcoming. "Noel said Derek was found by an old lady with a dog."

"She's known up there, walks the dog at night, says she hardly ever sleeps," said Jason, without turning around. "Got home and called 911."

They arrived at the car. Kyra told Noel about the B&B reservation. "Oh," he said. After finger-dashing around a Campbell River lodging site he'd found them two possible B&Bs. Now Kyra—or Linda—had one-upped him. He closed his laptop.

Jason got into the front seat, Kyra in back. Cindy slumped down beside her. Can't be twenty yet, Kyra thought, but what a drawn, weary face. "He's a strong young man, Cindy. Give him time to pull through."

Cindy nodded. "I hope."

The tension between Cindy and Linda still echoed in Kyra's memory. "Being with him lends him your strength. But he needs time to find his own strength too."

"I know." She sniffed. "I do know."

Jason turned to the back seat. "Which way, Cindy?"

Cindy gave directions—back out to Dogwood, a left, pretty soon a right on Merecroft. Just before the end of the road Cindy said,

45

"Over there." They pulled up in front of a cedar-shingled house set back from the road. To one side stood a small cabin.

"Nice place," said Kyra.

"Thanks," said Cindy. She got out. "Thank you." She started from the car, turned, said to Jason through the open window, "He's going to be fine." She nodded to herself. "Just fine." Quickly she headed toward the house.

"Make a U-turn," Jason said. Noel did. After a couple of minutes he pointed his thumb over his shoulder "That's the Beaver Lodge Forest Lands beyond there. Lots of trails and deer. A few bears, occasional cougar." A couple of silent minutes later he added, "We're close. Take the next left."

Noel turned on a road called McPhedran. Another turn, Evergreen. The homes looked middle class, some upper middle. He wondered about the economy up here now that the Elk Falls Pulp Mill had shut down, any logs left shipped out raw, no value-added wages here. Most of the fish canneries had closed, too few salmon to keep the locals employed. The Honda reached the end of the road, cement blocks blocking auto entrance.

Jason pointed to a closed yellow gate. "Back in there."

Noel read, ACCESS TO TWINNED HOLDINGS PIT. "What's that mean?"

"No idea. But this is where the old lady found him. Her dog, really."

"Any way of talking with her?"

"Don't know where she lives."

Noel and Kyra got out, stepped around the gate, and studied the area. They saw trampled ground desiccated from lack of rain. Tacked to a scrawny maple, a piece of yellow crime-scene tape. They walked to a point where the old road curved. Only the privacy of the area spoke to Noel. He took pictures, to keep the crime scene in their minds.

As if reading his thoughts, Kyra said, "Out of sight from any houses."

"Yeah." Noel started back. "I'd like to ring some doorbells."

At the third house a woman in shorts and an oversized shirt opened the door. No, she hadn't seen anything the night of the attack, just the Mounties' flashing lights. The woman with the walker? Sure, Sarah McDougal, lives three houses down with her daughter. They thanked her.

Jason said, "I'll wait in the car."

"Jason." It was almost as if Jason was undermining them. "We have to ask you some questions. Stuff we need to know."

Jason shrugged. "Ask away."

"How well do you know Derek?"

"What're you talking about?" His voice held tight.

"Does he share things with you? His plans? His feelings?"

"We talk about what he wants to do." He laughed, grimly. "Sometimes about what he doesn't. About what he's done that he's glad he's done. That the sort of thing you mean?"

It's going to take a while, thought Kyra. "What about Cindy, for example. How he feels about her."

"Mmm." Jason considered the question. "Don't really know. He likes her, you can see that. Doesn't tell me much. If he talked about her more, it'd be with Linda."

Like son, like father, Kyra thought. "I had a sense Linda doesn't find Cindy a total charmer."

"It's not so much she doesn't like her, it's—I don't know, kind of—see, they're both so young, Linda thinks Derek's got to finish his schooling, find a profession—he's good with big machines, but he needs to get work. Cindy's okay, but—you know what I mean?"

Could mean lots of things, Jason, but I don't know which ones *you* mean.

"Let's find Sarah McDougal," said Noel.

Jason returned to the car. Kyra and Noel went up the walk to a white-shingled house. Kyra rang the bell. From behind the door the sharp yips of a dog. Then a voice said, "My daughter's not here."

Kyra said, "It's you we want to talk to, Mrs. McDougal."

"What do you want?"

"We're investigating the beating of the young man. We hear you found him."

The door opened a crack, a chain across the space. White curly hair, thick glasses covering brown eyes above a red nose. The dog yipped harder. "Go lie down!" The dog shrank away. "You're not the police."

Kyra said, "No, we're friends of the young man's father, we're trying to help him."

"Well, come in." The door closed, re-opened wider without the chain. "This was once a peaceful neighbourhood." Noel closed the front door. Using a walker, she led the way into a living room to the right. She sat on a straight-backed red-upholstered chair. "Have a seat."

Noel and Kyra sat on a white couch. "Can you tell us about that evening?"

"Too many cars, too many."

"Cars?"

"Willie and I were going to take a walk—" she pointed to the dog, now lying on a blanket—"that's Willie. All these cars kept roaring by, right up to the cement blocks. And one across the street. And they parked there for a while."

"How long?"

"Ten minutes? Fifteen? I don't know, I didn't have a watch."

"Do you know what kind of cars?"

"And trucks. I told all this to the police."

Noel asked, "How many trucks?"

"That I know. One up there. And two cars."

"Old? New?"

"I don't know those things. I don't follow vehicle styles."

"And where were you?"

"Just outside the door. Willie didn't want to go for his walk with all those people there. Did you, Willie?" Willie looked up for a moment. "We waited till they left and—oh, we waited after that too. I think."

"And why was that?" Kyra spoke as gently as she could.

Mrs. McDougal squeezed her eyes tight. "I'm trying to remember . . ." Her eyes opened wide. "The other truck. Across the street. Somebody had got out. He was the second. He walked toward the first truck, I remember that. Then I didn't see him anymore. Then the other cars came, and finally they drove away. Roaring down the road. I just wanted them gone so we could go for our walk."

"But they didn't?"

"The cars, yes." She sounded confused. "I just said that, didn't I?"

"Yes, you did," Kyra said softly.

"Then the man came back to the truck here and got in and made a U-turn and he was gone too. But the other truck was still up there.

Willie and I waited. And then, I thought I'd figured it out—maybe the people from the truck had gotten rides in one of the other vehicles. So if nobody was up there it was safe to go for our walk. I said that to you, didn't I, Willie?" Willie thumped his tail.

Kyra nudged Sarah McDougal on. "So you headed up the road."

"Yes. And Willie was already there and barking his head off. I was hobbling along, but Willie had found that poor boy. He just lying there, there wasn't much light but I could tell he shouldn't be lying like that. And when I got close I could see what was maybe blood, and I was scared—wanted to get away from there quick as I could." She smiled, a sad little curve of the lips. "Which wasn't very fast." The smile went away. "But faster than usual, and I got home and I told Marcie, that's my daughter, what I'd seen, and she grabbed her cell phone and ran up the road and she called 911. Well, the police came, sirens and all the lights flashing. Everybody on the block was there. And the police asked me questions, but I was so upset I couldn't remember very much."

"Did they talk to you the next day?" Noel now, fearing Mrs. McDougal would tire.

"Oh yes, and once after that. I told them everything. The poor boy. How is he?"

"He's in a coma," Kyra said. "Is there anything else you can remember?"

"I don't think I know anything else."

Noel stood, and Kyra. She said, "Thank you, Mrs. McDougal. You've been very helpful."

Grabbing the arms of the walker she pulled herself to her feet. "Have I? I told all this to the police. Have they found out who did it?" She led them to the door.

"They're working on it."

She opened the door. "I can't remember . . ."

Kyra said, "What's that, Mrs. McDougal?"

"If I mentioned—the truck across the street. With a canopy on the back, or maybe it was a van. Can you ask them that? If I did?"

"We will. Thank you again. Goodbye."

They headed back toward the Honda, the foliage along the sidewalk thick but penetrable. A man in a second truck or a van. With the group? What was that all about? They walked past Jason in the car and approached the yellow gate. Noel said, "Three groups meeting. One of them is Derek. A fourth arrives earlier. Two, then the fourth, leave. Derek, left lying on the ground. How do you see it?"

Kyra studied the path ahead, the trees along the side. She walked to the curve and followed the road. Open but overgrown—not a place for a casual stroll. No broken branches or empty matchbooks advertising a locale the mayhem provider usually frequented. No footprints on the dry ground. She needed to pee; a little privacy? She came back to the gate. "Okay. Either Derek was beaten by whoever was in the truck and the car that parked up here, and then they left. Or they left and Derek was okay and didn't leave with them. Maybe waiting for the guy in the truck across the street, or maybe not expecting him but that's who beat him up."

"Right," said Noel. "Does that get us anywhere?"

"We've got a couple of hypotheses."

He grinned. "Moving forward, partner."

"We'd better find Derek's doctor."

In the car they told Jason what they'd learned from Sarah McDougal. He'd heard all that from the police. Including the second truck? He didn't remember. They drove down Evergreen. "Jase. Does Derek get along okay with most people?" asked Noel.

"What d'you mean?"

"Anybody who didn't like him? Enough to beat him up?" She watched as Jason's left shoulder slowly drooped. "What, do you suspect somebody?"

Jason's head shook, just a little. "No. I wish I did."

Noel glanced at him. "You think it was gratuitous? Derek just happened to be here? It could've been anybody passing by?"

"I don't know."

"What was Derek doing here?"

"I don't know that either."

"Who could've known he'd be here?"

Jason whispered, "I don't know."

Kyra said, "We'll need you to give us the names of his friends. Here in Campbell River and on Quadra."

"Sure. But they wouldn't have anything to do with it."

"They might guide us in valuable directions."

"Anyway, the Mounties have already talked to them."

Noel slowed the car and pulled into a commercial parking lot. "Look, Jase. You got us up here. We need information or we're stymied. And you've got to tell us who to talk to about Derek's life. Or we go back to Nanaimo tonight." He opened his computer.

Jason sighed. "It's just, it feels like—like I don't have much of a brain left."

"So let's take it one bit at a time, okay? Now. His friends."

Jason rubbed his chin. "On the island he used to hang out with a couple of guys, Nigel Meredith, and Sam Bristol, friends since grade one. And sometimes with The Demon—that's what they called him, Demosthenes Catokis—except he's the gentlest guy you can imagine. I'll give you addresses and phone numbers at the house."

Noel typed. "Any girls?"

"He dated Bertina the last year before he went to the college and until this spring. But then he met Cindy and Bertina was history. We all liked her. Bertina Anderson."

"Pretty name," said Kyra. "We'll talk to her. What about Campbell River. Friends at the college?"

"I don't know them but Derek used to mention a couple of guys. Mike Campbell, he's in the heavy machinery department too. They're close. Hockey buddies too. And Joe Daimley, another hockey buddy. Derek'd hang out with Joe and a friend of Joe's, Gaston something—Gaston, French last name, Robitaille, that's it. Gast Robitaille." A rueful smile from Jason. "They drank a lot of beer together."

Noel typed. "Anybody else?"

Jason thought. "They were the closest." He thought some more. "Linda might know. Timmy too. Probably not Shane, he's away a lot."

Noel closed the computer lid and started up the engine again. "Thanks. That'll be a start."

Kyra said, "Who're the Mounties who've been working on the case?"

"Huh? Oh, Dorothy Bryan. She's good. And Harry Latiche. Hard man. Professional, I guess. But I've seen him off duty and he's way more relaxed. Hell, long as he does his job."

The names Albert had given Noel. "We'll talk with them after the doctor."

Linda unlocked Jason's Corolla and got into the driver's seat. Alana tried to sit in back with Shane but Tim opened the other door and slid in. Alana sat up front.

Linda drove onto 2nd Avenue. To the back seat she said, "I hear Austin's back."

"Yeah," said Shane.

"They were in the office when Dad and I got there," Tim volunteered.

"Oh? What'd he say?"

"Not much."

A mystery conversation to Alana. Why didn't Shane want to participate?

Tim said, "T. Shorty asked if I was playing hockey this year."

"He pick you up at the ferry this morning, Shane?"

"Yep."

"T. Shorty Barlow runs the Zamboni at the rink," Linda informed Alana.

"Wow. I'd love to drive a Zamboni." Alana laughed.

"Sometimes Shorty gives rides," said Tim. "Or I could. I know how to drive it."

"How do you know that?" his mother asked.

Alana turned around. Tim had his cap on backwards. He shoved at it. "Oh, Shorty showed me." His voice rose on *me*. He took off his cap, turned it around and pulled it over his face. Alana grinned.

In the ferry lot Linda passed a plastic card to the ticket-taker and got it back with their fares subtracted. She drove into the lineup. The BC ferry, with its blue and red stripes over white, glided into its berth.

"What did Austin say?"

"That he'd come to see me skate."

"Well, duh." To Alana, Linda explained, "Osborne has been sponsoring Shane."

"Do I recognize his name? Wasn't he an Olympic champion?" She'd look him up as soon as it was polite.

"Yeah. Late nineties," Shane said, as if it didn't matter much.

"Wow!" Definitely check him out.

"He usually drops over." Linda started the engine and put it in gear.

52

Amazing, thought Alana. All these famous skaters.

Parked on board, Tim got out and slammed his door. Wow, is she ever pretty. Shane sat silent, staring out the window. Tim walked up to the front. Not the prow, he knew—the ferry ran forwards and backwards. He stared for a few minutes at the Quadra shore approaching.

"Hey Tim."

He turned. Randy, the guy who sometimes helped his dad. "Hi Randy."

"How's it going, fella?"

"Pretty good." The ferry approached the dock's guide rails.

"How's your brother doin'?"

"Not so great." What the heck was Randy on about? He had a sense Randy didn't much like Derek—cool vibes between them when Randy had helped out on the woodlot the last couple of autumns. "Still unconscious."

"Damn shame," said Randy. "Sad."

Randy didn't sound sad. "Yeah." Tim started back to the car. "See you, Randy."

"Right. September in the woodlot, right?" The ferry scraped against the barrier. A crewman reached for the attaching cable.

Wrong. "I don't think so."

"No?" Randy's brow furrowed.

"No. Dad's got his friend Zeke to come in."

"Oh," said Randy. "How about that."

"See you."

A minute after Tim had left the car Linda pulled out her cell phone. "Hi Barb, I've got Jason's friends, the detectives I mentioned ... Oh the same. Vital signs stable ... Thanks, we do too ... On the next ferry, I think. Your rooms still open, I hope? ... No, I didn't ask." She looked at Alana. "Would they share a room—?"

Alana quickly shook her head.

"No, two ... Don't worry about the breakfast part, they'll eat with us ... Thanks, Barb. Oops, we're unloading."

Linda pocketed her phone just as Tim slammed back into his seat. She looked back at Shane. "Did Austin say when he might come by?"

"No."

She turned around. Shane was sitting with his arms crossed tightly over his chest. She had never seen him sit so still for so long. Linda started the engine.

Dr. Pierce was running late. Would they be able to come back at five?

Noel turned to Jason. "How's that for the ferry to Quadra?"

"If we have a short chat with the doctor, and if the ferry's running a little late we can maybe get the 5:25. If there's no overload. Otherwise it's the 6:15."

"We'll be back at five," said Noel to the receptionist.

Kyra saw a sign: Washroom. "Catch up with you." Pregnant, demanding again.

"We'll wait," said Noel.

She reappeared shortly. They walked out to the car.

Jason said, "I'm betting on the 6:15. Pierce is often late."

"What's his specialty?" asked Kyra.

"Internist. Good guy, by and large. Not nearly as bad as McPherson, Derek's surgeon."

"Fits all the clichés about the surgeon-god?"

"More like surgeon-king. Campbell River's not big enough for a god."

Noel said, "Time to see the Mounties."

"I'll call, see if either is in." Jason found his cell phone and pressed in a pre-set number. Constable Bryan could see them.

Linda drove through an evergreen forest, trees speckled with slanting sun. Alana was not used to trees this towering, and this green. San Diego was more brown, and pastel-colored houses and palm trees. This road was narrow; at home there'd be an eight lane freeway cutting through the trees.

After many curves Linda turned onto a narrow graveled driveway and pulled up in a carport beside a two-storey log house. They all got out. Shane stalked to the door, opened it and disappeared. Linda, watching, frowned.

Alana set her purse-strap over her shoulder. A large vegetable garden lay to the right of the house. Clematis entwined a trellis to the roof. "What a pretty place!"

"Thanks," said Tim. "It's okay." His hat was on backwards again.

"Come in, Alana." Linda led the few steps to the door. The back door, Alana realized.

Linda and Tim kicked off their shoes onto a pile of others. So Alana did too.

Another door opened into the kitchen, a large room with an ell-shaped counter, stools at one side, walls with pictures and posters tacked up. There were dishes in the sink, on the drainboard, stuff on the counters haphazardly tidied into piles. A comfy house, Alana felt.

Linda shucked her knapsack onto a chair by a TV and rummaged out two food containers. "Tim, take off your hat and show Alana the house."

Tim whizzed his hat at the rack and it caught. "Hat trick! Come on," he said to Alana.

He whirled her through the living room—another comfortable mess—a den with another TV and a computer, bookshelves, out the window a slanting sun, trees, vines, upstairs to bathroom, "Shane's room," the door tightly closed, "Derek's room," door also closed. Tim put his hand on the knob, breathed in and bit his lip. He turned away. "My room." The door was open and Alana saw a jumble of bedclothes. "Parents' room," he pointed. A stained glass window at the end of the hall refracted the sun's rays.

"Is Shane in a bad mood? Or is he always so silent?"

"Just another grumpy teen." Tim smirked. So Alana did too. A conspiracy.

Back in the kitchen, Linda was poking about in the freezer. "Would you like a pop or something?" he asked Alana. "Or a beer?" He raised his eyebrows.

He was a cute kid. About as tall as Shane, fuzz on his upper lip, a few blackheads he'd likely tried to squeeze this morning. The sophomore look. "If you have some juice—"

Linda shouldered the freezer shut and backed away. Tim dove into the fridge. Alana said to Linda, "May I help you?"

Linda plopped containers on the counter. "We can have pasta with clam alfredo, have to nuke these and boil the noodles. Tim, please go pick salad stuff."

Tim handed Alana a glass. "Blueberry cranberry." He took a bowl and headed outside.

"When he comes back, you can wash the greens," Linda said. "I'll make some dressing and get the pasta started."

"Is Shane always this quiet?" Alana asked.

Linda lifted a container lid and looked inside. She'd have been really pretty when young, Alana thought, dark hair, curvy figure. She wasn't bad even now, probably forty, a few wrinkles, streak of grey. "Oh well, teenagers have phases," Linda said, "I don't suppose I have to tell you."

"Yeah, I guess."

A few minutes later Tim banged back in with a bowl dripping greens—lettuces, arugula, cilantro, mustard. Mostly leaves Alana didn't recognize.

She started washing. "Did you say someone's helping Shane's career? Or does he get grants and things?" She'd heard Canadian athletes got government grants. "Is there a foundation like in the States?"

"Sort of. He's carded so he gets some federal funding but it's darn small. He's got a sponsor." Setting the table, Linda asked Tim, "Did you speak to Austin at the rink?"

"Not much. He and Shane pretty much stopped talking when Dad and I came in. Like they'd been arguing. You want a beer, Mum?"

"That would be nice." She smiled at Tim. "In a glass, please."

"Coming up."

Alana thought of Derek, the lump under the covers at the hospital. And Shane, upstairs.

Immediately beside the arena, Campbell River's RCMP headquarters. Five cop cars sat in front. A large flag rippled in the wind, its red maple leaf proclaiming, You Have Reached An Official Place. They walked in the front door. At a desk Noel asked for Bryan. Kyra asked for the bathroom and disappeared. By the time Dorothy Bryan, taller than Noel by at least half a foot, walked toward them, Kyra had returned. She reached out her hand. "Jason. How's it going?"

"What we want to ask you. Dorothy, this is Noel Franklin and Kyra Rachel."

"Kyra. Noel." All shook hands.

About thirty, thirty-two, thought Kyra. Broad in the shoulders, good rounded face. Attractive enough except for that crew cut. "Thanks for seeing us."

"Come on back to my office, a little privacy." They followed her through a doorway into a common area, desks, a two-way radio, several computers, file cabinets, to a door which she opened and gestured for them to enter. They did. She grabbed a couple of folding chairs, followed and closed the door behind them.

They all sat, Bryan at her desk. The surface, Kyra noted, held mainly a thin computer screen and a keyboard. The screen sat on two Victoria phone books which raised the screen by four inches. Head level for a tall woman?

Jason said, "Dorothy, these are the detectives I told you about."

"Jason says he's hired you. Great, we're glad to take help."

Kyra said, "What can you tell us about Derek's case?"

She pulled a file from a desk drawer and opened it. "We got a 911 call at 11:19 PM, somebody was lying on the ground out at the end of Evergreen Road. That's—"

"We've just come from there," said Kyra, thinking, that file is pitifully thin.

"Good. So you can picture it."

"The call was from Marcie something?"

She glanced at the file. "Yes. Marcie Williamson." To Kyra, "You've been busy."

"We just spoke with her mother. Sarah McDougal."

"Right. The lady with the dog. She said she'd stay till we showed up. We got there—that's my partner Harry Latiche and me—a couple of minutes after the first responders. It was a code three for us, which means they can't touch the victim till there's an officer on site. So we checked out the wounded kid. Unconscious. The first responders stopped most of the external bleeding, covered him with a blanket. Couple of minutes later the ambulance arrived, it's a code five for them. They got there quick, considering it's got to be a local driver that takes the ambulance out—first responders can't do that. The medic examined Derek and figured it was bad enough to get him to Victoria ASAP, so they brought him to the helipad and whirred him off. Unconscious all the time down there. They patched him up as best they could. Nothing more to do so he's back here."

Noel said, "You spoke with Sarah McDougal, did you?"

"Of course. She told us about some cars that stopped where Derek was beaten. She waited till they left before going for her walk."

"Two cars," said Kyra. "And a truck."

"That's right. The truck belonged to the victim—" Bryan glanced at Jason—"to Derek."

"And," said Kyra, "the other truck."

Bryan looked her way. "Go on."

"Mrs. McDougal mentioned another truck or van parked across the street. She wasn't sure if she'd mentioned that to you." Kyra described what they'd learned.

"Interesting. Anything else?"

She presented Bryan with their two hypotheses.

"I'll go have another talk with Mrs. McDougal. Thanks for shaking that loose."

Noel asked, "And your investigation? Where are you?"

Bryan shook her head. "Front burner. But we've talked to his friends, his girlfriend, his family, his teachers. Nobody can guess why anybody'd want to do this. We got his DNA in case there was somebody else's blood on him, his medical records, his credit card and bank card, his phone records—the whole family's phone records for the previous month."

"The whole family?"

"Yeah. No leads there either." She grinned at Jason. "The Coopers have a quiet telephone life. No long distance calls except to Shane when he's training or competing. Shane's made a couple since he's been home, to his sponsor in Ottawa. And that's it."

"Nothing helpful in Derek's truck?"

"Nada. Course if anything was stolen it wouldn't be there."

Being sly? "And?"

"We taped off the crime scene and searched the area but it was a dark night and we didn't have any big beams. A team came out in the morning, walked the grid, sent stuff over to the lab. If any of it's relevant we can't figure out how."

"The lab's where?" Kyra was thinking, non-relevant evidence, no sense of possible theft, friends and family know nothing. And I don't believe it.

"Vancouver."

"What happened to the truck?"

"We taped that off too, notified next of kin—that'd be Jason—then towed it to a secure bay. We checked it out. Nothing out of place. It's back at Jason's."

"Anything else?"

"Wish there were."

Noel stood. "Thank you."

"You learn anything, you let us know."

"Will do." The others got up and followed Dorothy Bryan to the front desk, and went out.

"See?" said Jason. "All dead ends."

"Got to scrape at ends," said Kyra. "Sometimes they're not dead, just hidden."

To Jason, Noel said, "Think she knows more than she's saying?"

Jason paused. "She told me once about a kind of information that's called holdback evidence. The kind of stuff only a suspect would know. If they have any of that, they wouldn't be telling me. Or you."

Noel checked his watch. 4:23. "Jase, where do his Campbell River friends live?"

"I can find out." Jason went back into the station, returned a couple of minutes later. "Got phone numbers and addresses for Joe, Mike, and Gast. Check to see if anybody's home?"

"We've maybe got time for one of them, if he's close," Noel said.

Jason pressed in one of the numbers. Ten rings, no answer. Second number. "That you, Joe? ... It's Jason Cooper, Derek's dad ... Yeah, so are we ... Listen, can I come over for a few minutes? ... No, right away, we're so worried about Derek ... Okay, I've got a couple of friends with me, they're helping ... Okay, see you in five." He closed the phone. "He lives up on Peterson. Real close."

Right on Dogwood, left on Evergreen, right on Peterson and they arrived in four minutes. A small low house with a long wide porch. Two young men, one with a shaven head and the other with long brown hair, sat in plastic chairs, drinking beer. Noel, Jason and Kyra headed up the short cement path to the porch.

The long-haired one got up and waved. "Hi there!"

Jason led Kyra and Noel up the steps. "This is Joe, Derek's friend." He introduced Kyra and Noel.

Joe said, "And that stewpot sitting there's another friend, Gast Robitaille. That's real shit what happened to Derek."

"Noel and Kyra are trying to find out who did it. They want to talk to you both."

"Sure," said Joe. "Here." He opened three steel folding chairs and they all sat.

Noel would have preferred to interview the two separately. No choice now. "Joe, you're good friends with Derek?"

Joe looked over to Gast, who said, "Three of us are—were—god, I hope not—are best friends."

"When was the last time either of you saw Derek? Before he was beaten, I mean."

"Musta been three or four days before that."

"We used to hang out a lot. Less in the last coupla months."

"He has this girl that he's hot for."

"She's pretty hot for him, too." Gast leered at Kyra. "Cindy."

"Day before he got hit, they went to her grad dance. And the evening before that they were together, too. Long evening, Derek said."

"So you talked to him, but didn't see him."

"That's it," said Joe.

"Yeah," said Gast. "Yeah."

"What did you talk about?"

"Shootin' the breeze," said Joe.

"Anything about being in trouble, problems at home?"

"Naw," said Joe, "he was pretty easy at home."

"What about at school? Trouble with teachers, other students?"

"One guy he didn't like—Prof Smothers. Teaches in HDCTM. He's—"

"What's that?"

"Heavy Duty/Commercial Transport Mechanics. That was Derek's program. He was about to start his apprenticeship. Just before he was hit."

"What about this professor, Smothers?"

"They just didn't get along. But it didn't matter he didn't like Smothers, Derek was still acing the course. Acing most of his courses."

Kyra broke in. "What's your sense of Cindy?"

"She's okay," Joe said.

"Just okay?"

"Okay for Derek."

"You like her?"

"Hey," said Gast, glancing at Joe, "that's Derek's business."

"The day he was beaten, did you see him or talk to him?"

"No," said Joe, as Gast said, "Yeah."

"Yes and no?"

"Hey," said Joe, "you couldn't have. We were working on your car all day."

"Come on, we talked on the phone. You remember? We had to ask him—dunno—it was more'n three weeks ago."

"And when you talked," said Kyra, "how did he sound?"

"Like Derek. Why d'you want to know how he sounded?"

"Worried? Scared? Angry?"

"Maybe kinda excited," Gast grinned. "Like he was in the middle of a big project."

Joe turned to stare at Gast. "What project?"

"Cindy! Like he was in the middle of Cindy!" Gast giggled.

Joe shook his head. "Give it a break, Gast."

Noel glanced at his watch. "Thanks for your time, guys. You think of anything else, get in touch, okay?" He handed them each an Islands Investigations International card. "Use the cell numbers."

Through the whole interview Jason had said nothing. They returned to the Honda and followed Jason's directions.

Kyra said, "Too casual by half."

"They're kids," said Jason. "Derek spent a lot of time with them."

"Until Cindy came along," said Kyra.

"I think she was settling Derek down, cooling him out."

"What was he like before?"

"Just a normal kid."

"Drinking beer, smoking pot, having lots of sex?"

"I guess. Twenty years old, that's what they do."

"But after Cindy came along?"

"Oh, more responsible. Like the guys said, acing his courses."

Noel glanced at his watch. 5:05. Into the office parking lot. They got out, walked in, and Jason said to the receptionist, "We have an appointment with Dr. Pierce."

She scowled, recognizing him. "I'll tell him you're here."

Kyra said, "Looks like the 6:15."

At 5:25 a kid with a stethoscope about his neck approached Jason. "Hello."

Jason gestured to Noel and Kyra as he introduced them. "This is Dr. Pierce."

Kyra hoped her shock didn't show on her face. The man looked barely twenty. Tall and skinny, ruddy face, thin eyebrows blond like his hair, small hands. She pulled herself together. "We're investigating the Derek Cooper incident. What's his condition, medically?"

Pierce turned to Jason. "You're okay with my answering their questions?"

"I brought them here for that."

He led them to his office and closed the door. "I've told the police all I know."

Kyra said, "It'll help us hearing you directly."

He nodded. "Derek endured a major trauma. Major traumas. He has severe traumatic brain injury, as well as injuries on his ribcage, pelvis, shoulder and both upper arms. As you know, Jason, it's something of a miracle he's still with us. He must have a powerful will to live."

"I think he does." Jason's voice barely above a whisper.

"What's actually happened to his brain?" Noel asked.

"Well, there's bilateral damage done to the reticular formation of his midbrain, but in terms of treatment that gives us as much information as saying you need flour to make bread."

"What does it say on his chart, about the kind of treatment he first got?"

Dr. Pierce squinted at Noel. "Why do you ask that?"

"I'm wondering if he was conscious when he was found. Did he say anything? Was he tested on the AVPU scale?"

Kyra stared at Noel.

Pierce smiled. "I'll get his chart." He consulted his computer.

"Noel, what are you talking about?"

"It's a scale I read about—goes from being Alert to receiving Vocal stimuli to feeling Pain stimuli to being Unconscious."

Pierce read a file on his screen. "No, when he was first received in Victoria they did an RLAS test on him."

Noel nodded. "That's way more complex, isn't it."

"Yes," said Pierce. "It has eight separate categories, or levels. It's used early on and it can measure shifts between levels. Sometimes they change back and forth between higher and lower. Let me see—" he scrolled down and shook his head. "With Derek, the coma deepened until it finally leveled out one level before the lowest. And no—" he glanced at Noel, "no mention of anything he might have said. Sorry."

"And his prognosis now?"

"Comas on the average—and I'm speaking statistically here—last from between a couple of weeks to just over a month, and I—"

"So he could be coming out of it soon." Jason spoke quietly.

"Some comas last much longer, I have to warn you. Some patients progress, if that's the right word, to a vegetative state. Others do die while in a coma."

"And someone in a coma as deep as Derek's?" Kyra's voice was hushed.

"Depth of the coma isn't always a predictor of the chance of recovery. Somebody with a low chance might still wake up."

Jason sighed deeply. "So what can we do, Dr. Pierce?"

"We can and will take care of him as best we know how. We've got some excellent people here. You can wish or hope or pray or whatever you do best. Visit him, one or two people at a time. Patients who've come out of a coma have reported they were aware of loved ones and friends in the room and that gave them more strength to come out. Time's the only thing we have on our side right now. And Derek's natural strength."

Noel nodded, and said, "Has deep brain stimulation been considered?"

Kyra squinted at him, but said nothing.

"It's the wrong kind of injury," said Pierce. "No one I've consulted thinks DBS would be of any value here."

Noel glanced at his watch. "We've taken enough of your time, Dr. Pierce. Thank you." They shook hands with Pierce and left the building.

Back in the car Jason said, "Thanks for asking those questions. Now I know more about Derek's condition." He smiled ruefully. "Not that it helps."

"But Jase, Linda's a nurse. She must've asked questions like that."

"I think she has. I just haven't asked what she's learned."

"Why not?"

"I think—I was afraid of what she'd tell me." He paused. "And of watching her tell me. With Pierce, it all came out more—objectively? And it looked like he thought he was talking to a professional."

"I guess," said Noel as he drove into the line leading to the ferry booth. Jason passed Noel a plastic card. "What's this?"

"A fare card. They subtract money that's credited on it."

Kyra couldn't believe that Jason hadn't talked with Linda about all this. Kyra would have wanted to know everything, the tiniest detail.

"Here they are," Linda announced as the back door opened. Kyra, Noel and Jason added their shoes to the sprawling pile. Jason pulled on slippers. Noel wiggled his sock-clad toes. Kyra took in the sun slanting across the wooden cabinets, the dinner preparations, Linda bending over a pasta pot on the stove.

"I see a beer there," Jason noted. "You two like a drink before dinner?" He looked at Kyra, Noel. "Could be gin and tonic, scotch—"

"Gin and tonic would be terrific," Noel said.

"You got juice or a pop?" Kyra asked.

Jason got down glasses, found mixings, cut limes, clinked in ice, poured and handed. They thanked him.

"Where are the kids?" Jason asked Linda over the sound of water coming to the boil.

"Shane's in his room. Don't know about Tim and Alana."

Jason invited them into the living room.

Another pleasant light-filled room. Kyra sank into an overstuffed sofa, thinking, I like this house. Electronic beeps and whizzes emanated from around a corner.

"Sounds like they're at the video games," Jason explained, half apologetically.

Noel raised his glass to Jason and Kyra. "Cheers." He sipped, and walked to the window. The woodlot trees began about sixty meters away. A hill rose beyond them, the land cleared. "Are those sheep up there?"

Jason looked out. "Alpacas. Their wool brings more than sheep's wool and they crop the grass to no-never-mind the same." Kyra got up to see.

"Supper's ready!" Linda called. "Shane!"

"Coming," Tim yelled, over whizzes and beeps.

"Shane. Now!"

Jason strode to the foot of the stairs. "Shane!" He gave Noel and Kyra an exasperated look. Upstairs a door opened.

Tim and Alana appeared and they all entered the kitchen. "Sit anywhere." Linda cocked her chin at the long refectory table. Tim and Jason slid into what probably were their accustomed places. Two more placemats looked used; Noel, Kyra and Alana took places in front of crisply folded napkins. Shane arrived and sat, his face a cipher.

Linda placed a steaming bowl of penne on a trivet, reached back to the counter—

Alana stood quickly. "Let me help." She grabbed the salad bowl and brought it to the table. Linda added bread, butter, grated parmesan.

"This looks great," Kyra said, picking up the pasta server. "Alfredo?"

"Clam alfredo," Tim informed her. "We collected the clams yesterday."

Clattering of dishes and cutlery, passing of bread and salad, munching.

"What's your first competition this fall, Shane?" Alana asked.

Her tone was sprightly, as if she'd practiced the question in her head. Noel looked up. Her face was flushed.

Shane gave her a shadow of the smile his family knew from competitions. "September 24th. An Olympic qualifying event."

"That's exciting! Where will it be?"

Kyra wished Alana would tone the worship down a bit. But maybe she had. Maybe this was mild. She hadn't leapt onto his lap. Yet.

Shane kept his smile on her a moment longer: rewarding the fan. "Germany. If I go." He forked another mouthful of alfredo into his mouth.

Kyra saw a glance pass between his parents.

"Whaddya mean *if*?" Tim's voice squeaked and he coughed.

Stuffing in a last mouthful, Shane pushed back his chair and left the table. His footsteps banged up the stairs.

Linda called, "Shane!"

Tim said, "Woooweee!"

"Timothy. Behave."

"It's Shane who's gotta behave," said Tim.

Jason said to Noel, Kyra and Alana, "I apologize for him. But he'll apologize to you too."

"Jase, no need. We were all eighteen once and—"

"Eighteen's plenty old to be civil. He goes out on the ice and he smiles at the whole world." Jason glared. "So we know he knows how to smile."

Tim said, "He thinks he's the great Shane. What he really is is the great Shame." He giggled.

Alana tried not to. She covered her mouth. Tim caught her eye. She made an effort to sit straight and look serious. She rolled the two rings on her right thumb.

"Whatever else he is, Tim, he's a member of this family. And tonight it's his turn to do the dishes." To the rest, Linda said, "Have more. There's still dessert."

"Let him miss it. Let him be hungry." Tim drank his water.

"This is delicious, Linda." Kyra helped herself to more salad and bread. She passed the alfredo to Alana, who shook her head and passed it to Noel.

"Maybe I shouldn't have asked him about his next competition. I'm sorry."

"It's not your fault," Jason reassured her. "Shane knows better."

The rest of the meal passed in strained small talk. Linda brought strawberries from the fridge, ice cream from the freezer. They finished. Linda stood. "Jason, please tell him he has to be down here and finish his supper."

Alana, getting up, said, "I could do the dishes." She reached for a dessert plate.

Linda glanced at Alana's ringed fingers. "Thank you, but this is Shane's responsibility. He'll clear, too. You three go to the den, that'd be best."

Jason got up. "I'll get Shane."

The three guests stood and left the table. Tim followed them.

Linda realized she felt more worry than anger. Even when he'd come home last Christmas, Shane had been easy to spend time with. Proud of his skating, of course. Though the terrible fall, that must have unnerved him. But he'd got up, and seemed okay. Still, this business of living mainly inside himself, acting as if no one else were around, this wasn't her Shane. She'd already let herself wonder, could it be some form of depression? She worked occasionally with patients diagnosed as bipolar. Shane didn't act like those people, but some symptoms were similar. Did it have anything to do with Derek's beating, that Shane wasn't around to defend him? Except Shane was so rarely at home— If she still smoked, this would be the time for a cigarette.

Jason climbed the stairs and knocked on Shane's door. "Shane?" No answer. He knocked harder, spoke evenly. "Shane. You coming out?" Again no response. "I'm coming in." He turned the door handle.

Jason flicked the light switch. Shane lay on his bed, staring at the ceiling. The walls were covered with posters of skaters, Dick Button, Tim Wood, Toller Cranston, Austin Osborne, Brian Boitano, Johnny Weir; and a few women, Gretchen Merrill, Peggy Fleming, Michelle Kwan. And three smaller posters of Shane—including, Jason knew, Shane's favorite, costumed as a faun—a vest across his chest designed to look like curly hair grew on it, tight pants that gave the same effect, skates designed to look like hooves above the blades. The spectators, a year ago last spring, his first try at Juniors, had gone wild. He'd made it to the podium with, as he said it, only a bronze medal. But he'd become the darling of the crowd.

Shane hadn't seemed to have noticed his father, let alone the light coming on. "Shane." No answer. "Shane!"

Now Shane turned slowly and looked over to Jason. "Yeah?"

"You okay?"

"Fine."

"That was very rude."

"What?"

"Stomping off from the table."

Shane squinted at his father. "Sorry."

He didn't mean he was sorry, and Jason's anger grew. "You may be the idol of millions on the ice, but here you're my son and my guests are your guests. You're coming down to apologize." Shane stared at Jason, slowly shook his head, got up and headed for the doorway. Jason followed him downstairs. They passed the den, Noel and Kyra, Tim and Alana deep in conversation. Jason said, "Later. Into the kitchen."

Linda sat at her desk. She glanced at Shane as he came in. "Your evening for the dishes."

"Dishes? I haven't done dishes in a year."

"Exactly. And do not speak to your mother like that."

"It's okay, Jason." Her tone mellowed. "Shane, what's wrong?"

"Why should anything be wrong?"

"Derek comatose to the world is pretty darn wrong."

Shane sighed, hard. "Yeah. That is."

"Is that why you've become so—so withdrawn? Worrying about Derek?"

"Yeah, maybe."

"Look, son," Jason said, "We all are. But we have to go on with our lives, and be part of each other's lives too."

Shane tightened his mouth, a look of exasperation.

"So put on an apron. Dishes into the machine. And wash the pots."

A large dramatic sigh from Shane.

Linda said, "You're worrying about more than just Derek. Something to do with your skating?"

"Why do you say that?"

"I'm asking you."

"I've just got to keep training. That's all."

"Austin said you looked great on the ice today."

"I didn't feel great."

"What didn't feel great?"

"Everything I tried. My axels, my loops, split jumps, everything."

Linda put her hand on his arm. "Are you still upset about the fall you took?"

"No! For godsake, leave it alone."

But he'd been upset. He'd gone about cursing himself aloud. Word about that had gotten around because Shane never cursed. "It wasn't your fault, Shane—"

"Mom, I was the only one out there, okay? Nobody tripped me. I misstepped. I blame me, okay? Nobody else."

Jason put a hand on his shoulder. "Tell me, son. You afraid you'll fall again?"

Shane took a couple of steps backwards. "Look. My legs didn't do what I told them, what I've told them to do hundreds of times, thousands, and they always do. That one time it didn't happen. Okay? It's that simple."

"Still, if you're worried—"

"Stop it! Just leave me alone about my skating." He grabbed an apron. "I'll get this place cleaned up. Just leave the kitchen! Okay?" He glared at both of them.

They exchanged a glance, headed for the back door and out. On the deck Jason turned to look back. Shane, as if in slow motion, tying the apron. Linda said, "I'm worried about him. Was before he came downstairs."

"Yeah," said Jason.

"Think he should see someone?"

"Like?"

"Maybe Dr. Materoff. Or Dr. Lum."

"I don't think he'd go."

"So what do we do?"

"How about a walk? It's a pleasant evening."

"Just around the garden, then. I've got to take Kyra and Noel over to Barb's."

"Okay." Jason took Linda's hand.

In the den, Kyra and Noel had been interviewing Tim about Derek. The friends Tim listed were the same names as those they got from Jason and the Mounties.

With a glance at Kyra and Noel, Alana asked, "Who was his closest friend?" No one commented on the past tense.

"Sam Bristol," Tim said. "Since way back. Derek sometimes helped out in their greenhouses."

"You like Sam?" Alana continued.

"Yeah." Tim cracked his knuckles.

Kyra thought: *Go Nancy Drew*. Someone had to. Kyra was flesh-and-bone tired.

"Where's their place?" Noel took out his laptop.

"Up the road. On Fir. Off Triggerbrook."

"Derek sounds like a neat guy to have for a big brother," "Nancy" observed.

"Yeah."

As laconic as his father? Noel wondered.

Kyra took back some reins. "You and Derek and Shane, the three of you hang out together?"

"Not much, not since Shane started competing. Before that we all played hockey." Tim stared at the computer, at the abandoned game sticks.

"What about Derek's girlfriend? Cindy?" Alana asked. "You like her?"

Tim shrugged. "I liked his last one better. Bertina. She joked around."

"Where's she live?" Noel asked.

"On Pidcock Road." Tim looked at him. "It's not far."

"What about his friends at school?" Noel checked his computer. "Gaston? Joe?"

"They're okay."

No enthusiasm, Kyra noted. "No better than okay?"

"They drink a lot of beer, and all."

"What *all*'s that?"

"Oh, they're a couple of dopeheads."

"A lot of toking?"

"I don't know."

Seconds of silence till Alana observed, "Cindy seemed keen on Derek today."

"She usually drapes all over him. Glad Mom put some limits on her visits."

"We'll call on her tomorrow." Noel closed his laptop.

Linda, Shane and Jason came in. "We interrupting anything?" Jason asked.

All of them shook their heads.

"Sorry I was rude," Shane said, eyes cast down. "I got a lot on my mind."

"I bet you do," Kyra acknowledged. "Training for an Olympic trial."

"Please excuse me." Shane moved toward the stairs. "Goodnight."

A moment's silence as controlled footsteps ascended.

"Alana," Linda stated, "you can stay here tonight. You're very welcome. Barb only has two rooms."

Alana looked at her uncle. "Okay with you?"

Noel looked at Linda, who added, "She can have Derek's room."

Kyra caught Tim's downward eyecast.

"Yes," Uncle Noel acquiesced.

"Thank you. And thank you for a lovely dinner."

In spite of the dyed hair and tight midriff-baring top, nothing wrong with Alana's manners, Kyra thought. Unlike mine if I'm not poured into bed instantly. "If that's okay, maybe we could get along to Barb's." Please, please, before I sink to the floor right here.

"Tim," Linda's tone no-nonsense head nurse. "Please make up Derek's bed. The maroon sheets." A small painful glance passed between her and Tim. She cupped his shoulder. Noel saw, fleetingly, the face of the man he was becoming.

"I'll help you," Alana said.

Tim reached for the peak of his absent cap. "It's okay." He left for the stairs.

They were momentarily quiet, held by Tim's footsteps, the squeak of the linen closet door, the opening and closing of Derek's door. The sadness, Tim's pain, Linda's and Jason's, become audible.

Linda broke the silence. "I'll take you to Barb's. It's not far." She meant both of them, but looked intently at Kyra.

"Our suitcases are in the car," Noel stated. "We'll drive so it's there in the morning."

"I'll go with you and walk back. Oh, Barb's not feeding you." From the freezer Linda took two chocolate croissants and put each in a sandwich bag. "These should hold you till you come back." To Jason: "You'll be around?"

"Yeah, in the woodlot. Coffee'll be on and the door open."

"Thanks," Noel said. "We'll collect you in the morning, Alana." He gave her a hug.

"Oh! My backpack's in your car." She went out to get it.

Kyra begged to use the bathroom for a minute.

FOUR

THEY GOT INTO the car, Linda in front beside Noel. She half turned. "I need to repeat, I'm sorry for Shane's performance. He's usually a charming young man."

Noel started the engine. "Everyone's allowed a black mood once in a while."

"He comes into a room and sucks all the energy out. A walking black hole." She sighed. "Turn right up ahead."

"Was he so black in Vancouver? In his training?"

"I can't imagine Carl—that's his coach, Carl Certane—that Carl would let him get away with it."

"Maybe he's just exhausted."

"No, something's changed."

"Can you pinpoint when it started?"

"Not really—here to the right."

Noel turned right. "'Not really' isn't no."

"Okay, he took a nasty fall in competition a few months ago. But then he seemed better. And now, much worse."

"Could he have hurt himself? Something undiagnosed?"

Linda snorted. "Only his pride."

"No, I mean like hairline fractures."

"He had a thorough exam. Physically he's fine."

"Has he fallen before?"

"Not in competition. Well, not since he was twelve. In practice, of course. It happens when you're pushing yourself." She pointed. "It's over there, other side of the road."

Noel stopped the car on the verge. Too much talk about Shane, not enough about Derek.

"You can drive right in."

"Linda, what's your sense of the people around Derek? Who are his friends?"

"The guys on the island? Two of them are at UBC and now they've got summer jobs in Vancouver, so Derek hasn't seen much of them.

Sam's the closest right now. He went over to the hospital a couple of times. Sam Bristol."

Kyra pulled herself forward. "What's your sense of Sam?"

"Good kid. Works with his father, they have greenhouses and supply restaurants and markets on Vancouver Island."

"Where can we find him?"

"Bristol Greens. Up on Fir Lane, end of Triggerbrook Road."

"And in Campbell River?"

"Well, Cindy of course."

"What's your take on her?"

"A pleasant young woman." She paused for a moment. "She does seem to adore Derek. We may have to get used to her."

"You looked irked with her this afternoon."

"Well, she can be a bit much."

"How about male friends? At the school?"

"He's friendly with Gast Robitaille, and another called Joe. And Mike, I always remember his name, Mike Campbell from Campbell River."

"What's your sense of them?"

"They seem okay, too. Though why some men shave their heads . . ."

Noel said, "I got the sense from Tim that he doesn't much care for Gast and Joe."

"I don't think he really knows them."

"Enough to make him wrinkle his nose."

"I suspect he's a bit jealous. Of the time they spend with Derek. Derek and Timmy always were close. Eldest and youngest."

"So recently Tim hung out less with Derek?" Kyra offered.

Linda nodded. "I had the sense Gast and Joe treated Timmy like a little kid. Which I suppose someone at twenty might think of a fifteen year old."

"Tim called them the dopeheads," Noel stated.

"As in pot? Or harder stuff?"

"Pot, I think he meant."

"And Mike Campbell from Campbell River?"

"The kind of young man any mother would be proud of. He's in the heavy equipment course with Derek. But he's not around this summer either."

"Thanks, Linda. Anything else, Kyra?"

"No." Just get me a bed.

Noel turned into a gravel driveway, passing a sign, Steller's Jay B&B. A square two-storey cedar-sided building with a covered porch running the length of the front sat to their right. As they got out, a robust woman wearing jeans, a light-colored shirt and sandals stepped onto the deck.

Linda called, "Hi Barb." Barb, late fifties, came down the steps.

Introductions. Noel and Kyra grabbed their suitcases and followed Barb into the house, Linda trailing. In the hall, the sky-blue walls peppered with Steller's jays, Kyra said, "Thanks, Barb. Can I get to my room? I'm exhausted."

"Of course, dear. Follow me" She headed down the stairs, Kyra following.

Noel turned to Linda. "I'll take you back."

"I'll walk, thanks. Clear my brain."

"Want a ride into Campbell River in the morning?"

"No, thanks again. I ride with a friend. Ferry price for the car every day, it's become prohibitive."

"Yeah, we've noticed."

"And do you know how long you'll be staying?"

Does she think this is a pleasure visit? "Until we learn who beat up Derek, and why. We'll have to leave for a couple of days. But we'll be back."

"You can stay as long as you want, Barb said. It's a quiet summer. Oh, and I told her we'd cover the expenses but she said no, find out who did this to Derek, that's all the payment she wants."

"That's very kind—"

"She dotes on Derek. And he adores her. His honorary Aunt Barb." She started to leave, then turned back. "Please find out who hurt him so." She looked squarely at Noel, tears welling.

Noel nodded. Which Linda didn't see as she strode out the door.

He took his suitcase and descended the stairs. Barb came out of one room and pointed across the hall. "You're in here."

Alana Franklin turned on the light and closed the door. She glanced about. Derek's bed, twin sized—one of a pair? did Tim or Shane have the other?—had been made up. The window faced the ocean, pretty in the fading blue light. Beneath the window stood racked weights, 20 pounds, 10 and 5. Derek a bodybuilder, or was this for exercise? Beside the window, a desk, bare except for a computer and printer. She could email Sonia, find out what she was up to. And Jerry. When she'd arrived at her grandparents' Alana missed Jerry. But after a few days it was okay without him—back home he seemed to be around like all the time.

Shane. What a gorgeous hunk. If she got him alone she'd open him up, easy making guys relax. Jerry was uptight when she met him, now it'd be better if he retightened some. Shane's sponsor's Austin Osborne, cool! She remembered Sonia talking about Osborne, one of the greats, on the Olympic team maybe three times? Pairs. Who'd he skated with? Alana couldn't remember.

She opened her backpack and took out her night T-shirt. How were Kyra and Noel working on this case? She knew about detectives, she'd seen movies, but in movies things got rough. Were her uncle and Kyra up to violence? They both seemed too gentle. Somebody'd been pretty ungentle with Derek.

Could she be of help? She'd wanted to meet Shane Cooper to make Sonia jealous. Now if Sonia asked what was he like, all Alana could say is mopey. Like, not real exciting.

Across from the bed, bookshelves and closet. What did Derek read? Auto racing. Hockey. Coastal boating. House building, hunting, sky-diving, football. Yep, some kind of jock. Closet? You can learn a lot about people from their closets. She slid open the door. Flannel shirts, some dress shirts, three red hockey shirts with a yellow 23 on the back, corduroy pants, flannel pants, jeans, couple of jackets, one leather and a red team jacket—Campbell River Cougars. Shoes: runners with cleats, without, red and black highsiders. Black dress shoes. Hanging from hooks by their tied-together laces, two pairs of black hockey skates.

She backed out and pulled open the chest drawer. Sweatshirts, T-shirts, socks—

Tap-a-tap. Alana jumped back and squeaked "Eeeh—"

Linda's voice: "Alana?"

She pushed the drawer closed, slid the door to. Her breath was coming fast. She opened the door. "Hi."

"Would you like something warm to drink?"

"Thank you, but I'm fine."

"Is there anything you need?"

"Okay to use Derek's computer? I'd like to write a couple of my friends." She hoped Linda hadn't noticed her iPhone.

"Of course. I hope it's working. The RCMP took it looking for leads for finding whoever had beaten Derek."

"Did they learn anything from it?"

Linda shook her head. "If they did, they haven't told us. Shall I turn it on?"

"I can, thank you."

"Well, good night."

"Night. And thanks for letting me use Derek's room. It's nice."

Linda smiled. "Yes it is." She closed the door.

Alana checked the door handle. No way to lock it. What were the Mounties looking for on Derek's computer? Maybe she could find something. Something to help Uncle Noel—she had to stop thinking of him as Uncle Noel—and Kyra. She turned on the computer. It came to life very slowly—must be at least four years old. She took off her rings except the little pinky ring Jerry had given her—not because it was from Jerry, just it was difficult to get off. After a minute the screen finally brought up the wallpaper, a hockey arena, a game going, lots of people in the galleries—looked like the arena in Campbell River. More minutes till the icons came on. God, this was boring. What should she check out? His music? His pictures? His documents? She tapped on My Pictures. She tapped on Last Year: Finals. She opened the door and looked out. Dark and silent. She closed the door. Try the top drawer. Official looking papers—school grades, he'd done okay in high school, Bs and B+s mostly; a birth certificate; a passport—where would Derek go? Play hockey in the States somewhere? Photos, half a dozen of a very pretty young woman with long brown hair and a sweet smile; ten or so of Shane, skating, professionally taken—god, the man was beautiful, elegant bum and gorgeous legs and a mouth that sure looked good; a couple of his parents at a party.

She glanced over to the computer. Still no pictures. Next drawer. More underwear, jockstraps, socks. She ran her hand beneath the clothing—nope, nothing there. A sound like a squeak from the hall? She froze. Silence. An old house, shifting. She shivered. Is this what happens when Uncle Noel and Kyra look for evidence? The drawer below, sweaters. She felt underneath. Nothing. What did she expect, a note, Derek—join the Deaths' Head Rangers or we'll beat the shit out of you? Not likely on this island.

She pushed the drawer closed quietly. The computer had opened the Finals page. She clicked on Slide Show. Photos flashed by of a hockey game, focusing on number 23. Derek in the thick of things. The next set, Shane/Juniors. Again the long wait. Back to the closet? Again she listened, again silence. She re-opened the closet door. Trouble with trying to help Kyra and Uncle Noel—Noel—she had no idea what to look for.

Maybe something in a pocket of one of the jackets. She felt around in the leather one. Tissues, yuck. Anyway, if the police had searched this room they'd have found anything important. They must have, they took his computer. Still, people make mistakes, and even cops are human. She fished her way through all the jacket pockets. Nothing. In the shoes? Nada, nada. She lifted both pairs of hockey shoes from their hooks, turned one upside down—no way was she going to stick her hand in there—another, the other pair— Clunk. Something had fallen. She backed to the side and felt around. A memory stick? She picked it up. No neck cord, just the technology.

She returned to the computer. Did this ancient machine have a USB port? Not at the front. The back? Yay, two USB ports, one to the printer. She plugged in the stick. She sat, hoping for patience, unable to find it. Out in the hall, footsteps. She sat completely still, not even breathing. The footsteps passed her door, heading down the hall; Shane or Tim going to the bathroom? Did the parents have an ensuite? She breathed, shallow now. She'd wait till the footsteps passed again. Hey, she had no choice, E drive hadn't come up yet. She counted to 40-50-60. Forever. Okay, it took more than a minute to pee. The footfalls again. She forced herself to keep breathing. She waited, even though the screen now showed the E directory. Then only the light hum of the computer.

She moused it open. One file: Shane. She clicked. A list of dates, with dollar amounts:

June 15, $3000.
June 30, $3000.
July 15, $3000.
July 30, $3000.
August 15, $3000.
August 30, $3000.
Total, $18,000

Huh? Alana dug her notebook out of her knapsack and copied the figures.

Kyra crossed the hall to Noel's room. Its walls were a moss green, the duvet forest with lighter trim. He was unpacking his shaving kit. Green bathroom too. She yawned.

"Just get my laptop out." Noel rummaged, sat on the bed, kicked off his shoes and plugged in the computer.

Kyra yawned again. "Don't know how long I'll last."

"Okay. What do we know?" Noel typed in date and place.

The whole day jumbled in Kyra's brain, flash of Noel's parents mixed with Linda at her kitchen table, hospital lump, machinery, washrooms, police, Mrs. McDougal— "I can't do this. It's all a fuckin' muddle and I'm going to cry if I don't go to sleep."

Noel looked at her, concerned. "The fetus thing?"

"I guess so. I've never felt so tired in my life."

"Okay." He looked at his watch. "If we're up and dressed by eight, we can get a coffee and talk driving out to Sam Bristol of Bristol Greens."

She tried to smile. "Goodnight." She left.

Noel thought. Twilight had disappeared outside the sliding glass door. The ground must slope, house a back-to-front split level. Although he doubted there was anyone to see in, he closed the green vertical blinds, flicked on the bedside lamp, plumped up the pillows and stretched out, laptop on his stomach. What do we know?

> 15th June s.o.? hit D. coma
> 20 yrs., North Island College, good kid, everyone likes,
> close-knit family, no crim. rec. Friends: Sam, Joe, Gast,
> Mike, g.f. Cindy

79

2 bros. S. 18, v. prom. figure skater, worried? Ma worried about him? Sponsor Austin Osborne, ex-fig. sktr. part-time Q res.—T. 15, nice kid
Mo. L. nurse full-time, to hosp. daily
Fa. J. 400 ha. woodlot, self-employed—

Fifteen minutes and Noel found himself in a reverie. He and Jason had kept in touch after high school, Noel had introduced Jason to Brendan—and before him, to William—and Noel and Jason had shared all the missing years. He chewed his cheek ruefully, glad Kyra wasn't there to tease him.

Why would a well-liked kid with a stable family get beaten up? Drugs? This part of the world, BC bud. Growing? Dealing? Doping? No one said a doper, Joe denied Derek toked.

Random? Wrong place wrong time?

Cindy's old boy friend, jealous?

He typed *drugs?* after *D. coma*, saved and closed the laptop. After bathroom things, he located his book.

He was sure now. Absolutely convinced. It had come to him last night after his sixth beer—Charlie had cheated. That's the only way he could have got the thousand off him, a thousand of the kid's money he was going to clean up his debts with. Charlie had palmed an ace, no doubt about it. He replayed the game his mind. There! Charlie—his thin unmoving face, its permanent sneer, his balding skull above rimless glasses, the fast move of his hand to his lap. Earlier in the evening he'd thought nothing of it, assumed Charlie had a itchy crotch or thigh—hah! Charlie had a fourth ace stashed, he was convinced. Charlie had to be taught a lesson.

He'd gone to Canadian Tire. The chatty checkout guy had remarked, "Late in the season to buy a bat, in't it?" and he'd said, "Oh well, you know, pickup and kids—" and the clerk said, "Yeah, if they're breaking 'em, get aluminum." He'd said, "Ehh," and was outa there.

No masks for sale tonight. Good thing he'd bought a bagful last Halloween.

Charlie'd parked his car down the street from Saddleman's. He felt a flare of fury, rush inside, bash his head in right there, blood and brains splattering the table. Harder than he'd hit the kid. After all, the kid hadn't done anything to him. This, with Charlie, was personal. But he contained himself. If Charlie was in a game, he wouldn't be out soon. And who was he fleecing tonight?

He'd go home and plan. He didn't know Charlie's address. Nor where he worked, if he did work. Or his movement through his world. A beer called. He started the car.

Kyra rolled over. The clock said 1:43. She'd been checking since 12:48. Asleep since 10:30, she'd been awakened two hours later by her bladder, peed, crawled into bed and prayed to fall asleep again. The sheets under the duvet were cool except at her previous warm nest, which she squirmed into. Light from the full moon flooded the room. She burrowed into the pillow.

Her mind wouldn't shut off. One baby scenario after another: a small bundle of blanket smelling like sweet powder, dark hair under a cap—boy or girl? A toddler steps off the curb, a car approaches, she grabs for the child, misses— Kyra shivered and moaned against that image. She'd never seriously thought about having a child though she and Sam had discussed it. Before things went rocky.

An abortion. Only six weeks, hardly too late. Then she wouldn't have to wonder what sort of parent she'd be. She wasn't a right-to-lifer, was she? No. Every woman had a right to control her body, didn't she? She didn't believe life was sacred as such, but she did believe life should be protected. Not forfeited easily.

How to look after a baby and work? How to pay for day care? How to choose a good day care? All stuff she knew nothing about. How to work while pregnant? Suppose they were in the middle of a case, a stakeout, and she went into labor? A stakeout miles from anywhere? Yes, she should have an abortion.

No, you can't prepare for life. It's not like studying for a test. Life just happens. Maybe a baby comes under that heading. She should just accept it. But a baby is very permanent. Suppose you invest all that love and effort into the baby, the child, and something happens to it? Like Derek, lying comatose.

Kyra rolled over to shed her memory of an intubated lump, Derek on the hospital bed. The Coopers poured love into Derek and look what happened. A senseless, random act?—scary in itself—but I bet Derek was doing a drug deal. All that effort into a kid and it turns out a bad one. Kyra felt unbearably sad: disappointed and betrayed by her teenage druggie-child.

Maybe Tim knows something. Or Sam Bristol with the greenhouses. Hope Derek's just dealing BC bud, not anything else.

Kyra felt hot, twitchy. Her hair clung to her forehead. 2:29. She raked it back with her fingers, flipped the pillow to its cooler side. Close the venetian blinds? No, watching cloud wisps drift across the moon should be sleep-inducing.

At 8:00 AM, a knock on Noel's door. Kyra, open yellow shirt over red tank top and black jeans, hair wet from the shower, looked more herself again. He'd been for a long walk. "To suss out the lay of the land." He offered her a sandwich bag holding a croissant.

"I'll pass for now," she said, suppressing a look of distaste.

He opened his, and took a bite.

She looked out the patio door as he munched.

Another knock at the door. Barb. "I heard you, so here's coffee." She passed over a tray—insulated carafe, milk, sugar, two mugs.

Noel took it from her, smiling. "Just what we need."

"That's a wonderful bed, Barb." Kyra said. "I slept and slept." Yeah, finally.

Barb smiled and closed the door.

"Coffee?" He poured himself some.

Kyra stared at the tray dubiously. "Maybe if you put in a lot of milk?"

Noel did. She wrapped her hands around the mug. He opened his laptop. "Okay, what do we know?"

"Did you get anywhere last night?"

Noel read her his notes.

"You're thinking drugs?"

"A hypothesis. What else is more likely around here?"

"Old grudges?"

"Everyone says he's a nice guy."

"Means we haven't dug enough." Kyra sipped slowly.

"Well, some people are just nice."

She raised her eyebrows. "Tell me that when the case is solved."

Noel changed tack. "I propose this line-up for today: Sam Bristol; Shane when we collect Alana; then over to Cindy's."

"Yeah. I'd like Alana's impression of Cindy. Also, I've mulled some more and I think something's fishy about Joe and Gast. Remember when we asked if they'd seen Derek that day, one said *no* and one said *yes*? Also Tim didn't think much of them. I think I trust his intuition. We should re-see them." She sipped more coffee, realized it was half gone.

Noel added the itinerary to his notes. He nodded toward Kyra. "How're you feeling?"

"Maybe I'll try a bit of croissant." Noel handed her a sandwich bag. She opened it and broke off an end. She chewed slowly, swallowed. Noel realized he was watching her belly with extreme concentration.

Kyra noted this and grinned. "You look like a cat at a mouse hole." She tore off more croissant. "Anything else strike you?"

"Mike Campbell of Campbell River is supposed to be another nice guy. This set is littered with white hats."

"We should talk to the Zamboni driver."

Noel made a note. "Shorty Barlow. We'll have time to pass by the rink."

"I'd like to see Shane skate and," her tone changed, "how do I know so would Alana?"

"Come on. You had crushes when you were a teenager, right?" Noel, defending his niece.

Right. A monumental crush. But she wasn't going to tell Noel. Ever. Since it had been on him. "I'll brush my teeth and be back, ready to beard Sam in his greenhouse."

"Okay." Noel stood and gave her a firm hug. Kyra returned it.

Kyra said, "Thank you."

Austin Osborne pushed the plunger down into his Italian coffee maker and poured a cup of thick black liquid. He took a sip. Good. When Austin was in residence, Randy usually appeared at 9:00 AM. It was 9:10.

He strode through the open-plan kitchen, dining, living area to the foyer and opened the front door. He stopped as he always did on his first morning back and admired the flagstone entry and vine-covered gazebo. Then he admired the navy blue Porsche in the carport. Ah, here came Randy, slouching, swinging his arms. Waving a salute.

Austin looked at his watch. "Twelve minutes late."

"Island time." Randy smiled, on top of the situation. He was taller than Austin's six feet by a couple of inches. When Austin had hired him as caretaker, he'd made him cut his ponytail. Randy had grumbled. But Austin's deal was pretty good, including bi-monthly haircuts at Sylvia's Emporium. Therein lay a story Austin didn't know and Randy wasn't about to tell. Randy's hair, red-brown, was even coiffed. This morning he was newly shaved. Ready for Shu-li when she got in? Hmmm.

"Come up, have coffee." Austin said.

"How's Ottawa? You keeping those asses in Parliament in order?" Randy said this often when Austin arrived.

Another repeat: "I order them to keep in order." A bored tone.

Randy didn't think Austin paid any more attention to politics than he did.

Normally Randy had the place to himself, nice one bedroom cabin, lots of firewood, check on the big house a few times a week, do what Austin ordered from Ottawa. After Austin's absences his easy smile was the first thing Randy noticed. Out of show-biz skating for two years now, Austin still kept himself trim. Hard to do; running the big skating equipment organization he'd built up from nothing kept him on his duff most days.

During visits to Quadra Austin entertained the same people, Steve with his Dutch accent who kept taking pictures of everybody, Shu-li; an Asian woman with a Canadian accent. And a looker, like to look her all over one day.

Sometimes when Austin arrived Randy needed to fetch him from the airport. This time Austin had rented a car, driven himself over. But Randy had been ordered to go out and shop. Austin had sent the grocery list in advance, two hundred dollars' worth of groceries, twice that for booze. Randy didn't need a list; he knew what Austin liked for himself and for his guests. Sometimes he'd buy some delicacy he knew Austin and his guests would enjoy. Now there was beer in the fridge, whisky in the cabinet, wine in the closet. "What's up for this visit, then?"

"Shu-li's arriving today, I'll pick her up. You meet Steve at the airport, one o'clock tomorrow."

"Sure." Why can't Steve get a floatplane to Quadra? Randy kept his face impassive. He admired Austin. Mostly. Less when he breezed onto Quadra and gave orders: meet, fetch, carry, shop, drive. More when he and Austin could talk about how the world worked, how to understand those living on the island, how to make use of them. Best when he and Austin understood each other without spelling things out. Some workers took the commands they were given and followed them—this happened occasionally to Randy, like now upon Austin's arrival. But Randy worked best when he could help Austin out without being asked, when Randy understood what Austin needed even before Austin realized what he wanted. That was satisfying.

"Place looks great, Randy."

"Good." They surveyed the vista, from perennial beds near the house and paths around it, the gazebo by the small grassy plot with chairs and table in front, down the swoop of carefully thinned Douglas firs to the bay. To the right and the left the land rose higher, ending at cliffs sixty feet above the ocean. "I cut the grass yesterday." Randy's little nemesis, the patch of lawn with chairs and table to lug about and reposition each time he cut it.

Austin breathed the sweet, dewy air and took a sip of coffee. "Good to be back on Quadra. No place like it."

Something else Austin often said on arrival. And with this Randy completely agreed. He'd moved here four years ago, after a career of unfinished degrees and dumped jobs. He'd grown up in Prince George, dropped out of school in the spring of grade twelve; his girl had jilted him—obviously not *his* girl—and his heart was broken. He'd worked in the bush logging pine-beetle-infested trees, then at the mill. Laid off, he qualified as a mature student for the new university and almost got his high school equivalency. Half a dozen more menial jobs, then off to Fort McMurray and the tar sands. Liked the money but nothing else and so to Calgary and construction. Good money there too, and women and booze. And coke. Year and a half, there went the money. And his nose, sinuses, esophagus. Nothing left of those days except a framed picture of him, Randolph Dubronsky: Employee of the Month. Randy took off with everything he owned in his Ford 250 and pulled into a deserted campground in Yoho. He spent two weeks coming clean; when he'd stopped jittering and howling he loaded up and headed west. Someone in a gas station in Osoyoos mentioned Quadra Island. Randy just kept driving.

"Did you get fresh lemon grass and the other stuff on Shu-li's list?"

"Yeah." Thank god he didn't have to cook it. Shu-li liked to. He sipped his coffee and involuntarily looked over toward the lush cucumber vines crawling up the trellis behind the flowerbed. He'd planted cucumber seeds beside the mint when he'd noted, last year, that Austin had taken to drinking Pimms with cucumber and mint. He kept the plants well watered and they'd rewarded him with fast growth. Some sweet peas had benefited too. He'd had to prop those up, bit of a drag. Watering gardens in summer, even on a big island like Quadra, had to be kept to a minimum. So far Austin hadn't noticed he could have this afternoon's Pimms with his own cucumber slice and mint.

Randy thought Austin felt easy with him; he'd found Randy through a bulletin board notice: "House-sit, Pet-sit, Jack of all Trades, Do Anything, Leave number at store, Will phone. Refs." The refs, faked, had been more than adequate so Randy was installed in Austin's cabin with a stipend for caretaking.

Randy leaned on the railing and looked at the view. He did enjoy it. The tide was in, lapping softly at the rocks. Sky reflection on water-covered weeds, bottom-feeders, scuttlers, the general nastiness of underwater life and death. He had the same view from his cabin, which was a major reason he'd taken the job and why he put up with Austin's requests.

"Sure is nice, isn't it?" Austin finished his coffee. "Winter days in Ottawa, thirty below with the snow blasting, I think of this."

Randy set his empty cup on the railing. "Why don't you move here permanently?"

"Can't yet. Some day."

Why not, Randy thought, but he didn't probe. He'd learn when he needed to know.

"I hear the Coopers have hired a couple of detectives," Randy said.

"Detectives? What for?"

"The guys at the pub figure to find out who beat up Derek."

Austin tapped his fingertips on his coffee cup and stared into the far distance. Perhaps at the passing sailboat.

Going at a fair whip, Randy thought. Not anchoring in this bay. "Better get to it."

Austin watched Randy head off to the front of the house and disappear around the corner. He would wait to plan the meeting with Shu-li and Steve. Harold Arensen wandering about in Austin's mind too often transformed his mood from temperate to manic, so he worked hard to keep Harold away. But the purpose of these meetings was their plan to destroy Harold. So there'd be no avoiding him. Still, Austin needn't begin to let Harold into his thinking till they were all together.

Kyra sat next to Noel, the map in her lap. A left at West Road, past the village, up Heriot Bay Road to a tangle of small roads, and in a few minutes they drove under an arch that announced: BRISTOL GREENS. At eye level another sign said: CLOSED.

"You don't get much business being closed," Kyra sniffed.

"It's not nine o'clock yet."

The driveway was dirt, slightly rutted. Noel slowed. To the right a modular home fronted by a cedar deck held three folding chairs. To the left, a pickup and a mid-sized white van. Beyond the house opaque plastic-covered greenhouses stretched in two sun-reflecting rows. Beyond them grew tall firs, cedars, broadleaf maples. The Honda crawled along. They looked about for signs of human activity.

"That door's open." Kyra pointed to the fourth greenhouse on the left.

Noel stopped. At the slam of their doors a head appeared through the doorway. Under a ball cap bearing the words "Bristol Greens" were light blue eyes, a narrow nose and a three-day fuzz beard. A pleasant young face.

"Hi, you Sam?" called Kyra.

"Yeah."

They walked toward Sam. "We're friends of the Coopers." She held out a card. "May we come in?"

"Better I come out." Sam pulled the door to behind him. "The fewer people in with the tomatoes, the better they like it." He smiled and took her card.

"Oh, yes," Noel said, remembering a case with a greenhouse that had the same stricture. "Noel Franklin. My partner, Kyra Rachel. We're asking around about the assault on Derek Cooper. Have a minute?"

"Sure. I'll get my coffee." He disappeared, reappeared with a travel mug. "We can sit over there." He pointed to a bench and a strapped deck chair between two greenhouses. His T-shirt sleeves, folded up, revealed developed biceps crossed with veins and sinews. On the left, two small tattoos, a blue rose and a purple daffodil.

"Derek's a really good guy." Sam took off his cap and scratched at his scalp under a red-blond crew cut. "Breaks me up to see him so out of it." His voice sounded strained. He put his hat back on.

"Yeah, people seem to like him," Kyra said. "Any thought of who might have done it?"

"I've been over it and over it. All I can think is some guy just wanted to bash somebody and Derek was in the wrong place."

"Some guy?"

"Maybe."

"You know if he ticked anybody off recently?"

"Nope."

"How about that new girlfriend, was she with somebody before Derek?"

"Cindy? Jeeze, I wouldn't know, she's over in Campbell River."

"You met her?"

"Yeah, coupla times. Derek brought her over."

Noel asked, "What do you think of her?"

Sam shrugged. "I dunno her well. Pretty. Smitten with Derek."

"Derek broke off with an old girlfriend to date Cindy."

"Bertina." Sam smiled into his coffee mug. "She's great."

"Was she angry?"

"Like, would she try to hurt Derek? No way. Bertina's the gentlest kid."

This wasn't getting anywhere. "What do you grow here?" Kyra asked. "Tomatoes?"

"Yeah. And sweet peppers, all colors, jalapenos and Scotch bonnets. Lettuces, arugula, some flowers. All organic. We supply a lot of the Big Island now and just signed a deal with Whistler. The Olympics, we lucked out. And," Sam rolled his shoulders making his biceps flex and the flowers dance, "we've got a federal contract for medical marijuana. Now that's a lot of work."

"Different from the tomatoes and jalapenos?"

"Each plant makes its own demands but for the feds you got to do it their way. You have to follow nutrient formulae, different for different species."

"Who do you supply?" Noel asked.

"Compassion clubs. We take it to a distributor in Campbell River. He takes it to the clubs."

"Does that bring in much money?" Kyra asked. "Sorry to be nosy, but it's an occupational hazard." She smiled at him.

"It's okay. Thing is, it's steady income. My dad and I are partners, and I've got a share in the mortgage too, so it really helps."

"So your heart's in the business?"

"Yeah, my heart, my hands, nearly all my time. But I love it. Wouldn't do anything else."

Noel asked, "You wouldn't, uh, cut a little bud and deal privately?"

Sam jerked up straight, slopping some coffee. "Are you kidding? Think I want to jeopardize this contract?!" He glared at her.

"Just exploring."

Sam calmed a bit. "Besides, medical growers are all bonded and we have to account for each plant, and besides again, the local Mounties know us."

"Apologies," said Noel. Sam's righteous indignation sounded authentic.

Kyra looked around. "Is your dad available?"

"He's shopping."

"What's his name?"

"Brant Bristol."

Noel stood. The day was heating up. "Thanks, Sam. You think of anything, give me or Kyra a call."

"It's a damn crime."

Kyra stood too. "I'll look for Bristol Greens in stores."

"Thanks."

Back on the road Kyra said, "I've never known a case with so many nice guys. Where the fuck are the villains?"

"Yeah, a black hat would be refreshing. You believe him about the dope?"

"You mean impossible to rip off fed meds? No idea, but he made a good case."

"Using the medical stuff to camouflage his own?"

She thought. "It's possible."

"Even nice guys like a bit of weed."

They drove back, quietly mulling. As they neared the Cooper land, Noel said, "Shall we stop at the B&B and tell Barb we're likely staying till Friday?"

"Likely?"

"Unless we figure this out before then." After a moment he added, "You know, you could stay here and probe some more."

"Yeah. Maybe."

"I really better get Alana back to Qualicum. I could be back late Sunday."

"Hmm." Kyra considered that. "Let's see what happens tomorrow before I decide.

"I'd have to rent a car."

"No problem."

"Except we're not being paid on this one."

"I'll rent it for you."

"Be careful you don't run through all of Brendan's money."

Not possible, thought Noel. Brendan, a stockbroker, had left Noel well cushioned. And with Brendan gone—dead, dammit!—Noel had found a new broker. Who had advised Noel to put the largest part of his inheritance into bonds. Best financial advice Noel had ever received, even including Brendan's. Wonder where Brendan would have been on the present recession? A few months ago Noel had checked into those equities he'd banked out. If he'd have held on to them he'd now be worth sixty-five percent less. To Kyra he said, "I always try to be careful."

At the B&B they told Barb that Noel would be staying until Friday morning, Kyra maybe longer. Noel would be coming back.

On to pick up Alana. In the drive, Jason's Corolla was gone. Linda's Mazda sat there. They found Shane at the kitchen counter hunched over a bowl of fruit-topped cereal. His short brown hair was water-slicked back. He wore a black T-shirt, white jeans and white running shoes. Noel said to him, "Morning, Shane. Breakfast of champions?"

Shane gave Noel a you're-weird-man squint. "Breakfast, yeah."

"Seen Alana?"

"Taking a shower."

Kyra said, "I'll go see how she's doing." She left the room.

"So. What's on for you today, Shane?"

"Practice."

"Same every day?"

"Yep." Shane took a small bite of cereal.

Blood from pebbles time. "Any theories about what happened to Derek?"

Shane shoveled cereal into his mouth.

"Shane?"

"Why should I have any theories?"

"Anybody can have theories."

Silence from Shane.

"As Derek's brother, you might have clearer theories than other people."

"I wasn't here." More cereal, stoking the skating muscles.

"You and Derek, you're good friends as well as brothers?"

At last Shane looked up. "We're close. I love Derek. I love Timmy. Now will you let me eat my breakfast?"

Mighty recalcitrant. "Look, Shane, your father's asked us to try to find out why this happened. Anything you tell us might be helpful in ways you wouldn't realize."

A heavy sigh. Shane shook his head and turned his face back to the cereal bowl.

"What?"

"I don't know why Dad asked you."

Behind Shane, Noel noticed Tim standing at the den door; not wanting to disturb?

91

Shane went on, "What do you think you can do that the Mounties can't? They know this area, you don't know a thing."

"We're looking at this with new eyes, and if—"

"Just go away and leave us alone."

"Shane, was Derek involved with people who could get him in trouble?"

Shane's voice gruffed up. "How the hell should I know? I hadn't seen him for months."

"Do you know if he was involved with anything illegal?"

"Derek? Derek wouldn't do anything wrong."

"Illegal, I asked."

Shane shook his head.

"Was he part of a gang?" More silence from Shane. "Did he do drugs?" No response. "Pot? Coke? Crystal meth?"

Suddenly Shane stood. "Will you please stop? For godsake, leave it alone!"

"Maybe he was a dealer? How does he support himself? How did he?"

Shane glared at Noel. "You know, you're messing with my inner balance."

"Your what?"

"Leave us all alone." He was backing toward the den door. Tim had vanished. "You're a menace to our family. Go away and stay away." He disappeared around the corner.

A thump of running shoes headed up the stairs. It'd be worthwhile to go watch Shane skate. All this self-absorption could lead to an impressive performance. Energy like that put into something productive? Wow.

Kyra reappeared. "Heard the last of it. I didn't want to interrupt."

"He's a piece of work all right. Alana ready?"

"Couple of minutes, she said—" A sudden triple clang of a large bell. "Doorbell?"

A few seconds, and Tim led a man with longish blond hair into the kitchen. Familiar, but Noel couldn't place him.

Tim said, "Austin, these are my Dad's friends, Noel and Kyra."

"Oh yes," said Austin. "Good to meet you, Kyra." He smiled, just for her, he reached out his hand. She took it. Firm but gentle. The slightest flirtation? He turned to Noel, an equivalent now manly smile, "And Noel." A strong grasp of Noel's hand. "Welcome to our island."

"Ah," said Kyra, "you live here?"

"Whenever I can. Otherwise I'm in Ottawa. But I come here as much as possible. You know Ottawa." A small gentle grimace.

"I've visited," said Kyra.

"And what brings you to Quadra? It's a beautiful island, of course."

"Derek" said Noel.

"Terrible. If someone beat up a person close to me, I'd—well, I don't know what I'd do."

"We—" Noel began.

Kyra interrupted. "Noel and Jason have been friends since high school."

"Then you know the pride he takes in his sons. Each in their ways."

Kyra said, "You've been a great supporter of Shane."

Austin smiled self-deprecatingly. "I've tried to help."

"And your support of him has paid off."

Austin's brow furled. "How do you mean?"

"He's becoming a first-rate skater."

"With the best coaching, he stands to become one of the greats. He's already a competitor for others to measure themselves against."

"He has good coaching now?"

A smile. "Sure does. Carl Certane."

Pronounced with a soft *a* and a sounded final *e*. Unlike Linda. "I've heard of him."

"I persuaded him to take Shane on. Though once he'd seen that young kid skate, he didn't need much convincing."

Noel broke in. "Is Derek a skater, too?"

"Hockey." Flatly said. "Not that there can't be some greats in that world, too. Like Gretzky, obviously. He could have been a superb figure skater, he had the grace and the power. And especially the timing. Most hockey players rely only on brute force."

"You saying that's how Derek played, too?"

Austin shrugged. "Never saw him play."

Noel broke in. "Do you know him at all?

"As well as the rest of the family. I don't think he had—has—

anywhere near Shane's discipline. Discipline's at the base of all great work. Without it— Ah, Shane," Austin beamed as Shane appeared. "Ready to go?"

"Without what?" asked Shane.

"Discipline, Shane. What it always comes back to."

"Yeah." Without enthusiasm.

"We've talked about it before, we'll talk about it again."

Shane's eyes half closed and he nodded, looking at the floor.

"Ready to go?"

Shane headed for the door.

Austin said to Kyra and Noel, "Good to have met you again. Come see Shane at his practice." He followed the young man out.

"Just what I was thinking," said Noel.

"What were you thinking?" Alana, her hair still damp, arrived clutching her backpack.

"That we might go watch Shane skate."

"Yeah! I'm for that."

"After we make some inquiries."

Out to the car. Down the drive to the road. Just before the B&B Kyra said, "Stop for a couple of minutes, please. Need to go to my room." She grabbed her purse and fled.

Noel turned to the back seat, Alana lying across it, leaning against the door behind the passenger seat, her head clamped together with earphones. He started to speak, then thought better of it. And Kyra had to speak to him about the baby. The elephant tooted quietly. Minutes, and Kyra was back. "Better?"

"Always. As of late, anyway."

"What're you thinking? About the case, I mean."

"Like I said, so many nice guys. Jason, Sam, Derek, Mike by all reports. Tim."

"You're not mentioning Shane."

"You're right."

"What about those two guys we talked to yesterday?"

"Yeah. Something about them. Don't know what."

They drove in silence, each musing. At the ferry dock they drove into line.

Alana pulled the phones from her ears, stretched and opened

the door. "You think Shane and Austin are up there somewhere ahead of us?"

"Alana, stay here. Leave them alone."

"Hey, I wasn't going to—"

"Good. Close the door." He turned and sat on one leg to face her. "Tell me what you think is going on. With the family. With everyone you've met since leaving Qualicum."

She stared out the front window. "You mean did one of them beat up Derek?"

"Or two or more."

"I thought about that before going to sleep. I was pretty tired but I was stoked, too. See, there's this computer in Derek's room. I'd gone online to research Austin Osborne. Oh—" seeing Noel's glare, "Linda said it was okay."

"People you've met. Firsthand impressions."

She grinned. "I see what you mean. Okay. Linda. I like her. She's straight with you, she seems kind to everybody. I think she's a good mom to Shane and Tim. Maybe she's a great mom to Derek but I haven't seen them together. But I bet she is. By extrapolation."

"Good. Go on."

"Jason, I don't know. I just saw him at dinner. But I think he's a good dad and he's gentle with Linda. He'd have to be or you wouldn't be his friend all these—"

"You've seen Jason and me together, just talking, when no one else was around?"

She thought. "You're right. But what I've seen and heard from him, he seems okay."

"Not someone who'd beat up his son."

"If he would, he didn't show it since I've known him."

"Shane? Tim?"

"Shane's just gorgeous. But he's, like, not there. He's inside his head. I want to see him skate but I don't want to get to know him. If you've got to be like that to be a great skater, hey, forget it." She fiddled with her earpieces. "Now Tim, he's a good kid. Kinda young for me, but just to hang out with? Way up on his older brother. And there's no way he'd hurt Derek. And Shane couldn't've, he wasn't even around. He thinks too much of his body to want to get into a fight with anybody else's."

Noel studied her face. "Good, Alana. Smart."

"Thanks. Now can I tell you what I found out about Austin Osborne?"

"Sure."

"He's, like, had this great competitive skating career, won everything in sight. Then one day he was out. Overnight."

"Why?"

Kyra said, "The line's moving."

Noel swung himself around, started the engine and followed the car in front up the ramp. He stopped a foot behind it. An officious ferry worker gestured Noel further on. He started the engine again, inched ahead until suddenly Noel was facing the palm of the ferry worker's hand, stop sign. Noel slammed on his brake, a nano-span away from the forward car. He muttered under his breath.

Kyra said, "Never mind." Turning back to Alana she said, "So he was out of competitive skating. You find out why that happened?"

"Couldn't get a hold on it. Couple of people I read said 'cause he and his partner had been cheated out of a gold at the Nationals about the time he stopped competing. Hey, he got the silver, and that's pretty good."

"Maybe not good enough for him."

"Or maybe he was involved in that scandal when some of the judges traded votes so that their skaters won when they shouldn't have, and maybe Osborne thought he'd been cheated and gave up. Nobody actually said that and maybe I read it wrong, I was pretty tired. But he was awesome. And then he went with the Ice Follies and made lots of money. And now he owns this big skating equipment company."

Noel thought, first-rate researcher.

Kyra said, "That's all good to know. No, no—" seeing Alana's sudden troubled look, "it really is. Valuable context."

"Oh. Okay."

"Anything else about him? Or anyone else?"

"No. Not really." Alana lapsed into silence, her left index finger playing with the two rings on her right middle finger.

"But?" Kyra waited.

Alana looked up. "I tried to get a handle on Derek."

"Oh?"

"Well, there I was in his room, it had to be able to tell me something about him."

Kyra liked this. Herself, she believed in the narrative power of medicine cabinets. "What did you learn?"

"The room was real neat, shirts in the closet, sweaters aligned in his drawers, desk clear except his computer and printer, shoes lined up on the closet floor."

"And what did this tell you?"

"Well, either he's a neat freak, or Linda cleans up after him."

Noel laughed. "Very good."

"But I don't know which."

"You'll have to study the situation further." He beamed at her. "So everything was in its place, and you figure—"

"Well, one thing wasn't."

"Okay. Tell."

"In the closet, he had his hockey skates, two pairs, they were hanging from the wall by their tied-together laces. I turned them upside down and a memory stick fell out."

"And?"

"It was kinda weird. Why'd he put it in his skate?"

"You were curious."

"Yeah, like really. So I stuck it into his computer and booted it up. Really really slow computer, took forever."

"But you finally got see what was on the stick."

"That was weird too. All that memory, and just one file."

"What did you find on this purloined file?"

"Yeah, I did kind of purloin it, didn't I." Giggle followed by small malevolent grin. "A list of dates. I copied them out. If the computer was that old, the printer was probably a loud cranking dinosaur." She took a folded piece of paper from her pocket. "After I thought I was such a smart detective, what's on the file? Just a bunch of dates." She handed the paper to Kyra.

Kyra and Noel read it. Six dates, the fifteenth and thirtieth of the month, mid-June to the end of August. After each date, the amount of $3000. Added together, $18,000.

"Like, just so unimportant. I really tried to find something."

97

"Most of what we find is unimportant. So we keep on looking, trying to see a pattern." Kyra turned to sit forward. Noel's niece had the makings.

The ferry closed in on the Campbell River dock.

Austin Osborne had guided his Porsche convertible onto the ferry at 1 mile an hour. He'd noted the lip toward the end of the lowered ferry ramp rose a couple of inches higher than the ramp itself and the chassis of this Porsche, a fine vehicle, was low-slung enough to bottom out. Usually he rented a large safe sedan, but he'd been feeling sporting so had chosen a sassy motorcar. He hoped his good spirits would remain—some heavy-duty decision-making in the next couple of days.

He and Shane had talked little after leaving the Cooper house. Which was fine. They'd have their chat on the ferry. Which was now.

Austin was silent. Shane felt relieved. If Austin talked, he wanted something. Shane wasn't in a giving mood. He knew he'd have to tell Austin how the situation had shifted. So Shane kept his own counsel. The roof of the Porsche stayed closed. Good, he didn't want people to see him with Austin, not right now. Over the years Shane with Austin had been a great thing, it made Shane proud. And his friends kind of jealous.

The Porsche stopped behind an SUV, built like a tank. Nearly three times as high as the Porsche. If it rolled backwards, it'd crush them. But surely it wouldn't. Lots of other things were less certain, way less. What could he do? What in the world could he do?

Austin turned to him. "You're worried."

What was he leading to? Which of the thousands of things Shane might be worried about was he talking about? "Yeah."

"That's okay. Worry can be good."

"Then I should be in great shape."

"And you don't think you are."

"Do you? You saw me yesterday. I looked like shit. I sure felt like shit."

"Everyone can have an off day."

"And I feel way worse today."

"Oh? Something new has happened, has it?"

"You might say that."

"Whatever it is, it's solvable."

"Yeah?"

"Everything is solvable, Shane. You need to put your trust in me. As always."

"Maybe." Not true. Austin knew this. Shane hated it when Austin lied to himself.

"Listen to me. My words, but more than my words. My voice. Close your eyes and listen to me. Relax your head. Relax your shoulders. Relax your spine."

But Shane sat stiffly upright. Usually Austin's voice did its job. Not today.

"My oh my, you really are tight. Will you tell me?"

Shane knew he would. He didn't want to. "Something my father's done."

"What's that, then?"

"He's really pissed off at whoever beat up Derek."

"Can't say I blame him. But—?"

"So he's hired a couple of detectives. The two you met at the house."

"The man and the woman are detectives?"

"And they're poking around."

"So? Isn't that their job?"

"Except they're saying all kinds of things about Derek. That maybe he ran with gangs. That maybe he's a dope dealer, a meth dealer."

"Is he?"

"Come on, Austin, Derek's no dealer. Or part of any gang."

"How do you know? Have you talked to him? Before the beating, I mean?"

Shane had. Couple of times on the phone. Derek was his brother and he was going to take care of Shane. Said it twice. Loud and clear. "No."

"If the Mounties haven't built any leads, what can a couple of outsiders find?"

"I don't know. I just know that the kinds of questions they're asking, the kinds of insinuations they're making, the Mounties didn't do any of that."

"Not with you, perhaps. Possibly with your parents."

"They'd have told me."

"Oh?"

Shane closed his eyes. His head ached.

"I suspect they wouldn't have imposed another worry on you. And if the Mounties had learned something negative about Derek, they'd have followed such a lead, and maybe by now found out who did this to him."

Maybe Austin was right. Maybe this was one item he didn't need to worry about. Except he was worried. And he feared he knew why. He could feel the worry, right under the skin of his arms, and his legs. It was a worry that could fuck up his technique, he knew this. Because he knew Derek did sell pot. Just in little amounts. To his friends. And why was he telling all this to Austin anyway? Wrong question. There was no way not to tell things to Austin. He had looked up to Austin for so many years. And Austin did relax him, soothe him. In little psychological ways, in his muscles and his stamina. When he was fifteen and broke his elbow in three places, hitting the ice wrong, Dr. Bremer the surgeon said it'd take the best part of a year before the elbow would mend enough to allow Shane to skate with his previous balance. Austin had suggested that his own body held the power to heal the elbow, fully. That he needed to bring every aspect of his conscious and unconscious body to bear on that elbow. Austin had taken leave from the Ice Follies. Every day for seven weeks he had spent an hour with him in the morning, an hour in the afternoon, speaking softly, suggesting what he needed to do, bringing Shane to visualize the cracks in the bones of his elbow, look below the skin, with his imagination bring the small and larger bone fragments together, keep them warm, let them melt into each other, make them whole again. The hypnosis focused the healing power of Shane's body onto one small space in that body.

In the eighth week Shane and Austin told Dr. Bremer that Shane was going to compete in three weeks. Dr. Bremer exclaimed Shane would do no such thing—no skating till he was completely mended. But he was, Shane insisted. Impossible, the doctor declared. Austin told Bremer to test the articulation of Shane's elbow. Bremer was surprised. He ordered X-rays. The X-rays corroborated what Shane claimed—he was one hundred percent fine. Dr. Bremer announced he didn't believe in miracles, that the break couldn't have been as substantial as he'd assumed, that perhaps his previous diagnosis was exaggerated. Austin suggested Bremer look at the earlier X-rays. Later that day Dr. Bremer pronounced Shane ready to skate again. That's what Austin had done for him. And the same thing with a smaller break two years ago. Austin had that gift. And Austin controlled Shane with the gift, Shane knew this. So Shane's worry deepened.

What was Austin saying? The Mounties? Why did he keep going on about the Mounties? "Austin. It's not the Mounties I'm worried about. It's the detectives."

"I don't think you need to worry." His voice, never harsh, softened as he said, "We've got another few minutes. Push the seat back. Lean back."

Shane did. Now he'll say, *Close your eyes* . . .

"Close your eyes. Good. Let your shoulders relax. Good. Let your jaw relax. Good. Now take a deep breath. A deeper breath. Breathe in so deeply you can feel the air going right down to your stomach . . ."

Shane knew it all, the flow of the words, the way his body responded, most of the time completely, but always with increasing ease. It felt good to relax his responsibility and allow his body to ease away the sharp edges, the painful corners, the jagging heat. Austin had taught him how to do this. And when Austin wasn't around Shane could bring these states onto himself. Except he'd not done so in the last two weeks, not since he'd come home after Derek's beating. Why not? Part of him said he'd been too distracted. But more that—it was as if it'd be, somehow, something sacrilegious about using Austin's method for changing his body's state of being. Except when, like now, Austin spoke in that gentle fashion, it seemed almost okay.

Austin's voice came almost as a whisper: ". . . and you will, Shane, you will. With your discipline, you can, you will. You'll see, it'll be easy, you'll see . . ."

Would he? Maybe. He should know. He didn't know and it scared him. Maybe he had to. If he didn't? That scared him more. And he didn't even know if he had any reason to be scared. Which made it all worse.

Shane felt the ferry slowing. They'd be closing in on the Campbell River dock.

FIVE

T. SHORTY BARLOW stood on the porch of his 1950s mill-worker's house and surveyed the garden. It occupied most of his half-acre on a Campbell River hillside facing southeast, with a view of the Cape Mudge reserve end of Quadra Island across the water. And how were land claims going, how was Zeke managing the politicos?

The broad beans were nearly over. Tomatoes needed re-staking. Green beans looked okay, so did the lettuces and arugula. Might be a good crop of apples this year, but he needed to thin. He would come home early.

He cast a glance at the espaliered peach. Little tiny green balls, how did they grow such a big hard stone in so few months? The peach fruit around the stone didn't amaze him, the seeds of raspberries, strawberries, even apples weren't as startling as peach stones.

He set his empty coffee cup on the railing and clumped down the stairs, opened the deer-proof gate and surveyed the garden from there. The smell of it all made his heart smile—the moist earth warming, the radicchio and lettuce unfurling, the various squash extending tendrils. Hell, he could practically see it happening.

Loathsome weeds sprouted every day, shoots flourishing in the loose soil as if they didn't care. He squatted and pulled, the sun already hot on his neck. Slugs of course, thanks to the rain. The little ones, the most destructive, left brown holes in the lettuce. Shorty examined each leaf in the row and picked the white buggers off. These guys had emigrated from England or somewhere, not like the indigenous banana slugs that knew to stay in the bush and eat there. Shorty squished the little bastards between his fingers; he hated the slimy feel, then wiped the slime off in the dirt. The dirt clung to his fingers. "I know," he said to Perky, who'd stalked up. "I should have put gloves on. Why in bloody hell can't you look after the slugs?"

Perky rubbed against his side, said, "Miaow," and rolled over on the warming soil between the vegetables, inviting Shorty to rub his belly.

"Bloody hell," said Shorty. "I'm busy."

"Miaow." Perky was black with a white shirt-front.

"Fuck off." But Shorty knew this routine could go on for a while. Perky licked his paw.

Shorty gave in and, with the back of his hand, rubbed his stomach. Perky arched, and purred. "Okay, cat, you look after the veg, I have to get to the rink." He stood, locking his creaking knee. On the porch he scooped up the coffee cup between his palms. No way not to get dirt on the door handle, damn. Cup on kitchen counter, on to the bathroom. He scrubbed his hands, took a cloth from under the sink, wet it, went back and cleaned the door handle. Perky still lay between the lettuce and beans, rubbing his back in the soil. Cats should weed, or at least learn to make the bed. A good life. Long as you're not a cat in a research lab.

His other cat, Tabitha, a tortoise shell, looked up from the sofa, her usual place. She rarely went outside. Maybe fifteen minutes at dusk.

"You could do the dishes," Shorty told her.

She rolled over and purred.

He rinsed the cloth, came back and punched the answering machine replay button. "Hi, Shorty, it's Shane. Austin's driving me over. See you at the rink."

The ice was good. He'd had the icing team check it yesterday, right temperature for figure skating, slightly warmer than for hockey. Not many players practicing now, July. Just Shane on the small rink—and that little girl, Emily, only eight, so keen. Sometimes Shane gave her pointers. But he, T. Shorty Barlow the Great, was the Ice Meister of Campbell River.

Shorty got into his Toyota pickup, shoved in the key, backed out of his driveway. That Shane, close to Olympic material. He'd read a book, *Outliers*, which stressed the route to success was made up of luck and work. Being born in the right time and place, then ten thousand hours of practice. And have someone like Shorty around: keep the ice the right thickness and temperature, pick Shane up at the ferry when he didn't have a ride, be nice to Austin when he was around, he was bloody paying for that super coach in Vancouver. Ten thousand hours of practice. Hell of a number, but it was spread over years. Shane did it, just like Yo Yo Ma probably had with his cello. *Outliers* talked about hockey players, how most top players had been born in the first few months of the year. Like race horses the cut-off date was January 1, so children born early in the year had a physical advantage. They got picked for rep teams, had more practice time, and so on. Shorty knew Derek's birthday was early spring because one year his friends had surprised him with a cake at the rink. Didn't know when Shane's was. Maybe it wasn't so important in figure skating.

Shane. His attitude had changed. His skating was very good, but increasingly mechanical. Last year's sparkle had faded. Too much pressure now in Seniors?

T. Shorty Barlow the Great had watched Shane for thirteen years. At four and five he'd wobbled around the rink after his older brother, as Timmy had later behind both of them. The little kids, their desire, innocence, will to learn, always brought a lump to Shorty's throat. "Way to go, guys!" he'd yell, year after year, from a low bleacher seat close to his Zamboni garage.

Ten thousand hours of practice and every advantage. Shane had that, a loving family, not too much hassle for switching from hockey to figure skating, and Shorty to keep the ice in perfect condition. Yeah, and Austin to pay the bills. Shorty therefore should be in cahoots with Austin, right? Yeah, right.

Noel, not having Cindy's last name nor knowing where and if she worked, drove first to the hospital. Maybe she'd be back with Derek. But in Derek's room, no visitors. Derek lay as still and silent as yesterday. At the nurses' station he asked for Linda, she might have a sense of Cindy's whereabouts. But Linda was in the OR today, wouldn't be available for hours. So back to the car, Alana waiting, Noel and Kyra disagreeing whether Cindy had told them to turn right or left after leaving the parking lot. "Left, I think," Noel said, "because we got back on that main road—Dogwood, right?" He turned left, Kyra insisting he'd gone wrong. After only two wrong turns he managed to wind his way to Cindy's home. His mind kept coming back to the list of dates and the $3000 notations. They arrived at Cindy's home as she was opening the door to a tan Tercel. Kyra and Noel got out of the Honda. Alana stayed: more than two interviewers could intimidate the subject. Alana had sulked, then acceded.

Kyra waved. "Hello, Cindy!"

Cindy, tight jeans and a red T-shirt, whirled. "Oh. Hello."

"We'd like to talk to you about Derek."

"I'm just on my way to sit with him."

"We'll only take a few minutes."

"Well, okay." She closed the car door and leaned against it.

Noel propped his elbow on the car roof. Kyra faced them both. Not maximal interrogation circumstances, Noel thought. "How long have you known Derek?"

"Oh, five months?"

"And you've been dating since then?"

"Oh no, only since maybe March?"

"You know him pretty well, then?"

She looked down. "We were getting to know each other more."

"He's a good guy, is he?"

She gave Kyra a thin smile. "A great guy." Her eyes were welling.

"Did you get to know his friends?"

"Some." She pulled a tissue from a pocket.

"Who was he close to?"

"Well, couple of guys over on Quadra. Here at the college, Mike Campbell, it was Mike who introduced Derek and me." She giggled.

"Is that funny?"

"Well, no. Before I started dating Derek, I was going with Mike."

"I see. Was that hard on Mike, your leaving him for Derek?"

"It wasn't like that. I wasn't going to be with Mike much longer anyway."

"Did Mike know that?"

"Yeah. Well, sorta." Cindy wiped her nose. "Why do you want to know this?"

"Anything we can learn about Derek and his friends might help us. You want us to find who beat him, don't you?"

"Mainly I want him to be okay again."

"And when he's okay, you don't want anything else to happen to him, right?"

She sighed, close to a sob in her outbreath. "No. Please no." She looked Kyra in the eye. "Ask me."

"Was Mike angry when you started dating Derek?"

"No. Course not." She stared at the table again. "Why should he be?"

Noel said, "You're a very attractive young woman. Any guy could be upset if you shifted your affection."

"Are you saying Mike could've done this to Derek? He's not even in town."

"We're just asking questions, Cindy."

"No. There's no way Mike would—he's a gentle guy. No."

"Tell us about his other friends."

"Gaston Robitaille and Joe Daimley. They drank a lot of beer together. Too much, I thought. Gast specially, he got real loud after a few."

"Is that what they mostly did together?"

"Beer, and they played hockey. And sometimes we double-dated, Derek and me, and Gaston and Kelly. Or Joe and whoever he was with and— Shit."

"What?"

She put her hands to her mouth. "Won't be doing that for a while."

Noel made the connection. The list of numbers— "Did Gast and Joe do drugs with Derek?"

"What?"

"We think they were. More than just doing."

"What d'you mean, more?"

"Dealing?"

"Derek? No way."

"We've learned a few things, Cindy."

"Come on. Not Derek."

"If you know something about drugs, now's the time to tell us. To help Derek."

"I do want to help Derek. But how can this help?"

"Tell us what it is, and if it helps, then you've helped."

"It's not—oh, I don't know." She wiped her nose again.

Kyra smiled encouragingly. Noel looked stern. Cindy wouldn't meet their eyes. She rolled her shoulders. She rubbed her right hand with her left.

Kyra leaned toward her. "What?"

"I don't know. I'm sorry, I just don't know."

"We're not the police, Cindy. If it's not important we'll forget it. I promise."

Cindy took a deep breath. "Derek did it because he really cares for Shane. He did it for Shane." She paused. "He could get some good weed. Gast and Joe, they found the guys to sell it to. They were supposed to meet up that night."

Out of the corner of her eye Kyra noted Alana, leaning out the window of the Honda, listening intently.

"The three of them were going to meet these buyers. The meet was up at the end of Evergreen Road. Where he was found." Tears welled again. "Then Derek was coming over here. We were going to be together." She sniffed hard and wiped her face with the decomposing tissue. "He never came here, he was lying up there. I waited an hour then went looking for Gast and Joe. I found them at the Riptide, they were pissed. I got Joe outside and he told me they'd done the deal and they'd left Derek up there. He was fine when they left him." She sniffed, and wiped her nose.

Kyra found a pack of tissues in her purse and handed one to Cindy.

Cindy took it, wiped her cheeks and eyes. "Thank you." She stared at the hood of the car. "Except then—I drove to Evergreen but I never got that far, I saw cop cars, their lights flashing like crazy, and I just turned around, if he was okay he'd be fine and if he wasn't—anyway, I came home and took some sleeping pills and the next morning Linda told me."

"You said Derek was doing this deal for Shane. What do you mean?"

"There's a chance that the guy who's been supporting Shane's going to stop."

Noel said, "Austin Osborne?"

"Yeah."

"Why?"

"The stock market's tanking and Osborne lost money and maybe couldn't afford to keep on supporting Shane."

"Maybe?"

"They had to wait and see what happened to Osborne's investments. But Derek didn't want to take the chance. So he did what he figured he had to."

Kyra said, "Where'd he get the weed?"

"I don't know."

Kyra glanced at Noel, back to Cindy. "Thanks for telling us."

Noel straightened up. "Did you inform the police?"

Cindy blinked hard. "No."

"Because?"

"Because I didn't want to get Derek into trouble!" Now nearly shouting.

"He's already in trouble."

Kyra touched Cindy's shoulder. "We'll do all we can for Derek."

Noel said, "Is there anything else you could tell us?"

Whispering: "I've told you everything."

"It may help Derek. If there's anything else you think of, please phone us." He handed her a card.

"What're you going to do now?"

"Continue the investigation."

"Will you talk to Gast and Joe?"

"Probably."

Cindy grabbed the door handle. "Please don't tell them I said all this stuff."

He glanced at Kyra, who nodded. "We won't tell them."

She moved toward the house. Turned, looked from Kyra to Noel, went inside.

Kyra raised her eyebrows. "Impressive. How come you zeroed in on Derek's dealing?"

"Little things. Tim calling those two dopeheads. Derek's oldest best friend Jim growing marijuana—"

"Which he said he'd never deal, he'd lose that license—"

"But which he might deal if the close friend was desperate. But mostly it was the schedule Alana found. First date on the list was June 15, the day Derek was beaten. Is three thousand dollars a good price for a kilo of marijuana?"

"Sounds cheap to me."

"And six more kilos to go. With medical marijuana Jim would make sure he always had a fresh supply ready to harvest. What's a kilo when you're getting fifteen or twenty kilos every few weeks? Does Jim's father know exactly how much is maturing?"

"We don't know. We don't even know if Derek got the stuff from Jim."

"I'd bet on it." He walked back to the Honda. "We should revisit Jim."

Kyra said, "Right now, back to Gaston and Joe."

"I'd guess Derek's partners in crime weren't the ones who beat him."

They got into the car. Alana said, "Did you learn good stuff?"

"Didn't you hear everything? Your curious head was obvious." Kyra found herself liking Alana more and more.

"Derek took Cindy away from a Mike, and Derek did the deal for Shane because Osborne may have money problems."

"Good ears." Noel started the engine and pulled away. He inverted the arrival route, back on Dogwood. Again on to Evergreen, then Peterson, and there was Joe Daimley's house. On the porch no chair was occupied.

Kyra said, "Alana, this time keep the windows closed and stay low in the seat. We may have to confront a couple of guys here."

"You mean—you mean they might try to fight you?"

"We don't know."

"Uh, Uncle Noel? Do you have a gun?"

"No, Alana. We don't carry guns."

"Shouldn't you?"

"We don't work that way."

"What if they have guns?"

"We'll walk away and they won't use them."

"Please be careful."

"We try very hard to be careful."

And sometimes even succeed, Kyra thought.

Kyra and Noel got out and walked toward the stairs. Noel said, "Plans?"

"Confront them with the deal they made, find out who the buyers are."

"You lead." They crossed the verandah. Noel pushed a doorbell. Ringing inside. Silence. Another ring. Nothing.

Kyra tried the doorknob. Unlocked. "Want to look around?"

"No, Kyra, I do not."

"If they're not there, no big deal." She pushed the door open and stepped inside. "Hello!"

"I'll wait here." He hated it when she did this. He stared at the car. Alana wasn't visible. Good. A couple of cars drove past. He sat in one of the chairs. What the hell was taking her so long? Probably peeing, on top of everything else. She had to get serious about this baby. At the very least a medical exam. Where the hell was she? He squeezed his eyes tight. A headache coming on? Damn. He breathed deeply.

A voice said, "Hi. You looking for me?"

Noel's head jerked and his eyes opened. Joe Daimley, backpack slung over one shoulder, same jeans and T-shirt as yesterday. "Yes."

"All by yourself today?"

"No. Kyra's inside."

"The house?"

"Yes."

"What's she doing in there?" Irritation building.

Investigating, stupid, that's what she does. "The door was open and—"

"Open?" Joe's eyes narrowed. He pulled his long hair off his neck.

"Unlocked, and she went in. She had to use the bathroom. I'll call her." He leapt from the chair, opened the door, "Kyra! Joe's arrived! You done in there?"

"Thank you!" A calm voice. Followed a few seconds later by Kyra, adjusting her T-shirt. "Hey, Joe. We've been waiting for you. Is your buddy around?"

"He's at the college."

"We'd like to talk to the two of you."

"About what?"

"More questions about Derek."

"Ask away."

"We'd like your double insight."

Joe shrugged. "I can try calling him."

"Good."

Joe took a cell phone from the front of his pack, pressed in a pre-set number. "Hey, Gast . . . Yeah, look, those two guys from yesterday . . . Yeah, and they want to talk to us, can you come over? . . . Oh, yeah, sure. Hold on." To Noel and Kyra: "He's got a class in forty minutes. But we can meet him at the college. The bookstore."

Kyra looked at Noel. He nodded.

"Great. Be there in ten."

Noel said, "We can drive you."

"Naw, I'll check out some stuff for my hydraulics class. I'll drive myself."

"We'll follow." Down the stairs to Noel's Civic and Joe's Echo.

Noel whispered to Kyra, "Joe's a trusting fellow."

Kyra said, "You're right. These guys wouldn't have bashed Derek around."

They got into the Honda. Noel started the engine and drove off behind Joe. He asked Kyra, "What did you find in there?"

"Nothing. He's got a bedroom, clothes on the floor and books in piles and graph paper all over the place. Looks like he's studying heavy machinery too."

"Not the room of a criminal."

"Only if mess is a crime."

From in back Alana said, "Did you just walk into that house and look around?"

"Sure."

"Why?"

"Because the door was open."

"Huh?"

"It was like being invited in."

"Oh," said Alana.

"Like your taking a memory stick out of a hockey skate."

"It fell out, Kyra!"

"Same difference."

Alana sat far back in her seat. "Unc? Why didn't you go in, too?"

"Somebody has to stand guard."

"Oh." Smaller voice.

Under ten minutes to North Island College. Alana had to stay in the car. Objections, but that was how it would be. Or she could go to the cafeteria. She stayed. They followed Joe to the bookstore. It was a new campus, meticulously landscaped, one side the college, the other the high school Tim attended.

Gast, shaven skull gleaming in the sun, waited at the door. "Hey, what's up?"

"Just a few more questions." Noel looked at the grassy slope between the buildings and the parking lot. "Want to sit on the grass?"

They did. Kyra said, "Now look, guys, don't panic, okay?"

Gast raised his eyebrows. "About what?"

"You'll likely come out of this okay. We know you two and Derek met a couple of people up on Evergreen and sold them some dope. How much did you get?"

Gast was on his feet first, then Joe. Gast said, "Fuckin' nerve, accusing us of dealing."

"Sit down," said Noel.

Joe: "What the hell's this about?"

Kyra: "Sit down and we'll tell you."

The two guys glanced at each other, and sat.

Noel said, "The first thing you need is a lawyer. The second is to go with us and your lawyer to the Mounties. Your lawyer will make it clear that you've come in freely and want to help in the Derek Cooper case."

Joe and Gast stared at Noel, saying nothing.

"Your lawyer will also make it clear that all potential charges regarding the sale of an illegal substance must be dropped. Say nothing till the Mounties agree. Then you tell them everything you and Derek did that evening. Understand?"

Gast turned to Kyra. "Is he serious?"

"Very. The Mounties are going to be much more interested in what you have to tell them about the buyers, and about what happened before Derek was beaten."

"We got to talk." He stood again and moved away ten meters. Joe followed. They spoke in whispers. Kyra and Noel heard a few words: "...kill us...give them up...Soy and Gagnon...looked mean...The two came back."

Joe said, "Okay," and Gast nodded.

Kyra asked, "You know any lawyers?"

Gast said, "My aunt."

"Call her."

He did. A few minutes and he clicked off. "The cop shop at one."

"Kyra and I'll be there. Make sure you are." They walked back to the Honda.

"We're getting closer," said Kyra.

"Want a sandwich and status session? I saw a place near the ferry terminal."

"Good. I'm starving." They parked in front of a sandwich place. Kyra rushed in; Noel and Alana followed more slowly.

Alana said, "Is Kyra okay?"

"Yeah, she's fine."

They each ordered a shrimp, tomato, and sprout sandwich. Kyra reappeared from yet another bathroom and chose the same. They crossed the road to a waterfront park bordering Discovery Passage and found a picnic table. Two kids were tossing a ball. A toddler toddled by, pushing its stroller; the mother hovered. Their table was protected from the noon sun by a shady maple.

Kyra took a bite as Noel said, "Okay. What do we know?"

"This is a good sandwich," said Kyra with a full mouth. "The one truck belonged to Derek, the car to Gast and Joe, the other to the buyers. Which means whoever messed Derek up parked across the street from Mrs. McDougal. A truck, a van?"

"Whichever. And it means the guy intended to beat Derek up."

"Why?" Alana asked, wolfing her sandwich

"That's the question." Noel took a bite. For a few seconds they all chewed.

Alana swallowed. "To rob Derek of $3000?"

"Did the attacker know a deal was happening? Money changing hands?"

Kyra said, "We don't know how much he had on him. I said three thousand was cheap for a kilo and we don't know if he had more dope."

"I have a feeling," Noel said, "that any money was a bonus."

"You mean someone just wanted to beat him up?" Alana looked at her uncle with large eyes.

"Maybe. We don't have a motive. Could be anything. Till we know more."

They finished their sandwiches and stared past the ball players to the water. The toddler's job of shoving his stroller had apparently fatigued him; he was ensconced in it as his mother pushed it briskly.

"Thank you." Harold Arnesen put the phone down. Strathcona Gardens, the ice rink in Campbell River, had informed him that Shane did have time booked tomorrow, ten to twelve. He'd been in today, had just left.

He sat back in a large black captain's chair behind an ornate dark brown oak desk. It held a flat computer screen. He re-read some reports he'd printed up, needing to deal with their implications. He loosened his tie. Only when he came into the Vancouver Island Skating Union office did he wear one. These days ties choked him. In Ottawa he'd never been without one. Another reason to be pleased with his move west.

The ample office had maple walls covered with pictures showing the successes of his skaters. Even a couple of himself as a young competitor. Sadly he'd never advanced to celestial reaches; a case of bad vertigo came over him at eighteen. No physiotherapist could cure it—a vestigial disorder brought on by the spins and axels of performance itself. Nonetheless, he'd remained close to the sport, developing a number of fine talents. In BC they'd seen it as an asset to ask him to become Head of VISU. Well, honorary head.

Tomorrow he'd drive up to Campbell River. He should have called Vancouver yesterday, checked on Shane's schedule there, saved himself a trip. He'd never liked calling ahead; arrive silently, get to see what's going on with nobody knowing. Tomorrow he'd admire the remarkable technique young Cooper had developed.

Harold needed some good news. On return from the ferry he'd found two biannual scouting reports regarding his skaters in Baie d'Urfée and Toronto. Danielle Dubois was evolving well, though not as quickly as her trainer wished. The Toronto problem was Graham Pauley. He looked recalcitrant, as if he were fighting his coach all the way. Harold wondered if the problem wasn't his sponsor. Steve Struthers had always been a shame, a publicly accused doper who wasn't kicked out. Worse, Skate Canada had allowed him to sponsor the occasional skater. If Harold still lived in the east he'd have seen to it that Pauley not be allowed to let Struthers call him his protégé. Part of Harold's problem, so far from headquarters, grew from lack of daily contact between members and the Board.

Part of a larger quandary. He needed the young people he backed to succeed. Four years ago, while Chair of Skate Canada, he had been partial to three men and two women. He had pushed regulations a bit on their behalf—better ice time, grant money channeled their direction, additional press coverage. They deserved it but he'd let his diplomacy become visible. Board members had approached him, saying his favoritism was inappropriate. After some heated discussion he had accepted this—not that he'd done anything wrong, just that public apprehension of partiality might cause an image problem for Skate Canada. Unfortunately the conversation had leaked out. He hadn't resigned, but he hadn't sought a second term.

Though stepping down as titular head, he'd lost no real power. Also without the Chair role he could be more involved. As his young skaters collected Junior and Senior golds, he'd be recognized for the visionary he knew himself to be.

Tomorrow he'd drive up to Campbell River. He'd never taken the Island Highway that far north. He looked forward to the journey, leave early, stop for breakfast in one of those quaint little towns along the way. He'd spend the night in Campbell River. He turned on his computer to find the best lodging.

The family sat around the kitchen table. Linda had returned immediately after shift change, she and her nurse driver-friend picking up an uncommunicative Shane. Tim had located his dad in the north woodlot, limbing the fallen trees he could access. Tim said Kyra and Noel wanted to meet with the whole family as soon as everyone got home.

Tim was delighted to be here as part of the family council, and that no one had suggested he shouldn't be here. He wondered how Alana felt, an outsider, more than Noel and Kyra; as investigators, their role was central. That was another good thing. He, Tim, had entered into a first-name relation with the detectives. So they saw him as an adult. Then he had a dreadful thought: were they treating him as a Derek replacement? He glanced at his mother, his father. He saw increased worry on both their faces: still because of comatose Derek, more now because of what Noel and Kyra might tell them. His mom had insisted on tea, had just poured for Alana and Shane. Shane stared at it. Alana gazed out over everyone's head.

Damn, Tim thought, she has the most beautiful face. He wished he were two years older. Heck, here he was at the council, maybe he was her equal.

"Tell us what you learned," Jason instructed Noel.

Noel did, explaining first that he and Kyra were present at the full proceeding; since they'd set up the confession, the Mounties and the kids' lawyer had agreed on their right to be there. Noel described their conversations with Gast and Joe, mentioning Tim's clever suspicion—Tim felt his ears grow red, and Alana gave him a smile. "The truth is that Derek went to the meeting on Evergreen to sell pot to two dealers. His source was to get half the $8000, his contact guys got $1000, and he kept $3000."

Linda breathed in deeply. "You believe Gast and Joe?"

"I do," said Noel, "and so do Kyra and the Mounties."

Jason grabbed Noel's arm. "Did they know anything about Derek getting beaten? Did they do it?"

Noel shook his head. "They were so scared of getting arrested they held nothing back. Their lawyer, Gastòn's aunt, Julienne Robitaille, impressed on them the importance of telling the Mounties every detail."

Linda frowned at Noel. "Do the police think the buyers beat up Derek?"

Kyra broke in, "We're assuming not. They'd have nothing to gain. If they wanted to buy more pot, Derek would be a good source. Besides, they drove off first. Derek was fine when Gast and Joe left. There was another vehicle, according to Mrs. McDougal."

Tim fussed. Why would Derek break the law? Where would Derek find $8000 worth of dope? What would he do with the $3000 he kept? Then Tim understood, with horror, Derek did sell the pot. And he knew where Derek got it. "What happened to the money?"

"Derek paid Joe and Gast $500 each." Noel said. "That left Derek with $7000."

"Whoever beat Derek stole $7000," Tim concluded. Which meant the supplier had lost the money and was probably furious. Uh-oh!

Jason asked, "What'll happen to Derek's contacts?"

"Mounties are questioning them. As long as they keep cooperating they won't be charged. The Mounties are more interested in the buyers, two persons of interest. See who the buyers lead them to. And the growers. The in-between guys didn't know."

Linda whispered, "Who are they?"

"We've been told not to mention their names, Kyra said. "And you probably wouldn't know them. Not even Derek did."

"What happens now?" Jason asked.

"The investigation continues. Somebody other than the sellers or the buyers beat up Derek."

"All we know is what we don't know?"

"We know more than we did a couple of days ago."

Jason glared at Noel. "Now do we have to thank you for learning Derek dealt dope?"

"He's committed a crime, Jason. When he comes out of the coma, likely he'll not have to serve time. Probation. Some rehabilitation. This was his and Gast's and Joe's first sale." Noel had had to force himself to say: *When.*

Jason stood. "I hate it. Why the hell'd he do it! Goddamn!"

Shane, Tim noticed, was staring at his father. Then Shane covered his face with his hands. With the heels of his palms he massaged his eyes. Linda stood and embraced Jason. Alana looked from Tim to Shane and back. And a little smile for Tim; he forced an equally small one.

He got up and went out the door. He mounted his bike and pedaled up the drive to the road. He turned right, pumping hard. It'd be a stiff ride, uphill and winding a lot of the way. At least the sun still hung high. He needed to know why Derek had dealt dope. His eyes were heavy with tears. A dark green van pulled out of a logging road behind him.

Shane stared out the window of his room, seeing nothing. Derek had sold the pot so Derek's goddamn brother could have the money he needed for his friggin' career. In case Austin stopped supporting Shane Cooper! All done for Derek's asshole brother. Poor goddamn Derek. Shane felt tears rolling down his cheeks . . .

"We'll eat around seven," Linda said to Kyra. "Would you like to go back to the B&B?"

Kyra very much wanted to lie down. But Noel said, "We should spend the time talking to Derek's friends here on the island. You mentioned some names, Jase?"

"You've already talked to Jim Bristol, right? There's Harry, if he's around. I heard he's working at two jobs on the big island, so he probably wouldn't know much about Derek."

"What about his ex-girlfriend? Bertina, you said? Bertina Anderson?"

"Sure, I've seen her in Heriot Bay so she's probably on the island. You could call her, Hon, introduce Kyra and Noel?" To Noel and Kyra: "She lives pretty close by."

Linda found Bertina's number. Bertina herself must have answered because Linda immediately told the person at the other end about Noel and Kyra. She set the phone on its hook. "Bertina says she'll meet you at the plaza, at Food and Funk." She described Bertina. "I'll call Jerry, too. But with his schedule, you may have to meet with him in Campbell River when he's on a break."

"Thanks, Linda. Come on, Kyra. Alana, want to join us?"

Alana looked about the kitchen. Shane had gone to his room, Tim was nowhere in sight. Learning that their son was a dope dealer, Harry and Linda might want to talk alone. "Sure."

The three of them got into the Honda and headed up the driveway, Alana again in back. Kyra said, "I am so absolutely wiped."

"We'll talk to the girl, then you can go back to your room. You don't have to bother about supper."

"But I'm starving too."

"We'll eat and leave. Sleep would be good for all of us."

Silence until Noel said, "We should've stopped by the girl's parents' place."

"Yeah," said Kyra.

"Why?" asked Alana.

"Because now she's prepared."

"Maybe that's a good thing."

"It can cut both ways," said Noel. "But we're more successful just showing up at the door."

"How do you know? Maybe if someone had time to get ready, you'd've learned more. You can't clone the situation? Do it two different ways?"

Noel laughed. This niece was not half bad.

They reached Heriot Bay Road. Nothing coming, just a cyclist riding away. From behind it reminded him of Tim Cooper, then he noted a van behind him and accelerated across. At the plaza he stopped in front of Food and Funk. There she was, as described—small, rich head of brown hair glowing in the angled sun, pug nose. Jeans, sandals. A T-shirt saying THE BEATINGS WILL CONTINUE UNTIL THE MORALE IMPROVES. Noel thought, maybe not so nice after all. Or a fine sense of humor.

Bertina was staring at the approaching group. No, mainly at Alana, Noel realized.

Kyra said, "Bertina Anderson?"

The young woman nodded.

Kyra made introductions. Bertina said to Alana, "Are you a detective too?"

Alana smiled. "Just tagging along. Learning the ropes."

Bertina pointed to some tables. "We can sit right here."

The moment Bertina sat, Alana placed herself across from the girl, leaving Noel and Kyra to sit across from each other. They caught each other's glance: Not ideal.

Bertina sought first Noel's then Kyra's eyes. "So this is about Derek. How is he?"

"Unchanged."

"Oh, he's changed. From the Derek I used to know."

"You knew him pretty well?"

"You could say that. We spent a lot—a *lot*—of time together. A year and a half."

"What was he like when you knew him?"

"Sometimes sweet, gentle. Sometimes moody. Or way more than moody."

"More?"

She shrugged. "Angry."

"At you?"

She thought for a moment. "In those moods, at whoever happened to be nearby."

"Was he a tough guy?" This, suddenly from Alana.

Noel wondered, during the second it took Bertina to answer, would she respond to a question from the trainee?

She did. "Tough, yeah. He could hold his own. I thought about that when I heard he was beaten. Somebody must have blindsided him. Maybe two or three of them."

"Mean, sometimes?"

"No, not mean. He honestly liked people. Most of the time."

"Can you think who it might've been?"

"To beat him like that? He could tick people off but nowhere near enough for that."

Alana again: "Did he ever tick you off, ever?"

Bertina stared at Alana for fifteen silent seconds before saying, "Not at first."

"But later?"

"Yeah."

"About what?"

For more silent seconds Bertina kept her eyes focused on the table, elbows on it, chin on her fists. "Lotsa things."

"For instance?"

"Just stuff."

Alana leaned across the table and spoke softly. "Like seeing other girls?"

Bertina looked up. "Not while he was going with me. He wouldn't have dared."

"So he ticked you off about—?"

Bertina waited for a couple of seconds. "I have to go. My mother's waiting supper."

Alana reached over and took Bertina's forearm. "Did he get ticked off about sex?"

Bertina's lips twitched. "Why're you asking that?"

"Lots of guys get ticked off about sex."

"Derek never did." She shook her head. "In the beginning."

"And after?"

Bertina pulled her lips in. Then she sighed. "Yeah."

Noel and Kyra watched. Two teen-aged girls in normal conversation . . . ?

"What'd he want?"

"You know..."

"I know about some guys. I don't know about Derek."

"He—he wanted more. And more. Not like early when we were going together. We'd hike, we'd swim, we'd go to the movies and sometimes we'd fuck or just hang with other kids. But more and more, sex was all he wanted."

Alana whispered, "Insatiable?"

"Yeah. We never did anything else."

"And?"

"No *and*. I told him, if we couldn't do other things too, get lost."

"Off he went, just like that?"

"Yeah. After a year and half, off he went."

"Did you try to patch it up? Did he?"

"It was like we were both worn out with each other." She stood. "I really do have to go."

Kyra said, "You can't think of anyone else he might have got ticked off at?"

Bertina shook her head.

"How about his family?"

A short snort. "He'd do anything for his family. He thought his father and mother were saints. He was so damn proud of his brothers. He'd do anything he could to make their lives better. Like Shane, for example— No, I've got get home." She stepped over the bench.

Kyra repeated, "He'd do anything for Shane? What did Shane need?"

"It's nothing. Look—"

Kyra said, "It could be important. For Derek. You cared for him, once."

"Cared?" She sniffed. "I loved him."

"Because he was a great guy. To his family. To Shane."

"Yeah. Shane. Lotsa worry about Shane."

"But Shane was—is—in a great place. Maybe going to the Olympics."

"Yeah. Maybe."

"Isn't it certain?"

"Only if he keeps getting the support."

"But he's had it for years. Austin Osborne thinks Shane is as good as there is."

Bertina sighed. "Austin's had some bad luck lately. Financially. Like the whole world, right? All those companies going broke. That's where Austin's money is. Was."

"Derek told you all this?"

"Yeah. Just before we split up. The recession hit Austin hard. I said I'd heard Austin had whacks of money, he'd been supporting Shane so long, why would he quit now? And Derek said something else Shane had told him, that maybe Shane didn't want Austin's support any more."

Was this the Shane Kyra had seen, the Shane that had to be supported in order to take the skating world by storm? "Why would Shane say something like that?"

"I don't know. I don't even know if he did. Derek was rambling about Shane."

"Did Austin actually say that to Shane? That he's going to have to stop supporting him one of these days?"

"I guess it depends on the economy." A rueful laugh. "Isn't that what everybody says, it all depends on the economy?"

At West Road Tim turned up hill again. Then down, and eventually left onto Heriot Bay Road, more steep sections. At least the young trees let a lot of light onto the road—clear cut, his dad had told him, the year he was born. He went everywhere on his bike, his legs were strong. He was on the school track team, ran the hundred meters in just over eleven seconds and was the fastest of the four in relays. He was headed away from the ferry, few cars trying to pass but lots coming toward him. He hated it when two cars met right beside him. He was still pedaling hard as he passed under the Bristol Greens arch over to the house. "Yo, Jim! You there?" No answer. In one of the greenhouses? He called into sheds one to five. No one. In six he found Jim picking green beans. Large full bags lay in the cart beside him, each bag marked ten kilos. Tim wondered how much Jim and his father got for a bag of beans. "Hey, Jim!"

Jim whirled around. "Oh. Tim."

It was like he'd scared Jim. "How you doin'?"

"Fine, great. What're you doing here?"

"Thought I'd go for a bike ride."

"Well. Nice to see you. Everybody okay at your place?"

No, nothing was okay. What the heck was wrong with Jim. "Not too great."

"Derek's stable?"

"Yeah. Stable." He didn't know how to ask Jim except to ask straight out. "Some detectives Dad hired found out Derek was up at the end of Evergreen to sell pot. Eight thousand bucks' worth. You have any idea where he got it?"

"He went there—? He was selling pot?"

"You're his best friend. Did he ever say anything about dealing?"

"What're you talking about?"

"I'm talking about my brother getting beaten up. Where'd he get the pot?"

"Tim, believe me. I don't know." Jim's neck flushed red.

"Did you give him the pot to sell?"

"Course not. That'd be illegal. Our marijuana is medicinal. We're not allowed to sell to anyone except Compassion clubs. It's all controlled. You know that. God, how can you even ask me if I gave Derek the pot. That's not allowed. Don't go spreading rumors! We could get in trouble if people starting thinking that way! Hear me?"

Yeah, Tim heard. The command, and the fear. Maybe it hadn't been a great idea to ask him straight out. Better back off, get the hell out of here. "I wouldn't start any rumor, Jim. I'm just upset about Derek."

Jim took a deep breath and blew the air out his mouth. "I know that, Tim. Just go home now and don't even think those things. Okay?"

"Okay. I won't." Except how can you unthink something once you've thought it, something so obvious? "We eat at seven. I need to be home. See you. Happy picking." He walked out the door, then turned. Jim hadn't moved. "Take care."

Now he ran to his bike, jumped on and again pedaled hard. Out under the arch, out onto the road. Okay, he'd made the suggestion. Really only a question. Jim said no. Explained ten times too hard. Kept on talking. Yeah, Jim was scared. Maybe not because of the question. Maybe he'd been scared before Tim got there. Maybe he'd worried about being accused ever since Derek got beaten up. So was it really Jim who supplied Derek with the pot? If so, he's out $4000 and really pissed off. Maybe Jim was in Campbell River—? No way, not Jim! Maybe when he got back he should tell the detectives his suspicions? He slowed his pedaling. They could follow it up.

    He felt rather than heard the roar behind him, glanced over his shoulder. A van, coming on fast. He pulled onto the verge, soft earth—not too far, the ravine looked ragged. Boy, that van was driving way too fast for this road. And way too close to the verge—didn't the guy see him? Oh god, he did, he was aiming at him! Tim pulled as far toward the ravine as he dared and still the van was coming on, the right fender looked huge, it struck the bike and sent it and Tim flying into the ravine—an instant idea in his brain: Jim, trying to kill him—

SIX

EARLIER, BEFORE FIVE, Austin had anchored the *Layback*, his thirty-two foot Bayliner, in the shallows of the inlet off Rebecca Spit. The surface was as flat as any along the eastern shore of southern Quadra, so no problem for the floatplane to set down, the water in the bay mirror smooth.

The Cessna Hawk landed a couple of hundred feet from the *Layback* and glided toward the boat. Fifty feet away the pilot cut the engine. The left pontoon eased to the side of the boat and touched the bumpers. The pilot's door opened. Molly dropped from the cabin onto the pontoon. She threw a rope to Austin. He wrapped it twice around the boat rail. Standing on the pontoon she opened the door to the rear compartment. Of course, Austin thought, Shu-li wouldn't sit in the co-pilot's seat. She wasn't that sort of girl. But he knew she wanted to be with him today, as much as he wanted her here.

First came her suitcase. Molly handed it to Austin. Then Shu-li, wearing jeans, a white tank-top and sandals, stepped down the two-slat ladder. Backwards, holding on tight. A view of her he enjoyed.

The sheen of her long black hair reflected late afternoon sunlight. She stood on the pontoon beside the pilot and turned, her smile bright. "Hello, Austin." She reached out her hand, he grabbed her wrist for support and she stepped on board. Transfer complete.

"Hello, Shu-li," said Austin. "Thank you, Molly. Back on Sunday, right?"

"Three PM the order says," said Molly. "Right here."

"See you then." He released the rope from the rail and pushed the plane away.

Molly climbed back into the cockpit, pressed her starter, engine on, the propeller whirled and the plane slid away.

Austin watched as the wing cleared the boat, then turned to Shu-li, opened his arms wide and she came to him. They hugged, a long hug. They kissed, a quiet kiss. "I'm glad you're here," he said. "Let's go." He turned a key and the twin Mercruiser 470s sprang to life. He pressed a button and the anchor lifted from the sea-bed, climbed up against the starboard side of the prow and settled into its slot. He sat on his plush white chair behind the wheel and engaged the engine. Shu-li reached for his free hand and squeezed it. He set a course for another inlet, smaller, just north of Heriot Bay.

The trip took twenty minutes. He carried her case from his dock up the trail to the house and into the bedroom beside his. Steve, when he arrived tomorrow, would have the bedroom in the other wing. But Shu-li would not spend tonight in her bedroom. Friday and Saturday she'd at least start out there. As if Steve would care. At any rate they would all be here together. To destroy Harold Arensen. Difficulties remained, but do it they must.

God, how Austin hated that man. They all did, but Austin felt he could smell the hatred each time the man's name passed through his mind, taste the hatred each time he had to speak it. Not merely for what the man had done to him.

Austin and Harold had little communication but even that was too much. The man intruded into Austin's life with innuendos and lies. Unbearable moments. But soon, as plans worked out, such situations would be eliminated.

Two months ago, in Ottawa, Austin had picked up the phone. "We have a problem."

"We, or you?"

"Both of us."

"Harold, get to the point."

"The point is your man, Randolph."

"Randy isn't my man. Just a guy who works for me."

"And lives on your land. This is a matter of perception, Austin."

"What about Randy?"

"He's been trying to place bets."

"He's a betting man. It's his thing."

"Not when it's betting on figure skating competitions."

Not good. "What are you talking about?"

"Randolph went to a bookie and laid a bet on the last comp. You know that's not allowed. And being your man, he might have had insider information."

"He's not my man. Talk to him, not me." But if it were true that

Randy had tried to get odds on a skater, Harold was holding a gun to Austin's temple. Betting on skating was forbidden. Absolutely. Unless you placed a bet with an off-shore bookie. In Bermuda or St. Kitts, say. But why should it be true, what Harold claimed?

"Talk to him immediately. That's all I have to say."

Austin had slammed the phone down. Damn that man to hell! Calling from his throne, so calm.

Austin had phoned Randy immediately. Randy had waited seconds before answering. Austin's guts curdled.

"Yeah. I did try."

"It's illegal."

"Hey, don't stick your poker in the stove. I'm a betting kind of guy, you know."

This was the worst, Harold right. "What did you think you were doing, asshole?"

"Betting. It's how I live, and don't call me asshole."

"I can't believe you'd do that. You are totally stupid."

"Don't call me stupid." An offended voice.

"Randy—"

"Look, Austin, you've done a lot for me, setting me up and all. If betting on skating messes you up, I won't. Hell, I never even placed the bet, they wouldn't let me."

Austin had calmed. Randy occasionally acted foolishly, but his promises were honest. "Okay, Randy. Stick to horses and poker. I'll be out in a month."

"See you then." Randy's tone was icy, but Austin felt reassured.

How had Harold learned about this event that hadn't happened? Because he snuck around everybody's blog and tweet and Facebook?

Now Austin was at home on Quadra Island. With Shu-li. He didn't want to think about Harold. Tomorrow they would talk about Harold. Soon Harold would fall.

Shu-li unpacked her suitcase. This weekend she'd have to tell Austin her part of the plan was maybe unraveling. Her skater, Miranda Steele, would take two years easily before she was ready. Miranda at thirteen had shown such promise—grace, strength, stamina. Last year something in her shifted, more attitudinal than physical but visible to anyone who'd watched her before. Her glides were looking labored; her axels ended as they should, but it looked like the girl was working hard. Judges had begun to notice and she lost points. In the last months Shu-li had spent extra time with Miranda; perhaps she'd grow beyond this strange technique block. Telling Austin would not be easy.

She changed. When she met Austin in the kitchen, she saw they matched each other in shorts, T-shirt and Dockers. She'd cook dinner, their ritual. He told her what the fridge held, thanks to Randy. Soon she placed before them scampi and mussel linguini, steamed asparagus, baked stuffed tomatoes. Also sliced filone from the Lovin' Oven. For dessert, a quarter honeydew melon each. And a three-year-old Rosewood Pinot Gris, a fine Okanagan wine.

They sat on the deck, a pitcher of Pimms as *digestif* on the table between them, sipping from long-stemmed glasses. He watched as her tongue flicked up the mint, her teeth brought in the cucumber, her throat opened for the liquid. He did love her, even if they were together only five or six times a year, and then for only a few days. Three years ago they'd spent a week on the Mayan Riviera, but after four days she'd somehow withdrawn. Someone as lovely and gentle as Shu-li. He didn't understand. Three days seemed to be her comfort time with him. He'd often asked why. She would reply that she didn't know; the timing was something her body felt.

They sat in silence watching the flow and ebb of the ocean. Shu-li asked, "Have you had any more dealings with Harold?"

He'd enjoyed her voice from the moment she arrived. Her words seemed washed with melody. After a few weeks apart the sweetness of her speech would fade so that when they were together again her words and her voice sounded new. But now he turned to face her. "Let's not ruin this evening."

"Of course not. It's just, I despise him so."

"That's why we're here, why Steve is coming. For now, let's talk of other things."

She nodded, and sipped her drink.

She often repeated, like a mantra, her loathing of Harold Arensen. She had every right to hate him; he'd ruined her skating career. When the rumors finally stopped, it was too late. Austin had been able to trace them back to Arensen, a memo from him to several coaches in the Toronto-Ottawa-Montreal sweep. No evidence, just innuendo: from Shirley (her ice name) Waterman taking male hormones, to her being born with abnormally male characteristics, to her having had a sex-change operation, to her actually being a boy. Anyone who saw her in dance costumes would recognize these insinuations as lies: flawless skin, small but obviously feminine breasts, no bulge between the legs. True, she was five ten; hardly unusual for a young well-nourished North American woman. Strong, yes, but the strength of any serious female athlete. The rumors flourished for months, Skate Canada made its inquiries, the insinuations proved to be lies, but the harm was done. Austin, for all his detective work, could not convince the powers that controlled the figure-skating industry that Harold Arensen should bear the blame. The man had too many allies—then as now.

He also had enemies, chief among them Shu-li, Steve and Austin. Each had good reason for regarding Arensen a nefarious adversary, still perilous after these many years.

"Shall we cool our feet in the water?" That lovely mellow lilt.

"Great idea. A refresher of Pimms?"

"Please."

Glasses refilled, they walked down the trail, fingers intertwined. When they reached the gentle stroking water they slipped off their footwear. She led him to a flat stone bar at the left of the rocky beach. When the tide was up and at the right height, as now, they could sit on the bar and let the water lap their feet. They sipped their drinks. He put his arm about her shoulder. She let her head rest against his. An evening of peace.

He rarely felt such moments of tranquil excitement. It started seven years ago, she then nineteen, he thirty. He'd seen her skate and was enraptured. Her short program was grace in motion, the revelation of sudden loveliness enhanced by a red silk scarf about her neck flowing behind her to contrast her long raven hair. He had to meet her, and he did. She, flattered that the great Austin Osborne had taken an interest in her, agreed to have dinner with him. And each was quickly in thrall to the other. She spoke of their living together; he was uncertain. They spent time with each other when she was free, a day here, two days there. He had never been married, never lived with a woman—or even had a housemate. Despite how much he cared for Shu-li—which he called her from the moment she told him her Chinese name—he had to be mostly alone. She found this strange and told him so. He agreed, but couldn't change himself.

Then, one day, out of nowhere, the rumors about Shirley Waterman had begun. At first her skating was thrown off stride. Soon she was hospitalized for psychic exhaustion. She returned to the ice, the rumors quelled, but she could practically hear whispers from those who had believed the lies. She had increasing difficulty with her routine. She did not get the points. One day she decided it was useless and gave up her career as a competitive skater. She moved to Calgary where she easily found work as a coach.

Austin would visit, two days, sometimes three. They did try the Mexican holiday. Not the cure she needed. She turned to face him and kissed his lips, gentle as the setting sun. She drew back lightly and whispered, "Shall we go in?"

Shane came into the kitchen. "His bike's not there."

"Where'd he go?"

Shane shrugged. "He didn't tell me."

Linda hovered about the stove stirring a chicken casserole, wooden spoon in her left hand, half-empty beer stein in her right. The potatoes and carrots were ready. Alana had made a salad. Noel and Jason sipped red wine, Kyra and Alana cranberry spritzers.

"He knows better," said Jason. "He's a responsible kid."

Noel glanced at Jason. "Visiting a friend?"

"He'd be home by now."

"Worth a call to wherever his friends live?"

"I don't think—"

Linda said, "I'll call Robbie and Turk and Leo, they'd be the most likely." Avoiding the phone on the kitchen wall, she went into the den.

"Does he have a girlfriend?" Alana asked.

"No!" Jason knew he'd spoken too loudly. He looked away. "No."

Noel crossed to the stove, took up the spoon and stirred. He didn't want this great-smelling casserole to burn. He glanced at his watch, quarter after seven, still more than two hours till dark. "When we drove off to meet Bertina, I saw someone on a bicycle heading up Heriot Bay Road."

Jason turned to face Noel. "Was it Tim?"

"Could have been. I only saw him from the back."

"What kind of bike?"

Noel shrugged. "I don't know bike brands."

"Dirt bike? Mountain bike? Color?"

Noel closed his eyes. "Thick tires."

"Timmy's is a mountain bike. We got it for him last Christmas."

Kyra excused herself, lay on the living room couch, closed her eyes. She set one hand on her belly, which felt comforting. Except Pregnant didn't go away. What to do about little Pregnant? And when was her empty stomach going to receive some of that delicious casserole? Had she ever considered abortion seriously? Not that she believed abortion was wrong, just if someone had to be blamed and punished it was her. What kind of a mother would she be if she treated the fetus as if it really were a problem? Kids.

Like Jason and Linda's kids; each was more of a pain than the next. The first a dope dealer, the next completely self-engrossed, and the youngest can't even get home in time for dinner. What if the baby turned out like one of them? Or all three? Or worse? Come on, your baby could turn out a lot better. Yeah? Why? Because I'd be raising it. What makes you think you could be a good mother? Better than Jason as a parent? Better than Linda? She closed her eyes and saw a baby all wrapped up, just its face visible. Would a boy or a girl be better?

She heard voices in the kitchen. Then Linda's return and report that none of Timmy's friends had seen him, and that they'd now eat with or without Timmy. Kyra stood and ambled to the table. She was truly weary.

Linda served. They ate. Good casserole, great carrots; that from Alana. Linda noted they'd come out of the garden this afternoon. Nearly 8:00 PM.

Noel felt the press of silent fear at the table. The parents weren't about to admit to it. Shane was unlikely to show concern about his brothers. Alana surely knew it was there, she was good at picking up nuances and states of mind. Kyra? The poor woman just looked wiped. He had to break into the mood. But that wasn't what they'd been hired for. Oh, do it for Jason as friend, forget job. "There's still a couple of hours of daylight left. Let's go look for Tim."

Linda closed her eyelids before she looked up. "We could. Let's finish here and head out." A sudden energy took the table as they all, Shane included, scraped the last of the casserole off plates and cutlery and drained their drinks.

Kyra felt the energy too. Fed, so anything was possible. Alana stood and began to clear the plates but Kyra said, "I can do that." Dishes and cutlery in the washer, pans in the sink. She said to Jason, "Where should Noel and I be looking?"

Jason thought for a couple of seconds. "He liked to bike down to April Point. Sometimes he sat up there and read. You could try in that area. Linda and I could start at the village and—"

"Mom? Dad?" Shane was at the door. "I think I should go. Noel could go with you, Dad, and I'll go with Kyra. They don't know the island, there ought to be someone from here in each car. You better stay, Mom, for when Tim calls or gets back. Alana, you okay about staying with Mom?" Alana, alone allowing her surprise to show, nodded. Shane turned to Kyra and Noel. "You guys have cell phones?"

They both did, and left their numbers with Linda. Kyra's glance caught Noel's and watched his eyebrows shrug. "Okay if I take your Honda?"

He handed her the keys. "Don't get any scratches on it."

She tchhed at him and turned to Shane. "Let's go."

Noel followed Kyra and Shane out the door, watched them get into the Honda and head out the drive. Jason searched for keys. Shane's notion, that Kyra and he should split up—and where had that ping of intelligent analysis come from in surly Shane?—made good sense. Still, Noel didn't like her going off by herself. Well, with Shane. Likely Shane could handle most island situations. But in her condition, she needed to be—what? Protected? By him? Too often she protected him.

"Found them," said Jason. They got into his Corolla. Shane had said he and Kyra would check out the area between here and April

Point. That left Quathiaski Cove, both harbor and village, or up toward Heriot Bay.

At the end of the driveway Jason turned left. Noel said, "What's to the right?"

"Road dead-ends at Gowlland Harbour. A couple of lodges—Seascape Waterfront Resort and the Gowlland Harbour Resort. They're both nice without being too fancy. Timmy's had a summer job at each and doesn't much care for the guests they get."

"Fishing, whale and bear-watching, that sort of thing?"

"Yeah. Big on kayaking. All guests get their own kayak."

"Tim's not big on kayaking?"

"Looking at water's what he's best at. And running."

They drove in silence for a minute. Noel said, "How are we going to do this?"

"Depends on why he didn't come for supper."

"Yeah." Noel nodded. "He didn't head off to see his usual friends. His less usual friends maybe?"

"No idea who they might be."

"You reacted pretty abruptly about a possible girlfriend. What was that about?"

"I just couldn't see Timmy with a girlfriend already."

"He's a big kid. Kind of private."

When Jason didn't respond, Noel went on, "Okay, Derek whom he admires is messed up around drugs. That hurts. So Timmy's gone somewhere to lick his wounds."

"I think that's what it is." Silence. "Hope that's what it is."

"Or he's gotten into a fix, maybe hurt, somewhere he can't help himself."

Jason sighed. "God, I hope not."

"So? You want to go to Quathiaski Cove Village and ask around? You know some of the merchants?"

"Yeah. Most of them."

They reached West Road. Jason pulled off. "Got your cell phone?"

"Yeah, 'course."

"Get Linda. She can call around over there. We'll head the other way, toward Heriot Bay. Check the sides of the road. Keep your eye on the right, I'll look left. And we head down side roads. There aren't a lot, though. Pretty heavily wooded through there."

Noel powered his cell phone. Searching for signal. Searching... searching... "No signal."

"Wait till we get to higher ground." They drove up a hill. "Try now."

Yes, a signal. Noel poked in the number. Linda picked up. No, nothing from Tim. Yes, good idea, she'd call the merchants at the village. He closed the phone. Jason made a U-turn.

For the first minutes Kyra and Shane didn't speak except for his telling her to head left at the top of the drive. Her jeans felt tight around the waist—too much food, or the growing occupant? Kyra tried to make conversation: When's your next competition? A date and silence. How much time a day do you spend on your programs? Four to six hours. Any skating friends around Campbell River? No. When are you coming in from outer space? She didn't ask that. But she was getting there.

Shane said, "Turn right."

She did. She kept trying: "You figure Tim's okay? You worried about him?"

"Timmy can take care of himself." He paused, adding, "Usually."

"What's that mean?"

"Just what I said."

"He doesn't need a little help from his friends?" But from Shane's face it was clear he didn't get the reference. From before she was born, but her parents shared their own popular culture, The Beatles a large part of it. She wondered what Jason and Linda shared with their kids. Or did their lives revolve only around figure skating and hockey? What would she share with her kid? If. Right now she had to pay attention to the oncoming traffic—lots of it. Probably the ferry unloading. Narrow road. She glanced in the rearview mirror. Just a van, far enough back.

"Everybody needs help. Sometimes."

Hey, Shane actually spoke. A curious inflection, or was it a catch, in his voice. "Yeah, that's true. I need help a lot of the time. You need help?"

His head jerked her way. "Me? Why should I need help?"

"You just said it. Everybody does, at some point."

"Mmm."

"You got a problem, Shane?"

"Turn right up ahead, before the road curves. Balsam."

She slowed, made the turn, accelerated. "I asked, you got a problem? Something you want to talk about?"

"What makes you think I've got a problem?"

"You don't exactly act relaxed. You act tense and worried."

"How do you know what relaxed is for me?"

"I can figure relaxed for lots of people."

"I'm not lots of people."

"No, of course not. You're special. You get to mouth off at your parents, you get to be rude to your father's friend who wants to find out who beat up your brother, you get to ignore a cute young woman in your house. That does make you near to extraordinary."

Shane slumped in his seat. "I don't need this, Kyra."

The van behind her was coming on fast. She slowed and pulled onto the verge. The van roared past—too much of a damn hurry. She turned to Shane. "You can tell me to mind my own business. I'll be gone in a few days. But you'll be here and right now you're wreaking hell on a few good people who don't need that from you."

He stared straight ahead. She pulled out and drove on. Nothing. No bike. She glanced at him. Keeping his face cool but something sure was burbling in there. She figured he wouldn't let himself, but he looked close to crying. Maybe she'd pushed too hard. She peered down side drives, no Tim, no bike. Shane, slouching in his seat.

"Turn right at the Tee."

She did. April Point Road, winding and twisty. She had to pay attention so didn't glance Shane's way. "Sit up and check the sides of the road." Shane did as he was told. Slowly and defensively, but now he flicked his eyes from right verge to left and back again. Few driveways off the road, she realized. An ultra-lonely island.

"That's a good place to stay." Jason pointed to Quadra Island Harbour House B&B. "Good friends of ours run it. Great garden."

"Stop by and ask if they've seen Tim?"

"They're in Vancouver, wedding of a couple who've stayed with them often. Place is closed for a week. Imagine—high season."

They drove into Heriot Bay, west side of lower Quadra. Resorts, more B&Bs, vacation rentals, the ferry to Cortes Island. Jason stopped the Corolla at a gas station, got out. Jason talked to a man with curly red hair going to grey. No, hadn't seen Tim since last week. Back in the car, to the dock. Conversation with a rotund woman; no, no sight of Tim. At the kayak rentals a young woman in tight jeans and a halter top also said she hadn't seen Tim. To Noel, Jason said, "Sonia. She and Derek dated for a couple of months." Similar negative answers at the Heriot Bay Inn and the Heron Guest House.

The pub at the Inn looked inviting, summer guests enjoying the warm evening, a light meal, a couple of beers. Noel was beginning to sense futility. Needle-on-an-island kind of thing. He checked out some postcards, one of an impressive stretch of peninsula called Rebecca Spit. "Think Timmy might have gone out there?"

"A long ride on a bike. Timmy doesn't much come even as far as Heriot Bay."

Then why are we here, Noel heard his growing irritation ask. Not good investigative practice, beginning with the long shots. "Give Linda another call?"

"Sure, but if she'd heard anything she'd've called."

Noel responded by poking at the phone pad. No, no signal.

To the right a road led down to the April Point Marina, moorings for private boats. Shane said, "Let's try down there."

Kyra turned down a slope to the water, parked, they got out. An old warehouse, piles of crab traps. A dozen salmon fishing boats in the water. Kyra wondered if Noel would ever fish again. Not Brendan's kind of pleasure, so Noel had given up the fishing passion for a far greater one. Brendan was now gone. Maybe Noel would return to, at least retry, the lesser one.

Shane walked down to the docks, gave the moorings a cursory glance, and came back. "No sign of him."

Kyra pointed to what looked like an RCMP vessel tied to the near dock. "Let's see if the cops are around." They stood beside the Mountie boat, a large Boston Whaler with a small central enclosure. No one there. Shane noted someone leaving the warehouse and jogged up to him, a guy about his age. Kyra watched their conversation as she approached them. Shane nodded, and the other kid walked off. "Anything?"

"You don't know with Dean. We never did get along. But I think if he'd seen Tim, he'd've said."

Three actual linked sentences from Shane. "Let's keep looking," she said.

Back in the car, less than half a mile to the conglomeration of buildings that made up the resort and the point itself. A gravel road to the left featured a sign saying, PARKING. Hardtop to the right led down to the office. She pulled up into the lot, found a slot among the dozen cars. They got out, glanced around.

Shane said, "Timmy liked to go up there." A path led to a ridge above the resort at the water's edge. At its entry stood a small round of fir supporting a rusted commercial tomato can which held a yellow and white plastic cup. From the cup rose a small sign:

EXTREME FIRE HAZARD
PLEASE EXTINGUISH
YOUR BUTTS

Kyra followed Shane along a wooded path. After a minute it narrowed, then dwindled to nothing where the ridge fell off the cliff. Discovery Passage lay in front of her.

"Timmy'd come up here to stare at the water." Shane glanced about. "Sure isn't here now."

Peaceful place for staring, Kyra thought. Across the water the sun hung low over Vancouver Island, hitting black clouds sideways and burning them orange. Below lay several buildings with rooflines that swept up just before their gutters, pagoda-like. The largest, set in the middle of a pond, featured bridges leading to platforms. Two guests sat on the near platform, drinking beer from bottles. She'd prefer vodka-tonic but even a beer would be good. Not for nine months. "Maybe Timmy's down there."

"Doubt it. He doesn't like tourists."

She could spend a few days in a place like this, chirping birds and lapping waves. "Okay. Let's keep looking." Along the trail to the car. "Where to now?"

"Maybe April Point Road toward the village. New territory."

"Okay." She looked at the sky. "Going to be dark soon."

"We can get home easily from the village."

They drove down from the parking lot and headed the way they'd come. "Wonder if your dad and Noel had any luck."

"They'd have let us know."

"Yeah. Still, I think I'll give Linda a call." She pulled her iPhone from her purse.

"Hey, you shouldn't be using a phone while you're driving."

"You're right. But there's no one around and I'm going slowly."

"Lots of curves, Kyra." He glanced in the passenger side mirror.

She pressed three buttons—

"Anyway, there is someone on the road. A green van and he's coming up fast."

Kyra checked the rearview mirror. "Damn fool." The van was barely fifty feet behind and catching up. She set the phone in her lap and slowed the Honda.

Shane had turned to see what the van was up to. "Damn! He's going to pass us! He can't see around—"

The front of the van was beside the driver's side rear bumper, beside the rear door, it bashed against them. "What the hell—" They swerved toward the narrow shoulder. Kyra's hands squeezed the wheel and pulled the car straight. But the van was there again, a harder push, they were driving one wheel on the shoulder, ahead a gully filled with peckerpoles. Now the van was parallel and Kyra turned to see what the crazy guy was doing and she saw his face, something wrong with it— He hit them again, they were off the road heading for the scraggly trees, Kyra yelling "Hang on—" as the Honda dropped into the gully, one braked but speeding wheel after another, half-dozen scraggly trees ahead, car cutting a path between them, bouncing off tree trunks, slowing. Stopped.

"Oh my god, thank you thank you. Yes, we'll be right there." Linda put down the phone.

"What?" asked Alana. "Tim?"

"Yes, oh thank god yes."

"And he's okay?"

"Well mostly. He's banged up but they don't think anything's broken. Oh, but he's okay, yes," and suddenly she was hugging Alana. "Yes, he seems to be okay."

Alana's arms went around Linda. "That's wonderful, that's great!"

Linda pulled away. "I didn't think I was that worried."

"You sure didn't show it."

"Let's get over there."

"Where?"

"Medical clinic." She grabbed the truck keys.

"Um, shouldn't you let Noel and Kyra know?"

"Oh. Yes. Of course." She found their cell phone numbers on a slip of paper. She dialed Kyra first. The staccato buzz of a busy signal. "That's strange."

"What?"

"Busy. Who's Kyra talking to?"

"Noel maybe?"

"Yeah. But if it's busy isn't an answering system supposed to cut in?"

"All these phones are different."

Linda pressed the off button and connected again. After one ring Noel picked up. Tim was okay. At the clinic but okay. She was on her way. She'd tried Kyra but the line was busy. They'd meet at the clinic. She cut the connection and tried Kyra's number again. Still busy. Damn! Who was she talking to?

Shane opened one eye. Then the other. Where—? He felt a seat belt. The strap dug into his neck. In a car? Hurt. Right shoulder, shit— He closed his eyes. That van, it shoved them off the road! He tried to stretch out his left leg. It seemed blocked. His right— Aaarghgh!! Shit! Shit shit shit! Ogodhurting! Shitshitshit! He felt some kind of material along his arms, plasticky stuff. Yeah, a green van. Kyra. He spoke the name aloud: "Kyra?" No answer. He tried to turn his head, slowly. Yeah, there she was, slumped forward. Same plasticky stuff. He spoke louder: "Kyra!" Nothing. Well, he was alive. Was she? Breathing? He reached over to her slowly and touched her shoulder, shook it lightly. "Kyra?" Unconscious? And suddenly felt cold. Way too cold for a summer evening. Going into shock? Maybe already there. Got to get out. Got to do—something. Open the window, shout for help. He looked at the window. He nearly giggled—didn't have to open, it wasn't there. The windscreen—spiderwebbed. He turned to the window. "Help! Help!" He listened. A breath of wind. "Help! Somebody! Help!" Nobody out there. Shit. Double shit. What the hell was he going to do? He touched Kyra's shoulder again, shook it a little. She groaned. Hey, she's alive! "Kyra? Can you hear me? Can-you-hear-me?" Another groan. Her head sagged, chin against her chest, a deep breath. She raised her head. At least her neck wasn't broken. "Kyra, you okay? Kyra?"

She opened her eyes. "Where're we?"

"Middle of the woods."

A look of horror on her face, eyes and mouth wide open. An intake of breath as she realized the awful thing she'd done. "Noel's car!"

"I—I think it saved our lives."

"What?"

"Air bags."

"Air bags. Saved our lives." She turned to look at him. "How are you?"

"Cold. Scared. I think my leg's broken."

"Oh god, Shane. We've got to get out of here."

"Good idea. How?"

"We've got to get help. Call for help."

"I tried that. We're in the woods."

"My phone, where—?"

"You were making a call when the van started pounding us."

"My phone?" She looked about. The air bag material covered everything. She slowly released her seat belt and sat forward. "Oh. Ooohh. Damn." She breathed out a sigh that came close to a sob. She took a deep breath in, and again out. "I hurt."

"Where?"

"All over. Can you move?"

"Not a lot."

"Got to find the phone. This air bag stuff— Somewhere."

Shane reached over and pulled the material off his side. Kyra did the same. She leaned forward, stared at the floor of the car. Something there, between gas and brake pedal. She stretched her foot as far as it could go, couldn't reach it. "I think the phone's—there. Got to get out, grab it." She reached for the door handle, noted the smashed window, pulled at the handle— No give. She shoved at the door. Blocked. "Damn it!"

Shane said, "Maybe—I can—" He glanced at the pedal area. "Really think it's the phone?" He released his seat belt.

"Nothing else in the car I can think of."

Shane looked at the windscreen. The rearview mirror had been knocked off. "Maybe I can—get down there."

"You think—?"

"Let's—see." He bit his teeth together hard. It was going to hurt. He shifted his weight onto his left buttock. His right foot edged toward the door and he gave as much of a scream as could escape through his teeth. Another shift and his elbow was on Kyra's lap. She flinched hard but beyond a small "Eeep!" said nothing. Had to get between her legs and the damn steering wheel. Now he grabbed her left jean leg below the knee and pulled himself further forward till his left ear rested on her lap, his right shoulder partially blocked by the steering wheel. He forced his shoulder by the wheel. Ooohh! New pain. He reached down, further, further— His right foot shot against the passenger door and he screamed. She held his right shoulder and he felt and appreciated the support. He reached, his finger on the brake pedal, he grasped it and pulled himself down, his head on her knees. His fingers felt the object, grabbed it. The goddamn mirror! Shit and double shit. He dropped it to the carpeting and it clanked. On carpet? Or the stem of the brake or gas pedal? He felt around with his fingers. The pain in his right leg had made his fingers sweaty. His face and whole body too. He reached out. Something else down there? Something— His index finger found the other object, no pedal stem, something loose. He brought his thumb further down. He grasped it. Felt like—felt— Maybe. Yes! "I think I've got—" He heard her breathe in and out sharply, as if she hadn't breathed in a while. He lay there, the phone grasped in his palm.

"Can you pull yourself up? I can help, I think."

Gravity had taken him down. Up was a different matter. But she gave him a hand for leverage, another to draw him up. His head reached the steering wheel. He breathed, yanked, but his head stayed stuck. She grabbed his head by chin and forehead. His hair scraped against the wheel but there was too much of his skull to go through the opening.

Kyra let him go. "Can you punch in 911?"

"From down here?"

"Yes."

"I can try." He tried to flip the phone open. But his fingers were too fat, too sweaty, too weak. His sense of feel was disappearing. He tried again, the phone slipped a little, he grabbed at it. It slid from his sweaty fingers, dropping to the floor. "Shit! Shit!"

"What?"

"Dropped it." He felt close to weeping. He clenched his teeth again. "I'll try—find it." Again he lowered himself, groped about, his little finger touched it, knew it was the phone. He shifted his hand and held it again. "Got it! Got it."

"Good. Great. Hold on."

He didn't move. He breathed deeply. The pain in his right leg was sickening and he felt his stomach turn over. He didn't want to vomit, not right down here. He felt her pulling at him again. "I—I don't think—"

She relaxed her grip on him and he slumped down again. They stayed unmoving.

What the hell were they going to do. If only— Maybe— "Shane. Hold on."

He felt her reach down to the side of his head. He heard her grunt. Her seat slid back four inches. He heard her giggle. And he blurted out a laugh. He felt her hand on his shoulder again, grasping him by the armpit, pulling. It took minutes until he could hand the phone to her. He lay sideways, his head on her lap, he heard the numbers she punched, three of them.

Kyra said, "We've been in . . . a car accident . . . Where are we? Shane, where?"

Linda drove the truck quickly, Alana beside her. They sped down to the village square, parked in front of the clinic, rushed inside. No one in the waiting room or behind the reception desk, but they heard voices from the back. Down the short hall to an examination room, two women standing by and a man talking with Timmy who lay on the exam table. Linda rushed past the man. "Oh Timmy, you really are okay?"

"I'm fine, Mom." Tim looked embarrassed. "Really."

He didn't look fine. Cuts on his hands and face. A nasty gash on the side of his neck, stitched up. The cuts had been cleaned. Why wasn't the gash bandaged?

Introductions for Alana's sake. The younger of the two women, Dr. Kellerhals, mid-thirties, trim, bright eyes, said, "Nothing's broken, Linda. A few days and he'll be healed up."

The other woman, Janet Bragg, a nurse, said, "He's been very brave."

Sam Mervin, one of the island's RCMP constables, smiled. "Good you got here so quickly, Linda."

"Jaspon's on his way. Can Timmy come home?"

"After I've talked with him some more. This was a strange accident."

"What happened?"

Bragg turned to Tim. "You want to tell her? We might as well hear it again."

Tim explained: He'd gone for a ride because he'd been upset about Derek—not mentioning in front of a policeman about Derek and drugs, just Derek having been beaten—and he'd ended up at Bristol Greens, and had talked for a while with Jim, and then he ridden back and suddenly this van was behind him and coming on fast, and at first Tim thought the guy didn't see him so he stared hard at the windshield and could see the driver and it looked like he was a clown or something his face was full of colors and then Tim knew the guy could see him and before he could think anything else the van wiped him off the road and sent him flying into the ravine like the guy had done it on purpose and he bounced a couple of times and then lay there, air bashed out of him, scared, wondering if he'd broken anything. Wondering too if the guy was coming back to hurt him or if it really was an accident to try to find him to see if he was okay. But nobody came and after a few minutes when he was breathing more easily again he pushed himself up and then had to sit down afraid he'd fall. After a few minutes he started crawling back to the road and wondered if he could ride his bike. It seemed to take a long time, getting to the road, and when he got there he felt wiped. He looked around for his bike and saw it back down in the ravine really busted, the frame and one wheel bent. He heard a car or something coming and he stood up and balanced himself carefully and when the vehicle, it was a brown pickup, could see him he put both hands up and waved hard and it stopped. George Pete, Zeke's son, and George called his dad at Cape Mudge Village and brought Tim down to the clinic really fast, Tim trying to explain what happened. "Zeke said he was going to come by here." George left because he had to get the truck to his father.

Linda let out a breath of air. "That's good."

Mervin said, "You really think this van hit you on purpose?"

Tim nodded and immediately winced. The doctor said, "Head still, Tim."

"Okay. Yes, on purpose."

"Did you notice anything else about it?"

"Dark green, and it was flat in front, I remember that. It wasn't new."

"Did you recognize it?"

Alana thought, Recognize? So few vans on Quadra that Tim just might?

"No. It was coming too fast. I just wanted to get out of the way."

They heard footsteps in the reception area, a voice, "In back," and Jason came through the door, Noel behind him. Jason, instantly at Tim's side, hugging him. Tim, wincing. Introductions for Noel's sake.

Dr. Kellerhals's phone rang. She picked it up, listened, said, "Okay. Yes, I'm already here. Good." She closed the phone.

Jason said, "Tell me what happened, Timmy."

Damn, why didn't his father call him Tim in public. Another repetition of the story, Tim sounding braver this time. He alone knew this was for Alana's hearing.

The doctor asked to be excused. First responders were on their way, she and Janet had to prepare the two other exam rooms. An auto accident up by April Point, they'd be here shortly. "You might want to stick around for this, Sam," she said to Mervin.

Noel had a sudden sense of unease. "What happened, doctor?"

"Car went off the road. Couple of people, man and a woman, banged up."

Mervin asked, "Not taking them to the hospital in Campbell River?"

"Al, he's the first responder on tonight, thinks maybe we can handle it here. Maybe some broken bones. I'll know more when they get in."

"Did they say what kind of car?"

Kellerhals looked surprised. "No, that wouldn't concern me."

Noel nodded.

Jason said, "Can we take Timmy home? Make room for the people coming in?"

"I'd like to keep him under observation for another hour anyway. And don't worry, we've got room. But if this keeps up—" She sighed. "Usually it's quiet here."

Again sound from the reception area. Zeke Pete. "Timmy! You okay?"

"Okay," said the doctor, "everybody out except Jason and Linda and Janet. You can stay for a minute, Zeke, then you'll have to go."

Jason called out, "Noel, you and Alana can take the truck back to the house if you want, or to the B&B."

"Thanks." Noel walked to the reception area, sat, took out his cell phone. Alana followed. He pressed the code for Kyra. It rang and rang. Where the hell was she? Again. Same result. Back to Tim's examination room. "I'll stick around for a while, Jase."

Janet the nurse said, "Please wait outside."

In the reception area he said to Alana, "I can drive you back if you want."

She said, "I'll wait with you."

After a minute Linda joined them. "You don't have to stay, you know."

"I know," said Noel, and Alana nodded in agreement. The three sat in silence. When Zeke came out, Linda got up and returned to Tim.

Zeke said to Noel, "Can't tell you how much it means to Jason, you being here."

"We haven't done much."

"More'n anybody else."

Had Jason confided in Zeke about Derek's doper friends? "Wish we knew more."

"Sometimes it's hard to know."

Noel glanced at Alana. Earphones in again. She wasn't looking his or Zeke's way, but she seemed to be paying attention. "Right," said Noel.

Zeke said, "It's like there's a curse on the family."

Noel laughed nervously. "I hope *curse* is bit strong."

Zeke sent Noel a grim smile. "Lots of bad-weather coincidence, then."

In the distance, a wail of sirens. Dr. Kellerhals came into the reception area. "Two injured people are coming in. I have to ask you to stay well out of the way. Please sit over there." The three of them shifted as far from the door as possible. The klaxons grew louder, till the ambulance and the screaming stopped in front of the clinic door.

Noel stood, but stayed at the far end. Jason joined them. The doctor opened the door and went outside. Through the window Noel could see the driver get out and confer with Kellerhals. Red and blue lights continued to flash. The driver pulled the back doors open and stepped inside. Noel couldn't stand it any longer, strode to the door and dashed out. Jason followed him. To the driver Noel said, "Are they okay?"

The driver, tall, wearing a T-shirt with a faded logo, said, "Who are you?"

"Someone who's worried about who you might have in there."

"They'll be okay."

"A woman in her thirties, a kid in his late teens?"

"Yeah. Could be. But you better—"

Noel pushed by. He stepped up on the ambulance bumper. Two raised stretchers, each with a person lying there. Dr. Kellerhals was administering to the one on the right, a paramedic was calming the one on the left, a woman, crying. Noel shouted, "Kyra!"

The doctor turned to him, anger in her face. "Please get down, sir."

"That's my partner!"

Now Jason stepped onto the overcrowded platform. "Noel, is it Shane too?"

Kellerhals turned her stare at Jason. She looked like she wanted to be hard but her body wouldn't let her. "Jason, give us room to work. Yes, it's Shane. He's in shock and we don't know what else. Please, Jason. You can talk to him in a few minutes."

"Doctor—Kyra—is she—"

"In shock as well. Please, sir, we have some work to do here. Wait for us inside."

Glum, Noel and Jason returned to the reception area. To Zeke, Jason said, "Could you ask Linda to come out?"

Zeke nodded and returned to Tim's room.

Linda appeared. Jason told her it was Shane and Kyra. She strode outside, held back when she heard a cry of pain, spoke to the driver, a first responder, an acquaintance. "How serious, Al?"

"They're banged up pretty good. But they'll live, both of them are tough."

"May I talk to Shane?"

"Maybe in a bit. I think the doc figures we got to take them over to Campbell River, find out what's happened internally."

Linda's eyes welled up. "Could I ride over with Shane? I am a nurse, you know."

"Have to ask the doc, Linda. She's the boss."

Noel and Jason joined Linda, and they waited. Ten minutes, fifteen.

At last Dr. Kellerhals came out and conferred with Al, the driver. Then she spoke to Noel and the Coopers. "They're both stable, and sedated. Shane has a broken leg and I don't know what else. The woman, Kyra Rachel is it?" Noel nodded. "She doesn't have any overt problems except where she got cut with window glass, but she has to be examined fully before we can release her. They're going to Campbell River. I suggest you follow in your cars."

Both Jason and Linda said, "Thanks, Erika."

Noel added, "Yes. Thank you." And thought: *Wonderful she's alive and going to be okay.* And then: *I don't have a car anymore.* And: *Who is destroying the Cooper family? Why?*

SEVEN

SHU-LI WOKE EARLY. If others were in the house she would move to her bedroom and rumple the sheets before showering. Today she wanted an early morning walk along the shore—well, not so early, the clock on the mantle told her 7:25. She slid from her side of Austin's bed. Nothing lost if she woke him but she wanted a half hour alone in the clear morning light.

Last evening they had avoided discussing Harold Arensen. Never mind that he was a powerful member of the Board of Directors of Skate Canada, and Honorary Chair of VISU, the Vancouver Island Skating Union; mainly he was Harold, destroyer of careers, and a too large part of her reason for being here.

In her room she slipped out of her red silk nightgown and saw her body in the mirror. She hadn't changed much since the glory years of international competition. Her hair, still long and glossy black. Her face, less make-up these days than when she'd been on the ice. Oval eyes from her father, her mother's high cheekbones. Small breasts, her contribution to the rumors that defeated her. Still slim of waist, lucky that she had such an active metabolism since she enjoyed eating, another legacy of her mother. Good crotch and all it implied because she was a great devotee of sex. Though increasingly she found herself longing for sex with only one man. Sadly, she was beginning to understand she couldn't have him for always; settling for sometimes? She slipped on panties, didn't need a bra here, a green short-sleeved blouse, khaki shorts. Her legs, still strong and slender as ever—as a coach, she had to demonstrate every move to her students. Runners on, and ready.

She crossed the landing and whipped downstairs, wishing no floorboards to squeak; they rewarded her. Out the door, down the trail cutting between high cliffs to the beach. Again waves lapped the shore, though today the tide was further out. She breathed the tangy salt air deep into her lungs. She sat briefly where last night she and Austin had dipped their feet, high and dry this morning. Where would his mind be this weekend? How long would he stay close to her? With Steve here he'd be distracted, the three of them planning.

She wished she fully trusted Steve and Austin on the topic of Harold. She sure didn't have an alternative plan. Maybe Austin would ask her to stay on after Steve left. She'd arranged her ticket not to return to Calgary until Tuesday; the float charter could be rescheduled.

She stood up and walked fast. Down the rocky beach twenty minutes, twenty back. The squawks of gulls broke the regular wavelet pattern. Now she'd take a shower. Up the path to the porch and into the kitchen where Austin had coffee going, the last of the glugs saying it was just ready. Its thick scent wafted her way. She thought she heard him speaking. Or maybe the radio.

"Austin?" No answer. She poured a mugful. Wondered if he'd like coffee now. Poured a second mug and walked along the hall toward his study. The double glass doors stood ajar.

He sat at his desk, the phone in his hand at his side; no more talk.

"Coffee?" She noted his face: ashen. "What's wrong?"

He looked up. "All our plans." And repeated: "All our plans."

"What?" She set the coffee mugs on the desk. "What's happened?"

"Shane—a car accident."

"What? Is he okay?"

"Last night. That was his father on the phone."

"Shane's okay? Isn't he?"

"His leg. Two breaks. Femur and shin."

"Oh Austin. Oh shit." She slid a coffee mug toward him. "Will he heal?"

He stared at the coffee "I'll help him, of course. But the breaks are bad."

"Did Jason say that?"

"Yes."

"You mean they won't heal in time?"

"He's got to qualify, for petesake. I have to get over there. The hospital."

"I'll go with you." She sipped coffee. "Do you want breakfast?"

"We'll get something there."

"Is the other brother still there?"

"Yes."

"Do you think—uh, will Harold know? Yet?"

"Word gets around. It's a tiny culture. My guess would be, yes."

"Maybe I won't go with you."

"I don't think we'll run into him." He stood. "Tiny culture, but careful too." He started for the door, thought better of it, came back. "Ready in a couple of minutes."

"Let me have a fast shower." She walked through the doorway into the hall.

In the kitchen, pouring coffee, smiling to himself, stood Randy. He was Austin's man so she tolerated him, even made a show of liking him. "Hello, Randy."

He looked up, saw her, beamed. "The lovely Shu-li. How good to see you." He strode over and hugged her.

She hugged him back. His hug lasted a second too long. She stepped away first. "Good to see you too."

"Austin around?"

"Getting ready to go out."

"Gorgeous day to go out into." He beamed.

She never knew what to say to Randy. "Want milk for your coffee?"

"Doing fine, thanks."

His face was lean and tanned except where he'd shaved off a beard, growing into cragginess. About forty, she thought. His smile stuck to the middle, in his eyes as well as on his mouth. "We're off to Campbell River. To the hospital."

"You okay? Austin?"

"No, we have to visit Shane Cooper. You know him. He was in an accident."

"Shane? What accident?"

"We don't know details. A car went off the road."

"No—"

"His leg's broken."

"That's terrible—"

Austin appeared from downstairs. "Morning, Randy."

"That true? About Shane? A car accident?"

"He was looking for his brother, he'd disappeared. With one of the detectives his father hired. The woman. She was driving, must've lost control and crashed into the woods. The car's totaled. She seems to be mainly okay but Shane's smashed up."

Randy slumped onto a kitchen chair. "That poor family." He shuddered suddenly. "It must've been the detective's fault. Was she drinking, does anyone know?"

"We don't know anything. We're going to find out. Don't worry about picking up Steve. I'll be over there, I'll get him."

"Oh. Sure."

"Just make certain everything's ready here. His room, his chocolates especially. Then you can take off. I won't need you till Monday." He headed for the door out.

"Yeah. Okay." Randy picked up his coffee cup.

Shu-li following Austin, turned and gave Randy a smile. "See you, Randy."

Randy smiled after her. She felt good where he'd held her. No bra. Maybe one day he'd be able to do more than just hold her. She smelled good too. Off to Campbell River. Not today or likely even tomorrow. Maybe—? That accident? Stupid woman driving.

Then Shu-li came back. She headed upstairs. Did she want him to follow her? He sipped coffee. Minutes later again downstairs, now skirt and blouse, clutching her purse. She smiled and waved as she passed. What? Oh yeah, fuckin' Steve's chocolates. He'd bought them already. Then the whole day off. Lots he could do with a whole day off.

Noel had slept or something like it sitting beside Kyra's hospital bed. He'd awakened just after six, and splashed water over his face. He felt ratty in the jeans and shirt and underwear he'd had on for nearly twenty-four hours, and three hours till he could get to a toothbrush. He returned to his chair. He'd been present when the Mountie, Bryan, was questioning Kyra and Shane. They'd agreed, a dark green van had forced them off the road. Why? No answer. Noel would find an answer. But, irritatingly, only after he got back from seeing his parents and brother. What the hell was happening to Coopers? Derek, then Tim, and now Shane. Whoever was doing this, at least he, or they, hadn't killed anyone. Yet. Both van brushes could have killed the two boys. And Kyra. And Derek was still in a coma. What more was coming?

He watched as the sun traveled up the sheets on Kyra's bed and crossed over her arm to her face. He studied her curly dark brown hair, which he realized was longer than he remembered. It lay on the pillow awry, but that was how it looked even when she combed it. With no lipstick and her face washed clean, she seemed much younger, all tender innocence smashed around by a rolling car. His car.

The sunlight reached her nose, she wrinkled it, opened her eyes, blinked. "What—where—" She sat up, saw Noel, and slumped down again. "Yeah. I remember."

"You slept well."

"You've been here all the time?"

"Of course."

She sighed and turned to face Noel. "Have you seen Shane?"

"Not since last night."

"Would you check on him, please?"

Noel stood up, leaned over and kissed her on the forehead. "Good morning."

She reached out and took his wrist. "Thank you."

He headed down the corridor and some stairs. In Shane's room Linda was sitting in a chair. "Hi. How's he doing?"

"Very unhappy."

Noel gestured for Linda to come into the corridor. She followed him. They walked a few paces from the door. "What do you make of this?"

"Of—?"

"These attacks on your sons. On your family."

She shuddered. "No sense. Scares the hell out of me."

"It must make sense to someone. Someone who wants to do you harm? Scare you? Someone who wants revenge for something?"

"Noel, I just don't know."

"We have to assume that you—maybe all of you, maybe just your sons—have something someone wants. That they'll harm you to get it?"

"We don't have much of anything. We've got the house, we've got the woodlots, Shane has—we hope he has—an exciting career ahead of him. Derek doesn't have anything." She stared at Noel, her face flushed. "I don't know anything."

"Try to think, Linda. Who might want to harm you, and why."

She nodded, and turned.

Back in Kyra's room, she now had a breakfast tray. "Shane's as well as he can be." He glanced at his watch. Just after seven. "I'm heading out for a while. They aren't going to serve me breakfast. You feeling okay enough to leave here this morning?"

"No question."

"I'll talk to the nurses on my way out."

The kitchen phone rang again. Jason Cooper picked up. "Hello?" He listened. "You're right." He listened some more. "Okay, I'll tell her. We'll be on the ten o'clock." He set the phone down.

"Noel?" Alana asked, half-standing, her hand still holding her coffee cup.

"Yeah. He'd like you to pack up then we'll go to the B&B and you can get Kyra and his stuff and I'll take you over to the hospital."

"Can I go too, Dad?" Tim pushed his chair back from the table and stood.

"How're you feeling?" Jason studied Tim's face and bruised arms.

"Good. Great. Rarin' to go."

Two black eyes, bruising on the lower right cheek and the left side of his neck, a bandage covering the stitches on the right side, small bright red scars forming on the boy's bare arms, the middle three knuckles of his right hand covered with Band-Aids. "You don't look great."

"Inside I'm doing fine."

"Okay." To Alana Jason added, "We'll head out in half an hour."

"Did Noel say anything about Kyra?"

"She spent an easy night. They're releasing her this morning." Jason paused. "Shane didn't have a good night. He's on painkillers. His leg's in a cast."

"Oh." Tim grimaced. "It's really badly broken?"

"Bad enough. He'll stay in the hospital at least one more day." Jason heard what Tim was thinking. They'd leave that unsaid, for now. Jason turned to Alana. "Noel's still planning on heading to Qualicum before your parents show up. He's rented a car."

"Has he talked to Kyra? Or Shane? Did they say how it happened?"

Jason didn't want to answer. But Tim and Alana would find out soon enough. "Yeah, they said. A green van forced them off the road."

153

"Holy shit," said Tim.

"Tim—!"

"Sorry, Dad. But—the same green van?"

"Hard to know. The Mounties are checking with Sam Mervin here."

"This is really weird!"

"Yeah. Really." Jason pulled himself together. "I need to pack stuff for Shane. Get yourselves set." His eyes met Alana's and Tim's. "Wear a long-sleeved shirt, Tim. Cover up your arms." He left them.

Alana said to Tim, "This is pretty awful."

"No coincidences, you figure?"

"Like someone's out to get you guys."

"Yeah, like that."

She walked around to Tim's side of the table and gazed at his face. "I'm real sorry, Tim."

Tim looked over her shoulder, his eyes suddenly welling tears. "Oh god—"

She hugged him for a few seconds, her cheek against his. She whispered, "It'll be okay. Noel and Kyra'll figure it out and end it, and make them pay."

Tim's arm went around Alana, and held on. She squeezed him and let go. He stepped back. "Thank you."

She smiled. "I'd better get packed."

"It makes no sense," Linda said.

Shane agreed. He and Derek, that could be a coincidence. But Timmy too? It couldn't all be Shane's fault. No one wanted him to break his leg. Maybe more than his leg—who knows what happens when you're in a car and it rolls like the Honda did.

He glanced toward his mother. She'd been sitting in that chair all night. Real handy for her, two of her three battered sons close at hand. She'd been here since they brought him; he'd barely slept. A broken leg. No Olympics for you, Shane. Kiss your damn future goodbye. He could feel tears gathering. No way his mother should see him cry. He grabbed a tissue and blew his nose. He let his eyes slide shut . . . He'd be in the den watching televised Olympic skating. Petro Sagan, a perfect triple axel. Petro was good. Maybe almost as good—

"Hello, Shane."

Shane's eyes opened slowly. Damn! Austin. "Hello."

And Shu-li. She swept around Austin and up the side of the bed, arms wide. She hugged his head. "Oh Shane, Shane." She relaxed her hold. "Are you in pain?"

"It's controlled."

On the other side of the bed, Austin's hand clamped Shane's shoulder. "We got the ferry soon as your dad called. We have to start working on that leg right away."

"It's not just the leg, it's—"

"We'll deal with it. Like last time."

"Hello, Austin," said Linda.

He turned, made noises about healing Shane. He introduced Shu-li. They'd met once before. They should get better acquainted, go for tea and croissants. Austin and Shane would begin working right away.

Shane wanted to be healed, but when Austin got like this it could be scary. Shane knew how good Austin was at hypnotherapy, maybe he could bring on a miracle— It wasn't possible. He might be able to skate by the Olympics, but he wouldn't be ready to qualify in the fall.

He said nothing. His mother and Shu-li were leaving. He wanted to call, keep his mother here, but she was gone.

Austin pulled up the chair. "Tell me what happened."

Shane did, the van tailing them, forcing them into the ditch. "Dad says it might be the same van that knocked Timmy off his bike."

"Timmy?"

"Yeah. Smashed the bike. Smashed Timmy too, a lot of bruises."

"That's terrible, Shane."

Shane examined Austin. He saw no emotion, no awareness. Austin, already preparing for hypnotherapy.

"Yeah." He drooped lower into the bed. No choice, it would happen.

"Close your eyes. Take a deep breath . . . good. Another breath . . . good . . . another . . . and again . . . breath in the relaxation . . . breath out the tension . . . very good . . . now continue . . . relaxation in . . . tension out. Feel the relaxation in your feet . . . legs . . . hips . . . stomach . . . chest . . . neck . . . face . . . scalp . . . Good. Relaxation in . . . tension out . . ."

Shane could feel it working. Austin excelled at this. Shane breathed tension and hurt out, ease and relaxation in, tension and hurt out... He rode on Austin's voice.

"See your leg through the cast... Let your mind penetrate the skin... See the bone... See the fracture... Good... See the tiny spaces between pieces of bone... Bring the pieces together... Tight together... Breath deeply... Hold the bones together with your mind... hold them tight together... breath deeply... deeper... deeper..."

Noel agreed to have his poor Honda towed to the Quadra RCMP station. An insurance assessor would come over from Campbell River. No need, he thought, it was totaled, but the insurance people needed to play the charade. "The rental's being delivered here about now," Noel told Kyra. "Honda Civic. I said to the guy it had to be that. Get back on the horse. I want to check around before we leave."

"Check what?"

"Go to the rink. Talk to the Zamboni driver. Shorty something."

"Why?"

"He seemed to know more about the Coopers. A talk with Jason's Mountie. Back by 10:30. Alana should be here then."

Kyra swung to her feet. "Why are we rushing off?"

"Not rushing, just—"

"You think the family's still in danger?"

Noel clenched his teeth. "There's—something off about this case. But no, I sense whoever attacked those kids won't try again soon."

"Why?"

"A feeling."

"My rational friend Noel the computer whiz responds to his feelings?"

"Yeah, until I can grasp what the feeling's about. When we get back maybe bits and pieces will have gotten rearranged in some pattern."

"When will we come back?"

"Soon. I don't think we should spend the whole weekend in Qualicum. Seth and Jan get in this afternoon, we'll see them today and tomorrow. They'll be here a week."

"I could stay, talk with whoever—"

"No. We should work together."

"Noel, are you worried about me?"

"Always." He smiled. "I'll get a doctor organized to check on you and release you. How do you feel?"

"Okay. A bit stiff."

He glanced at his watch. "Car should be here by now. See you in a couple of hours." He squeezed her hand and walked out the door.

At the hospital entrance, his rented Honda, metallic grey. The driver opened the door. At the rental office he signed papers and asked for a breakfast suggestion.

What did he and Kyra know about this case? The Cooper sons had been attacked. Derek dealt marijuana. Shane was perhaps a great skater, but so self-centered. Osborne was Shane's patron. Jason worked a couple of woodlots, Linda worked shifts at the hospital. Dedicated, middle class. Did these pieces fit together? They knew damn little.

Eggs, bacon, toast and coffee, and he was re-fueled. Arena first, see Shorty.

He parked in the lot, glanced at the police station. Later. Into the foyer, out to the first rink. A Zamboni, pulling a conditioner. Noel leaned against the glass wall. The Zamboni glided along the ice, almost floating, nearly silent. It curved around the end and drifted toward him. He saw the driver now. Noel waved. The Zamboni slid to a halt. "Hey there."

"Morning," came from behind the huge walrus mustache. The man climbed down.

"Noel Franklin. We met a couple of days ago, I was with Jason Cooper."

"Yeah."

"I'd like a few minutes of your time, Mr. Barlow, ask you about—"

"Everyone calls me Shorty, Noel."

"Shorty." Noel did not ask this tall thin man why. "Shane Cooper. You know him pretty well, do you?"

"Better'n some, not so good's others."

"That'll do. I can't get to know him at all."

"That's not him."

"Mmh?"

"What you see is a kid transformed."

"From?"

"Gentle and gritty, generous, hardworking. Dose of footwork genius on the side."

"That's impressive."

"He is impressive. Was." He tilted his head. "Ever see him skate?"

"We were going to watch him yesterday, but we got held up."

"Should see him on the rink. Fills it up by himself."

"Wish I had. Hope it's not too late."

"No, you can't squeeze talent back in the bottle."

Should Noel mention Shane's accident? Shorty would hear about it soon enough. "What happened, to make him so—so—"

"Cantankerous? Don't know, but he's been crabby his whole time back and the only thing I know about is that fall he took in the spring."

"If he's as good as you say, he should've just bounced back."

"Not as good as I say, as good as he is."

"I'll take your word for—"

"Don't have to take my word. I can show you."

"How?" Noel's brow furrowed. "You going to demonstrate?"

"Don't have to. I got tapes every time Shane was on television. First time at Juniors, when he got his first bronze, other events, here, Germany, Istanbul, Skate America, gold at the Juniors' four months ago, that slide and fall, I got them on tape. I get off at five. Come by the house, I'll show you."

"Hey, thanks, Shorty. Can't today, I'm gone for a couple of days."

"Give me a call."

"Thanks." Definitely better to tell Shorty now. "There's some other news about Shane. He was in a car accident. My partner Kyra was driving. A van forced them off the road. They're both okay, sort of, but Shane's right leg is broken."

Shorty squeezed his eyes shut. "Oh shit."

"He's in a cast."

"Double shit. Forced off the road?"

"Yeah."

"Oh man . . ."

"He's at the hospital."

"Don't have to keep a guy in the hospital for a broken bone. What else?"

"That's all I know."

Shorty turned to the Zamboni. "I'll go see him. My lunch break." He bashed his fist against its side. "Shit!" He turned back to Noel. "Why didn't you tell me right away?"

"I should've."

"Yeah." He climbed into machine. "You should've. And call me."

"I will," said Noel.

The Zamboni floated across the ice.

Noel left the sports complex and crossed to the RCMP headquarters. He asked for Dorothy Bryan. Out of the office.

Noel had said Alana would bring Kyra's case with clean clothes. Kyra shuffled down the hall to Shane's room.

She didn't go in, but became a fascinated audience. She'd not watched a hypnosis session before, didn't know whether she thought it was hogwash, valuable for its entertainment value—would Austin have Shane oinking like a pig?—or was this doing some good? She'd read hypnosis worked for back pain and recurrent headaches.

Now in the doorway she felt chilled, only a hospital johnny under a thin dressing gown pulled tight, legs bare and feet in paper hospital slippers. She turned to go just as a large man in a white polo shirt, tartan Bermuda shorts, and sandals, elbowed into Shane's room. Hair too black for a man in his mid-sixties. Florid face, painted by beer and whisky.

"Shane!" the man grunted. "What's happened to you, son?"

Shane's head snapped up as if yanked forward by some invisible cord. He was suddenly breathing hard, his hand on his chest. He pulled his eyes open. He blinked.

Austin turned. "Harold, we're busy."

"What're you doing here?"

"Helping Shane relax."

"Relax? He's lying down. He is relaxing."

"Harold. Please go away."

"Hey, I came up from Victoria to see my favorite skater and at the rink they tell me about a car accident and he's in the hospital. I'm here to help."

"You can be most helpful by going out that door."

The ruddy face smiled at Shane. "Nope. I'm going to talk to every

159

bone doc in this place and if they can't fix him I'll fly him to Vancouver. We're going to get him healed."

"Shane, keep breathing," said Austin. "I'll be back when Mr. Arensen leaves."

"Shane doesn't want me to go away. Do you, son?"

"I guess," said Shane.

"What happened?"

Austin stood, turned, headed out. He noted Kyra, didn't recognize her, then did. "You okay?"

Kyra nodded. "I'm leaving. Today."

He checked her up and down, clutching at a dressing gown. "You look cold."

"I'm okay."

"Take care."

She nodded, and he walked away. She glanced into the room. Shane was out of his trance. "Kyra! Hi!"

She shuffled in. "How're you doing?"

"I'm okay. You?"

"Okay to be leaving."

"Leaving?"

"Down to Qualicum, Alana's parents are arriving."

"You coming back?"

She glanced at Harold Arensen. "Yes. We are."

"That's good." Shane actually smiled at her.

"Who's this, Shane?"

"Kyra. She's a friend of my parent's."

"Harold Arensen. Great fan of Shane's."

Shane said, "Kyra was driving when we went off the road."

Arensen's face flushed. "You caused Shane's accident?!"

"No, no! We were forced off. Kyra controlled the car so it wasn't lots worse."

Arensen scowled dubiously.

Kyra glanced back at Shane. "Get better, Shane. Noel and I'll be back." She shuffled out.

It had been years since Shu-li had seen Austin so angry. Not a fiery surface anger, more abdominal fury. She knew this way of reaction, had felt much the same. When the rumors about her had first surfaced, she turned the anger onto herself. Something was happening, a major change in how people saw her. Due to her own actions? More important, how could she bring herself back on track? Not able to figure it out, she'd blamed herself. Only after, when the terrible insinuations surfaced, did she search for their source. And directed her anger to where it belonged: Arensen. It had remained with her. Yes, she had held it in. In the room when Arensen tried to take Shane over, only Austin had felt the brunt of Arensen's malevolence. He'd said he was okay. He was lying to himself. Driving to the airport he began to lose control. She'd been actively frightened, had to concentrate safe thoughts at him to keep the car from dumping them. "I could drive."

Austin glared at his watch. "How can a plane be late without a cloud in the sky?"

Steve Struthers's flight from Vancouver was twenty-five minutes overdue and counting. The delay had not improved Austin's mood. Something specific that Arensen said that got to Austin, or had just seeing him again been enough? He'd ruined Austin, had done the same to Steve. And to herself, of course. Austin believed Arensen would ruin Shane as well. For the time being Arensen was treating Shane as his private star, but that would inevitably change.

Arensen had been least direct with Steve. Rumors of doping was how it started. Then the discovery of androstenedione in Steve's suitcase. Some joker had smuggled it into the luggage. He requested a medical exam: clean. But Skate Canada put him on a list. A week before the Junior Grand Prix in Obersdorf, Steve tested positive. Impossible! He'd never taken dehydroepiandrosterone. Had it been slipped into his food? He'd never take any steroid, but a heavy dose showed up.

Months later he found someone had alerted Skate Canada he was on an illegal substance. The informant's name seeped out. Steve confronted Arensen, tried to punch him out. It was then that Austin suggested another plan—more long term, but more thorough.

"It's coming in now." Austin and Shu-li leaned against the hood of the Porsche and watched the plane taxi toward the terminal. They went inside and greeted him, Austin with a handshake and an arm around Steve's back, Shu-li with a hug and a kiss. Steve, carrying his camera case, was tall with a longish nose and a blond crew cut. Shu-li noticed his abdomen newly bulging over his belt. Small talk while they waited for his luggage. Steve dragged a large suitcase off the carousel. How much does he need for three days, Shu-li wondered.

To the Porsche, the two men in front, Shu-li squeezed behind the seats. Hard to talk with the wind blowing by the speeding open car, though Austin and Steve shouted at each other. She heard only an occasional word. Austin seemed in greater control now, the car tracking a straight line as it hurtled forward.

Harold Arensen and Austin Osborne: a long bitter story. Mid-nineties, Austin a teenager in Kanata near Ottawa, Harold head of the Ottawa Skating Association. Harold had heard talk about the young skater, had driven to watch him, was impressed. The next week he returned to offer Austin membership in the OSA. This would give Austin desirable ice time—mid-afternoons and weekends—and coaching time with Ralphie Belliveau who had trained half a dozen medalists. Within a year the lithe fifteen-year-old Austin had become a smooth and muscled skater. A body with enough power to support a partner. Harold and Ralphie would transform Austin into half of a pairs champion.

The Porsche turned onto Jubilee Parkway, a wooded stretch of road. Austin, Shu-li had heard, tried to resist—he'd been trained to work routines himself since he was eleven, had earned a reputation. No, they had argued, nothing on ice lovelier than a striking young man and a stunning young woman. Still Austin resisted; anyway, who would want to skate with him? Harold's instant response: Tilly Danforth, his niece. Austin had met Tilly, had watched her skate. She was self-possessed and pretty.

Onto South Dogwood, past the Beaver Lodge Forest Lands, North Island College on the right.

Tilly Danforth and Austin Osborne, Austin had told Shu-li, not only skated well together, they dated. They "lost" their virginity with each other.

Harold Arensen worried: dangerous if young skaters who on the ice depend on each other one hundred percent get involved emotionally. Emotion distracts. This thing between them had to end. But Tilly and Austin, now eighteen and legal, refused. The only distraction was Harold's ravings. They worried Harold, a powerful figure in Skate Canada, might do them harm. But why would he? They were good. They would be great.

Under Ralphie Belliveau they rose in the pairs rankings. Bronze in the Nationals, silver at Lake Placid. On their way to the top, anyone could see it. Spectators adored the striking duo as Austin and Tilly swept down the arena, loved their pleasure as they met the other's eyes, radiated joy, a glorious young couple utterly in love.

The Porsche slowed as they entered urban Campbell River. Shu-li hoped Shane's fate would not parallel Austin's. In Nagano in the final round he'd raised Tilly high, threw her higher, she fell back into his arms—and he dropped her. A gasp from the overflow crowd. Nothing broken, he swung about, helped her up, and they completed their routine. They lost points for the fall, gained points for the recovery. Not enough. Didn't get to the podium. Fourth.

The Porsche entered the ferry parking. Steve and Austin discussed lunch. "No no," said Steve, "let's get to Quadra. I'm tired of traveling."

Shu-li agreed. Austin parked. Next ferry in twenty minutes. Time to stretch their legs. Shu-li said she'd walk on to the ferry. Austin and Steve walked toward the terminal building.

With Tilly's fall the last hint of respect between Harold and Austin ended, he had told Shu-li. Emotion! Harold had thundered. You weren't concentrating, you were dreaming! Austin owned it was his mistake—Tilly's extra lift had been marginally off. No, the fault was hers, Tilly insisted—she knew her balance was off and she hadn't compensated. Whichever! was Harold's relentless response. Whichever is true, you were both in error!

They continued to skate together, a strong pair for the rest of the season: two bronzes, a gold, then a silver. Falling back to silver, Harold had fumed: The gold was at your fingertips but you weren't concentrating! You were each distracted!

Then in Istanbul, again. A different routine, another admiring audience. Austin whirled Tilly before him, was supposed to break her spin with a strong arm to her waist. But her arm struck his hand, threw her off balance, she crashed into his side, and they both went down. As before, up instantly, but this time Tilly's right leg wouldn't hold her. He supported her as they skated off the ice to the admiring applause of the crowd.

Harold Arensen forbade his niece ever to skate with Austin again. You can't do that, Austin had insisted, she's an adult, she can skate with whomever she wants. But not you, he had smirked. If she skates with you, she loses my support, official and financial. Beyond his personal malice Harold's maneuvers within Skate Canada brought sanctions against Austin, taking away his right to skate in pairs competitions for two years.

Austin would return to men's singles. But it felt wrong. Without Tilly he felt clumsy, naked. He tried to remain in love with Tilly, and she with him, but without the skating they found they had little in common. They edged away from each other. When he joined the Ice Follies, their relationship ended.

"Ferry's here," said Austin, as he and Steve climbed back into the Porsche.

Steve was not looking forward to the weekend on Quadra. Odd: he'd enjoyed previous stays at Austin's house. Since Shu-li was there and insisted on cooking, the food was superior. And until recently he'd been pleased with their plot to bring down Harold. But back in Toronto his work with Graham Pauley was unraveling. His protégé had great talent, could manipulate his body with ease, had won more than his share of medals. But three or so months ago something had gone out of him. To Steve it looked like he'd lost his enthusiasm, the will to win. A month ago he had accused Graham of this: You don't seem to care anymore, young man. He should never have said it. Such balance as there'd been between Graham's hard work and Steve's delicate stroking came apart, to the point where Graham had now twice skipped practice. This weekend Steve would have to tell Austin and Shu-li about this turn of events.

EIGHT

NOEL STEERED THE rental Civic off South Dogwood and onto the Island Highway. Other than color, it was exactly like his own.

Kyra peeled her white knuckles off the chicken handle. Last night Shane had sat in the passenger seat, the car falling, the splat of airbags, helpless as they rolled—

Noel watched sideways as Kyra lay her hands across her stomach. Acknowledging the elephant? Breathing deeply, nearly panting. She crossed her legs, businesslike: "So this Harold guy burst in, Shane was jerked out of a trance, Austin got coldly quiet, told Shane to keep breathing deeply and stormed off."

Alana leaned forward. "I have a friend who's learned hypnosis and she says it's dangerous to yank someone out of a trance. Changes the brain waves too abruptly. From alpha to beta or something. Weird Austin left like that. If he was the hypnotist, I mean."

"He just about knocked me over." Kyra crossed her legs the other way. "Harold nearly knocked me down too, rushing in. You want invisibility, wear a hospital gown."

Noel speeded up by eighty kilometers per hour to pass a beater truck. Kyra reached up to the chicken bar again and held on. Noel swerved back into the driving lane. "Do we know who this Harold is?"

"I don't think so. He said Shane was his favorite skater—" She pulled out her iPhone. Alana did too. "No reception here otherwise I'd search him," Kyra said. They were passing an ELK CROSSING sign: antlers, arched back, four legs in simulated motion.

"Hi, Sonia," Alana said to someone far away. "I don't have good reception, can you look up Harold Arensen for me?" She spelled the name. "Based in Victoria, BC. Thanks."

How does she do it? Kyra fussed.

"Oh yeah? ... Really? ... Thanks, that'll get us started." She closed the phone. "Arensen is head of the Vancouver Island Skating Union, VISU. And a director of Skate Canada."

"Big-time guy."

"How did you get reception when I didn't?" Kyra asked.

"More powerful instrument? I phoned, didn't try the internet?" Alana shrugged.

Kyra shoved her phone in her pocket. "Head of VISU shouldn't have a favorite skater, should he? Or was that just a figure of speech?"

Ten minutes and they were across to Quadra. Austin, calmer, kept to the sixty kilometers per hour limit. Soon they were back at the house, the three on the deck, late afternoon Pimms in hand.

"So," Steve began, "a setback." He templed his fingertips and rubbed them together.

"A ridiculous one, but monumental," said Shu-li. She'd forgotten how irritating she found Steve's habitual gesture.

"The accident, it's unexplained?" Rub, rub. "Out of nowhere? Hit and run?"

Austin glanced from Steve to Shu-li and back. "You suggesting something else?"

"Someone trying to hurt Shane?"

"But why?"

"I have no idea."

Shu-li said, "Someone trying to hurt the detective?"

"What precisely was she here to inquire into?"

Austin stared at Steve. "The beating of Shane's brother. Who did it, and why."

"Well then." Steve folded his arms above his spreading paunch.

"No, must be someone who wants to harm the whole family."

"The sons, at least. From what you said."

Shu-li shook her head. "We won't get anywhere speculating on who did what. We need to talk about what we're going to do. About Shane. And soon, about Harold."

Austin nodded. "You're right. I'll spend three hours with Shane every day. His mind will help him heal his bones."

"Good," said Steve. "How quickly can it happen?"

"I'll try for speed. The mind is tricky, but Shane'll work hard."

"When can he be ready? In time for the Olympics?"

"In time to qualify, you mean?"

Steve tented his fingertips together. "Can we cut corners, do you suppose?"

Shu-li raised her eyebrows. "What do you suggest?"

"Something perhaps—painful. Harold Arensen is a first-rate corner cutter."

She squinted at him. "Are you out of your mind?"

"It's Harold's obsession with the boy that we can turn to our advantage." Steve smiled ironically. "Shane's advantage, I mean."

Austin said, "You're suggesting that one of us goes to Harold and says, dear Harold, could you cut a corner or two?"

"I would be unable to do that. Could you, Austin? Shu-li?"

Shu-li shook her head. Austin exploded a breath.

Steve set his fingers and palms together, as if in prayer. "Perhaps someone else . . ."

Austin grinned widely. "Carl."

"Carl Certane, Shane's very own coach, admired by Arensen."

"Think he'd be willing? He's pretty straight arrow."

"Carl believes in Shane. For Carl it won't be cutting corners, it'll be a matter of righting wrongs. Very honorable."

"Okay," said Steve, "who's going to talk to him? I barely know him."

Shu-li shook her head in mock-weariness. "You make great tactical suggestions, Steve. But when it comes to carrying them out . . ."

"He wouldn't take suggestions from me. But he admires you."

"He admires my body."

"We all do. Which doesn't mean we can't restrain ourselves." He stared over the water. The ferry from Cortes was approaching. "Some of us, anyway," he muttered.

"Okay. I'll see him on my way back." She held Carl in high esteem; he'd been one of the greats. And was a remarkable coach. Carl could admire her body. She thought highly of his talents. "If the cut corners and the hypnotherapy work, Shane can still do it. Right?"

Steve said, "Maybe."

"Definitely," Austin said. "Refreshers on Pimms?" He took their glasses and went to the kitchen. Yes, he enjoyed Shu-li's body, looking at it, loving it. And the woman herself. What a shame that she had such a hard time staying with him for longer than three days. Always in a rush to go somewhere. Or hurrying to get home to Calgary. Calgary! Poor Shu-li. He would have loved her to stay on Quadra a few more days. If she ever really committed herself to him, that'd be the moment he'd leave Ottawa forever.

The band meeting ended at 9:00 PM. Three years ago when Ezekiel Pete became the convener of the Negotiations Team he insisted their gatherings begin punctually and finish two hours later—most people's brains weren't up to concentrating in meetings longer than that. At first the other team members mocked him: you got loose brains, Zeke? Won't hold together more than a couple of hours? Put more meat on your bum, Zeke, so you can sit longer. But they soon discovered that a concentrated meeting produced clearer results than when consultations dragged on. Now he was known around the island for this tactic, and other groups used the pattern as a model. He also ran an organized meeting, which helped.

Before the evening's session he'd signaled to Dano and Charlie, stick around after the meeting. When the others left, he said, "Lisa and Jake at home tonight, Dano?"

"Lisa's on the last ferry and Jake's shacking up with his girlfriend these days."

"Let's go to your place."

Charlie said, "Why, Zeke? We can just stay here."

"Yeah, but Dano's close, he'll give us a beer." Zeke grinned at Dano. "Right?"

"No problem."

"Besides, I don't want the others to see us talking."

"Big conspiracy?" Charlie clamped on his hat. "We gonna take over the world?"

"Kinda. Let's go."

They left their cars at the Center and walked in silence past the red-roofed open shed that protected the war canoe. An old green van passed them from behind and headed down toward the southern end of Cape Mudge Village. Zeke glanced at the totem pole flat on its back next to the museum parking sign. Such a shame. After another hundred and thirty feet they reached Dano's house, a low clapboard rancher. Dano turned on the living room lights even though it wasn't dark yet, and headed for the kitchen. Charlie sat in the middle of the couch. Zeke dropped onto the old La-Z-Boy to glance out the window towards the Passage. Water always eased him, no matter the situation.

"Here you go, guys." Dano handed them cans of Molson's, opened his, turned a straight-backed kitchen chair and leaned forward on the backrest. "Okay, Zeke, what's up?"

Zeke let out a small sigh. "Matthew's boy Amos didn't get the scholarship."

"Shit," said Charlie.

Dano added, "Yeah."

"I don't get it. He had the grades."

"Yeah. He was good in high school. Matt shoulda made him go right to the U after that."

"Whatever," said Zeke. "He worked hard at school. He stayed out of trouble till he had nothing to do. Now he's signed up for that joinery course, it's part of the parole agreement. But he's got no money. And Matt's already paid the tuition deposit."

"So what's your idea, Zeke?"

"We've got to raise the cash."

"Amos isn't going to take our money. Anyway, Matthew wouldn't let him."

"No gift. A loan."

Charlie thought about that, then nodded. "Maybe."

"Definitely. At low interest rates. And he'll work harder, to get it paid back."

"How much?"

"A thousand'll cover the courses."

Dano said, "I can do a hundred."

And Charlie, "Me too."

"Then we're nearly a third of the way there. If we each talk to four elders we should have the cash for him by the end of the week."

"That kid's gotta go to school," Dano said.

"He'll pay us back." Zeke hoped he wasn't just dreaming. "Joiners make good money."

They came up with a dozen names and divided them among themselves. They finished their beers. Charlie walked south to his place, Zeke headed back to the Center. It was deep dusk. He noted the green van, parked on the west side of road. Zeke knew most of the vehicles on the south end of the island. This one he didn't recognize.

Great. The guy was leaving alone. He didn't want to tackle two of them. He slipped on the rubber mask, a death's-head that covered him from scalp to under his chin. He glanced inside the cab, key in the ignition ready to go. He grasped the golf clubs, a five- and a six-iron, with gloved hands, hefted them and waited for the Indian to pass the van. The guy'd be able to describe it later, maybe even remember the plate, but he'd been wearing gloves each time he borrowed it from old Marlton, off in Mexico. First those damn clammy medical things all the way over on the ferry, now these green gardening ones. Well, they both did the job. Guy was walking right toward the van, no way could he see, too many shadows. Wait till he's gone by. Rubber-soled shoes, never hear anything.

 He watched as Zeke approached. Couldn't see his face clearly. Short-sleeve shirt, no protection from that, skinny arms. Light-weight pants too. He'll be hurting for a while.

 He squatted beside the van, passenger side. There the guy went, on the other side. The fuckin' ess-oh-bee, what he'd done, wasn't gonna get away with it. Past the tail, couple more steps. Now! He stepped out of the shadows, six-iron high, lunged angling it onto the guy's neck right by the ear. Yeah! A whump, and he went down on his knees, hands catching him, all fours. Step up, swing, and that was his nose, good squish— Yeah, way to go! Another bash, right across his chest, but the guy must've sensed something coming, he slipped to the right and the club slid off his hip. Another whack caught him in the lower leg. The guy rolled again and came around standing facing—bet the death's-head got him scared now, Indians're all scared of spirits and this face was back from the dead. He pulled the club around and came about but the guy had shifted positions again, he was out of reach but lots of blood coming out of his nose. Have to charge him hard, come in swinging, club back and over and down— Damn if the guy didn't catch the thing as it came down and wrench it away, goddamn! He pulled back and shifted the five-iron to his right hand, up around and down but the guy caught the shaft with the six he'd just stolen and something in his other hand glinted—fuck, he had a knife, where the hell—? How could he still be on his feet? He pulled back on the five, swung it at the knife and caught him on the wrist and the knife skittered away on the dirt. Hah, even again. He swung hard, got the Indian in the ribs just as the guy landed one with the six, shit! just above the hip, damn— But the guy was flat while he was still standing.

Okay, enough punishment. He ran for the van, door open— He glanced back. The Indian was up, running, more like reeling toward the van. In, turn the key, gas, outa here— In the mirror he saw the guy grabbing for the rear door handle, holding on, but the van sped up and if the guy didn't let go he was gonna get dragged— Yeah, he could see the guy sprawled on the dirt road. Now get off the island, dump the club overboard. He checked the clock. Just make the last ferry off. He lifted the mask over his head. Better. Mask'll go in the drink too. His brain felt lots better now, job that needed to get done. Nobody to answer to but himself, no taking orders, nobody else unhappy. Not this time. Over to the other side, into the woods, onto that side road in the park, get some sleep. In the morning dump the van near the ferry, wouldn't use it again—the cops'll get it back to Marlton if he ever got back from Mexico. Then get on the 7:30, pick up his car from the lot and be home for breakfast. That bash the guy landed right above the hip felt sore, prickly. Couldn't be blood, skin didn't break. In the ferry washroom he'd see what it looked like.

Shane had never felt such pain. Not from the leg; they'd set the broken bones, treated the outer wounds and locked it in a cast-like apparatus that could be removed to check the healing. The painkillers they'd given him had sent him away from the small world of the hospital room to deep inside his head where his memories crept along the valleys of his brain. He lay on his back trying to drive flaming lances of thought from his mind by staring at the dim ceiling. He saw only flat space. No relief, because the pain came from so deep inside. Alone tonight. His mother had gone back to Quadra. She hadn't slept much the night before. Alone, except for the wheezing guy in the next bed.

He should never have decided to become a figure skater, let alone try for greatness. What hubris. A kid from a nowhere small island should be playing hockey like everybody else. A kid who didn't know anything about the demands made on the narrow elite superhighway.

In Vancouver he had not only Carl his superb coach, but also James his physical trainer, Mel his dance instructor, Larry his psychologist, Liane his chiropractor, Trent the costume designer, and any number of other people— No one should be coddled like this. Not even thinking about how much it cost. Austin paid for it all, and that wasn't right either. Increasingly Shane felt he had been bought and now belonged to Austin. Austin had said, No Shane, you belong to the world of beautiful motion.

Right now Shane felt all the pain of what he'd done. To his parents, what they'd given him—their unquestioning love, their unending time, what little money they could invest in his career. To his brothers, standing aloof from them, his career more important than coming home the moment Derek was attacked, than spending time with Timmy who loved and respected Shane and what did Shane give Timmy, locking himself in his room when Timmy needed him. He felt too the pain of what he'd done for Austin. Pieces in his brain were locked in a terrible agonized battle. No correct position to take, not any more. Had there been an acceptable way of handling himself, earlier? He hadn't found it. Now he wondered, if he'd dealt with it right away might there have been a better choice?

He tried to roll onto his right side but before he got there his encased foot jammed a line of coal-hot pain from toes to hip. Despite the painkillers. He stared again at the ceiling.

Maybe he could talk to Harold, Harold had always been kind to him. No, that was a betrayal of Austin. Maybe if he pleaded with Austin, I can't go on, please don't make me . . . But he'd tried that, three times. Each time Austin said, consolingly, Of course you can, Shane. It's essential. Consider the consequences if you don't.

He'd acceded to Austin once. He wouldn't again. And what consequences then?

He twisted to his left. Some pain, but less than the other way. Possibly by staring at the curtain that hung between him and the old guy in the next bed, sleep would come. He lay still. He took deep breaths trying to breathe the pain away. But it was Austin who had first taught him about breathing, and now the exercise was contaminated with Austin. Maybe Carl's exercise: stretch the muscles, then relax them. Head muscles, neck, shoulders, arms, fingers. Chest.

Stomach— He gave up. Because somewhere in his brain, Austin was grinning, whispering, Shane, it's not going to help, you will of course acquiesce.

In the past Shane might have shouted, No! But right now he didn't know what to do, or even think. His leg throbbed. He shifted again to his back. Small tears slid down his cheeks. He felt his chest begin to shake, realized he was panting. Not good, stop! But he couldn't. Derek, he thought, Derek!

Outside light began to brighten the room. Safer out of the dark, he slept.

After lunch Noel and his brother walked down to the beach. Despite Seth's declaration that he and Jan would get to his parents' place by mid-afternoon yesterday, they hadn't arrived until after dinner—a two-ferry wait in Tsawwassen. Why, on just an average summer day? Paul Franklin explained: in July and August, Friday afternoon is, by definition, not average; there's always an overload on the ferries between the mainland and Vancouver Island. People don't like whichever side of the Strait they're on so they have to cross to the other side. Seth and Jan got to the house exhausted. They'd spent breakfast, the morning and a superior two-quiche lunch with salad and wine catching up, family stories that Kyra participated in too; she'd gotten to know the Franklins well during summers on Bowen Island. Now, while the Four Superwomen, as Paul called them, Astrid, Jan, Kyra and Alana, cleaned up and gossiped, and Paul took his nap, Noel and Seth walked.

The beach, today pocked with seaweed debris tossed ashore from what may have been a storm somewhere north of Seymour Narrows, stretched for miles. The water lay flat, broken by splashing children and the occasional whisper of incoming tide. Only strong winds could create breakers; this afternoon the air hung still. When Seth and Noel spoke, their words were quiet. They talked about Seth's work with NASA, he'd been seconded to an Astrophysics lab at UCSD. And what was he doing there? His specific role was classified, national security kept him from saying more. But life was good. And Jan's work with autistic kids? At the start wonderful to do so much for these children, after a year depressing as she watched them make so little progress, then satisfying when she realized she was helping.

Their son Keith, at Stanford, had spent two weeks with them earlier this month.

"And you?" Seth asked. "The work's good?"

"Yes. Interesting. A pleasure working with Kyra."

"How about personally? Anyone new there?"

Seth had of course known Brendan, and had liked him. Now Noel said, "No, and I don't think there will be."

Seth said, "You're not looking?"

"No." Noel shrugged. "If someone appears, who knows."

Seth carried on, "Kyra's okay?"

"Sure. Why?"

"She seemed a little tuckered over lunch."

"She has a right to be." Noel told Seth about the car accident. "Not two days ago."

"On Quadra, right? Alana was real excited to go with you. She didn't get in your way, I hope."

"No, she was helpful, and a delight. She's got a good inquiring mind."

"What's the case? Can you talk about?"

"Sure. It's not covered by national security."

"Okay, okay."

Noel repeated what they had so far discovered, ending with the green van that had sideswiped Kyra and Shane, and forced Tim and his bike into the ditch. "Both kids are more or less okay. Shane's broken leg may keep him from the Olympics. That must hurt a whole lot more than the wounds."

"Tough on both of them."

"Kyra and I've been trying to figure if somebody's after the three sons, or if it's a coincidence."

"Similar green van doesn't sound like coincidence."

"And the three of them being harmed within three weeks doesn't either."

"You've told the RCMP?"

"Yeah. They're checking out all vans registered on Quadra."

"The lady with the walker saw a bunch of vehicles?"

"Right. And— Hey, she called one of them a truck, then said it was a van."

"Maybe less and less of a coincidence."

"We'll have to get back to Mrs. McDougal. Maybe she had a better look at the guy who got out of the truck, or van, than she thought."

"Worth asking."

"But why? Why try to kill the Cooper sons?" Noel chucked a rock in the water.

"They hurt someone and the guy wants revenge?"

Noel nodded. "Could be."

"Or maybe the Coopers have something this guy wants? Money? Property?"

"Not money. Jason gets by, but without Linda's salary it'd be harder times."

"Their land?"

"They've got their woodlot and licenses on two others."

"I don't know anything about woodlots. Any money there?"

"I wouldn't have thought much."

"Maybe someone who wants the woodlots. Another tree farmer. Or a developer."

"No idea. I'll ask Jason."

"Or maybe there's a creep out there who just likes hurting people. Which doesn't explain why he wants to hurt these three brothers."

"If it's the same van, then one time he came from the van and attacked with a blunt instrument, and twice he attacked with the van itself." Noel stopped walking and stared out at the smooth sea. He mused out loud: "Timing of the attacks. First, after dark. Second, at dusk. Third in the dark."

"One three weeks ago, the other two the same evening. Is he getting desperate?"

"And— Damn."

"What?"

Noel kept his eye on the sea, as if an answer could be found just under the surface. "There's something but I can't grasp it."

"Maybe not desperate but scared. Something the Coopers are doing that—"

"No. Wait. Let me think." Noel closed his eyes and rubbed his temples. Derek in the dark, Tim at dusk, Shane in the dark—

"How could the Coopers harm—"

Seth went on. Noel didn't hear him. A shudder took him. Zeke Pete saying, maybe a curse on the Cooper family? Hadn't felt right. Why not? Derek in the dark but out of his truck, recognizable in the moonlight, Mrs. McDougal had said. Tim in the twilight, identifiable. Shane in the car, invisible. How did the van guy know Shane was in the Honda? Night, and the windows were tinted. Which meant— Another shudder. He was after the car. He'd tried to kill Kyra and himself. Not Shane.

Take it easy. Just a hypothesis. Try it on Kyra.

"Isn't it nice, the boys out for a walk," Astrid observed. "They so rarely see each other."

"Uncle Noel comes down to San Diego at least once a year," Alana pointed out.

"I meant a walk from home, from this house, on the beach right here—" Astrid, flustered, looked out the screened sliding door, past the patio, north along the beach.

"It is lovely," Jan soothed, "for them to have a good natter. Let's get these dishes under control and go for a walk too." She was an inch taller than Kyra, nearly Seth's height. A handsome woman radiating calmness and good will, she frequently touched another's shoulders, arms, cheeks. More than Kyra liked, but her touch was soothing. Now Jan stood by her mother-in-law at the door, her arm across Astrid's shoulder, while Kyra and Alana cleared the table.

On a trip to the kitchen Kyra looked at the tableau of the women's backs, their heads tilted toward each other, and felt a pang of desire for her own mother, Trudy. She was back now from Turkey—she'd been teaching Canadian Literature, seconded from Simon Fraser University. On her way off Vancouver Island, Kyra would phone her.

My god, this embryo will turn *me* into a mother! Kyra nearly dropped seven plates onto the tile floor. Of course she'd known that fact, but it was emotional reality hitting her now. A mother. Forever and ever. Here she was, thirty-six, wanting her own mother. Did you ever stop being a mother? A child? That marriage commandment, *till death do us part*—the parent-child commandment never said it as such, but it was much more of an absolute.

Dishes stored in the chugging dishwasher, Alana scrubbing

quiche pans in the sink, Kyra wiped down the counters and wrung out the dishcloth. Jan and Astrid entered the kitchen, offering to help. Offer rejected.

"To the beach then. Meet the boys." Astrid said. "Paul won't be up for an hour."

"Men," Alana mouthed. Kyra caught it, and smiled.

They collected hats and rubbed on sunscreen. The condo owners were expected to go out the communal front door to the paved path to the beach. But Paul, since their unit was the farthest corner one, had built stairs down from their patio. His unapproved action had brought on some raucous strata meetings, until common sense prevailed: nothing really wrong, and they were handsome stairs. The women walked down the path.

"Where are your parents, Jan?" Kyra asked, as they attained the beach.

"Dead."

"I'm sorry." Kyra meant sorry about both—dead parents, and that she'd asked.

"They were daredevil skiers and got caught in an avalanche. I was twelve."

"How did you manage?"

"Boarding school, an aunt in the holidays." Jan's tone was even. She smiled and squeezed Kyra's forearm. "Sounds worse than it was."

"Then you got married and had children."

"Well, I did a few other things, but essentially, yes."

"How did you find motherhood?" She shouldn't be a bulldog. But intensity of the moment made her hold and drag and shake the subject.

"Fine. I love it." Jan smiled at Alana, and Astrid smiled at both, at all.

"No, I mean really."

"Are you thinking of having a baby, Kyra?" Astrid asked.

Kyra looked out at the Strait. Two fishing boats. An enormous cruise ship in the hazy distance on its way to Alaska. She pressed on. "A friend cites biorhythms, she's older than I am, if she wants a baby she'd better get on with it. I don't feel that way"—*didn't she?*—"but she keeps talking about it." She paused to excavate a pebble from her sandal. The other three waited. The sun was hot on their backs and heads and the saltchuck glistened too brightly to look at. Its salt and pepper smell stung their nostrils. Adjusting her hat, Kyra persisted, "What's it really like, being a mother?"

Jan said, with asperity and another arm-squeeze, "First you're pregnant and then you don't sleep for a number of years and then you have a person you keep coping with."

"Sounds awful!" said Alana. "Why would anyone?"

Astrid laughed. "That's a truncated version. There are things they don't tell you in the pre-natal classes, but the rewards are greater than the drawbacks."

"Mom, you didn't find Keith or me that bad, did you?"

"No, dear, not at all." Jan drew Alana into a hug. "Just a bit frantic at first."

"Is your friend married?" Astrid asked.

"Well, sort of," Kyra hedged. "How about you, Alana? Do you want children?"

"Sure. But not alone. I don't want to be a single parent. I know a girl who got pregnant last year and the guy ditched her and she dropped out once the baby was born even though the school tried to keep her in. Too difficult to do both, she said."

"My friend's worried about labor."

Jan cast Kyra a hard look. "Most women survive. At least in the US and Canada."

"You tell your friend," Astrid contributed, "once through labor, you forget it."

"How were your labors?"

"Seth had a shoulder in the way so he took hours, and that was a bit of work. Noel was a breeze. Look, sweetie," Astrid smiled at Kyra in a way that made Kyra think Astrid didn't believe in the friend, "You tell your *friend* that women are built to give birth. Muscles adjust over pregnancy and the pelvic structure loosens up. After nine months the only thing you want is to have the inside lump outside."

"She'll be pleased to hear that, maybe," Kyra said. She didn't feel very pregnant. She wasn't tired and right now she didn't have to pee urgently. Her breasts were tender, but so what. She felt the sun and prickles of perspiration in her armpits and a discomfort in her gut.

Maybe she shouldn't have had the second helping of quiche.

"Look, there are my boys!" Astrid waved at distant figures who waved back.

Alana rolled her eyes.

Noel sidled in beside Kyra and, *sotto voce*, asked her to stop on the patio for a brief confab. There he suggested the guy in the van had been out for detective blood, no way of suspecting Noel was not inside. He mentioned the woodlots—enough value for someone to commit personal attacks?

"If somebody was after us, then the woodlot isn't the issue," Kyra said. "Conversely . . ."

"Yeah, that's right. At least maybe, from what we know."

"We've got to talk to Jason. And Mrs. McDougal." Kyra winced.

"What? You okay?"

She shrugged. "Guess so."

"Maybe you walked too far?"

"Hardly. It was okay. Who knows?" She looked strained.

"Kyra, you really want to keep it? Raise it by yourself?"

She took a breath, exhaled. "Right now I think, absolutely. Earlier, in the kitchen, I knew I had to get rid of it. Back and forth like that, three times this afternoon. Schizzy."

"How're you going to decide?"

"Toss a coin?"

"Be serious."

"I don't know how I'm going to decide. And I don't know if I will decide."

"If you just let it go—"

"I know, I know."

"I wish I could help, Kyra."

"Don't you dare."

"What?"

"Try to convince me one way or the other."

"You don't have to tell me not to dare. This one's all yours."

"Thank you."

"But if you want to do any out-loud thinking, I can react or not, your choice."

Her eyes misted up. He put his arms around her. "Whatever you decide, it'll be the right thing." Her head nodded against his shoulder. "Ready to join the others?"

She found a tissue in a pocket, dabbed her eyes. "Let's be sociable."

Inside, the kitchen smelled of the large forty-cloves-of-garlic stuffed chicken that was roasting. Paul offered drinks. Noel and Seth allowed how vodka-tonics would be just right. Kyra, with a wry smile, asked for juice.

Alana said, "Vodka-tonic for me too."

Seth mock-glowered at her. "We let you go away for a week, and what?"

Paul interrupted. "She can have a thin one."

"Thanks, Grandad." She turned to her father, wrinkled her nose at him, grinned as well.

Kyra thought, *Family is good*. She had that kind of relation with her own father, teasing and joking. With her mother, starting with returning home for vacations from Reed College in Oregon, she'd been a bit more formal. Why? Was she to blame? Or was her mother blaming her for something and she was withdrawing? She'd wondered if her mother had disapproved of her serial husbands, Vance whom she'd left after a few months when she discovered he enjoyed slapping her around, Simon the depressive who'd killed himself, most recently Sam who'd told her that to be happy she needed to live her own life and when she did, as a detective, he'd turned so jealous of her work he'd become impossible. But then her mother had taken up with a millionaire car salesman. Maybe she'd never figure it out. And what would her mother think of this pregnancy?

". . . to being all together," Astrid was saying, raising her glass of red wine, followed by a chorus of "Yes!" and "Cheers!"

Kyra watched Noel. He looked happy, but was part of him feeling, like her, that there was work to be done on Quadra and Campbell River? The idea, that the green van man was trying to stop Noel and her from investigating Derek's beating, gave her pause. No fear, not yet, just desire to get at the real situation. She sipped cranberry and soda water. It softened the squirmy feeling in her stomach.

They moved to the table where they found chicken, vegetables, potato casserole, salad. Noel said, raising his glass. "Another first-rate meal, thanks to all of you." Astrid smiled, gratified, and said it was easy, she'd done most of it before they got here. More glasses on high. They ate. Desert appeared, crème caramel. Noel's phone rang. He got up.

Paul dipped into his crème. "Excellent!"

Noel stepped out of the room and raised the phone to his ear. "Yes? ... Yes? ... You mean now? ... Sure, of course." He waited, listening. "Okay. See you there." Back to the table. The others, except for Kyra who was watching him, were deep in conversation. He squatted by her chair. "Jason says Derek is coming out of the coma."

"Whoo. Let's go." She stood.

Noel stood too. "Sorry, everyone. Major doings. We have to go back. Now."

Seth: "What's happened?"

"Derek, the man in the coma. He's coming out. He might remember things."

Astrid said, "His parents must be so relieved."

Alana too got up. "May I come with you again? Please?"

Noel thought, if the van guy is after Kyra and me, it'll be dangerous for you. He didn't say this aloud. No one should know there might be a risk. For anyone. "You haven't seen your parents for a long time, Alana. Let alone your grandparents."

"I really want to come with you."

"We don't know if Derek is really coming around. Could be a wild goose chase."

"I've started on this case. I want to see what develops."

"We'll report everything—"

Seth said, "How long will you be gone?"

"It could take a while."

"Alana, you can go with Noel and Kyra for two days. Noel says you're helpful. If they're not finished with the case then, you get on the bus and come back by yourself."

"Daddy—"

"Two days. Your grandparents see little enough of you."

She tucked her lip behind her teeth. And conceded.

NINE

SETH HAD SAID, "She's very keen to go along."

Noel had said, "She's useful."

"Thanks, bro. We'll look after the folks." He patted Noel's elbow, then put his arms around their parents' shoulders.

Bro. How Californian. If they were gone three days, Noel would avoid a chemotherapy trip to Victoria. He backed out of the parking space. North, then west, turn and onto the new Island highway. He speeded up.

With a glance at the back seat—Alana absorbed in her electronic device—Kyra said softly, "Any thought of why Green Van wanted to push two investigators into the bush?"

Investigators. She'd used his preferred word, not hers: *Snoop.*

"Someone worried about us snooping. Taking over the woodlot business was a notion but, if Shane wasn't the intended victim, that perfectly good theory's shot."

Kyra inhaled, and winced. Her stomach had been crampy off and on since brunch; shouldn't have eaten so many garlic cloves? "What is the Coopers' most prized or valuable thing?"

"The woodlot?"

"Shane." Alana, from the back seat, one earphone out.

"Huh?" Kyra swiveled around.

"Sponsorships. If you've won major prizes, Worlds or Olympics. Shane's worth more than a woodlot. In money. I don't mean love and stuff. I bet he'll be worth megabucks when his leg heals." She re-anchored her earphone.

The miles sped by. Kyra ignored creek signs, Elk Crossing signs, extensive fences. "Who benefits if Shane is out of competition?" More cramps. Did she have to pee, was she going to dribble?

"A competitor?" Noel finally ventured.

"There were those two American women, one slashed the other with her skate blade. A real scandal."

"I remember." He mused. "Needs Internet investigation."

The first exit to Campbell River appeared. Good thing, Kyra

thought, she was feeling crampier and squirmy and—was she going to throw up? No, she was peeing, no she was— "Noel, I'm bleeding!"

Noel glanced over and the car swerved to the right. "Bleeding?!" He looked ahead, straightened and slowed.

Alana, earphones down, leaned forward and touched Kyra's shoulder. "Do you hurt?"

"Don't know yet. Quite bloody." She shifted to look at the car seat. "Yep, bloody. A rental car. I don't have any pads— Damn!"

"Hospital, next stop." Noel speeded up.

They wouldn't let Noel see Kyra after they'd put her in an Emergency cubicle. She needed privacy, the nurse said. Alana agreed to stay in the waiting room while Noel headed upstairs to find out about Derek.

Jason was slumped on a chair across the hall from the room. When he heard Noel approach his head jerked up and he half-smiled. "Hi. You made good time."

"Yeah." Noel checked his watch. Just after 8:30. "How is he?"

"None of his doctors are on and the nurses won't say. Not even to Linda."

"He was coming out of the coma?"

Jason's checked shirt and khaki pants looked disheveled. "He moved, his toes twitched. His eyelids fluttered but they didn't open . . ."

"And?"

Now Jason stared at Noel. "That's it."

"Does that mean the beginning of the end of it?"

"Linda thinks maybe."

"That's great!"

"Shit, he was almost back. And then—" Jason threw his hands open, giving up.

"Tell me what happened."

"Timmy was here. Linda and I'd gone for a snack, then we'd checked on Shane. Oh god— His doctor says it'll take months before he can skate. If he doesn't heal completely before he tries anything, he could mess up his leg and limp the rest of his life."

"I'm sorry, Jase—"

"Linda stayed with Shane and I came back and Timmy was stroking Derek's arm, and crying. He grinned, he said, 'Derek's coming back.' That's when I saw his eyelids fluttering. They stopped and he lay still. Just like the last weeks. Timmy told me about his toes, he'd moved his right leg a little."

"It's the right direction, Jase."

"Yeah, I was thinking that so I told Tim to go to Shane's room and tell him and his mother, and get her over here. I sat with Derek and nothing more's happened."

"This is a good hospital and they've been doing all they can for Derek and Shane. And now for Kyra." Noel's specific anxiety climbed.

"Kyra?"

"She's in Emergency. She was pregnant and miscarried."

"Oh god— The car accident?"

"Likely. She's staying overnight."

"For a miscarriage?"

"Something else might have happened. What the accident did to her insides."

"Oh Noel, I'm so sorry!"

"It's all pretty bad."

"How're you doing?"

Noel shrugged. "Worried. I adore Kyra. I wasn't the father. Case you wondered."

"Oh." Jason's looked up. "I hadn't thought."

"I'll look in on Derek."

"Linda and Tim are there."

"Just for a second. Let them know we're back." He entered the room.

Tim sat on the bed, Linda in a chair. She said, "Jason told you?"

Noel nodded. He stepped over to the bed. "Derek, hear you're coming around. That's great!" No response; Noel hadn't expected any. He said, "I know about the visitor limits. You have my cell number. I'll leave the phone on."

In the hall Jason said, "Linda's staying the night. I'm going back to Quadra with Tim on the 11:30, they've got the late run tonight. You and Alana can come with us. She can have Derek's room again. You can have Shane's or go to Barb's."

If they released Kyra . . . "Thanks, Jase. I've got an errand. Won't be long." He left, glanced at his watch—8:57—and headed down to Emergency. He felt useless. Nothing to do for the Cooper kids, and he couldn't see Kyra. Or—?

Alana was sitting in the waiting room, eyes closed, ear plugs installed, twitching to her private music. He touched her shoulder.

She bounced into consciousness. "Hi!" She smiled. "How's Derek?"

Noel explained. "And Kyra? Have you seen her?"

"No. It's only been twenty minutes since you left."

No one at the nurse's station. He marched toward the curtain hiding Kyra's bed. He stage-whispered, "Kyra?"

"Yeah. Come in."

He slid the curtain open. "How you doing?"

"I don't know what they want me in here for." She hiked into a half-sitting position. "I'm okay."

"You didn't look okay before. How're you feeling?"

"I'm fine."

"Shit, Kyra, I mean about losing the baby and all."

"The baby? What baby. A few cells. No name attached."

"Don't—"

"Don't what? I feel grungy. Morose. Relieved. Empty. Like myself again? I don't know how I feel. My womb doesn't ache, if that's what you mean. Does my soul ache? I don't know. But I do feel like I want out of here."

"Yeah."

She slumped against the pillow. "How's Derek?"

He told her. "I'm going to have another chat with Sarah McDougal."

Kyra didn't want Noel to go. Not without her. "If she's still awake."

"It's still light out."

"Okay. But find out when I can leave and come back."

He leaned over and kissed her forehead. "I will."

It took fifteen minutes to find someone with information about Kyra's fate. She was definitely being kept overnight; they were waiting for a bed upstairs, ready shortly. He returned and told her this. "You want Alana to stay?"

"Yeah. If she wants to."

He squeezed Kyra's hand. "See you soon."

Alana paced, as if eager to head over to Kyra's bed but not daring. "How is she?"

"Wanting out but they're keeping her overnight. I've got to check something out. I'll be quick. You willing to stick around, make sure Kyra stays okay?"

"I'm planning on being here all night if she needs me."

"Thanks, kiddo. You're great. They'll take Kyra upstairs. Try to go with her. It may not be allowed, but try anyway. I'll meet you there. Or here."

She hugged him. "When will you come back?"

"Under an hour."

Noel sat in the car figuring out what he knew, what he had to do. Set up an appointment with Shorty Barlow. He opened his cell phone, stared at it— He'd fought this piece of technology when Kyra had given it to him, became used to it, and then bought up for one with a camera. He located the number, and poked the keys.

"Barlow." Grunted.

"Shorty, it's Noel Franklin."

"Back sooner'n you thought."

"Your invitation still open, to watch those videos of Shane?"

"Sure, but not tonight. I got a visitor."

"Couldn't do it tonight. How's tomorrow, mid-morning? You working?"

"I'm off, that's fine." He gave Noel the address. "Ten-thirty. I'll have coffee going. You want it with brandy, you'll have to bring it."

"See you then." Noel closed the phone, checked the map and erred his way to Sarah McDougal's place. On the north side of the street with the sun low, Mrs. McDougal sat on the porch with a younger woman, both sipping something. He strolled up the walk. "Hello Mrs. McDougal. Remember me?"

"Asking about the kid who was beaten? This is my daughter. Like some ice tea?"

"No thanks. That vehicle across the street that night. Was it a truck or a van?"

"It was dark, and my old eyes..."

"You said there was a moon. Will you close your eyes and try to see it?"

Sarah McDougal closed her eyes, "Say, this is interesting..." She nodded again, and opened her eyes. "A van."

"Can you see what color?"

"It was night." But she closed her eyes again. "Grey maybe, or green. Not blue or red, nothing bright. Not black. Yes, grey maybe. Or green. Maybe grey-green."

"Thanks," said Noel, "that's a help. Enjoy your tea."

On the way down the hill he saw an open store and decided to treat the bloodstained seat to some enzymatic cleaning product. He was provided with a "guaranteed miracle" product. He bought a roll of paper towels too.

Back at the hospital lot, he left the door open to keep the overhead light on. He scrubbed at the blood with the product. He wouldn't know until morning if it worked. But the rental company probably dealt with blood and guts every day.

He didn't like Kyra alone in a hospital room. He had no choice. After visiting hours, Alana had been told, no one was allowed upstairs—not to see Derek or Shane, let alone Kyra. So he and Alana waited for Jason to appear. He'd take an early morning ferry back. Alana could stay on Quadra or come with him. Likely come, Noel figured. To see Shorty's tapes of Shane skating.

Which is more or less how it worked out. Tim and Jason appeared, Linda spending the night in Derek's room. With two sons in the hospital, the administration wouldn't send home a caring mother and a nurse who knew the place intimately. None of them, Jason made it clear, would be any help tonight. "Let's go get some sleep." They left the rental Honda at the hospital and headed to the wharf in Jason's Toyota. The ferry plowed across the Strait. They arrived at the Cooper house.

Alana and Tim went to their rooms. Jason offered Noel a nightcap: "Laphroaig?" Noel accepted. Jason poured. He raised his glass. "To Kyra's health."

"To Derek's and Shane's."

They sipped. Noel remembered the smooth peaty taste. He and Brendan had made a trip to Scotland and they'd been side-tracked from castles by single malt discoveries. Home in Nanaimo they bought the bottles they remembered best. But outside Scotland it tasted different. They'd gone back to vodka-tonics.

Noel and Jason sat in silence until Noel asked, "What's a woodlot worth?"

"To buy? Or lease?"

"Buy."

"Depends on the size, where they are, quality of the timber, how much you're allowed to cut. Here, you can probably get a quarter section for $250,000 to $600,000."

"Hundred sixty acres?"

"Usually measured in hectares now. Our land might go for $400,000. Not that I'd sell it, hope the boys won't either. And I'd never give up the licenses."

Noel sipped more Laphroaig. "Look, ol' bud," he said, "we think whoever hit the car didn't know Shane was in it. We think he thought Shane was me. He or they think we're sniffing too close to whatever."

"Noel—that's terrible. I'm so sorry. Never thought I'd be putting you in danger."

"Comes with the territory." He had tried to sound tough but it came out softly. Yes, he could easily have been in the car.

———

In Derek's room Alana found the bed just as she'd left it yesterday. Barely thirty-six hours ago. Poor Kyra. That accident, then a miscarriage. Kyra's conversation on the beach with her mother and grandmother and her now made more sense. Could the accident and the miscarriage be connected? Come on, Alana, don't be stupid, a woman gets rattled around like that and of course she's going to lose a baby. The accident hadn't phased Kyra much, at least from how she talked. But what would a miscarriage do to her? Kyra seemed tough. Maybe she'd cope.

———

He'd felt it build as he drove off the ferry, his neck first, sliding down his shoulders, upper arms, hanging in the biceps seconds before hitting elbows and forearms, tingling his wrists, then hands. He flexed his fingers. Springy, ready to grab and bash. Weird how that came over him sometimes, the tingle that needed action. Lucky being in Campbell River tonight. Safer than on the island. More privacy there, but if you want a car in town you need the ferry and anybody can see you. Action in town safer than action on Quadra.

Good coincidence, this need for action and Saturday night. Charlie went to Saddleman's Wednesdays and Saturdays mostly. Now, how to get Charlie out sooner rather than later. Bad idea to go inside, who needed a roomful of witnesses. Charlie played late into the night, waiting for him in the truck would look suspicious.

He reached over to touch the bat. Sweet smooth oak, wouldn't crack in contact with a hardball. Or a skull. Better than golf clubs. He liked ribs too, three or four cracking from one blow. Charlie's ribs might be a little tougher to get at, that fat covering them. But everybody's got arms and legs—hell, elbows and kneecaps, good cracking sounds.

Gettin' late for alternative action? Just any sucker walking around? No, he wanted Charlie. Cheating at cards, immoral. No respect for the guys at the table, pretty low. Palming an ace, a corrupt soul. Maybe Charlie didn't have a soul to get corrupted. Just skin covering fat and bone. And shit. Soul-free shit. He grinned— Fuck! Cops.

The cruiser angle-parked in front of him. Goddamn it. He hadn't done anything. A Mountie opened the passenger door and came toward him. Roll down the window, smile. "Evening, Officer." Tall, vest over his chest, pistol, no hat.

"License and registration, please."

"Something wrong?"

"Need to see your identification."

Wallet for the license, glove compartment for registration. Pass them out the window. The cop takes them, back to the cruiser. Now he'll get on his computer . . .

Four minutes later the guy was back. "You waiting for somebody?"

Damn right. "No. I was thinking."

"Yeah? In public?"

"Is that illegal?"

"No overnight parking here."

"I wasn't going to think that long."

"Just move along, then."

"Okay."

The officer handed back the documents but continued to stand just beyond the window. Key into ignition. Start the engine. "You'll have to move your vehicle, Officer."

The cop turned back to the cruiser, got in, it was driving away. Bye-bye, cocksucker. He could still feel the tingle in his fingertips, but less so. Just enough to still want action. Maybe a different kind of action. He turned the corner onto Dogwood, up the hill a ways and into the Town Centre Inn. He liked to stay here. They had free and early breakfasts. Yep, a room. He could get back to the island early. He went upstairs. Not too late, he'd call Joanne. He set the bottle of Scotch on the dresser. She was a night bird. That tingle, definitely still there. Joanne liked it rough and tumble. That always got her off. He punched numbers into the phone. She answered on the second ring. Like she was waiting for him.

At the B&B, Noel had a hard time finding sleep. Tuesday Kyra had told him she was pregnant, four days later she wasn't. She must be going crazy in that hospital. He hoped they'd given her a sleeping pill. He hoped she wasn't feeling lonely, or abandoned. Or scared. Nothing he could do till tomorrow. Jason had said Linda would look in on Kyra.

Noel had never worked on a case like this, where instead of the parts moving towards a solution, the pieces were drifting apart, the situation going from poor to dreadful. Derek beaten, Shane's leg broken, Timmy smashed up, Kyra too, and then losing the baby. If she'd decided on an abortion, at least the decision would've been hers. And they were no closer to figuring out who had messed Derek up.

They stopped at the hospital to collect Kyra, check on Derek and Shane, knowing from Linda's phone call that nothing had changed since last night. Tim said he'd stay with them. He didn't need Shorty's tapes, he'd seen most of Shane's competitions. Kyra was dressed when they got to her room. She wanted out. Now!

Noel said. "How're you feeling?"

"Battered, but I'll survive." She smiled at Alana. Alana grabbed Kyra's suitcase.

Into the hall, to the elevator. Noel said, "There's time for a proper breakfast before our skating education."

The passenger seat of the rental looked better. Earlier, Jason had dug a blanket out of his car, and placed it beside the spot till it dried. Kyra, though impressed by Noel's cleaning job, chose to leave the blanket in place and opted for the rear seat beside Alana.

A night of bawdy games with Shu-li. In the early morning he kissed her brow, stroked her hair, apologized for leaving.

She understood: hypnosis for Shane's leg. "I'll expect you for brunch."

Austin was at the hospital by nine-thirty. Shane lay on his bed. "How're you doing?"

"Ehh," Shane said, and pulled the sheet over his midriff.

"Eaten?"

"Yeah, cereal and tea."

"Ready to work?"

"I guess."

Austin shut the door, hitched the chair closer to the bed, and sat. "Close your eyes and breathe, in, out, one, two—"

Shane had done this often. He settled quickly into a hypnotic state.

"Look at the places that need to knit— All your attention on your leg..."

A knock at the door. It opened. The doctor, Linda, and Jason entered. For god's sake, Austin thought, how am I going to get this leg healed?

"Oh, hello," Linda said, "you're here early." She introduced Dr. Bremer to Austin.

"Quite a skater, I hear." He checked Shane's cast. "How was your night, Shane?"

"Sore, but I slept. Thanks."

"What are you doing?" Linda asked.

"Talking about the breaks," Austin replied, "in a healing way."

"It needs time for the swelling to abate," said Bremer, "so we can adjust the cast."

Shane could hear the doubt in the doctor's voice. Bremer didn't have much belief in what he assumed Austin was, some faith-healer.

"Don't touch the leg."

"I wouldn't think of it." Austin exuded world-weariness.

"How long will you be, Austin?" Linda asked.

"Half an hour, forty-five minutes."

She looked at her watch. "We'll come back for you, Shane. We'll go to Derek's room for Sunday brunch." Linda kissed his brow and left.

The doctor listened to Shane's heart, took his blood pressure, and left also.

"Back to it, Shane," Austin said, his tone trance-inducing. "The skin on your shin, it's started to heal ... Your bones are protected by sinews ... The bone shards join with each other ..."

"Hi, Carl? Shu-li Waterman here. How you doing?"

He said her name, making it sound like Sheh-li, which was how she got to the anglicized Shirley for her skating name. They went a long way back.

"Good, yeah, me too. I'm over on Quadra visiting Austin, Steve is here too— Why don't you join us? It's a big house— Oh yeah, you wouldn't want to miss that ..." She laughed. "Listen Carl, bad news. Shane was in a car accident and broke his leg ... Right. It's terrible ... Three places ... Well, he might. He'll probably be ready for the Olympics, but not for the Fall qualifiers ... Yes, Austin's working with him every day— Yeah, you know Austin ... Right ... Carl, you ever heard of anyone skipping the qualifiers and going right to the Olympics? ... No, I never have either ... A damn shame, he's so good and you and he've worked so hard ... Would you ask around? Maybe Harold? ... Okay, we'll keep you updated ... You have the number here? ... Bye."

Shu-li closed the phone and looked at Steve sitting on the sofa in Austin's office. "That's the most I can do. Let him think for a few days."

"Stroke of genius, inviting him over," Steve said.

"A safe stroke. He hates the wilderness."

"And you left it open for more calls." Steve's tone was overly admiring.

"He cares for his star pupil, and Shane is pretty crocked." She stood up. "Would you like a hearty walk before I concoct something for brunch?"

Austin had just wrapped up when Jason appeared with a wheelchair. "Going to scoop the kid up," he said. "Feed him a good breakfast."

"Right," said Austin. "See you tomorrow, Shane."

"Yep."

His father wheeled the chair close to the bed so Shane could clamber onto it. It felt good to be upright. Semi-upright. "We're trying smell therapy. All Derek's favorite foods, and he's wired to an EEG and an ECG. We've discussed this with the doctors. For the rest of us," Jason put his hand on Shane's shoulder, "it's a normal Sunday brunch."

To Derek's room, Tim sitting on the bed. "Where's Mom?" Shane asked.

"Hey Derek," Tim said, "Shane and Dad are here. Mom's coming with the food."

"Think he hears you?"

"Who knows? He might. He might smell the food."

Shane looked at his brother, inert, head bandaged, tubes going in under the sheet. "Hey Derek, it's Shane. I have a broken leg and you have a broken head, but we'll make it, dude." He wheeled closer and grabbed Derek's hand.

Linda appeared loaded with takeout cartons, followed by a candy-striper volunteer who wheeled in two bed-trays, piled with dishes and cutlery. The smells helped Shane forget the earlier lukewarm oatmeal.

"Not hospital food, is it?"

"It's from The Comfort Zone. Let's eat while it's hot."

Waffles, bacon, scrambled eggs, perfecto hash browns, and local strawberries for the waffles, juice, milk, and rich-smelling coffee. Like coming downstairs on birthday mornings of Shane's childhood.

They all ate, watching Derek. "Hey Derek, it's really good, want some?" Tim touched his strawberry-laden spoon to Derek's nose. To his lips.

"It'll take time," Linda said. "Let's just enjoy a breakfast picnic together."

Back in the car, Noel handed Kyra the map, said the address, and guided them to Shorty's house, a one-storey bungalow. "What a gardener," he exclaimed. In front and at the sides, thriving green—lush vegetables, fruit, flowers. "Shorty Barlow believes in self-sufficiency."

A black and white cat on the deck meowed as they walked up the steps.

Barlow opened the door. "How do, how do." He checked Noel's and Kyra's hands. He shook his head, said, "No brandy, eh?" sounding disappointed.

Noel hadn't taken the hint seriously. "Sorry."

"Ah well, dry movies. Come in."

"My business partner, Kyra Rachel. And my niece, Alana Franklin."

Shorty ran a ship-shape house, Noel noted. Another cat on the sofa, a mottled one. Noel didn't hate cats the way Kyra hated dogs. He figured they couldn't help being cats, any more than he could help being human.

"Coffee? Juice?"

"Nothing, thanks," they chorused.

"Let's get on with it then," said Shorty. "I have carrots to thin."

"This is generous of you." Noel, making socially appropriate noises.

"Think nothing of it," Shorty replied. "The carrots can wait an hour or so. I'm trying to train the cats to weed, but it's like herding grasshoppers."

Alana laughed and sat on the brown leather sofa. Kyra looked at the cat, which yawned, stretched, curled around again. Kyra sat between it and Alana. Noel, thinking Shorty probably occupied the lazy-rocker, took an overstuffed floral armchair.

"We'll start at the beginning." Shorty shoved in a video and turned on the TV. "And proceed to the end. An hour or so." He backed up to his chair.

Their attention refocused from the sun-filled living room to the artificial lighting of an arena. Shane appeared, skated to the center of the ice, stopped, raised his arms, and smiled, waiting for his music.

"He's fourteen here," Shorty said. "First Junior Grand Prix."

Shane was wearing a powder blue, skin-tight one-piece costume, and blue skate covers. The music swelled, Shane waited three beats, swooped to the side of the rink and around the end, rotated and skated backwards, fast. Forwards, backwards, forwards, so fast it looked like he was twisting, then into a camel spin, down the side, and the turn for an axel, a double. The music soared, he was down the other side, a double axel, another.

"Wow!" Alana said. "He's so good. Even then."

More twisting bits, a lengthy spin, arms upheld, the music stopped, he bowed to the judges and skated off. The crowd applauded enthusiastically.

His marks afforded him third place, a bronze. Shorty fast-forwarded through the winners on the podium and the medal ceremony.

"That was his first major competition," said Shorty. "Now the next year—"

Shane, fifteen, a gold skintight costume with russet trim, an autumnal look. He'd gained in confidence and strength. He performed to "The Sting," quite a different program, but still containing spins and axels and other jumps Noel couldn't name. Shane won gold.

Third Junior Grand Prix. Shane in a tuxedo like Fred Astaire, his hair in longer coif. Even as he stood, waiting, it was apparent his confidence generated charisma. The crowd cheered even before he started to skate. Again a stellar performance, more and higher leaps to "There's No Business Like Show Business." Now he owned the rink.

"See what I mean?" Alana repeated.

Noel and Kyra nodded, not taking their eyes off the video. Shorty beamed like a proud parent.

In the next segment it was apparent Shane was the audience's darling. He appeared in rib-high brown tights, bare-chested with a slinky vest that showed his chest hair. He had on a brown skullcap with two little points above his ears.

"That's a radical costume," Kyra stated.

"I saw this on TV," Alana breathed. "Just wait."

"L'Apres-midi d'un faune" swelled forth and Shane skated, leaps, splits, twists, stunning smoothness. Taking lessons from old Nureyev films? Noel realized he'd been holding his breath.

"That blows me away," Alana crooned.

The gold again, to a standing ovation.

"Told you he was good," said Shorty. "Okay, last spring. Just turned eighteen."

Shane, as he looked now, skated to center ice, held his start position. He wore a space explorer costume, blue one-piece with red tabs on the shoulders. Zipper down nearly to his navel, curly hair peeking out. He smiled, waited, arms straight down. The first bars of something spacey. On the second beat he shoved into a glide, ran on his picks, pushed into a double axel then, at the other end of the rink, a triple.

"Just wow!" Alana couldn't help herself.

Up the far side, an extended spin—Shane fell.

The crowd gasped. So did Alana. Shane caught the ice on his hip, then elbow and back. Instantly he was up, not appearing hurt. The crowd sighed in relief. He smiled, carried on, catching up to his music, leaps and spins backwards and forwards, ice dust on his hip and back. He scored just out of contention, fourth. Off the podium, first time in five years.

"Every skater falls," said Shorty, "but a damn shame he did it in this competition."

Alana said to Shorty, "Would you run that again, please?"

"What? The whole tape? I got to get to my carrots."

"No, just the fall, please."

Shorty rewound. Shane finished the double, the triple, went into the spin—

"Stop! There!"

"What?"

"Can you do slow motion? Frame by frame?"

Uncle Noel kicked in. "What's up, Alana? We've taken a lot of Shorty's time."

Alana ignored him, continued to Shorty. "Have you watched the fall real close?"

"Just when it happened."

"Please, let's watch again, then in slow motion. It's so weird for him to fall."

Shorty raised his eyebrows, rewound again, Shane fell again, got up—

Frame by frame, spin, fall—

"See there on that toe loop? Looks like Shane's pick did something, or he dug it in and changed edges . . ."

"Where?" said Shorty.

"Run it again. Look hard."

Shorty rewound, then frame by frame played Shane's skate from the triple. Noel couldn't figure out what Alana was on about.

"There!" The cat bolted from the sofa. Alana stood, walked up to the TV, pointed. Shorty stopped the frame. "He's dug his pick in. And look!" She made a clicking motion with her thumb. Shorty obliged. "See? He should be on his back outside edge. But he's picked with his left toe and come down on his inside right edge. Then he falls. Weird."

Shorty backed the film up, ran the few frames.

"What are you saying, Alana?" Kyra asked.

Alana kept her eyes on Shorty. He re-ran the frames.

"What?" Kyra repeated.

The tension in the room sparked.

"You think he tossed it?" Shorty asked Alana.

"Strange mistake for someone that good."

"Everybody makes mistakes." Shorty ran the piece again. Shane came out of the spin, started his toe loop, raised his other leg as if to push off, shifted to his back outside edge, landed on the right, fell—

Noel was grasping for a sense of the sequence. "Did he just lose his balance?"

"Why would he do that?" Shorty asked, of no one. "It was a simple accident. Damn bad timing, that's all." He ran the frames once more.

Kyra shifted on the sofa. "Why would he do it? What does it mean?"

Shorty put the remote down. The screen blanked. He stood up, paced around. "It's a hard charge," he said to Alana. "Let's look at the beginning again." She perched on the sofa arm.

Shane in his space suit, arms raised, smile. Shorty rewound until Shane skated out to begin, slowed this to watch each frame. He wound back to the beginning of the faun-suit program. "He looks more present there," Kyra observed.

Back to the space suit. "Tense," Noel said. "Maybe."

Shorty shut off the TV and re-wound the tape. "Only thing to do is ask Shane. I won't believe he did that on purpose unless I hear it from him."

Noel stood. So did Kyra and Alana. "Are you certain, Alana?"

"Uh—," she shrugged. "He probably has an explanation." She bit her lip. "Maybe I shouldn't have said anything."

"We gotta ask him," Shorty repeated.

"We'll do that now. Shane's still in the hospital." Noel led the parade to the door. "Thanks, Shorty. Get to your carrots."

"I'm coming too. He's one of mine. Cats can do the carrots."

Kyra and Noel exchanged a glance. Kyra said, "The hospital allows two people in at a time. Noel and I'll talk to Shane. We'll let you know."

"Kyra's right."

Shorty frowned. He looked at Alana before he conceded. "You phone me immediately. I can be over in minutes."

Noel and Kyra nodded.

"You want to stay here?" Shorty asked Alana. "Do some weeding?"

Was he asking not to be left alone? He looked very worried.

"I'll go to the hospital, Shorty," Alana said. "I'll phone the minute I know anything."

"Shorty," Noel sounded tense, "what's your best analysis?"

The tall, thin, mustachioed man looked from Noel, to the girl, to the woman. "Suspicious." He turned to his garden. "Be easy with Shane."

Steve and Shu-li strolled from the house along one of the paths through the woods to the top of the southern cliff overlooking Austin's beach. Below to the right gentle surf broke against a line of craggy rocks. They stood a couple of feet apart, Steve steepling his fingers. "Think Carl will find a way for Shane?"

"I felt good about it when we were talking."

"Now?"

She shrugged. "Now I can't say."

"Not feeling optimistic?"

She stared out to sea. "I'd like to talk to you about something else." She turned to face him. Now he was splaying his fingers. Should she get into this?

"Aren't we talking now?"

"We've known each other for a long while, right? And I trust you."

"Well, that's good. Because I certainly trust you."

"Can I trust you not to talk to Austin about what I'm going to say?"

He tilted his head to look at her face. "If it's important to you, I will discuss nothing you tell me with Austin."

She believed him. She cared for Austin a great deal, but she had to sound Steve out. "How important is our project to you?"

"Taking down Arensen, making him bleed? Very."

She nodded. "Do you think it will happen?"

"What do you mean?"

"I'm worried. I think things are falling apart."

"Because of Shane's injury?"

"All of it. Shane, my Miranda—she's so young still. Your guy, Graham. You've haven't praised him since you've been here. Is he going to become one of our tools, Steve? Good enough for Arensen to want to take him under his wing?"

Steve remained silent. He interlocked his fingers and tensed them from nearly horizontal to right angles.

Shu-li put both her hands on his. "Don't do that, listen to me. You're not talking to Austin. This is just me. Will Graham be ready to play his part?"

He pulled his hands from hers and stared at the ground. "I don't know."

"Look at me." Steve did. "I want to destroy Harold. But we're not getting there. Shane was our real chance. I don't see it happening."

"Austin thinks he still can—"

"What, hypnotize Shane into mending? It's a multiple fracture. Austin's good, but he's fooling himself."

"But if Certane can get past that—"

"Carl's good too, but I heard it in his voice—we're on the wrong track. The rules are too tight, there's no wiggle room."

Steve's right hand grabbed his left fingers, started to massage them. He dropped them as he saw Shu-li eyeing his move. "What're you saying? We should call it off?"

"We have to talk to Austin. Make him see. Maybe try again later."

"With a new trio of students? I'm not sure I'm up to it."

"Austin has to listen to us. Stop telling himself everything's going to be okay."

Steve shook his head. "Normally I enjoy being here on Quadra with the two of you. The three days together gives me new energy."

"Yes," she said, "me too."

"But it's strange. By the fourth day I'm ready to leave."

Shu-li felt a sharp chill take her.

"Must be a throwback to my skating days. By the fourth day I wanted to get away from people like myself."

She forced herself to smile. "Even when you were in the final round?"

"Especially. That intensity." He nodded wistfully. "This time I'm ready to leave now."

The fourth day. Her heart pounded. She glanced down to the surf. All these years, was this why she'd felt such discomfort? "Come on, let's go back." She led the way.

Noel drove through the hospital lot twice. No space. He parked half a block away. Walking back, Alana said, "Please may I come with you?"

"It's an interrogation, Alana," Noel said. "Three on one doesn't work."

"I noticed the strange fall." She pulled back from a pout.

"Yes, you did. Thank you."

"We've got to take it from here," Kyra finished. "We'll meet up at the cafeteria."

Alana looked at them, their tones as businesslike as their demeanors. She dragged out her iPhone, plugged in the ear pieces, turned something on and walked away.

Shane was dressed, sitting on the edge of his bed. Tim sat in the visitors' chair. "Hi," Kyra said, "How're things?"

"They're letting me go home," Shane said with a smile. "Dad's getting me a loaner wheelchair and crutches."

Noel said, "We'd like to talk, Shane. Tim, Alana's in the cafeteria. Will you join her?"

"Oh." He looked at Shane, at Noel and Kyra. He took off his cap. "Well."

"We'll be down soon," Kyra said. Noel sat in Tim's chair. Kyra remained standing. Shane watched Tim leave, then stared at his cast.

Kyra closed the door. "Shane, we've watched the tapes of your competitions. You're very good. We also saw you fall. We watched that one about ten times. Frame by frame. We have some questions about it."

Shane swiveled his head from her to Noel, made as if to stand on his cast, flinched and squirmed back onto the bed. "Yeah?"

Noel said, "We watched the tapes with Shorty and Alana. They think there was something suspicious about that fall. They pointed out that you dug your pick in on the toe loop, which you started on the back outside edge and ended on the inside right. Shane, did you throw that competition?"

His face had turned pale. "What do you think I am, man?"

"A liar," said Kyra. "You're too good a skater to have fallen right there. Why didn't the judges pick it up?"

Sweat had formed on his brow "I don't know." His pupils contracted.

Silence, as all realized what Shane had admitted.

"Why, Shane?" Noel asked.

Shane shrugged, let out a sob, twisted so he could fall onto his pillow.

"Why, Shane?" Kyra watched his shoulders tremble. Some instinct drew her to rub his back, but she resisted. "You're too beautiful a skater to throw away a career."

Noel: "We know Derek was dealing pot to support your career. He's in a coma. We know someone sideswiped Tim, on purpose. We do not think someone hit the car you were in to damage you, but to get rid of Kyra and me, the investigators. You seem to be the crux of this. You and that fall. Why'd you do it, Shane?"

Shoulders heaving slowly. Mumbling.

"What did you say?" Kyra moved closer.

Now his chest heaved. Now she did rub his back. He was just a kid. When he moved on skates, a beautiful kid. After a few seconds the heaving subsided and Kyra drew back.

Shane sat up. Noel handed him the box of tissue. Shane blew and wiped. "The judges didn't catch it. They didn't disqualify me. I just didn't get a medal."

"Why?" Noel asked.

Shane took a deep breath. He stared out between Noel and Kyra. "Austin—" Shane's mouth stayed open. They waited. A whisper. "Austin told me I had to."

Kyra shivered. "But—why?"

"Because if I didn't fall he'd stop—" he sniffed a sob, "—supporting me."

They stared at him. Noel whispered, "Why did he want you to fall?"

"I don't know!" He shuddered. "I don't know."

Kyra now: "But what good did it do him if you fell in that competition?"

"I wish I knew. He said I had to fall, make it look accidental. That's all I know."

"I think you know something more than that," Noel said.

"What? What more?"

"You tell us."

Shane stayed silent. They waited. Ten seconds passed, twenty. Shane stared at the floor. He spoke but so quietly they heard no words.

Noel asked, "What did you say?

"I know something else."

"What?"

"He—wants me to fall again."

"When?"

"In September. First qualifying round." He breathed in hard, small gulps of air.

His tone acerbic, Noel said, "You won't be falling soon, not with that leg."

Shane squeezed his eyes shut. Tears seeped out. "I couldn't, I couldn't. I've been an asshole but I know what I can't do! I can't stand it!"

"He simply told you to fall, just like that?"

Shane shook his head. "When he took me on. When I was fourteen. He said one day I'd have to do something for him. He made me promise. He'd let me know when."

"And he waited, what, four years?"

Shane stared at Kyra. "Do you know how hard this is?"

"It'll get easier." Kyra could feel a great resistance in Shane, words he couldn't bring himself to say. "Just tell us all of it."

"He started pushing. A year or so ago. Then in the winter he insisted."

"But how could he insist?"

"He has the money. He bought me everything I needed. And—"

They waited. Noel prompted: "And finally you gave in."

A long sigh. "Yeah. I gave in."

"That's it? That's all."

"Isn't that enough?!"

"Is there something more you're not telling us?"

"I can't do it again!"

Noel said, "He can't make you. He can try to undercut your skating career, but he can't make you be untrue to yourself."

Shane mumbled, "Yes he can."

"Why do you say that?"

"Because I know him! I know he can."

"How?"

He closed his eyes again. "He says he can take pain away, and he's done it for me. He says he can cause pain just as easily."

"'Cause pain'? What's that mean?"

"I don't know. He's never made it clearer. 'Don't make me cause pain, Shane.'"

Noel glanced at Kyra. "Cause pain." To Shane: "Has he ever caused you pain?"

Hesitantly: "No. Not really."

"How do you mean, not really?"

"I mean no, he hasn't caused me any pain!"

Time to move on. Noel said, "Now what do you want to do?"

"What do you mean?"

"Are you going to tell your family?"

"About Austin?"

"All that you just told us."

"Do I have to?"

"It'd be best if you did. Otherwise we'll have to. At least your father, since he hired us."

Shane thought about this for a full half minute. Then he glanced from Noel to Kyra and back again. "If I do—when I do—can you both be there?"

Kyra glanced at Noel, who nodded. "It'd be best if you did this when they were all together. Say, this afternoon. In your home. We'll meet you there."

Slowly Shane nodded. "Thank you. Should I tell my parents when they drive me home?"

"That's up to you," said Kyra. "It might be easier if you only had to do this once."

Shane nodded again. "Yeah."

As if on cue, the door opened. Jason, pulling a wheelchair, crutches balanced on the seat.

"Hang in there, Shane," Kyra said. "We're getting there." To Jason she added, "Alana and Tim are in the cafeteria. Do you mind driving them over to Quadra? We've got a job to do. And then we should all meet at your house. About two?"

TEN

AUSTIN ROCKETED HIS Porsche smoothly down the driveway and came to a sharp stop, the sort he used to do on blades, slivers of ice arcing away, a bow and a little jump: his trademark. He closed the door, no thin tinny sound here, a solid comforting thonk. Everything would work out.

He found Shu-li and Steve on the deck. "Hi," Shu-li said, giving him a brilliant smile. "We're shucking oysters for Rockefeller—"

"He's coming for brunch?"

"Nit, oysters Rockefeller. My Asian twist."

Steve beamed. "Got them down below the cliff. What *richesse* you have, Austin."

"Two dozen for three people, that's enough." Shu-li stood.

Steve regarded the half shells they'd discarded. "Where do you put these?"

Austin made a dismissive gesture. "Randy chucks them back into the drink."

Shu-li picked up the bowl. "We'll eat in half an hour. You attend to libations."

"A dry white?" Austin said to Steve. They walked to the closet that Austin called his wine cellar though it was at ground level. "Vancouver Island Sauvignon." Austin presented a bottle to Steve. "Not this one, though. I have two cold." In the kitchen he took a bottle from the refrigerator, prepared an ice bucket and set the bottle in it.

Steve asked, "How is Shane?"

"The same. It'll take time. He's going to be fine."

Austin, fooling himself? "A true shame."

"Yes. But we'll work through it." Austin located a corkscrew and opened the bottle. He poured three glasses, put one by Shu-li, gave one to Steve. He toasted: "To a beautiful summer day."

They sipped, then Shu-li said, "Out. You distract me."

Steve and Austin moved to the table on the lawn.

Austin said, "How's your student doing? Graham?"

"So-so."

"He'll improve?"

"Of course. But he may not get there."

"You'll get him there. Won't you."

A threat? "I hope so. Yet—"

"Shu-li's girl's promising. She'll help."

"Shu-li thinks so. But the girl won't qualify for a year. We were counting on Shane." He sipped again. He knew Austin didn't want to hear this. "Shu-li phoned Carl."

"And?"

"Shu-li was brilliant. He's never heard of anyone getting to the Olympics without qualifying but he'll ask some pointed questions in the right places."

Austin scanned the panorama. He loved it: treetops, beach below, cliffs to the left and right. Waves breaking, seagulls squalling, flying after and above an eagle; stolen one of their babes for breakfast? "Carl's going to find a way to avoid the qualifiers. I can speed up work with Shane."

Steve put his drink down and rubbed his fingertips. "We need to have a re-think."

From the kitchen Shu-li called, "Nobody going to refresh my wine?"

At the rental car Kyra felt the seat. Nearly dry. She quartered the blanket and sat on it.

Noel got behind the wheel. "What do we know?"

"More than we did a few hours ago." Kyra blew her lips out.

"Shane may start to feel better with that off his chest."

"Confession good for the soul?"

"Sharing."

"I think there's more."

"More he hasn't told?"

"Yeah. He's been living with a lot of pressure. I think he's not out from under it."

"What makes you say that?"

"A feeling."

"Figure it out." Noel checked his watch and the ferry schedule. "Next stop Austin? Let him tell us what it's about?"

"Yeah. Maybe he's not committed a legal crime, but he's corrupted a minor."

"I think it's a crime."

"It should be. Makes me furious." Kyra's jaw clenched. "Let's get to the ferry."

Noel drove out of the lot. "We could make the noon. Unless you're hungry?"

"Not overly. If a donut passed by I'd be tempted. You?"

"I can wait."

"Onward, then."

They reached the ferry in time. Ten minutes later they drove off. Kyra said, "Do we know where Austin lives?"

"Jason pointed it out when we were looking for Tim." They headed up the hill, turned left at the shopping center where a flea market was in progress, and onto Heriot Bay Road. Something itched in Noel's mind, related to Kyra's thought that Shane was holding back. He couldn't grasp it.

Kyra asked, "You know where we are?"

On the island or in this case? "Pretty sure." After a few minutes he turned onto Hyacinthe Bay Road. "Look for a driveway with a sign OSBORNE. It's hard to miss."

"How do you want to handle this?"

"Businesslike. Tell him what we know and what Shane told us."

"Didn't someone, Linda, say he has visitors?"

"We'll find out. There it is." Above the entry a large cedar sign, OSBORNE, hung from a crossbar between two posts, each brandishing a single skate shape. Noel turned into a shaded gravel driveway. It wound a quarter mile through woods. Then the aspect opened into a broad meadow sloping toward the ocean. Another quarter mile until the house. Noel parked behind a dark blue Porsche. He wished he could remember what Shane had said that bothered him so.

Up three steps to an extensive roofed cedar deck. Around the corner of the house they found the front door and, on a small patch of lawn overlooking a stunning view of the sea between two cliffs, three people eating at a table.

Austin patted his lips with a napkin and stood. "Yes?"

"We met at the rink and the hospital." Noel repeated their names. "We have to talk."

"I'm eating with friends. I can see you later."

"Afraid not," Kyra said. "Time's running out. On all of us."

"It won't take long," Noel added. "Where can we go?"

Austin frowned, but turned to his companions. "Excuse me." He opened the door. "There's my office. Turn right."

A comfortable room with an elegant antique roll-top desk. At it a captain's chair, a loveseat to one side, a sofa to the other. Kyra sat on the sofa, Noel on the loveseat. Austin sat at the desk and turned the chair to face them. "What's this about?"

"We watched the tapes of Shane's competitions. We especially watched his fall last winter. It looked deliberate. We asked Shane. He said he'd fallen on purpose, throwing the competition. He said he did it because you pressured him into it."

"Corrupting a young man," Kyra threw in.

"He said if he didn't fall, you wouldn't continue to support him financially."

"We're asking you, Why?" Kyra finished.

"All outrageous." Austin's face remained impassive, his voice low and steely. "You know I help him focus through hypnosis? We've had sessions to prevent—*prevent*—him falling. You must have confused what he told you. Shane wouldn't suggest something so inane. But I'll speak to him. Thank you for letting me know." He stood.

Kyra wanted to choke the smug bastard, but didn't move. Noel remained seated. He said, "Shane told us that, when he was thirteen or fourteen, you said one day you'd ask him to do something he might not want to do. You waited till he was seventeen, then asked him to throw a competition. He wouldn't. You began to insist. In the end, he did it for you. It began to destroy him. And now you're insisting he do it again. That's no hypnosis misunderstanding."

Austin walked to the door and held it open. "Get out or I'll call the police."

"That would be very foolish," said Kyra.

"Very well. Make yourselves comfortable. But you're about to be thrown out."

"From now on it's simple. We know what you did. Learning why comes next."

Austin lifted the phone off its cradle and pressed a couple of buttons. "Randy, I need your help. I've got two crude detectives in my office who won't leave . . . Thanks."

Noel glanced at Kyra, who nodded. "Don't worry," he said. "We'll be back." They walked past him and out the door.

"What was that about?" Shu-li asked when Austin returned to the table. Good thing he'd finished his oysters, she thought, before he was called away. He looked a little grey.

"Shane told them I engineered the fall."

"Shit," said Steve.

"Yes." He glanced from one to the other. "They watched a tape of Shane falling. They either know a lot about skating or they had some kind of analyst with them. They accused Shane. He admitted it."

Steve plunked his fork down and stood up. His chair tottered. He steadied it.

"And—" a moment's pause, "they know we want him to fall again."

Shu-li finished her last mouthful of salad. She put her fork down. "Now what?"

Back in the car, out the driveway. Noel said, "And now?"

"Now we wait. Let him stew. He's one smooth dude."

"And a real possible danger to Shane. Someone should be with Shane at every moment for the next few days. I'll talk to Jason."

Kyra nodded. "I'd like to be a fly on the umbrella over their lunch, listening in. Think he'll tell his friends?"

"You mean, are they in on it? That's a stretch, but who knows." Noel was still searching for what Shane said that bothered him so. "Shouldn't we be getting over to the Cooper house?"

"Maybe eat first, not show up hungry. It's after one."

"There's that place in the shopping center."

"Let's go." She settled back as Noel drove. The case, at last surging ahead nicely over the past few hours, suddenly felt like a wall of mud. Waiting wasn't her favorite tactic. "What do you think he'll do? Austin, I mean."

"I don't know. But we've loosened a couple of his supports."

As, Kyra felt, something had pulled out from under her, too. The fetus was gone. Was that good? She honestly didn't know. She crossed her ankles. How really did she feel? She'd called it just a few cells, but it would have become a child. Did she want a child in her life? Now at least she wouldn't have to tell a child she didn't know who its father was. A worry gone. Save the worry for the case. "How do you read Osborne?"

"Smooth on the outside. Inside, pretty twisted."

"I bet skaters learn to create smooth. Like actors. Shane, turning on the charm at center ice. Remember Linda's comment? 'We know he knows how to smile, he does it for the world.'"

Noel wheeled into the village center and parked in front of the Lovin' Oven. They ordered sandwiches, and a salad to share. "I know it has to happen," he said, "but I'm not looking forward to Shane's confession this afternoon."

"One painful afternoon coming up. For the whole family."

"Yeah." Pain brought on by Austin. That was it! Shane had described Austin saying he could take pain away, and he could cause pain. How would Austin cause pain? Time to talk to Shane again. After he'd finished with his family.

At 1:45 they pulled into the Coopers' drive, the Corolla parked there and Derek's truck, hurtingly undriven for a while. They went into the kitchen. "Hello?" Noel called

Jason appeared. "Hello. What terrible news do you have for us now?"

"Let's talk in the living room. Linda and Alana and the boys are here?"

"Tim and Alana are on the computer. I'm making up the sofa bed for Shane so he doesn't have to climb stairs. He's practicing with his crutches. And acting odd."

Kyra, trying to lighten Jason up: "Is that something new?"

"A different kind of odd."

"Let's all go talk."

From the living room Jason called to his family. One by one they wandered in. Linda and Jason sat on the couch, Noel, Kyra and Alana on chairs, Shane in his wheelchair, Tim on the floor playing with his baseball cap. Linda offered tea. Everyone refused. They waited for Kyra and Noel to begin. Noel turned to Shane. "Go ahead."

"I have something to tell you." Shane addressed Kyra and Noel.

He sat straighter than Kyra'd seen him, his voice stronger. He explained how he'd fallen on purpose. Because Austin demanded it. Fall, or Austin would no longer sponsor Shane. "I know—I knew then—It was completely selfish of me, I know I've been an asshole. Especially this summer. But I haven't known what to do. I've been crazy." Shane teared up and blinked. "That's the reason I fell. I love skating, I want to get as good as I can. I'm sorry—" Big tears came now. "I've just ended up hurting people, everybody I care about."

Linda walked to Shane's wheelchair. She hugged him and kissed his cheek. "Sweetheart, we didn't know what pressure you were under." She hugged him again.

"Yeah, why you were being such an asshole," Tim elaborated.

With a cautioning glance at his youngest son, Jason said, "I wish you'd told us this months ago. Years ago."

How could he have, Kyra thought.

"There's more."

Linda backed away. "What?"

Shane leaked silent tears. "He wants me to fall again."

Jason stared at Shane. "I'm going to punch the fff— shit out of Osborne!"

"I'll go with you, Dad," said Tim.

Jason drove a fist into his palm three times and kicked a cupboard. "Ow!"

Linda said, "Jason. Sit down."

"We need to talk about what happens next," said Noel.

"Jesus effing Christ!" Jason straight-armed the counter. He kicked the cupboard again.

Linda put her arm around him. "Sit down. Please."

When bad things happen to good people, Kyra thought, uselessly.

"All right, now what?" Linda looked at Noel and Kyra.

Noel glanced at Alana. She sat blinking, trying not to cry. He checked Kyra: What he expected, the let's-go-for-it face.

"What do you know about Austin?" Noel asked.

"What do you mean?" Jason asked back.

"He's been around your family for years, you must know facts, impressions, whatever. What's he like?"

Tim put his cap on, twisted it front to back—

"Tim!" his mother said. "Stop with the cap."

Tim stuck it under his leg. He said, "I've always felt glad Shane dealt with Austin, not me. That's chicken of me," he looked at Shane, "but when it comes to Austin I'm a chicken. You're the brave one." Tim's tone a mixture of admiration and shame.

Kyra wanted to ask, *Why did Austin want you to do this, Shane?* Later. "What about the rest of you? Austin's been part of your lives, if indirectly."

"You're right." Linda marshaled her brain. "We couldn't understand why a man like Austin would want to contribute so much to someone he barely knew. We had serious doubts, you know, an older man, a young boy. We checked every source we could. Our friend in the RCMP got information from CSIS, from bonding agencies, even the FBI. But Austin had a perfectly clean past. Nothing negative."

Kyra glanced at the teenagers. They looked appalled.

"You did all that?" Tim squeaked.

"Do you expect," his mother said, "that either your father or I would let any of you go off with a stranger without finding out who he is?"

"So you know who he isn't." Noel kept his tone mild. "But do you know who he is?"

"We thought we did," Linda said.

Jason, beside her, took both her hands in his. "We did those checks with hockey coaches, too. Linda's right, we tried to protect our children."

Alana said, "Uh, Kyra? When I found out who he was, I googled him again. He started as a singles skater, but then moved to pairs with a woman, Tilly something—"

"Danforth," Shane supplied, his tone subdued.

Alana said, "Yeah. Pairs, that's where he got his reputation. And the Ice Follies, but that was later. They won four championships. But they had two accidents where they fell badly, and they stopped skating together."

"Good, Alana." Noël glanced about. "Anything else about Osborne?"

Silence. Linda said, "Some tea now?" A nod from Jason. Then Tim. She stood, at Shane's chair she gave him another hug, and left the room.

Noel said, "Shane."

Shane looked up.

"The big question remains. Why did Austin ask you to fall?"

Shane shook his head three times, as if he were stretching his neck. "I don't know. Thought about it, but never figured it."

Kyra picked up her purse and went to the bathroom. The bleeding had slowed, but she needed a new pad.

Noel sat beside Jason. He whispered, "For the next while Shane should always be with someone. For his own protection."

Jason looked at him, thought, and nodded. "You're right."

Noel stood and approached Shane's chair. "Let's go for a short stroll." He took the chair handles and pushed forward.

"I can do it." Shane grabbed at the wheels, turned, and rolled toward the door. "You'll have to drop it down one step."

Outside, a hot bright afternoon, Noel walked as the chair rolled. At first neither spoke. Then Shane said, "I don't know anything else. Really."

"Do you suspect anything else?"

"What d'you mean?"

"You said Austin said he could cure pain, and he could cause pain."

"Something like that."

"What kind of pain have you felt, recently?"

"You mean this leg?"

"The leg. What else?

Shane gave this a few seconds thought. "I don't understand."

"Has there been pain around you?"

"I don't know—you mean the pain I've caused my parents and brothers?—well, Timmy anyway?"

"That, yes. Any other pain?"

"I don't know. Derek maybe—but I don't know how much pain you feel in a coma." He shrugged. "I guess indirectly Derek's caused my parents and Timmy and me some real pain, wondering if he's ever going to come around again."

"Austin told you he could relieve pain but also cause it. When did he say that?"

"When? Couple of times, I think."

"The first time?"

"Maybe two-three months ago?"
"Before you fell?"
"I think so. Yeah."
"Did that scare you?"
"Scare me?"
"Do you think he meant, he could cause you pain?"
"Uhhmm—"
Noel waited.
Shane said, "It might've crossed my mind."
"Did he scare you when he said that?"
"I—can't remember." He squeezed his eyes shut. "Yeah, maybe."
"Enough to convince you that you had to fall?"
"I don't remember. Really."

Noel nodded. "The second time he said he could cause pain, when was that?"

Shane inhaled deeply and stared into the distance. "Maybe—a month ago?"

"After you told him you wouldn't deliberately fall in competition again?"

"Yeah. Right."

"A week or so before Derek was beaten?"

"About— No way, Noel. Austin wouldn't do that."

"You never thought he might have?"

"I—no, I haven't thought anything like that."

"Could you now?"

"I don't know. Shit, Austin's supported me for four years."

"At a price. A price you agreed to when you were fourteen ."

Shane said nothing.

"Think about it."

"I can't—I mean, he wouldn't. He just wouldn't."

"Lots of coincidences in the timing."

"Yeah. Maybe." He rolled himself forward. "I just don't know."

Steve Struthers got up from the table. He averted his face to keep from meeting his colleagues' eyes. He stacked the three plates and collected the cutlery. He walked them to the sink. He came back and sat again. He poured another glass of wine. He gestured the bottle to

Austin and Shu-li. Both accepted. He sipped, and sighed. "It's over, I think," he said. "It's unrescuable. It was a grand concept. But now we can never bring it about."

Shu-li glanced toward Austin. His face had darkened, now a slate tint; anger or despair, she couldn't tell. She mentally stroked his hand. A part of her said she must speak now, a part of her didn't dare. She waited for Austin to explode. But he only stared across the table at a point somewhere between her and Steve. She made herself say, "We have to talk this through."

Steve shrugged. "What's to say? We knew what we wanted. We built a scaffolding to get us there. Over the last four years we worked hard to reinforce it. We did all we could. Now is the time to simply walk away."

"You mean completely?" But it depressed Shu-li to realize she agreed with him. Her personal involvement? She'd find that hard to discard. "Hang the three of them out to dry?" She shook her head slowly. "I don't think I can, Steve."

"Do we have a choice?"

"You'd drop Graham, just like that?"

"Shu-li, when you agreed to support Miranda, a favor from the gods fell on her. What the gods provide, the gods also remove. She's had four years of training that would never have happened without you. Remember that."

Austin continued to stare.

Steve went on, "Now it will be safest if we withdraw."

"Let Harold Arensen get away with all his past evil?" Shu-li shook her head. "And whatever he might be plotting now?"

"Do we have a choice?"

"Austin, what do you say?"

Austin looked from Shu-li to Steve to Shu-li, got up and left the table. Shu-li pushed her chair back and made to stand. Steve caught her arm, shook his head. She sat again, watching Austin close the door to his study behind him.

Steve said, "He'll see he has to agree."

"You were abrupt."

"He has to be shocked into recognition. Wander around the point, you lose his attention."

"You certainly had it a few minutes ago."
"We'll see."

Austin sat at his desk and stared at the computer screen. The wallpaper, a publicity photo of Shane high in the air partway through a triple axel, his face aglow with pleasure, shone at Austin in accusation. When he'd met Shane he saw a young man who might became the champion Austin himself had been. He'd known as well, presciently, that through Shane, Austin could bring down Harold Arensen. Shane and two or three others like Shane. Through two or three others like himself.

He knew the three who could make it happen. Steve Struthers. Shu-li Waterman. Missie Kagasaki. Their fates had been parallel to his own, the ruin of their careers at the machinations of Arensen. Austin invited the three of them to Quadra Island. A day to become reacquainted: Missie and Shu-li had trained together but hadn't seen each other in five years; Steve and Missie had shared a coach for three years. Austin prepared a fine meal. They all had a good night's sleep. At breakfast the second day he told them his intention: destroy Arensen. Quick agreement: all had been devastated by the man. After discussing possible tactics, Missie wriggled uncomfortably. By noon she decided it wasn't her project. Yes, she'd like Harold punished, he'd conspired three times with four other judges to keep her off the podium. But she didn't want to replay the memory—trying to hurt Harold might mean contact with him and she couldn't bear that. She wished them luck. Could Randy drive her to the airport? Of course.

Austin had been sorry Missie had bowed out. Four were stronger than three.

That meeting set the blueprint for the next years. He, Shu-li and Steve sought the best young skaters in each of their regions—Steve in Montreal's west island suburbs, Shu-li in the Calgary area, Austin around Ottawa and on BC's lower mainland—and studied them for a year. After this each would choose the most promising for full sponsorship. With their backing, the skaters—Miranda Steele, Graham Pauley and Shane Cooper—would become, to the then head of Skate Canada, Harold Arensen, the promise of the Canadian Team. When Harold was fully enamored with these prospects, they would fulfill the contract that they'd agreed to with Steve, Shu-li, Austin. One after the other. Dominoes.

Staring at the photo of Shane on the computer, Austin recalled Shu-li's question: What's in it for the skaters? Austin had explained, first, the best training money can buy. Second, once Harold resigned, and resign he would after being accused by Skate Canada of pushing these skaters beyond their endurance into injury and depression, the youngsters would escape Harold's whims. The Quadra Cabal would not let Harold wipe out the careers of this new generation as he'd destroyed the careers of Austin, Shu-li, Steve. How, Steve asked, would Harold be so accused? Austin explained the three would employ one of Harold's own methods, create a whispering campaign. Only in their case they wouldn't have to lie as Harold had, just bring the truth to the skating community.

Harold Arensen, for reasons Austin hoped of health but cited in the press as a preference for balmy over sleet-ridden Februaries, had moved to Victoria. After only six weeks there he was offered, and accepted, the position of Honorary Chair of the Vancouver Island Skating Union. The Quadra Cabal could bring about Arensen's double fall from grace.

But now Steve asserted his protégé Graham was proceeding more slowly than they needed, and Shu-li believed that her Miranda might not be good enough.

And now Shane. The leg breaks would heal. But he'd told the detectives about the purposeful fall. Intolerable. Worse, irreversible.

Had the scaffolding broken? Would everyone learn that Austin Osborne had conspired with Shane Cooper? Likely the true reason for the pact would never become known. So the skating community would invent explanations. Austin shuddered. He knew the venom it could spit out.

Make his own statement to Skate Canada? What could he tell them? The truth might be the easiest. Would anyone believe the Quadra Cabal had conspired to bring down Harold Arensen? Surely there must be more to Shane Cooper falling than that. Some deeper and more complex machination, right? Which Austin would deny, because there was nothing else. And he would forever be accused of conspiracy.

At least there was nothing illegal in asking Shane to lose in a competition. At least he didn't think so. At least he was safe on that front. He hoped.

He stared at the photo of Shane on the screen. A beautiful skater. But Shane had betrayed him. No more support from Austin. No hope for Olympic gold.

Austin returned to the deck. The table on the lawn had been cleared. The others sat staring down at the ocean. He said, "I have to agree. The Cabal is dead."

In the bathroom Kyra sat on the toilet and shut her eyes. What she'd've liked best was not to open them again today. She brought a clean pad and a plastic bag from her purse, wrapped the used one in half a dozen tissues, dropped it in the bag and put that in her purse for later disposal. Then the tears came. At first she tried to sniff them away. No good. They glided down her cheeks, salty at the corners of her lips. Her nose too was running. She felt she didn't have the strength to reach for another tissue, for a whole bundle of tissues, no strength at all.

What the hell was wrong with her? Hormones shouldn't be that big a deal with the fetus gone. Should they? Hormones, that was the trouble. Fuck it, too much of everything. Too much of this case. They should've pushed Osborne harder, over the edge, not let him get away with— With what? What crime had he committed? What had he done they could get him on? What had she done to herself? Why were her innards so screwed up? She hated it all, this lack of control. More control now than if she'd had a baby? Her hand reached for the tissue box. She wiped her eyes and threw the tissue into the wastebasket, and found another, and one more for her nose. She had wanted to have that baby. She was glad the baby had aborted. She would have been a good mother. A mother? You crazy? No. Yes you are. No ... Another round of tears, and now the front of her head ached.

From the doorway Jason watched Shane in his wheelchair, some heavy conversation between him and Noel. He saw a brown Ford pickup come up the drive. Zeke's all-purpose. It pulled up to the house slowly; often Zeke slammed the brakes on at the last moment. The door opened. No one. At last a foot stepped down, another, and Zeke pulled himself to face Jason by holding on to the top of the door for support. Goddamn, Zeke was in pain! The bandage on his neck told a story, as did the splint across his nose. "What the hell—?" He leapt out of the doorway and caught Zeke around the waist.

Zeke flinched, went silent, then said, "We—gotta talk."

Jason helped Zeke limp toward the house. Dreadful; Zeke made a point of avoiding physical fights. "You sure you're up to walking?"

"Yeah. But not far."

"What the hell happened?"

"Hell is what happened." They stepped through the doorway.

Jason supported Zeke to a kitchen chair and gently sat him down. "Man, you sure you should be walking around?"

"I'm mostly okay. I've got to talk to you. You alone here?"

"Linda's around, the boys too. And the detectives."

Kyra, coming out of the bathroom, heard them speaking. She stopped to listen.

Zeke squeezed his eyes shut. He breathed out hard.

"You want something to drink? Ice tea?"

He opened his eyes again and smiled. "Bit of Scotch. Bit of ice."

Jason turned to the cupboard, fridge, came back with two drinks. "You should've called me, I'd've come over. You shouldn't be driving."

"Gotta talk to Timmy too. He here?"

"Yes. What about Timmy?"

"Can you call him?"

"Sure." Jason didn't like this—what did Timmy have to do with Zeke? Something about Zeke's son picking up Tim after that van hit him? "But first tell me what happened to you."

Zeke raised his glass and sipped. "There's a crazy man out there."

"Who?"

"I don't know."

"Where?"

"The village. At night. I walked past a van I didn't recognize, which should've warned me something wasn't right." He touched his neck bandage. "Guy came up and hit me with a fuckin' golf club. Four-five times, bashing me. I mean, a golf club?"

"You didn't see him?"

"Too dark. And here's the bizarre thing. He wore a mask like a skull face."

"What?"

"A Halloween mask. Scary. Except the club was even scarier."

"How'd you get away? What'd you do?"

Zeke grimaced. "Third or fourth time he hit me I grabbed the club. Don't know where the strength came from. But he had two clubs and he came at me again. I got a good bash at him and then it was like we were dueling with those fuckin' clubs."

"This is nuts."

"Tell me about it." Zeke's grimace grew. Then quickly his lips recoiled in pain. "I pulled my knife and that gave him a chance to get to the van. I tried to grab the door but I couldn't run." He sipped. "Dragged myself over to Dano's. Had to be the most hurting minutes of my life."

"You got there."

"Yeah. Dano called the doctor and he took me to the clinic. The doc checked me out. She didn't think anything was broken except my nose." He grinned, and winced. "First time since I was eleven. Then Dano drove to the hospital."

Jason's concern for Zeke kept him from noticing Tim and Alana listening from the door. When Linda came into the kitchen and exclaimed, "Zeke! My god!" he saw that others were around too. Both he and Zeke drained their glasses.

Linda's professional self knelt beside him, examining his neck. "How are you?"

"Just a broken nose. And maybe one rib chipped."

"The hospital let you out?"

Now Kyra was in the kitchen too.

"They kept me overnight. To be sure there's no concussion. There isn't."

Tim, Alana behind him, came over to Zeke's side. "Who did it, Zeke?"

"Yeah," said Zeke. "That's what I wanted to talk with you about."

"You think I had something to do with this guy?"

"When George picked you up, when that van knocked you down, did you tell him you thought there was something funny about the driver? Something about his face?"

"Yeah! He looked like a clown, a painted face."

"A mask?"

Tim thought. "Could be. Or just that his face was painted." He covered his eyes and waited. "I can't see it anymore. But I did say that."

Kyra said, "Excuse me." They all turned to her. "When Shane and I were forced off the road, I saw the man's head. It looked weird."

Jason said, "Weird how?"

"I don't remember. A flash. I was trying to control the car. Just, not a real face."

"What wasn't a real face?" Shane asked from his chair as he and Noel arrived.

Jason explained. Zeke added, "It's some crazy out there. And he's hurting people close to your dad."

Noel said, "Did you talk to the Mounties after you were beaten?"

Zeke nodded. "The doc said when someone gets mashed up without being in a bar fight she's got to call it in. I told them what happened."

"About the mask too?"

"Yeah, but it wasn't till this morning I remembered what Tim had told my George, and I came over here first 'cause I didn't want to tell the Mounties something I didn't get straight."

"Time to get back to Sam Mervin," said Noel.

The phone rang. Linda took it. "Hello ... Oh, hi Cindy ... He ... Yes ... Oh yes! ... We'll be over soon as we can ... Thank you! ..." She turned. They were all staring at her. "Derek. Cindy's with him. He's coming out"—she sniffed—"out of the coma."

"For real?" Jason was beside her, embraced her.

She spoke to him, and to the others over his shoulder: "They talked, he said, 'Hi Cynthia,' and she said 'Hi Derek' and they said a couple more things and then he closed his eyes and she took his arm and he opened his eyes again and she said, 'Are you here?' and he said, 'I'm here,' and then he said he was thirsty and she ran for a nurse and when they got back he actually took a sip of water, and then Cindy called here."

Jason released Linda. "Zeke, you okay to drive home by yourself?"

"Sure, no problem."

"Let's get to the ferry. Noel and Kyra, can you come over too?"

"We're with you," said Kyra.

As the others scrambled, Shane wheeled himself over to Tim. "Hey."

"Yeah?"

"I need a favor."

Tim suddenly distrusted Shane. What kind of favor could he do? "Yeah?"

"Come with me." Shane wheeled himself into the den.

Tim followed. "What's up?"

"I'm not going to the hospital. Can you stay here with me?"

"What the hell? Derek's coming out of the coma."

"This is important too."

"What's as important as getting Derek back?"

"This favor."

"What the hell is it?"

"Can you drive Derek's truck?"

"Of course I can!" Not having a license didn't mean he couldn't drive. "Why?"

"Tell you in a minute." Back to the living room. To Jason he said, "I'm going to stay home, Dad."

"What? With Derek coming back to life?"

"I'm exhausted. Tim said he'll stay with me—in case I need some help. Tell Derek I'll see him tomorrow."

"He'll be disappointed."

"He'll have enough of you."

"Jason, a word again." Noel drew Jason toward the kitchen.

"What's up?"

"If Derek is coming out of the coma, sooner or later he's going to remember what happened to him. That could be dangerous when whoever beat him finds out. Can you contact your Mountie friend Bryan, tell him about Derek, maybe provide him with protection?"

"Jeeze, I didn't think of that. Yeah, I'll call right away." He sighed. "I wish things could go back to how they used to be."

ELEVEN

THE HONDA FOLLOWED Jason and Linda in their Corolla. Noel said, "Strange Shane and Tim didn't want to go see Derek."

"Yeah," said Alana from the back seat. "I don't get it."

"I wonder how much Derek will remember."

"If he really is out of the coma," said Alana.

Kyra said, "We should have asked Linda to call the ward."

"We can do that if there's time at the ferry line-up." Alana took the iPhone from her backpack. "Want me to find the number?"

"I'd bet Linda has it memorized," Noel said with a smile Alana didn't see.

"Oh. Right." But she punched several buttons.

"Jason's pushing it hard." Noel accelerated, trying to keep up. The Honda screeched around a curve. Kyra grabbed the chicken handle over her door.

Alana leaned forward. "No rush. There's forty minutes till the five. We'll just be waiting in the line-up."

Kyra glanced at her watch. "She's right."

"Maybe Jason knows something we don't." He kept pace with the Corolla. "Like there's a lot of visitor traffic leaving the island late Sunday afternoon. Like there's always a possibility of an ambulance run and the whole schedule's thrown off. Like there was a convention at that place on Cortes and everybody left at the same time."

"Huh?" Alana grunted.

"Another island. You have to cross Quadra to get the ferry for Cortes."

"You do?"

"From Heriot Bay. Trip takes about forty-five minutes."

"Why would anybody want to have a convention there?"

"It's a beautiful island," said Noel.

"So is Quadra," said Alana, pushing more buttons.

Was he hearing island-fatigue in his niece's voice?

Kyra squeezed the handle more tightly and, to distract herself from the speed, said, "Something's wrong with Shane and Tim not coming to the hospital."

"Shane really looked tired," said Alana. "Like he said."

"Right, but I don't see Tim staying home too."

Noel said, "Didn't want to leave Shane alone?"

"It's not like Shane doesn't know how to be alone." Alana giggled. "He's good at it."

Kyra found herself with an increasing affection for Shane. Noel had told her about the conversation, Osborne capable of removing or causing pain. "He's been through a lot, today and in the last months." Still, odd not wanting to see Derek coming back.

They passed the village shops. As they turned to head downhill to ferry parking a minivan inserted itself between the Corolla and the Honda. One and a half lanes already full. They parked. They'd get on the ferry, but this was more than casual weekend traffic.

Noel opened his door. "I'll get Linda to call Derek's ward." He walked up to the passenger window.

Linda said, smiling while blinking away tears, "Just did. Derek comes and goes in small stretches but he's come back now four times."

"Good news," said Noel. He walked toward the ramp. What might they learn from Derek? Best not to prethink, let whatever happens happen. He stared over Discovery Passage, Campbell River on the other side, the hospital, a solution: Derek names his attacker, Triple I informs Mounties, case closed. If Derek knew the person or persons who'd beaten him, he or they would be worried Derek could identify them. But Jason had called the Mountie, Dorothy Bryan. Had Derek been in danger all this time, without protection? Indefensible. But no one had bothered him. Because Derek couldn't identify his attacker? No. Because the attacker had been masked! No coincidence. All the brothers, and Kyra, and Zeke, attacked by the same person. Austin Osborne? Noel couldn't picture it— "Noel?" Kyra at his side. "You were far away."

"Trying to work some stuff through."

"Me too. So I have an idea why Shane stayed home."

"Yes?"

"He may be going to confront Osborne."

"You think— And that's why Tim stayed home too?"

"I'd give it more than an even chance."

"I bet you're right. And if Osborne did beat up Derek and Zeke, and wiped out you and Shane, and Tim—"

"—then Shane and Tim could be in trouble."

"You really think Osborne would do them harm?"

She thought for a moment. "I do. I don't like the asshole but it's more than that."

"Okay." Now the ferry was approaching the dock. "Come on, we've got to go."

"What about Derek?"

"He didn't see the face. The guy would've worn a mask. It's the pattern."

"You're right."

"A kid with a broken leg and a fifteen-year-old boy. Not good." He turned and headed back to the car. "Alana should go with the Jason and Linda. She can take notes." At the Corolla Noel said to Jason, "Something important just came up here and we have to check on it. Take Alana and write down whatever Derek says."

"What's going on?"

"We'll tell you when you get back. No time now."

Jason noted the docking ferry. "You're not going anywhere till we start to load."

Noel looked back at the Honda. Hemmed in, front and back, nowhere to turn until the lines beside the car drove onto the ferry. "I'll get Alana." He headed back.

Jason called, "Kyra, what—" but she'd turned to follow Noel.

At the Honda Noel said to Alana, "We've got to stay here. We need you to help with interrogating Derek."

"What's happening?"

"Something we've got to do. Hop out and get in the Cooper's car."

Alana grabbed her backpack. "Is this dangerous and you don't want me around?"

Kyra said. "Don't worry. We'll tell you later. Listen carefully to everything Derek says. Take notes." Kyra could see Alana torn, her own investigative assignment against some important shift here that she wouldn't be part of.

Alana frowned at them. Finally she said, "Okay." She flung her pack on her shoulder and started to the Cooper car. She turned. "Be careful."

They watched as she got in the back seat. Arriving foot passengers and a few cars had finished off-loading. So slowly. Come on, come on! Departing foot passengers walked on. The row beside them began to roll. It emptied. Noel pulled into the empty line and accelerated ahead. Honks from the cars ahead of him—a line crasher! But they stopped when he U-turned and headed back up the hill.

"Straight to Osborne's?"

"We need to know, are we being paranoid." A shiver sped down his back.

Faster than their drive to the ferry they were back at the Cooper house. They walked quickly from the car, Noel shouting, "Shane! Tim?" several times. No response. Kyra, her head through the doorway, did the same. Silence. Noel looked around. "Linda's car is here but Derek's truck's gone."

Derek had let Tim drive the Mazda half a dozen times, but only on Gowlland Harbour Road and with Derek in the passenger seat. Nearly the same now, just a different brother. Except the pickup felt strange. Maybe because it was Derek's without Derek. Maybe lots of things. He wanted to be in Derek's room, see his brother's eyes open, talk to him, hear him. He wanted to be there with the rest of the family. But Shane needed him. That's what Shane had said: "Timmy, I need you to help me." He couldn't remember a time when Shane had admitted he needed Tim. He'd even used the word when he'd told their parents he was wiped, he'd see Derek tomorrow, all was going to be okay with Derek, today he'd feel better if he could be by himself, but would it be okay if Timmy stayed home just in case Shane needed anything.

Tim could tell his parents had found it a bit crazy, Shane and Tim not wanting to visit Derek in the hospital. But they'd let it go and left. Now here he was behind the wheel, Shane with his crutches beside him. He glanced over. Shane stared ahead. He'd not said much since they'd gotten into the pickup, just "Thank you" when Tim had boosted him into the seat, and a minute ago, "I appreciate this, Timmy."

At West Road Tim asked, "It's left, isn't it?"

"Yeah. Then left at the fork."

Tim felt a bit scared about this mission. He didn't know what Shane wanted to do, to say to Austin. Curse the man for forcing him to fall while skating? For insisting he do it again? Shane looked angry. Hit Austin with his crutches? "What's your plan?"

"No plan. I've got to ask him some questions, that's all."

And if Austin didn't answer? "What kind of questions?"

For seconds Shane stared ahead. Then, "If he was the one who beat up Derek."

The pickup lurched to the middle of the road. Tim felt as if he'd been slapped. Did Shane really think that? "You're simply going to walk in there and ask him?"

Shane closed his eyes. "There won't be anything simple about it."

Tim drove on. Austin beating up Derek? It didn't make sense. Tim didn't like Austin, but he couldn't imagine a smooth guy like him bashing anybody. "Shane?"

"Yeah?"

"What makes you think he'd do that?"

Shane thought for a moment. "Because he can."

"Huh?"

"I think it's how he works. He can heal, he can cause pain."

"Oh." But Tim didn't understand. Cause pain? Well, with words and while the victim wasn't looking, okay. But Derek's body had been badly beaten. Like Zeke. With a weapon in somebody's hands. And what would Austin say—do, even—when Shane asked? Because this'd be more than a question, it'd be an accusation. He tried to picture the scene—which was hard since he'd never been to Austin's house. But in his mind he saw a huge Austin looming high above Shane and a tiny Shane on crutches, Shane staring up at his sponsor. "Are you scared?"

Very slowly Shane nodded. He looked at Tim. "Of what he might say. And of what happens next."

"Oh. Yeah."

"But the first thing I have to do is ask why he wanted me to fall."

"Yeah, that'd be a good question too." Safer, too. Now the fork, the left branch. "This way, right?"

"Yep." And in a whisper, "To Austin Osborne's house."

Tim thought he saw Shane shudder.

A few minutes, and Shane said, "It's ahead. That drive there."

The driveway to the Osborne land couldn't be mistaken. Above the entry a large cedar sign, OSBORNE, hung from a crossbar between two posts. On either side of the name, the outline of a man's skate. The driveway, a tunnel in the woods, trees meeting overhead, branches on all sides, squeezed in on Tim. The gravel crunched beneath the tires for at least a couple of hundred meters as if it were dry bones. "How far's the house?"

"Pretty close now."

The trees stopped at a large sloping field, a house halfway down. Where the green field ended, the blue sea sparkled. Tim felt relieved. From here the house and view were pretty. He drove on. He stopped, got out, came around and helped Shane hobble down, handed him his crutches and let him go first. He didn't know how scared Shane really felt, but for himself his guts were trembling. They walked along the path to steps leading up to a covered deck. Tim helped Shane lurch up onto it. He led the way around a corner to the front door. Shane knocked. They waited. Tim wished they'd never come.

―――

At least Gowlland Harbour Road was halfway to Osborne's house. Up to West Road, left to Heriot Bay. Noel was getting to know this route well.

―――

The door opened. Austin Osborne, larger than life. "Shane! What a pleasant surprise. Come in. And hello, Timmy. Welcome."

"Hello Austin," said Shane. Tim stayed silent.

Austin let the brothers walk past him, watched as Shane hopped on one foot and the crutches, and shut the door. Immediately Tim felt trapped. Stop that, he told himself. Just because you don't like Austin, there's no reason to be frightened. Yet.

"We'll go to my study," said Austin. "I have guests in the living room." He led them along a hallway, opened a door and stood aside as Shane and Tim passed. He shut the door. Pulling it tight, Tim noticed. "Please have a seat."

They both sat on a sofa. Austin took a chair on the far side of his desk—his throne, Shane knew it to be. "How's the leg, Shane?"

"Healing, I hope."

"Good. It'll be easier to work on it now you're back on Quadra." He noticed Tim glance out the window, from the fine view of the ocean down the cliff at the bottom of the field, up to the right and left where the land at the edge of the forest was covered with salal and Oregon grape. "Yes, Timmy, beautiful, isn't it? But distracting. To get any work done, I need to keep my back to the view." He smiled. "Now, what can I do for you?" He looked from Shane to Tim. Both remained silent. Austin waited. "Shane?"

Shane stared at the desk between them. At last he raised his eyes to Austin's neck. "I have to ask you a question."

"Yes?" Austin's smile deepened.

"When you told me to fall. Why? Why did I have to do that, Austin?"

Austin's smile lingered until disappearing like the Cheshire cat's. "You asked me that then, Shane."

"And you wouldn't answer." Red splotches covered Shane's cheeks.

"Do you remember what I said? I told you not to question this. Just do it, I said. It's for your career. In the long term, this is important. And you asked me again, Why? And I said one day I'd be able to tell you. And you did as I asked. Which was good, Shane. Then and still now."

"So when are you going to tell me?!"

Veins on Shane's temples were throbbing. Tim hoped his brother wouldn't cry.

"I'll tell you now if you insist, Shane. Would you like a glass of water?"

"Fuck the water! Tell me!"

"Very well. To keep your career from being ruined by Harold Arensen."

For Tim all sound and all motion faded from the room. How could anyone ruin Shane's career? Tim had heard about Arensen, the head of the skating association. What did Arensen have to do with Shane? Why would he meddle with Shane's skating?

But Shane seemed to grasp what Austin had said. "You mean like he ruined you."

"Like that," said Austin.

"But I don't understand. How does my falling save me?"

"He's doted on your skating since he first met you. He sees you taking giant strides toward what he believes will be perfection. In his eyes, you do nothing wrong."

"So—I had to commit a big mistake?"

"In his eyes, you now have been blemished."

"You mean, one more fall and he'd never bother with me again?"

Austin nodded. "Exactly."

Now Shane looked straight at Austin. They locked eyes. Tim watched as Austin nodded slowly. Was this some kind of hypnotic move? Tim looked away from Austin and said to Shane, "He's full of bullshit."

Austin turned to Tim. "Fortunately, you're wrong."

"How can Arensen ruin Shane, anyway?"

"Harold Arensen has ways of harming a skater's career that have never occurred to anyone else. He chooses his method according to each of his victims. What would he do to Shane? I don't know. And I don't want to find out. I only want to protect Shane."

Shane let out a heavy breath, as if he'd been holding it. Maybe he had, Tim thought. Shane said, "Why didn't you tell me back then?"

"You don't need to deal with such problems, Shane. That's why I'm here. Your training is important. That's what you need to give your total concentration to."

Shane didn't respond. His shoulders slouched.

"What?"

"I don't know, Austin. I don't know."

"What don't you know?"

"Anything."

"But I know. You head home now and spend the day relaxing. Tomorrow we'll get back to work healing your leg. Okay?"

Shane nodded, and reached for of his crutches. "I guess." He started to stand—

"Shane."

Shane glanced at his brother.

"There was another question."

"I—I don't know, Tim . . ."

The study door burst open. Noel, with Kyra behind him. They glanced around the room. Noel said, "Are you guys okay?" He stepped up to Austin's desk. Tim sprang from the couch.

"What is this?" Osborne, now leaning across his desk. "Get out of here! Now!"

"We're fine," said Tim.

"You have no right to break into my house! Who let you in? Leave! Right now."

Tim said, "Austin. They stay."

Kyra and Noel glanced at Tim. Solid authority in that voice. Noel backed away from the desk and stood beside Kyra.

Tim said, "I was just about to ask Austin a question."

Austin sat down. "Ask away. Then all of you leave."

Shane said, "Maybe—maybe not now."

"Now." Tim leaned onto the desk. "Austin, did you beat up Derek so badly he's still in a coma?"

Austin's head jerked to the side, all his attention on Tim. "What did you say?"

"You heard me. You beat up Derek. Why?"

"You're being ridiculous. I would never beat up anybody."

"Except Derek's in a coma and I think you put him there."

"That's a very serious accusation, young man."

Kyra took a step toward Tim. Noel grasped her arm, holding her back.

Austin went on, "Be careful about repeating that. You could get in deep trouble."

"Austin, you're—you're—" Tim could feel himself already deep in trouble. Austin was right, they'd better leave now. "Shane, we're out of here."

Austin walked around the desk to Tim. "Listen to me, Timmy. I could no more beat up Derek than I could—than I could harm you. You've known me for four years. Do you really think I could beat someone up like that?"

No, Austin was right. Tim had known personal violence wouldn't be Austin's way. Yet Tim knew Austin was responsible for Derek's coma. And not by flinging words at Derek. Maybe—words to someone else? Had Austin paid someone to beat Derek up? Austin paid people to get things done. Had he—oh wow! Yes! "You wouldn't do it yourself. You'd get someone to do it."

Slowly Austin shook his head. "Now you really are going too far, Timmy. This is completely ridiculous. You and Shane have to leave now."

"No, not just someone." Tim knew now. It made total sense. "Randy. You got Randy to kick the shit out of Derek. Didn't you? Didn't you!"

"Shane, take your brother and go." He faced Kyra and Noel. "And you two as well."

"You did, didn't you?"

Austin shook his head. "I never ever would do such a thing." Sadness in his voice.

Tim heard the lie. "Come on, Shane, let's ride."

Shane shuffled to his feet, held himself supported with the crutches, and turned to the door. Tim held it open and they both passed through, Kyra and Noel behind them.

Austin followed the little parade. "Shane, I'll see you tomorrow. Timmy, take care of your brother. He'll be much better very soon. And you please watch your tongue. You don't want to say slanderous things in public."

Shane stepped outside. "So long, Austin."

Tim thought, *if that guy uses "Timmy" one more time I'll strangle him.* But Austin said nothing. Tim couldn't stop himself from adding, "Anyway, Derek's come out of the coma and he'll tell us who beat him up. We'll know soon, Austin." He put his arm around Shane's waist when they reached the steps and helped him down.

Austin closed the door and walked back to his study. He wasn't prepared to talk with Shu-li now, let alone Steve.

From bad to terrible. A dangerous accusation. That Timmy should think Austin Osborne capable of hitting someone, again and again.

Yes, he'd been angry when Shane refused to commit himself to a second fall. But that was normal. Angry because Shane didn't understand it was for his own good, for the safety of his splendid career.

Back then, a month, six weeks ago? Austin had felt thoroughly despondent. He had thought about picking up the phone, calling Shu-li. He didn't, not because someone might overhear, just... it wasn't the kind of conversation for the telephone. You speak face to face when worrying about plans going awry. Too much could be misunderstood if you couldn't watch the other person's expression.

He'd had no one to talk to. Need to think, need to think. He'd plucked some mint from the garden and found the cucumber in the fridge. He'd cut himself a spear, mint at the bottom of the glass, poured in the Pimms, dropped the cuke into the liquid. Randy knew how Austin liked his drink, always made sure to stock the refrigerator with fresh cucumber. He'd sat in front of the fire and let his mind wander. Shane must fall one more time, this was imperative.

When Randy had arrived Austin was into his third Pimms. "Randy, come join me, make yourself a drink."

"Thanks, Austin." He'd poured a Scotch and joined Austin by the fire. They talked of the projects Randy had worked on while Austin was back in Ottawa—the new flagstone walkway, the deck's roof repairs, replacement to a section of fence that kept the deer out. Randy was good at seeing what needed doing. So it seemed natural to speculate about Shane, the need for Shane to act as he was told. For his own good, of course. Sometimes one had to be taught a lesson, Austin hypothesized. "Don't you think so?"

"Yep, that's sometimes necessary."

"Of course we have to be careful with Shane. He's a valuable person. He shouldn't come to any harm."

"Yeah, that'd be terrible."

"Really terrible." A weariness to Austin's words: "He's sometimes so thick. I've warned him, if he doesn't follow my directions to the letter, someone might get hurt."

"That'd be bad."

"But he's doing just that."

"Just what?"

"Not following directions."

"Yeah. That's not good."

"So he has to be taught a lesson. He doesn't get it when I tell him things directly."

Randy had nodded. "Maybe he could figure it out indirectly."

Austin sipped his Pimms. "Maybe. Yes, maybe."

That was all. They'd each had another drink. Later Austin grilled himself a small steak and baked a sweet potato, he remembered. A couple of days later he headed back to Ottawa. Not until he'd talked to Shane a few weeks later did he learn how terribly Derek had been beaten.

And what now, with Timmy shooting off his mouth? Wild guesses. Stupid Randy. And the boy in the hospital, out of the coma. What if he figures out who hit him?

The four gathered at Derek's truck. Noel said, "That was a crazy, confronting Osborne, just the two of you."

"Scary," said Tim, "but not crazy. We learned something."

"You learned what you should have figured before, that Austin wouldn't tell you anything, just try to frighten you off."

"He told us why he wanted Shane to fall while competing. Before you came in."

"He did?" Kyra asked. "Why?"

Tim glanced at Shane, who said, "He was trying to save me from Harold Arensen."

"What do you mean, save?"

Shane repeated what Austin had told him. "And, I think, it's a kind of revenge for Austin. He wants to ruin Arensen's reputation."

Noel said, "That makes no sense."

"It's how Austin thinks. He makes these connections in his head and everything that follows from them is logical. In his terms."

"I don't get it," said Kyra.

"Tim," said Noel, "tell me about Randy. Who is he?"

"Oh, just a guy. He works for Osborne, all kinds of jobs around the house. He worked for my dad a couple of years in the woodlot. He gives me the creeps."

"Because of how he looks?"

"How he acts, how he moves. Sort of—stealthy, almost."

"What's he look like?"

"Normal. Taller than Austin. Maybe thirty-five, forty." He tried to image Randy. "He's strong, got big shoulders."

"And you think Randy hurt Derek on Osborne's orders?"

Tim nodded. "I'd bet on it."

Austin Osborne, standing on the top step: "Go! Leave!"

"Come on," said Noel. "Let's reconvene at your parents' place."

Tim and Shane drove together from the Osborne house, followed by Kyra and Noel. "Well," she said, "that was a show."

"Yeah, like opening Pandora's box."

"Dangerous for Derek?"

"Yes. But I told Jason to get a guard posted at Derek's door." They turned onto Hyacinthe Bay Road. "You believe Tim's right, that it was Randy who beat up Derek?"

Kyra considered this. "It's a hypothesis. Maybe we've found our black hats."

"What about that crazy reason for Shane falling?"

"It seems—I don't know. So minimal. Such a little thing causing such a mess. He wasn't even trying to fix a competition."

Noel's cell phone buzzed. Ah, network contact. He took the phone from his pocket, read call display. "Alana."

"You shouldn't talk on the phone while driving."

He scowled at her and pressed Talk. "Hi."

"Hi. I'm here just outside Derek's room. He's waking, then going back under. He's been doing it for the past couple of hours, Cindy says."

"He saying anything?"

"Some words. Not making a lot of sense. At least not to me."

"His parents understanding any of it?"

"They're just glad he's making sounds. Linda acts like he's back all the way."

"How're you doing?"

"I'm fine. Shorty was here when we arrived. He just left. You two okay?"

"All in control. Should we come over?"

"Not much going on."

"Okay. Keep in touch." He flipped the lid closed and reported to Kyra. She seemed off somewhere inside her head. They followed Derek's truck as it turned right toward the woodlots, and down the drive to the Cooper house. A couple of hundred feet behind the now parked truck, Kyra touched Noel's arm. "Stop here."

He squinted at her, braked and came to a halt. "What's up?"

"Randy. If he beat up Derek, who knocked Tim off the road and pushed me into the ditch? No, don't answer, I'll tell you. Randy. And Randy again beating up Zeke. The death's head mask. And Tim thought he saw a clown driving the van. Another mask."

"And it's all Randy..."

"And Osborne's giving the orders."

"But why Tim?"

"To push Shane into obeying Osborne. However ridiculous you and I think it is."

"Derek too?"

"That's where it all began. At least for Jason and Linda."

"And the Honda, that was because Randy or whoever thought I was in there with you. Why would Randy want to get rid of us?"

"Because Osborne thought we were learning too much about who beat up Derek."

"He sure was wrong there. If Tim hadn't been knocked off the road, we'd be nowhere." He sighed. "Okay, how do we test this hypothesis of yours?"

"We ask Randy."

"To admit it?" He was not liking Kyra's tactics, not at all.

"To see how he reacts."

"Whoever wiped out Zeke and Derek's a powerful guy. If it's Randy, I can predict how he'll react."

"There're two of us. And I've got my Mace. Let's go talk to him."

"You know where he lives?" Maybe they wouldn't find him.

"Tim and Shane will."

Noel accelerated and stopped behind the truck. Tim was still helping Shane get down. Yes, Shane knew where Randy lived—in a cabin on Austin's land. A left turn as you leave the heavy wooded area, along a small dirt road. "You going to confront him?"

"We just want to talk to him," said Noel.

Tim said, "If he's the one who wiped out Derek—"

"We'll be careful." Kyra said. "If we're not back by nightfall, send out the dogs."

Noel turned the car around and headed out the drive. "Back to where we came from."

"Not quite. A new bit of the geography."

"I don't get it. Osborne has a crazy notion about saving Shane from this guy Arensen, and it sets off a chain reaction." They were asking for trouble, he could feel it.

Not stupid Randy. Dangerous Randy. Shane's little brother, too smart by half, was he going to blab? Austin didn't think so. Timmy'd be scared of making accusations he couldn't prove. Kid shouldn't be spouting out wild guesses. Next thing, he'll try to use his hypothesis to explain everything that goes wrong. Randy didn't like those detectives, Austin had seen that. Especially the man. Had Randy noticed Austin's aversion to the flaming snoop? Randy often read Austin's sense of things. Certainly had that afternoon, last time Austin was here, the two of them with the Pimms. Used the older brother to show what could happen. Except, if the older brother could identify Randy— No, Randy would never allow that to happen, it was dark, he'd have been disguised—

Then Austin heard, inside his head, Timmy shout to anybody who'd listen that Randy had driven the van that pushed the detectives' car off the road, that Randy had brought on the accident which broke Shane's leg. That Randy was responsible for Shane not making the Olympics.

Wait. Don't give credence to the kid's wild guesses. Randy wouldn't dare injure the prodigy, he knew how valuable Shane was to Austin. He wouldn't have the guts to—

Not the guts. The malice? Possibly. Malevolence. He'd seen Randy angry. Those times Austin had confronted Randy about his gambling, his fury got mean. Turned against Austin who was trying to help Randy, keep him out of trouble. Betting on a skating competition, for godsake! With a Canadian bookie, so stupid. And Randy must've known that. Too bad Austin had to find out the way he did.

Which meant Timmy's voice in Austin's head might be making a too-good guess. Randy, responsible for Shane's injuries. Not a hypothesis to be carried around without testing. He reached for the telephone and pressed in Randy's pre-set number. Randy picked up. "Would you come over to the house? ... A drink together ... Half an hour? Fine." He broke the connection. Thirty minutes to explain his fears to Shu-li and Steve.

Noel had driven past the road taking off to the left both times he'd gone to the Osborne house without it registering. Now, there it was. He spun left onto the dirt track, smooth for the first hundred or so feet, then suddenly rutted. Forest to the left, high brush to the right, terrible road surface. Likely in the spring tires sank into mud here, leaving these indented furrows. Noel drove slowly, right tires on the verge, left on the hump in the middle of the troughed road. "Bet Randy drives a truck with big wheels."

"Or a jeep. Or maybe he doesn't take this road at all."

"Shane didn't suggest another way of getting in."

"Maybe he didn't know of it."

Noel concentrated. A raised ridge scraped at the undercoat. Just a rented vehicle, no problem. Slowly the track flattened again; a less wet area? The furrows disappeared giving place to two- and three-foot deep potholes. Now the road was relatively straight but it rose and fell twice, and again. The brush on the right crowded in, making it hard to see what lay ahead. Maybe half a mile later, around a small curve, the land opened into a large clearing. At its center stood a small cabin, cedar-sided like Osborne's house. Beside it, a Ford truck.

"As you predicted," said Kyra.

Noel parked the Honda on the thin grass beside the truck. Beyond the truck the brush had been cut back, leaving a view of the sea below what looked like an extension of Osborne's cliffs. "We go say hello?"

"We do."

"And then we ask him why, rather than if, he attacked Derek?"

"We do."

"Pretty brazen, aren't we."

"We are."

"And if he's got a weapon?"

"There're two of us, one of him."

"And your Mace."

"And my Mace."

Kyra grabbed her purse and led the way along a dirt pathway to two steps rising to a railing-free wooden deck. Gracing the deck to the right, a table and two chairs, one white plastic, the other a large cedar. To the left an old barbecue. The door had a window starting at waist level. She stepped up and knocked. No answer. Another knock. Nothing. With cupped hands she shaded her eyes and looked in.

"Anything? Anybody?"

"Living room, couple of closed doors. Nobody there. Let's look around back."

Noel could already feel himself not liking what she'd be up to in a minute, but he followed. The side of the cottage featured a few cared-for plants, some with knobby purple flowers, some orange lilies. At the back another deck, same as in front, more plastic chairs and table. No barbecue here. He glanced up at the sun. Likely the front faced west, good sunset evenings while Randy grilled his steak. From beyond the cliff came a dull roar, ocean beating against rock.

Kyra glanced through a window. A bedroom maybe, the bed a folded-out couch. She knocked on the door. No answer again. She turned the doorknob and pushed. The door opened. "I'm going to take a look inside. See what's in his medicine cabinet."

"Kyra, you know I don't—"

"Quiet. Just stay here and give me warning if Randy shows."

"Do I have to tell you every time that I can't stand it—?"

"Not every time or any time. Your job is to stand guard." She opened the door the whole way. "Randy?" No response. She stepped inside, leaving the door ajar.

He sighed. One day she'd get them in real deep shit. Usually her investigative methods were sane. But her natural instinct to snoop, to break and enter—okay, the door had been open this time—always gave him the shudders. He pulled himself straight and returned to the side of the cabin to spot anyone approaching without immediately being seen. He stared to the right where Osborne's house would be. No building visible.

In the living room/kitchen Kyra found a sink with dirty dishes, empty pizza boxes, frozen dinner packages, a cereal carton in the garbage. Beer cans, unwashed from the smell, whisky bottle, pop cans, two wine cartons in the recycling box. On the table an unfinished bowl of tomato-like soup. In the fridge, milk gone sour, leftovers from the frozen dinner packs, five part-emptied bottles of ketchup, unwrapped stale bread. More or less clean plates and bowls in the cupboards. On the living room end a fireplace, its glass screen blackened. Two stuffed chairs, one with the padding escaping from an arm. A footstool. Nothing on the walls except a color photo of a man over a caption, Randolph Dubronsky: Employee of the Month. Eyes close together, a stubby nose. A smile on the right side of his mouth. A stealthy smile?

In the bathroom, a dirty tub behind a plastic shower curtain, hair and soap particles clogging the drain. A dirty towel hung from a rack. In the medicine cabinet, four bottles of patent medicines, toothpaste and a brush. A dildo. A package of condoms. She suddenly felt lightly nauseated. She lay her hand on her belly and breathed deeply. A smell of old food hung in the air. An open package of latex gloves under the sink. Hmm.

On to the bedroom. The unfolded couch, sheets rumpled. A closet: shirts, pants, sweaters, shoes. A chest with three drawers. In the top, three packages of women's black knee-high stockings. Double hmm. Beneath them two heavy white plastic bags held closed with a drawstring. She opened one. Aha. Masks. Around-the-whole-head masks. A clown mask with a bulbous yellow nose, a red-white-blue painted face. Bingo! A Ronald Reagan mask, bushy eyebrows, real scary. A Donald Duck mask, complete with protruding bill. In the second bag, a Lone Ranger mask tied over a Lone Ranger face. The mask of a pink and white bear, its huge tongue lolling down to its chin. A skull mask, with grisly red tears running across the cheeks. "Noel!" No answer. "Noel!"

He heard her call. It sounded muffled. He ran around the corner of the house and stopped hard. "Oh my—" Kyra's body, but a black and white death's head staring at him as if the skull had swallowed the torso and was now disgorging it. He squeezed his eyes shut. Opened them. Kyra's grin, eyes and black curls appeared from behind the mask she was holding in two tissue-protected hands. "For cat-sake, Kyra!"

She'd wanted to wear it to shock Noel, but the ideas of pulling on the stinky plastic and of contaminating evidence stopped her. Still, Noel's reaction was gratifying. "See what I found?"

"Like in Zeke's story."

"Like that. And a clown mask from Tim's story."

"And now?"

She took out her iPhone. "I call Sam Mervin, he comes over to search the place—"

"And you tell them you entered Randy's home illegally and contaminated whatever evidence there might be here?"

She thought for a moment. "Okay, I call 911 and say we saw a guy beating up a woman, and he was wearing a skull mask. That should intrigue the Mounties."

"That's a lie. Just tell them to check. Do it anonymously. And we get ourselves out of here right away, okay?" He headed up to the car, Kyra phoning behind him. She finished and stowed it. Noel, impressed she'd found a signal here.

"We're going to Osborne's."

"Again? Why?"

"Where do you think Randy is?"

"What makes you think—?"

"His truck's here. He's not gone far. And I didn't see him tanning himself."

TWELVE

RANDY WALKED THE cliff trail, a path he enjoyed. When it rained he took the truck, or if he needed it after leaving Austin's. No rain today—a first-rate late afternoon, the sky clear except for sea haze to the south. Now to Austin's for a drink. Which was first-rate too. Steve Struthers would be there, too bad. Steve was a loser, unclear what kind but a loser for sure. Except without Steve there'd be little chance of Shu-li being around, they arrived together, two eggs in a nest. Didn't stay together, Shu-li was Austin's girl. Though recently he'd seen tension there. Which was fine.

    He stopped to stare at the sea, sixty-five feet below. The strong wind had given a dramatic surge to the waves. Maybe today a little background drama was a good thing. Usually here the channel, protected by Read Island up north and Cortes to the east, rippled more smoothly. He'd showered and put on clean clothes: black skivvies, yellow shirt, comfortable jeans, socks and sandals. Even a shave; wouldn't do to say hello to pretty Shu-li with yesterday's plus today's five-o'clock shadow. He patted the snippet of toilet paper on his neck where he'd cut himself. Dry, so he pulled it off. He touched the wound; yep, scabbing had started. He dropped the paper. The wind carried it inland.

    Even though Austin hadn't been specific, he'd invited Randy so he could show his appreciation in a ceremonial way. More than just a pat on the back. Hadn't been time for thanks since Austin got here, what with Shu-li and Steve arriving. Randy valued the invitation. Because Austin had reason to thank Randy, partly for all the jobs done that Austin didn't even know about, mostly for all those indirect requests. That was Austin's reason for calling Randy to come over now. Likely they'd ask him to stay for supper. Hot damn. Throw some charm in Shu-li's direction. Maybe sit next to her, or across from her and he'd look into her eyes. And she into his. If beside her, their hands could touch under the table. She'd understand. He'd tell her about his cabin, neat little place, she should visit. He'd show her around. Hell! What if she decided to come this evening? Place was a mess, a while since he'd cleaned up. But if she was so eager to see it she'd put up with the mess. In his living room he'd take her hand and hug her and they'd kiss deep. Or maybe she'd make the first move, run her fingers along his fly. Yeah! Either way, soon their clothes would be off and he'd see her naked like last fall from in the garden when she'd been in her room with the window open, running her hands down her little tits and nice curvy hips and sweet ass, having a great time. Man oh man. If Austin hadn't been a couple of rooms away— Man oh man.

Maybe. Maybe she'd tell Austin, Austin, I want to spend time with Randy. And maybe Austin would object. And she'd say, No, it's my life and I'd like to spend part of it with Randy. If Austin got tough, Randy would take her side, tell Austin he didn't control the lady, she'd do what she wanted. If he got rough? Randy could fix that. And maybe the fixing wouldn't be so nice. What it'd feel like, hurting Austin? He didn't want to hurt Austin. But sometimes you got to choose. Randy knew which way that choice would go.

He reached the dip in the path where it sloped to the little sandy bay. On the other side more cliffs, but down the trail Austin had easy access to the sea. Great place for a house, protected by cliffs, a lowland cut between them. Now the sea lay quiet, as if muffled by the cliffs on either side. Randy checked the razor cut on his neck. Crusting over well. He combed his hair back with his fingers, stepped onto the deck, walked around to the front door. He was after all a guest—no entering via the kitchen today.

"Come in." Fifty minutes ago Austin had said, half an hour. Randy was getting too casual.

"Hiya, Austin. Havin' a good afternoon?"

"Fair to middling."

"Yeah?"

"Come in to the living room." Austin led the way, Randy directly behind, a dog showing deference.

In the living room sat Shu-li wearing a yellow dress, hem at her knees, arms bare, and string sandals. Steve reclined on the sofa, black Hawaiian shirt rich with red and yellow butterflies, shorts and bare feet. Randy said, "Hey, Steve," and nodded in his direction. He turned to Shu-li and smiled broadly. "Hello, Shu-li. You're looking lovely."

She gave him a small smile. "Thank you." She sipped from a glass of clear liquid.

Randy noted Steve too held a glass, stubbier than Shu-li's, containing brown liquid and ice. "That looks good. I'll have whatever Steve is drinking."

Austin stared at him. Randy looked different. Changed body shape, unusual demeanor, more confidence? How to deal with this? Randy'd said he'd have what Steve had? Austin had asked him to come for a drink. Had Randy done all he was accused of?

"Glenfiddich on the rocks okay?"

"Great. Yeah."

At the bar Austin picked up a glass, dropped two ice cubes in, poured a finger of whiskey and handed it to Randy. Randy scowled at it, a tiny drink. "Thanks, Austin."

"Have a seat." He gestured to the sofa in front of Steve.

"I like to stand while I drink." Randy glanced from Austin to Steve, then let his eyes rest on Shu-li. She remained impassive. "Cheers, everybody." No one moved a glass in return. Randy sipped, walked over to the fireplace and set his glass on the mantelpiece.

"Randy," Austin said, "We want to talk to you." He walked over to the other side of the mantle.

Randy shrugged. "Whatever, Austin."

"Did you beat Derek Cooper to a pulp?"

Holy shit. This wasn't going right. What the hell was Austin doing? And what was he supposed to say? With these two here? Did he have Shu-li's attention? Time to turn on the charm? Damn well better. If Austin wants it this way, this is how it's gonna be.

The right side of Randy's mouth rose, a smile Austin recognized. Randy's finagling smile. "Did you want me to beat up Derek Cooper?"

"What kind of question is that?"

"Same as your kind. If you wanted me to beat up Derek Cooper then I did. If you didn't want me to, then I didn't. Okay?"

"It's a straightforward question."

"It's not a straightforward situation though, is it?"

An exasperated sigh from Austin. "You've worked for me for four years, right?"

"Yep. Plus a few months."

"You've done many helpful things."

"I hope so."

"Sometimes even when I didn't ask for them, right?"

"I know you, Austin. I know what you need right then and what you're gonna need tomorrow. That's what you hired me for, right?"

"Yes, well, I often—"

"You're not here, off wherever, something's got to get done, it gets done."

"Very good. Now, did you beat up Derek Cooper?"

"You wanted him beaten, boss, he got beaten." Yes, he'd caught Shu-li's interest. He gave her a large seductive smile.

"The Honda with the detective woman driving, did you force it off the road?"

"Hey! You worried about the detectives. Scare 'em, you said, scare 'em good."

"I never said anything like that. Never."

"Not out loud. But I heard you."

Austin squeezed his eyes shut. "My god." He opened them and glanced about the room. Steve and Shu-li hadn't moved. They looked as shocked as he wanted to look himself. He'd been right—a new kind of Randy, emerged while Austin wasn't around. A devious Randy. "You understand what you've done?"

"Everything you wanted done, boss."

"I wanted? You think I wanted Shane's leg broken? Are you out of your mind!?"

"Hey, Austin, I only—"

Austin threw the contents of his glass at Randy's face. "You bastard!"

Randy swiped at the liquid. "I thought it was the other detective. I didn't know Shane was in there. You can't talk to me like that." He sipped his drink.

"I can and I will! Steve, Shu-li, you heard Randy admit he beat up Derek, and hurt Shane and the detective. Right?"

Steve looked at Shu-li. She nodded and said somberly, "Yes, we did."

Austin stared at Randy as he said, "Steve, in my study call 911. Tell the operator to send the Mounties here."

Randy stared at Austin. "You crazy?"

"Never less crazy in my life. Steve?" Austin cocked his head.

Steve leapt up and started for the study.

Randy grabbed the poker from the fireplace, held the handle in his right hand and patted the shaft against his left palm. "Forget it, Steve. Stay right there."

Steve sat again. "Take it easy, Randy. Austin's just joking."

"You jokin', boss?"

Austin took a step toward Randy—

Randy threw the ice from his glass at Austin. "Stay right there, boss."

Austin, with deliberate slowness, wiped at the wet spot on his shirt. Calm. "Not joking at all. You have destroyed my finest creation. You have undone the career of Shane Cooper." And then he screamed, "You think I'd joke about destroying Shane?!" He turned on his heel. "Steve, keep him right there. I'll call the cops myself." He headed for his study.

Randy started after him. Steve grabbed his arm. "Stay here, Randy—"

But Randy had already swung the poker, a hard bash, catching Steve in the ribs, an audible thunk of bones cracking. Steve dropped, arms on the sofa, feet on the floor. Randy strode toward the study.

Shu-li grabbed his poker-free arm. "Randy, you're being foolish, don't—"

He stopped, lowered the poker. "You wouldn't call the Mounties, would you?"

"Of course not. The four of us can settle this easily. We'll behave like adults."

"Yeah." Randy gave her the half-lip smile. "Let's be adults. You and me." He took her by the shoulder with his left hand, poker still in his right, and led her to the study.

Shu-li called, "Austin, it's okay, it's—"

Austin turned, phone to his ear, and said, "Yes, the address is—" just as the poker caught his right elbow, and the phone fell to the ground.

Randy smashed it with the poker. "Get those cop ideas out of your brain. You call them, I tell them I was only doing what you told me."

Austin, holding his elbow, spoke quietly. "All right, relax, Randy. Nobody's going to hurt you, understand?"

"Yeah, I understand."

"Good. You'll be quiet, I'll be quiet, Shu-li will be very quiet." Shu-li looked as if she were about to speak. Austin put a finger to his lips. "We'll all be quiet, and easy, and relaxed. You should sit, Shu-li. You should sit, Randy." Where the hell was Steve . . . "I'll sit too, right here." He lowered himself slowly to his desk chair. Shu-li didn't move. Nor did Randy. "You'll be just fine, Randy. Think of your quiet cabin, the gentle woods around the cabin, soon you'll be there, very soon."

That smile again from Randy, "I'll be there. With Shu-li. That'd be nice. Shu-li?"

She said nothing. She stared at Austin.

"Maybe you'll be there with Shu-li, maybe."

"That'd be good, Austin."

"So sit, Randy, sit in the chair there by the window, sit and be comfortable, relaxed and quiet . . ." He watched as Randy, still holding the poker in one hand, Shu-li's shoulder in the other, walked slowly to the chair, and sat. And stared at Austin. "That's good, Randy. That's very good. Very comfortable, so easy. Are you comfortable, Randy?"

After a moment of silence, Randy said, "Yeah. Comfortable."

"Very good. You should be comfortable, relaxed." Austin waited five seconds, not too long . . . "Now, Randy, I want you to gently hand that poker to Shu-li. You want to hand the poker to Shu-li. She wants you to hand her the poker. Yes, so . . ."

He was slowly moving his right arm around, the poker in his grasp. Shu-li, equally as slowly, brought her arm around to the approaching poker.

"Very good, Randy, very good." Barely a whisper.

Something snapped. Randy jumped to his feet. "You son of a bitch, Austin, you can't hypnotize me!" He brought the poker down hard on the top of Austin's desk, smashing into the grain. Another smash took out the computer. Shu-li stood, frozen.

Austin jumped to his feet. "Randy." A command. "Stop it."

Randy brought the tip of the poker up against Austin's belly, blackening his shirt. "I'm going to skewer you with a poker. Like you tried to skewer me with words." He pushed the poker hard at Austin's stomach. Austin grabbed the poker's shaft and tried to twist it from Randy's hands. Randy stepped back, pulled the poker loose, raised it high.

Shu-li jumped, grabbing Randy around the neck. Randy swung at Austin. Austin stepped away and ran to the door. Randy bolted after him, Shu-li hanging on, "Randy! Stop this! Stop!"

Austin was out the door running. To the Porsche. No, Randy was now between Austin and the car. Shu-li, he saw, no longer had her arms around Randy's neck, he held her by the wrist, was dragging her along. Beyond them both came a car, out of the woods toward the house. Whoever it was would get here too late. He had to take care of this himself. And there, clutching his side, leaning against the wall of the house, Steve.

Austin turned again, now heading up toward the southern cliff.

"Some people outside the house," said Kyra, squinting. "Man and a woman." She tried to focus. "Good shoulders on the guy." They sped toward the house. "He's running." Peering harder up the hill. "The woman's being pulled along, I think."

"There's somebody else, farther off, running up to the cliff."

"Where?"

Noel stopped behind the Porsche. "Up there. Just where the trees begin." He turned off the ignition. They got out, both straining to see who it might be. Noel said, "Think it's Austin. Not sure."

Kyra felt more than saw movement by the house and spun toward it. A man. She called to Noel over the car, "Somebody's by the front door. Waving at us." They watched as the man by the door slid to the ground. She grabbed her purse. "Come on!"

They ran. Noel crouched beside the man. "Are you okay?"

"No—no... Broken ribs— Poker—"

"We'll call for an ambulance. How'd it happen?"

"Randy—gone crazy."

"What'd he do?"

"Just save Austin."

248

"Do the best we can."

Kyra had her iPhone out, for the second time in ten minutes calling 911.

Noel, saying to the man, "Don't move, the medics'll be here in a few minutes, they'll take care of you. Okay?"

The man nodded, and immediately winced. "Yeah."

To Kyra: "Come on." Together they ran after the man and woman. The lone man had already disappeared into the trees.

Kyra felt her gut, suddenly aching. Shit! Too much stress on a recently evacuated womb. If the baby were still there she'd never try this hundred-meter dash. Had to go on. Damn purse, heavy. Randy or whoever and the woman were no longer visible. Fuck! Noel wasn't in such good shape, eight years older but no trouble running uphill. Less trouble than her anyway. They reached the wood, tall firs, not thick. Ahead a couple of trails in. She was breathing heavily. "Which one?"

"You go left, I'll take the other one." She did. All the paths have to lead to the sea, right?

Noel loped along, stopping every few seconds, listening for human sounds. If Randy had some kind of weapon—what did the man say, a poker?—what to do? Randy was strong, Tim had said. And he knows how to use weapons, how to swing at people, make them hurt. Send them into a coma. He stopped. If anybody up here were shouting, he wouldn't hear against the roar of the waves. Onward. He saw open space, bits of hazy blue from the ocean. Then he was at the precipice, twenty meters down, craggy rock below, irregular breakers, rowdy as they receded. He stood on a promontory, cliff to the right, a break in the cliff to the left where the sea had cut through the rocky land, more cliff beyond—

There. He hadn't noticed them because they lay on the ground, not much of it over there, a platform like here. Three of them, a yellow dress and two men, one of them standing now holding a stick he swung—no, the poker, he smashed its point down hard, into dirt or flesh. He raised the poker again but the woman, risen to all fours, grabbed his legs at the knees and he struggled just as the other man got up and lunged at the poker man's hand—Randy, the other Austin?—and the poker fell to the ground.

The struggle brought the three within centimeters of the precipice. Randy tore himself away from the woman's grasp and pulled back, the woman and Austin at the edge. Austin now held the poker, his left hand flat, fingers bent forward, wiggling as if in invitation, Come hither. Randy stood motionless, then charged at Austin. Austin stepped aside but Randy caught his right arm, the poker dropped, together they fell to the ground, Randy at the edge between Austin and the craggy drop. Randy lay gasping, his breath knocked out. Austin shoved at Randy's right side, working him half off the ledge.

Randy grabbed Austin's shoving arm with both hands and pulled Austin toward him and the edge. Austin continued to push, Randy pulled, but slowly Randy from feet to waist slid over the edge. He stared up the length of his arms to Austin's hand and arm to Austin's shoulder, his chin, his nose. He shouted, "I go over, you go over!" and gave Austin the half-mouth grin. "Pull me up!"

Now the woman had the poker, she knelt and swung the poker down at Randy's forearms. He held on. Again. Now his right grip loosened, he let go. She brought the poker back again, and swung. She hit nothing.

Randy might have screamed on the way down but Noel didn't hear. He saw Kyra standing at the edge of the trees, the end of the other trail.

Kyra watched as Shu-li hugged Austin and squeezed her face against his chest. He held her to him with both arms. Kyra waited ten seconds, fifteen. As if planned, they broke their embrace at the same moment. She took his hand while she leaned over the edge and looked down. She pulled back and turned her head. Facing Kyra. "Eeeh!" She tugged at Austin's elbow to make him look in the same direction. "The detective!"

Austin saw her, bent down and picked up the poker. "What are you doing here?"

"Figuring out what's going on."

Brandishing the poker, Austin stepped toward her.

"I don't think so, Austin," Kyra said.

"What?"

"You're being photographed."

He smiled. "Oh?"

She point over to the cliff beyond: Noel, his camera poised. "And I saw it all."

He touched the ground with the poker and leaned on it. "So you know it was self-defense." Kyra just stared at him, at them. "Randy attacked Steve. He tried to kill me."

"Maybe."

"Shu-li." He put his hand on her shoulder. "Tell her."

Shu-li nodded. "He did. He came to Austin's house and hit Steve with the poker, he said he was going to skewer Austin." She put her arm about his waist. "And he beat up Derek Cooper and he's responsible for sideswiping your car."

Kyra stared from one to the other. "Why are you telling me this?"

"Randy admitted it. To Austin and me and Steve. Austin accused him of hurting Derek and then Randy admitted to all of it. Like he was bragging about it."

Kyra pointed over the edge. "Is he dead?"

"Must be. Dozens of spear rocks on the way down."

Austin said, "It's a long fall."

"Back to your house and call the police." Or maybe they'd already be there. "Give me the poker. Handle first." She plucked a packet of tissues from her pocket and pulled one out. Austin held out the poker. She covered her hand with the tissue and grasped the weapon. "Lead the way." She glanced to where Noel was standing. No one there now.

Austin and Shu-li walked past her, away from the cliff.

The ambulance had taken Steve Struthers away. Sam Mervin and another Mountie had scrambled down to the beach with police tape and secured the small bay where Randy's body lay to await the arrival of more Mounties; now they were questioning Shu-li and Austin in the den while Noel and Kyra sat in the living room. "Don't go anywhere until we've talked," Mervin had told them.

Stepping onto the deck didn't seem like going somewhere, so they went outside and sat at the table. "What do we know?" said Noel in a soft voice.

"Yeah, what?"

"We know Randy is dead, so he's not going to tell us much."

"Right. And we're told he admitted to all the mayhem against the Cooper family. If we can believe Osborne and Shu-li, and if Struthers corroborates." Kyra whispered too.

"I do believe them. What I'm less sure about is why Randy did all that."

"Right."

"He did it because Austin told him to?"

"And that'll be hard to prove." She stepped off the deck into the garden. Trails of busy ants shuttling back and forth. One crawled onto her shoe. She shook it off.

"We know Austin will probably walk away from the trouble he's caused."

She looked at the door behind Noel. "What do we want to see happen now?"

He thought for a moment. "We want the Cooper family to have a life again."

Kyra checked her watch. "Nothing from Alana." She took her iPhone from her purse and pressed in Alana's number. "Long distance via California." She waited. "Hi Alana, it's Kyra." She mostly listened. "Okay . . . Yes, at the Coopers'. See you then . . . Tell you later." She turned to Noel. "Derek. Still coming out and going back under."

"So let's say Derek's going to be okay. And Tim is fine. Linda and Jason will be all right if Derek's back to normal. That leaves Shane."

"His leg's going to heal, just a matter of time." She took more steps away from the deck, her small act of rebellion against the Mountie. Noel followed.

"His skating career?"

"There is that. He needs a new sponsor."

Noel said, "Or a revamped old one." Kyra raised an eyebrow questioningly. "I have pictures. Osborne will agree to continue paying for Shane's expenses."

"It's blackmail."

"Or justice."

"Blackmail is an offense. So is obstructing justice. This is a murder case." Kyra had another thought. "If you don't turn the camera over to the Mounties you become an accessory after the fact."

Strange. Usually he was the one with moral rectitude. Where had

Kyra's suddenly come from? "Any other notions to let Shane continue his career?"

"No," she had to admit. "But let's keep thinking."

"I think, not necessary."

The two Mounties appeared on the deck. "We told you not to go anywhere,"

"Sorry." Kyra smiled winningly. "We didn't think this was anywhere, as such."

"The atmosphere in the house is too close," Noel muttered.

They told and retold the story of the day's events, four times in all. At one point Sam Mervin's beeper rang. He stepped away from the others. The questioning continued.

Mervin returned. "I think we can wrap this up." He sat. "My colleagues have been to Randolph Dubronsky's cabin. Somebody called 911, mentioned a cabin of interest. No people but they found a bunch of rubber masks like the ones worn by the guy who assaulted Zeke, and maybe Tim. Maybe Derek too." He stared hard at Kyra and Noel.

"Oh," said Kyra. "That's very good."

Mervin squinted at her. "Any idea who might have made that call?"

Kyra's face filled with naive surprise. "How could I?"

"Just wondering," said the Mountie. "You might be interested to know, we found a green van in town like the one that ran you off the road. Paint scrapes on the side could be a match for the Honda."

"Any prints?"

"We're checking."

"Doesn't matter. We know who attacked us."

"Nice working with you two." He shook their hands. "Okay, that's all I need."

"We're leaving Quadra tomorrow morning." Noel handed Mervin an Islands Investigations International card. "If you need anything, those numbers will reach us."

The Mounties left. Kyra and Noel stayed at the table. They waited. Kyra set her purse on her lap, shuffled around inside it, and took out her iPhone. "Should I try the hospital again?"

"If anything shifts, they'll let us know."

She shrugged and dropped the phone into her pack.

Austin and Shu-li appeared. Shu-li shrank back. Surprise from Austin. "You two still here? Go." He snapped the back of his hand at them, two bothersome flies. "Leave."

"Sit down, Osborne. You too, miss."

"My name is Shu-li Waterman."

It felt absurd for Noel and Kyra to introduce themselves at this stage, but they did, Noel adding, "Please, both of you, sit."

They each took a chair. Austin said, "Okay, what?"

"We're concerned about Shane Cooper," Kyra said.

"His bones will heal."

"It's not his bones that worry us, Austin. It's his career."

"He'll have a career."

"If he does what you tell him."

"Of course. I don't—"

"If he doesn't want to do what you tell him, like falling on purpose in competition, or something worse, what then?"

"I would never ask him to do anything wrong."

"Never?"

"You have my word."

Kyra and Noel smiled, at Austin, between themselves. Kyra said, "Not good enough. He needs your support, not your control. Control comes off the table right now."

"What's that mean?"

"It means you place in escrow a cash deposit, the amount to be set this coming week by our lawyers, to cover Shane's annual expenses. The money stays in that account until he can support himself through endorsements and other independent income."

"This is ridiculous. Anyway, I don't have that kind of money."

Noel glanced about, the deck, the garden, the house. "Nice home you have here. One of many? Write them off as a business expense?"

"You can't be serious."

Noel sat forward, leaning across the table. "Very."

"What if I refuse?"

"The police may have to take a closer look at Randy's death."

Austin leaned back in his chair. "Complete self-defense. The Mounties are satisfied. Even you two said it was self-defense."

"We may have said so. We might have been wrong."

"Change your story? Lie?"

"We wouldn't lie, Austin. Not after we've looked more carefully at the photos I took. And shared them with Sam Mervin."

"What photos?"

"On the cliff. The two of you shoving Randy off the cliff." He took the camera from the pouch on his belt, flicked it on and showed Austin the final picture: Randy over the edge holding on to Austin's arm, Shu-li slamming the poker against Randy's hands. Noel turned the camera so Shu-li could see the photo. "Good work, Miss Waterman."

Austin lunged across the table for the camera, missed as Noel withdrew it. Austin said, "That doesn't prove a thing."

"Maybe not, but it sure would make good press. The great Austin Osborne, exposed to the world. Along with Shirley Waterman. Put that together with the story of Osborne demanding that for Shane Cooper to receive Osborne's support he would have to throw competitions. Because Osborne wanted to bring disgrace onto Harold Arensen. However that would have worked. Get it?"

Austin stood slowly. He pushed the chair back. "Give-me-that-camera." A growl.

"Sit down, Osborne. I emailed the pictures to two separate secure locations ten minutes ago. No one ever needs to see them. Put the money in escrow, nothing changes."

Osborne started around the table toward Noel.

Kyra bolted up, purse in hand, finding and grabbing her can of Mace. "Don't even think it, Osborne." She turned quickly as Shu-li lunged forward. Kyra's finger depressed the spray-guard and a waft of grey haze hit Shu-li in the face. She gasped and shrieked. She fell back against her chair.

Austin ran around to Shu-li's side and cradled her against his chest.

Kyra drew a package of tissues from her purse and tossed them on the table. "Use those. Then get some water. You'll get your instructions by registered mail. Look at me!"

Austin looked up.

"You'll follow the instructions. Sign where you are told to sign. Understand?"

"This is blackmail. You can't—"

"We play our part, you play yours. No further contact with Shane. Except the hands-off allowance from the escrow fund. The administrators of the fund will be Linda and Jason Cooper. You got that?"

"I can't—"

"You can and you will." She pointed the Mace at Osborne. "Tell us that you will."

"I—will."

"Don't ruin your reputation, Osborne. Some people respect you. Keep it that way." Noel stood. "Get some water for her eyes!"

Noel and Kyra were back at the Cooper house before the family and Alana returned from Campbell River.

"I'm for a hot bath and stiff drink," Noel said.

"Ditto drink, but shower and clean clothes. Let's go to the B&B."

Half an hour later, vodkas with a little tonic in hand, they sat on the patio outside their rooms.

"The more I think about that scenario, the more risky it was," said Kyra.

"Is. Still." Noel took a hefty sip. "How much do we tell the Coopers?"

"Randy is dead, Shane's career is guaranteed?"

"Yeah. No details?"

"No."

"Just—done."

"Yeah."

The view was stunning, a ridge of trees, a pasture with sheep. Or alpacas? A sweep of island-dotted bay.

"I had the shakes in the tub." Noel glanced sideways. "I always do, after."

"It was risky, but you pulled it off."

"If anyone finds out—"

"We won't let anyone."

Her tone reassured Noel. A bit.

She took out her phone, poked in Alana's number, talked. Cut the connection. "On the ferry," she announced. "Drink up and we'll get to the next act."

Tim took Randy's death harder than the rest of the family. "I didn't like him, but I didn't wish him dead." He blinked against tears, bit his lip, fumbled for his cap that wasn't there. "Tell me again how it happened."

"He got too close to the edge and slipped," Kyra said.

"That's a huge cliff," Noel added. "Austin needs to put up a fence."

Shane worried: "I still don't get how you convinced Austin to not make me toss a competition again."

Kyra shrugged. "From what he said, he'd half decided you didn't need protecting anymore. We helped him decide the other half."

"We can't thank you enough," Linda gushed.

"Yeah!" Jason enfolded Noel in a bear hug.

Next day, after a long, celebratory breakfast, another conversation with the Mounties, a visit to Derek—Kyra and Noel's first since he'd become non-comatose—then they and Alana started back to Qualicum. There'd been no point in rushing off early since Seth and Jan and Astrid had taken Paul for his chemo in Victoria. Noel elected to mosey back on the Old Island Highway, two lanes winding through picturesque towns on the edge of the Strait. They stopped for a long beach walk and lunch in Fanny Bay where Alana had her first-ever oyster. She wasn't sure, but tentatively ate another and then declared them her food find of the summer.

On the road again, Alana launched into a paean for Triple I. "You guys were awesome! How did you figure it out so quickly? I can't wait to tell my friends about this. And you're keeping Shane skating! Wow!"

Kyra and Noel both said, "Alana!" at the same time. Noel braked and pulled over. Kyra turned around to face the back.

Noel said, "You cannot tell your friends about this. You can't tell anyone. Clients' confidentiality is paramount. Do you understand?"

"But you were so great! Can I work on another case with you? Next summer?"

Kyra said, "We'll see. You were a big help. But the primary thing about this business is professional discretion. Do you know what that is?"

"Not saying anything? Even to my best friends?"

"Not saying anything that would identify the clients, right, Noel?"

"Right." He started up again.

"I think you could tell your friends," Kyra continued in an Uncle Noel voice, "that you met Shane Cooper because he was skating in Campbell River this summer, that he's broken his leg and won't be in these Olympics, but he'll be back. You may not say anything about the family or the case. Got it?"

"The rest is client confidentiality, Alana. Got it?"

"A secret?"

"A secret with grave consequences if you break it . . ."

Alana digested for a moment. "If I don't say anything, can I work another case with you sometime?"

EPILOGUE

FIRST THING MONDAY morning Noel had phoned his lawyer for a recommendation of a colleague in Campbell River, someone to sort out Shane's escrow account. His lawyer recommended Brian Sommers.

Noel had discussed the arrangements with Linda and Jason the evening before. They'd wanted more information. Noel and Kyra explained: with the work pressure at his factory, Austin agreed this was easiest. The four of them explained it to Shane. He was still afraid that Austin would have control over him despite the pact Noel outlined. "If he so much as tries to contact you, phone me immediately." Shane acquiesced. No more hypnosis from Austin, his leg would have to heal of its own accord. No participating in the trials for the Vancouver Olympics, no chance to skate for Canada in 2010—this was the heavy price Shane was paying.

A quiet Tuesday and Wednesday with Noel's family. Thursday Noel and Kyra headed to Nanaimo, inviting everyone to come down for dinner. He'd treat them to the best restaurant in town. On the trip he tried to convince Kyra to spend a couple of days at his condo, the guest room was going begging. They could take walks, eat good food together, something they did so well. They'd sit on his balcony above Nanaimo harbor at vodka-tonic time, take in a schlocky summer movie. She should rest, do nothing for a while, be checked by his physician and deal quietly with the trauma of the miscarriage after the distractions of the case. Noel wanted to go for a picnic to Newcastle Island just across the bay from his condo; he and Brendan had spent good times there and he couldn't make himself take the ferry over by himself.

This last argument convinced her. She would stay until after the weekend.

Friday afternoon Brian Sommers called to say Austin Osborne had just left a signed statement accepting the financial responsibility for Shane Cooper's career, the papers for opening an escrow account for Shane, an additional document which recognized Linda and Jason Cooper as the sole trustees of that account, and a check for the agreed-on amount. The arrangement would stay in place until Shane was twenty-five.

Noel put the phone down. "Well, it's done." He called Jason who, overwhelmed, said he'd be forever in Noel's debt.

Noel disconnected and plunked the phone on the table. "I have a bottle of Verve Clicquot. We can celebrate."

They sipped the bubbly on the balcony, overlooking the port. A small soft breeze tickled the warm air. Kyra said, "You were right. I'm glad I stayed on. Thanks. It's been fun."

He raised his glass. "To enjoying ourselves."

"We're pretty good at that." They both drank in silence. Then Kyra said, "Noel, I do want to have a child."

He couldn't tell, was she serious?

"Very serious," she said.

Not really?

"Believe me, sincerely serious. I've given it some thinking, and it's what I want." She raised her glass. "And with every passing day I get more serious."

He made a wry face. "You going to try another speed dating session?"

"I don't think so."

"So what, then? Pick up some guy in a bar and let him impregnate you? Shit, Kyra, you wouldn't. Would you?"

"No."

"Well that's something at least. So?"

"I think, artificial insemination."

"Oh, go to one of those sperm banks, find yourself a genius father for this kid?"

"Not that either."

"What's this, some sort of quiz show? Who're you getting as the lucky dad?"

"You."

"No way!"

Kyra smiled, and sipped.

Acknowledgments

WE WOULD LIKE to thank a number of people who helped us with their expertise. First, for many important insights into the world of competitive figures skating, Marilyn and Ian Wood; they spent hours with us, answering our questions and watching tapes of figures skating championships as they explained the meaning and quality of various moves. Also for her skating knowledge, Tina Leininger, who answered questions about the daily world of skaters. Thanks as well to Stacey and Peter Wisiorowski, for sharing with us their experiences as they underwent the complexities of speed dating—unlike Kyra's, their venture proved highly successful. Heather and Rolf Kellerhals, together with their daughter Erika (who appears as herself in the novel, the island's physician), provided us with valuable insight into the social texture of Quadra, and corrected some factual errors. And thanks to Dr. Barrie Humphrey, who taught us about the medical side of people in a coma. Finally, we much appreciated our conversation with Constable Mike Reid of the RCMP, who gave us a number of astute glimpses into police procedure on islands.

In addition, a number of people bought their—and others'—places in the novel by contributing to the Gabriola Commons (gabriolacommons.ca; check it out); the names they made their contributions for appear as characters. Dorothy Betts bought three characters: Bertina Anderson, Dorothy Bryan and Sam Mervin. Alison Douglas bought a place for Steve Struthers. Christine Gagnon and David Soy bought characters who now bear their own names. To all of you, our thanks and the thanks of the Commons.

We took artistic liberty with parts of Quadra Island and Campbell River. The Quadra ambulance takes seriously hurt people directly to the Campbell River hospital and not to the Island clinic. Do not travel the areas looking for certain fictitious roads and structures.

SANDY FRANCES DUNCAN is the author of ten award-winning books for children and adults, including *Gold Rush Orphan*, which was nominated for a 2005 BC Book Prize. Her articles have appeared in numerous literary journals, magazines, and newspapers.

A National Magazine Award recipient and winner of the Hugh MacLennan Prize for fiction, GEORGE SZANTO is the author of half a dozen novels, his most recent being *The Tartarus House on Crab* and *The Conquests of Mexico* trilogy: *The Underside of Stones*, *Second Sight* and *The Condesa of M*. He is a Fellow of the Royal Society of Canada. Please visit his website at georgeszanto.com.

Together, Sandy Frances Duncan and George Szanto co-author the Islands Investigations International Mystery series, which includes the titles *Never Sleep with a Suspect on Gabriola Island* and *Always Kiss the Corpse on Whidbey Island*.

Also in the Islands Investigations International Mystery Series:

Never Sleep with a Suspect
on Gabriola Island
978-1-894898-89-8
$14.95, Paperback

Always Kiss the Corpse
on Whidbey Island
978-1-926741-05-5
$24.95, Hardcover

Kyra Rachel from British Columbia and Noel Franklin from Washington State form the Islands Investigations International team. Together, they solve mysteries on the charming, but dangerous, islands off the west coast of North America.

In *Never Sleep with a Suspect*, Kyra and Noel are on Gabriola Island to investigate the murder of an art gallery groundskeeper. The island is spinning with rumors about the murder, but not everybody is telling the investigators the truth. As each falls prey to those they need to trust, Kyra and Noel learn that even charming island communities have deadly secrets.

In *Always Kiss the Corpse*, a Whidbey Island General Hospital nurse has supposedly died of a heroin overdose, but when his mother views the body at the funeral, she cries out, "That's not my son!" Kyra and Noel are on the case to find the missing nurse and figure out the truth behind the mysterious body in the casket.